Astounding Praise

The
CONDUCTORS

"Inventively mixing mystery, magic, and alternate history, Glover's nail-biting debut takes readers to Reconstruction era Philadelphia. . . . Glover is a writer to watch." —*Publishers Weekly* (starred review)

"*The Conductors* is a seamless blending of magic, mystery, and history, creating power and wonder with its rarefied glimpse of Black life in the late 1800s. The Vigilance Society and the magic-wielding couple at the core of this story are a welcome addition to the growing chorus of voices in Black speculative fiction. Glover's worldbuilding, characters, and attention to historical detail create a delightfully genre-bending debut!" —**Tananarive Due, American Book Award winner, author of *Ghost Summer: Stories***

"An Underground Railroad—but with magic. With compelling characters and wondrous worldbuilding, Glover weaves a tangled mystery of murder, spellwork, and freedom amid the remnants of slavery's lingering memories." —**P. Djèlí Clark, Nebula Award–winning author of *Ring Shout***

Remarkable Praise for

The
UNDERTAKERS

"It's fun, twisty, and richly detailed."   —*Publishers Weekly*
(starred review)

"Hetty and Benjy's camaraderie is the real star of the show, no matter how many spells they fire off at assailants. *The Undertakers'* historical fantasy vibe will appeal to fans of Alyssa Cole's Loyal League series and Maurice Broaddus' *Buffalo Soldier*."   —*Booklist*

"If you love genre blending mashups of historical fiction, fantasy, and mystery, you should absolutely check this out."   —*Courtney Reads*
Romance

The
IMPROVISERS

The
IMPROVISERS

A Murder and Magic Novel

NICOLE GLOVER

HARPER Voyager
An Imprint of HarperCollins Publishers

THE IMPROVISERS. Copyright © 2024 by Nicole Glover. All rights reserved. Printed in the United States of America. No part of this book may be used or reproduced in any manner whatsoever without written permission except in the case of brief quotations embodied in critical articles and reviews. For information, address HarperCollins Publishers, 195 Broadway, New York, NY 10007.

HarperCollins books may be purchased for educational, business, or sales promotional use. For information, please email the Special Markets Department at SPsales@harpercollins.com.

Harper Voyager and design are trademarks of HarperCollins Publishers LLC.

FIRST EDITION

Designed by Jennifer Chung
Title page plane art © liubov/stock.adobe.com

Library of Congress Cataloging-in-Publication Data has been applied for.

ISBN 978-0-06-329359-5

24 25 26 27 28 LBC 5 4 3 2 1

For Mom and Dad—for everything and more

RULES TO SURVIVE THE DRY SPELL

1. You may buy potions or enchanted tonics with a bona fide medical prescription.
2. You cannot store potions or enchanted tonics in any place except your own home.
3. You may use previously stored potions or enchanted tonics in your home or in the home of a friend when you are a guest.
4. You can only use previously stored potions or enchanted tonics among yourself, family, or friends.
5. You may get a permit to move potions or enchanted tonics when you change your residence.
6. You cannot give away or receive vials of potions or enchanted tonics as a gift.
7. You cannot buy or sell formulas for potions or enchanted tonics either on their own or in spellbooks.
8. You cannot transport potions or enchanted tonics by land, sea, or air.
9. You cannot maintain a garden that contains any Grade 3 herbs or 50 percent of Grade 2 herbs.
10. You cannot brew magic for money or exchange of goods unless you have the proper papers.

Courtesy of the *Eventide Observer*, January 16, 1920

When thinking of longstanding Black communities in the Northeast, eyes turn first to Oak Bluffs on Martha's Vineyard, Sag Harbor on Long Island, or Highland Beach in Maryland. While these are lovely places to live and visit, none can outshine Bramble Crescent. An island uniquely placed off the Massachusetts coast, Bramble Crescent has a vibrant history full of pirates, rum smugglers, war heroes, and revolutionary thinkers. The island has throughout its existence remained a safe harbor for those fleeing persecution, creating a place where magic is interlaced with every aspect of life.

A visit to Bramble Crescent in the summertime brings about traditional delights. Penny fairs, kite-flying contests, magic duels, and the stargazing festival named in honor of its most beloved guests—the mystery-solving couple Henrietta and Benjamin Rhodes, whose descendants found a place to call home here.

—From *Bramble Crescent, A History* by Seraphina Mills

Owl and Eagle Dispatch

Dillon Harris   **May 7, 1930**

A trip just outside the city leads to the rather interesting sight of planes, guided by nervous and untrained pilots, wobbling about in the air. The skies are polluted with the menace of the winged bird, and the scant few who can fly with any confidence perform reckless stunts that aim to distract from matters of greater importance occurring in our fair city.

Owl and Eagle Dispatch

Velma Frye   **May 15, 1930**

The High Flyers Club marries mechanics and magic in ways many have yet to see previously. To fly is to reach new heights—and to inspire the next generation. Which is why, contrary to certain opinions, Uriel Coffin's flight from Vancouver Island to Maine is a promising first step in the soaring heights that the Negro can reach through aviation. To claim otherwise reeks of a lack of understanding and getting key facts wrong.

Owl and Eagle Dispatch

Dillon Harris   **May 27, 1930**

The key facts are that the growing interest in aviation downplays a long-storied history of broom flight and, quite frankly, hardly does anything better. Planes are a costly nuisance and a fad for those with too much time on their hands.

Owl and Eagle Dispatch

Velma Frye   **June 5, 1930**

Some people disparage change, as their minds are too rigid to the possibilities out there in the world. What is new and innovative is deemed as a fad, as these individuals lack an imagination for future prospects. I am talking of course about the state of the airmail service. . . .

Owl and Eagle Dispatch

Dillon Harris   **June 11, 1930**

This weekend's air show was a smashing success. Quite literally, because there was an accident on the airfield. Cornelius Jefferies experienced a malfunction during flight, requiring an emergency landing. Such a dramatic landing resulted in no deaths, a broken arm for the pilot, a damaged plane, a roofless barn, three fainters in the audience, and figurative egg on the face of a certain columnist at this paper.

Owl and Eagle Dispatch

Velma Frye   **June 19, 1930**

To fly is to take on risk, but it's also to fly despite words of naysayers. Dillon Harris, if you have such a problem with planes, why don't you take to the air yourself? And not by broomstick, either. Come down to the field and test your mettle and bravery.

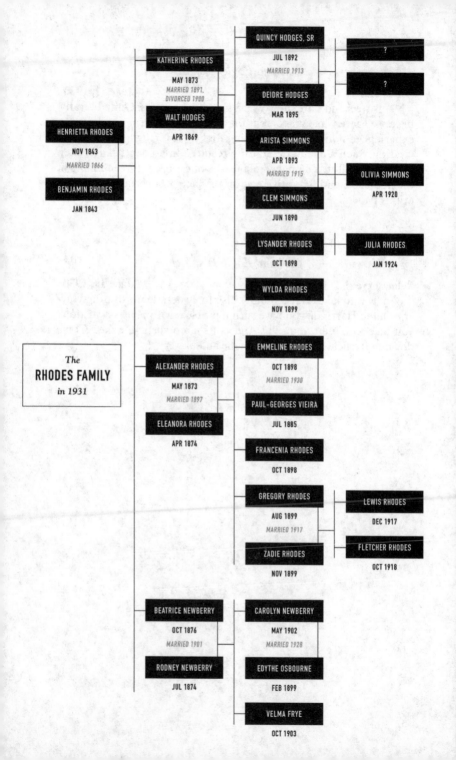

The
RHODES FAMILY
in 1931

HENRIETTA RHODES
NOV 1843
MARRIED 1866
BENJAMIN RHODES
JAN 1843

KATHERINE RHODES
MAY 1873
MARRIED 1891,
DIVORCED 1900
WALT HODGES
APR 1869

QUINCY HODGES, SR
JUL 1892
MARRIED 1913
DEIDRE HODGES
MAR 1895

?

?

ARISTA SIMMONS
APR 1893
MARRIED 1915
CLEM SIMMONS
JUN 1890

OLIVIA SIMMONS
APR 1920

LYSANDER RHODES
OCT 1898

JULIA RHODES
JAN 1924

WYLDA RHODES
NOV 1899

ALEXANDER RHODES
MAY 1873
MARRIED 1897
ELEANORA RHODES
APR 1874

EMMELINE RHODES
OCT 1898
MARRIED 1930
PAUL-GEORGES VIEIRA
JUL 1885

FRANCENIA RHODES
OCT 1898

GREGORY RHODES
AUG 1899
MARRIED 1917
ZADIE RHODES
NOV 1899

LEWIS RHODES
DEC 1917

FLETCHER RHODES
OCT 1918

BEATRICE NEWBERRY
OCT 1876
MARRIED 1901
RODNEY NEWBERRY
JUL 1874

CAROLYN NEWBERRY
MAY 1902
MARRIED 1928
EDYTHE OSBOURNE
FEB 1899

VELMA FRYE
OCT 1903

The

IMPROVISERS

CHAPTER 1

Chicago, Illinois
June 1931

L aughter escaped Velma as she brought her airplane out of a steep dive. The hardest stunts were behind her and now she got to do as she wished. With a steady but gentle hand on the controls, she immediately put her plane through a series of tight loops that turned the world upside down for her as she cut up the figurative rug in the skies. These were standard tricks for air shows and rather old hat for Velma, but for the crowd below, the same could not be said. Despite layers of metal and the rushing wind, Velma could hear the gasps of both anticipation and delight from the ground. These were the sounds she lived for and always hoped to coax out of the watchers below no matter if it was someone's first or fifteenth visit.

A High Flyers air show always drew a decent crowd. The shows were widely advertised in newspapers, and people came out of curiosity and interest for the promised spectacle above their heads. They also attended to see Velma, who had built up a sizable reputation over the years as a barnstormer.

Sometimes her stunts were silly—like her ducking and rolling as if the skies held an obstacle course. Other times she averted magical traps and star sigils hovering in the air, bringing to life the film reels playing in the theaters. On special occasions, she even did the dangerous stunt she was becoming known for, the one in which she jumped out of the cockpit, tap-danced across her wings, bowed to the crowd below, and then dropped back inside and kept flying.

While Velma enjoyed the applause, the cries of delight, and even the clucking tongues of disapproval, every time she flew it was for one person.

Herself.

Up in the sky only the miracle of flight mattered. It was just her, her plane, and the horizon calling her name.

Although flying for adoring fans was nice as well.

After one last pass over the crowd, Velma headed back for the ground, closing out the tricks-and-wonders segment of the show to thunderous applause.

The loudest came from her personal crew, who hurried up once it was safe to approach.

"Great flying, Velma!" Mona cried, grinning as Velma climbed out of the cockpit. "Not that it isn't always pretty swell!"

"Except when someone wants to try an experiment." Lester stalked around the plane, like a pesky storm cloud on an otherwise sunny day. "Don't encourage her, Mona, or she'll do something truly dangerous!"

"Yes, Uncle Lester," Mona said, pretending to be admonished before flashing one last smile at Velma.

Chuckling at the old man's bristling tone, Velma propped herself against the wing and pulled off her cap, fluffing up her cropped curls. "Why so dour, old man? You saw those loops I did—they were perfect!"

Lester huffed. "I got no fault with your flying. What I take an issue with is you using the alchemical fuel before it's ready! I told you not to use it! What if something went wrong? You didn't even do a trial flight!"

"Every flight is a trial. Also, I trust you wouldn't let me fuel up if you had major concerns."

"I trusted you would have the sense to keep a steady hand. Not go all out! We don't know how much of it would burn compared to the usual fuel. What if you did the show on fumes?"

"Life is about risks." Velma took out her compact mirror. Satisfied with her reflection, she then applied a fresh coat of her signature scarlet lipstick. "I wouldn't be here if I didn't take any."

"Any? You take too many! If you aren't sneaking off in the plane when repairs are half done, you're jumping into some wacky race. . . ." Lester's ranting picked up speed as he fell into a familiar groove. Velma had heard it all before and only paid it half a mind, letting him rant. The old man could fuss all he wanted, but he would never leave her employment. She had the best plane for miles around. A Ward Chappelle Kestrel-3, it was a low-wing monoplane with an enclosed cabin and modern instruments. Painted a darling midnight blue, her baby, the *Fowl Weather*, could reach 150 miles per hour on a good day, and that was before Lester got his hands on it. Under the mechanic's care, her plane could do wonders seldom thought of due to the enhancements etched on the wings. There were other pilots within the Flyers he could work for, but only Velma would ask him to reach for the clouds and then aim higher.

As she continued to study her reflection in her compact, Velma spotted the leader of the High Flyers, Cornelius Jefferies, heading her way in a rush. A dentist when not flying, Cornelius was a tall and plainspoken man who was the rare voice of reason among daredevil pilots. Velma had barely arrived in Chicago before Cornelius sought her out after catching sight of her plane. Their first conversation started and ended with him inviting her to join the club. She accepted not only to have the company of fellow pilots but because Cornelius was ambitious enough to start up a flight school with nothing more than a dollar and a dream.

"What's wrong?" Velma asked the reflection. "You look like you're chasing after someone who stole your shoes."

"Oscar is out for the showstopper!" Cornelius called.

Velma shut her mirror, twisting around to face him. "You mean the headliner that we advertised on? The one in which our main sponsor, Maryellen Prince, is flying her broom in a featured segment? The event we talked about all over town, because part of the proceeds of this event will go to Providence AME?" Velma said. "*That* showstopper? What happened? Did Oscar fall and break his neck in the last five minutes?"

"Issue with his plane," Cornelius said, no less annoyed, but no less serious. "He's not going to risk it, and I agree with him on that."

So did Velma, for that matter.

She didn't know what the issue was, but anything that could get Oscar, who was even more of a daredevil than Velma, to ground himself without a fuss had to be major.

"Don't tell me the show is ending early," Velma said.

"Hardly. I was thinking that you could replace him. You're the better pilot anyway, and this showstopper is key."

Velma looked over to where Maryellen stood holding her broom as she dazzled the crowd around her like the polished socialite she was. There were reporters from the *Chicago Defender* and smaller weeklies who were likely eager to see the greatly publicized showstopper. Although today the High Flyers Club was mostly pilots, the club started fifty years ago as the first all-Black broom-riding club in the area. Broomsticks had been an integral part of baseball for decades, and were a popular way to avoid the indignity of the Jim Crow train cars. That day's showstopper would playfully pit traditional flying with the newfangled, and hopefully bring in more potential pilots and financial support for the club—not to mention delight their usual fans.

"I'll do the showstopper," Velma said, the decision coming to her easily, as there was only one clear choice. "I'll need to fuel up first. Otherwise Lester won't be happy."

"You're the best," Cornelius declared, and ran off to put this plan into action.

"You owe me for this!" Velma hollered after him. She turned to her crew to give direction, but Lester was already darting back to his truck for the fuel cannister while Mona was bent over, sweeping her rag along the plane for a quick clean.

"Go help your uncle," Velma told Mona. "I'll finish this up."

Velma took the rag and climbed up onto the starboard wing. She had just started checking for anything that might have gotten loose when movement caught her eye.

Expecting Lester, Mona, or even Cornelius with more bad news, she found instead the last person she wanted to talk to at the moment. Or more correctly, the last person she wanted to talk to at any given moment. With a camera bag slung over his shoulder, Dillon headed toward her, pretending it was such a shock to see her. A spare, wiry fellow, he was always up to something. And today was no exception. Mud splattered his shoes and his glasses were in need of cleaning, but his hat was perched at a jaunty angle and there was some air of success to his stride. Because he was around the same height as her, Velma remained atop her plane to give herself an advantage, but if it made any difference to him, she couldn't tell.

"Dillon Harris," Velma called. "What foul winds brought you here?"

"You're cantankerous as ever, Miss Frye," Dillon said with good cheer. "I see there's a nice gaggle of reporters around. You brought them here like the pied piper, I take it? How many newspaper offices did you stroll into, announcing the day's event?"

Velma tried not to scowl. About two years ago she had done exactly that: strolled into the offices of the *Owl and Eagle Dispatch* decked out in her flight jacket, jodhpurs, and boots, looking to find a reporter to cover the High Flyers' first air show centered on planes. She got coverage for the event plus a weekly column to write about aviation, flying, and anything else tickling her fancy. Most of the paper's reporters accepted her with open arms. Dillon did not. As someone who investigated crime, curses, and corruption, he held a disdain for "fluff" columns and wasn't shy about sharing that opinion, especially in earshot of Velma. Dillon was, of course, the reporter assigned to cover that first High Flyers event, and while his article and his photographs helped make the club popular, his dismissive opinion about airplanes remained firmly entrenched. Not long after starting her column, Velma got into a battle of words with Dillon when he proclaimed Uriel Coffin's groundbreaking flight a stunt, and Velma couldn't let the insult—or the subsequent insults—go unremarked. She called him out in her column, he name-checked her in his articles, and they always found space to insult the other in minute ways. The small feud lasted nearly a year before a cease-fire was ordered by the editor, who found their public sparring an embarrassment despite the increase in sales. The feud, however, was officially over due to a technicality. Two months ago when the daily *Owl and Eagle* went from twelve pages to eight, Velma was let go. While this should have meant she never had to cross paths with Dillon again, Chicago turned out to be a much smaller place than she'd thought.

"I made no arrangements with the press," Velma finally said in return. "The event itself is a draw, but if you're going to write a story about me and my exploits, I want to see a copy of it first."

"I'm not here to write about you. I'm just passing through."

"That's code for you're on a story."

"If you want me to tell, just ask nicely," Dillon said. "I don't bite."

"You don't go around asking questions unless something's caught your interest."

A grin flashed in her direction. "You caught me. I'm here to see if Hounds McGee went aground in this neck of the woods. While I'm here, I figure I can kill some time and do a write-up about all of this." Dillon waved a dismissive hand at the airplanes and gathered crowd along the field. Flipping his notebook to a new page, he asked, "Got a quote for me?"

Annoyed as she may have been, Velma was not one to give up free publicity for the club no matter the source. "I'm subbing in for a showstopper that will be a preview for an event I'm planning later this fall," Velma said. "Nan Kingfisher, Hazel Cheung, and Pepa Ruiz are coming to Chicago to fly with the club."

"How nice it is to have friends in high places," Dillon said as he dutifully made a note. "What can people expect? Gimmicks like brooms flying along planes? Dangerous spins and death-defying loops? Diving into the crowd low enough to skim the hats off folk?"

Knowing he said that just to stoke her temper, Velma replied with great restraint as she met the bemusement dancing in his eyes, "The show's going to be nothing but good clean flying."

"Oh, so you're not taking part, then?"

"Are you implying I'm up to some trickery?" Velma bristled. "My tricks are genuine feats of wonder. No illusions involved whatsoever!"

Dillon made his eyes go wide and innocent. "I'm only asking for more information. You're taking offense where there is none, as always."

"As always, you're asking questions that will get you in trouble."

"Because you got nothing to hide, do you, Miss Frye?" Dillon replied. The seemingly innocent words had steel behind them, bolstered by the sudden intensity in his eyes as they locked upon hers. Eyes that had seen through all sorts of lies and misdirection over the years from lowlifes, scammers, and sleazy salesmen. "I'm sure you have no reason to hide why you were in an apple orchard last month with a bushel of Vivacious Twilight. An apple that is currently public enemy number one for its use at a dance-a-thon in Pottsburg, Ohio. Three people died and dozens ended up in the hospital."

"I didn't know people died in that," Velma said conversationally.

"But you knew about it."

"I just wanted to eat a purple apple. It's not a crime." Velma shrugged, hoping to put Dillon off. She couldn't lie—he would see through that—but she could misdirect or annoy him enough to keep him off the scent.

"No, it's not a crime," Dillon agreed. "However, it's awfully strange that you went all the way to *Missouri* to do such a thing."

"Well, I do have a plane. I like to travel."

In the space she left for further explanation of her flimsy excuse, a scream shattered the calm of the afternoon.

Before the sound could even echo in the air, Velma jumped off her plane and charged forward at a dead run.

When she saw what lay ahead of her, she ran even faster.

The other end of the field sparkled with the lights of spellcasting as two men lobbed blasts of pure magic at each other. Without the use of constellations or star sigils to give a spell form, this was magic in its rawest state. While it was less powerful and dissipated quickly, its effects were wildly unpredictable.

On the perimeter, a patchwork arrangement of wards made a barrier between the pair and the rest of the crowd. Held up by Cornelius and another fellow pilot, Janet Brown, the barrier spell was intact for now, but Cornelius and Janet were buckling despite the combined might, the light from the constellations they used fading quickly.

"Out of the way!" Velma yelled into the crowd as she drew star sigils to her side. People dove out of her path as the Ursa Major star sigil erupted into the air. The great bear with its furs shimmering with starlight charged ahead, beating away rogue magic flung in its direction. When it reached the barrier, Velma's spell threw itself right at it. The barrier surged upward, strengthened by the influx of magic.

"Thanks for the assist," Janet huffed as she concentrated on her spellwork.

"Anytime. What's going on?" Velma asked.

"No idea," Cornelius put in. "One minute Joey and Alan are talking, and the next they're at each other's throats. Gotta have something to do with money. Maybe they had a bet going on."

"Well, they need to find a better way to resolve that," Velma said.

"Quickly. This barrier won't hold," Janet added. "And if their spells get out of control—"

"I know," Cornelius said. "That means somebody's got to stop them."

Then he looked at Velma.

"You want *me* to do it?" she asked.

"Who else can?"

"Why do you got to be right?" Velma grumbled. "Can you two hold this barrier a bit longer?"

Janet nodded and Cornelius grunted his affirmation.

Trusting them to hold the barrier as long as they could, Velma jumped through the magic shielding to stop the misguided duel from truly getting out of control.

Velma had only one sister, but she had several older cousins she used to brawl with. Sometimes with fists and other times with magic. Both experiences were about to become quite relevant as she charged right into the middle of the fighting.

Noxious green-colored magic shot in her direction. Velma tugged back the sleeve of her left arm to expose her bracelet, bringing up her wrist to block the oncoming magic. The star sigils etched into the bronze metal gleamed at once, dissipating the oncoming spell in a puff of smoke.

Usually this sort of thing stopped people in their tracks. These men scarcely blinked before, as one, they flung more raw magic right at Velma.

Velma brought up her right arm, which was also clad in a matching bronze bracelet. Instead of merely rebounding the spell, the charms etched on this bracelet caught the oncoming magic, encasing it in a protective orb.

Velma flipped her hand around, and the orb landed in her palm. She waved her other hand over it, taking control of the magic captured inside. Gripping the buckling spellwork, Velma manipulated the spell and then threw the orb right back at both men.

Like a meteorite striking the earth, the resulting blast knocked them off their feet, flinging them onto the ground. Alan remained flat on his back, but Joey got up again. He lurched forward to attack Velma, but she had a sleep spell waiting for him. She flicked it in his direction. Joey froze mid-swing, struggling against the magic until he collapsed, putting an end to all this nonsense.

With both men firmly placed in the arms of slumber, Velma studied her bracelets for anything more than cosmetic damage, grateful that she had worn them today. She could do magic perfectly fine without them, but as she'd learned from her grandmother, carrying something that could store a few extra spells for you was rather handy.

As she caught her breath, footsteps hurried past. In front was Maryellen, who was also a nurse, as well as a few others who were friends with Joey and Alan.

"Nice work, Frye." Cornelius patted Velma's shoulder. "You good?"

"I'll manage." Velma jerked her chin toward Joey and Alan. "Try to keep them apart."

"We will," Cornelius said. "Rest up. You earned it."

Velma nodded, waving him off, and Cornelius left to take charge of the situation.

Left to her own devices, Velma surveyed the damage done to the field. The havoc unleashed by the unrestrained magic had ruined this part of the field, leaving the ground choppy and uneven. On the hunt for traces of lingering magic, Velma spotted a pocket watch lying abandoned on the ground.

Sterling silver in color, it was smooth from use, with only faint marks where it had gotten scuffed by accident. Velma reached down to pick it up and then flipped the watch open. She noticed first the cracked glass and the stillness of a clock frozen in time. Then her eyes drifted to the faint scratches on the watch's lid, only to realize they were a deliberate mark. Not a star sigil or anything she recognized, just some abstract mark made of circles overlaid one another like falling leaves.

Light winked across the mark and her bracelet—both of her bracelets, actually—reacted at once. They flared, forming a protective barrier between her and the pocket watch. Quick as it had begun, the magic faded.

How very curious.

A camera flashed behind her.

Velma whipped around. Dillon stood in the nearby knot of people around Alan and Joey. His pencil skated across his notebook as he nodded along, listening to Janet.

From the way his eyes drifted back over to Velma for the briefest of moments, she knew it was a ruse.

Shoving the pocket watch away, Velma hurried off, not wanting to be on the receiving end of Dillon's questions—at least not until she had answers herself.

CHAPTER 2
DETROIT, MICHIGAN

The field cleared out quickly. The spectators, reporters, and remaining pilots left so speedily, they kicked up a massive dust cloud as they headed back into town.

"People are spooked," Lester said as he rubbed the worst of the grease off his hands. He hadn't gotten all of it off, so black was still stark around his nails. He kept working to remove it, though, fuming with each rub. "You should be too, but you just jumped into that mess without a thought! If your folks knew about—"

"They'd understand."

Lester snorted his disbelief, but Velma was telling the truth. Her parents *would* understand her running into danger like that—but they would also fuss as much as the old man did afterward.

Velma stretched across the seats in her cockpit, her foot propped on the open door, gazing up at the hatch above her head. Reclined as she was, Velma studied the pocket watch. It belonged to Joey, it turned out. He'd bought it from a street vendor while on a recent trip. It never worked quite right and being kicked around earlier hadn't helped matters. He wasn't keen to have it back, especially after she asked him about possible enchantments on it. The mark scratched on the inside cover of the watch left her as nervous as a rabbit fleeing hunting dogs. The interlocking circles resembled no symbol she knew of. Something was off about this watch, and it went deeper than the gears tucked inside. Velma knew she had to call this incident in, but she needed more information than just an odd feeling.

Velma worked for the Magnolia Muses, a magic rights group that contested harsh laws that restrained magic and provided resources for those without. As part of the investigative arm of the organization, Velma was one of many field agents in charge of making inquiries about various magical mysteries out in the world. One of her most recent assignments had been to that star-forsaken apple orchard to bring in a bushel for testing at the main office. Bad enough she had gotten shot at for her trouble, but if Dillon had spotted her too, then that meant several years of careful lies had just gone up in smoke. The work she did was meant to be quiet, as it tackled the intersections of delicate magical relations, and Dillon was anything but delicate when he felt pertinent information needed to be shared with the world.

"That's it for me." Lester shoved the rag aside, apparently resigned to the remaining bits of grease on his hands for now. "We're headed home. Are you riding along with us, or are you going to risk neck and limb taking your bicycle back to town?"

A slight buzz from the plane's radio transmitter saved Velma from disappointing Lester once again. She sat up, knowing no one would hail her today without a good reason.

"You go ahead—looks like I have business to take care of." Velma reached into the compartment that held her purse and pulled out his and Mona's pay, with a bit extra. "Until next time."

Lester nodded, gratefully taking the money. His eyes were concerned as he glanced at the transmitter. "You be careful, now."

"You know me."

"I do, that's why I worry."

Velma waved goodbye to the uncle and niece and pulled the door to the cockpit shut as she answered the hail.

"Magpie here," Velma said as she turned on the receiver. "I hope it's serious, since it's my day off."

"We know, but this is important," dispatch answered. Velma didn't recognize who it was, but the cheeky tone suggested the dispatch officer was someone she'd run into previously at the Muses' office. "How was the air show?" the voice continued.

"Exciting," Velma said. "This is good timing, actually—I have something to call in."

"You can add it to your report. You need to get to Detroit."

"How soon?" Velma sighed, thinking of the warm bath she'd been looking forward to.

"You're needed right away," dispatch said. "A woman stabbed her sister during a dinner party. The woman is alive and expected to recover. When authorities arrived, they found so much magical residue that the entire household is being charged for indecent magic use, which means prohibition violations. Charlotte Allen is there for legal support to contest the charge, but she wanted an arcane expert to check on things. She's worried that the family might have been targeted, as the magic she detected was unusual."

"How unusual?" Velma asked.

"She used the word *sinister*," dispatch said.

Now this had Velma's attention. Charlotte was an excellent lawyer and a true believer in the Muses' work, but she wouldn't know a joke if it tap-danced in front of her. Her reports were dry and straight to the point, and the only colorful language she used involved literal colors.

Charlotte using any sort of adjective was cause for alarm.

Given some of the things Velma had been hearing about the latest hooded terrors in Michigan, perhaps it was an apt warning.

"I'll give it a look," Velma said, beginning prep for flight. "What's the address? I'm on my way."

The contact that met with Velma upon arriving in Detroit happened to be a friend of hers. This turned out not to be by chance—Yolanda had been the one to report the incident in the first place.

"No wonder dispatch called me directly," Velma said. "You used the card I gave you."

"I didn't want this routed through all the usual loops," Yolanda said as she drove them to the site of the incident. "Plus, I know you'll figure this out."

"Not much to figure out—there were several witnesses to the stabbing."

"It was all very strange," Yolanda insisted. "Belinda and Mary are very close and the fighting started up so suddenly. . . ."

Belinda Hayes and Mary Green were a pair of well-known but not particularly well-liked sisters in the community. Members of a family with a high social standing in town, they invited people to dinner parties and teas solely to ambush their guests with moralizing lectures. The party they hosted was another one of those lectures directed at hapless guests, until the sisters' quarrel suddenly broke out and Belinda took the knife used to cut cake and rammed it into Mary's hand.

"The stabbing, in fact, improved the party," Yolanda said. "Honestly, most of us were there expecting something like this. This is the first stabbing at one of Belinda's parties, but there's been fighting before. Three people have already gotten seriously hurt at her other gatherings."

"Three people?" Velma echoed. "And these parties are still well attended?"

"The incidents have only recently started. People were saying it was these new teacups Belinda got. That they must be cursed or something. She got them to flaunt her money to impress folk, as if nothing's changed for her despite the Crash."

"I don't know about cursed cups, but I'll find out otherwise."

Leaving Yolanda outside to stand watch, Velma walked into a house clinging to the sheen of great wealth, despite all the signs of cracks and tears in the veneer. After no one answered her knocks, Velma picked the lock and went inside.

Shifted furniture and upturned chairs led Velma to the dining room, where the stabbing had taken place earlier that afternoon. Deep scratches ripped apart an armchair like a tiger had made sport with it, a nearby lamp had been snapped into three pieces, and the walls were marred with ugly streaks of drying blood. This was interesting to note, yet the longer she stood in the room, those details fell away as she detected that feeling she had been warned about.

A feeling, not sinister, as the lawyer had described, but oppressive and suffocating. Sinister would have pushed Velma away. Instead this feeling seemed to tug at her, pulling her in . . . and under.

Velma let the feeling wash over her as she drew the compass star sigil in the air before her. Focusing the spell to detect that strange feeling, she finished up the sigil and let it go. The compass made of stars floated before her, and the arrow slowly spun to point to the side table. Or more specifically, a music box.

It was a small thing. A rounded wooden box that was wide as a book and tall as a stack of four such tomes. Time had dulled the polish, but the painted design of a sea coast was quite vibrant. Yet, it looked as if it might have been a victim of the strife that recently filled the room, due to a large unsightly chip on the lid's corner. Uncertain if it was broken, Velma carefully lifted the damaged lid. A tall ship bobbing in a busy harbor, clearly setting off on a grand adventure, was painted on the inside. There was also the music that played as the whole scene began to slowly revolve.

Instead of a soft tinkling tune, a pared-down piece from Mendelssohn's *Calm Sea and Prosperous Voyage* spilled out from the music box, bursting with all the fanfare of a ship being launched. It was as if a miniature orchestra were playing before her. As if she were in the audience—no, she was onstage with her piano and—

Velma's hand lifted to the air in search of the right notes, and something sparkled from the corner of her eye. It was her bracelet, pulsing to warn Velma of nearby danger.

Velma snapped the music box shut and looked around. She saw nothing and no one in the room, but the pulsing stopped.

Curious.

Nothing could have disappeared that quickly.

Unless . . .

Velma lifted the music box's lid once more. Barely a note escaped before the star sigil etched on her bracelet lit up, and Velma snapped the music box shut once again.

The third time Velma lifted the lid, she sensed it. That uneasy feeling she'd felt the moment she'd arrived—this music box was the source!

But did it encourage a woman to stab her own sister?

Was it the music itself? Did it put people under its sway?

The Mendelssohn overture was triumphant, but the beginning replicated the tension from waiting for calm seas to roil to life to begin a voyage. Music could compel many things, but *this* song? What enchantment was at work here?

Velma picked up the music box and flipped it over. There were no star sigils carved into the wood that reacted to her touch. No signs of any other magic systems. Sorcery was all incantations, so no traces would be left behind. Potion residue was often felt by the touch. All the other systems that ran through Velma's mind were unable to be seen with the naked eye or would have been more obvious. The wood was seamless as the painted seascape continued, save for a small, raised bump in the otherwise smooth paint not far from the box's hinge.

Locking her eyes on the spot, Velma pulled on the chain of her necklace, revealing a silver pedant of sweet violets. Velma twisted around the flower petals so the pendant split open to reveal a tiny magnifying lens.

Holding the lens over the spot she'd noticed, she studied the bump and the uneven lines radiating from it. She pressed her thumb against the lines, and a panel moved with a soft click.

The top layer of the lid popped up to reveal a hidden compartment. Not a particularly deep one. The compartment was just big enough for a folded scrap of paper to be tucked inside. With care, Velma undid the folds and read on the aged paper: *For my darling.*

Who wrote it and why was intriguing, given the implications of such a gift that inspired violence. Yet, it was not the most interesting thing at the moment.

Etched on the lid of this hidden compartment was a very familiar mark: circles overlaid like falling leaves.

Breath hitching ever so slightly, Velma carefully replaced the music box on the side table and pulled the watch out from her flight jacket pocket.

Holding the pocket watch next to the music box, she glanced between the items with a growing sense of unease and excitement.

"Stars and shards," Velma muttered to herself. "It matches!"

Erupting violence. Magical items with the same mysterious symbol. Incidents occurring so close together. It was all too much to be a coincidence.

Which meant someone *wanted* these items out in the world, sowing discord.

Given that nothing good ever came from objects with bad intentions, Velma knew the items weren't the only two of their kind. There were likely to be more, and if she were lucky, the objects were only sources of strife and chaos instead of death. But she wasn't always lucky.

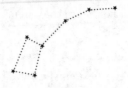

INTERLUDE

PHILADELPHIA, PENNSYLVANIA

May 1920

THE MOON HAD RISEN OVER THEIR HEADS BY THE TIME VELMA'S SHOVEL struck the casket.

"About time," Velma grumbled as she wiped her forehead with her sleeve. "I was starting to think no one was buried here!"

"Wouldn't be the first time." From her perch, Velma's grandmother tapped out a spell to brighten the lantern's light.

"Please," Velma begged, "no stories. I just can't handle them right now. I'm only out here because I didn't want to be at the funeral home. There're so many people around I have to share a room with Fran and Emmy!"

"Then why did you come home at all?" her grandmother asked.

Home was always Philadelphia. It was where her grandparents lived, where they ran a funeral home, and where they provided mystery-solving services for the most peculiar cases. The house on Juniper Street was where her grandparents would always be to help, heal, and aid their children and their children's children no matter how unusual the trouble might be. It was why, after Peter's funeral, this was the place Velma had gone to grieve.

Peter, her childhood friend, had died two months ago after suddenly taking sick. Shortly before he had confessed to being in love with her and Velma had gently turned him down. They were about to graduate from the Brambles School and her plans for the future didn't involve romance. Velma's sister had assured her that the events were not connected, but Velma had fled Bramble Crescent anyway with guilt and regret as traveling partners.

Now she had no idea what shape to make the rest of her life. With the war, the flu, and a summer where the streets ran red with blood, and now Peter's death—so much had changed, so why should Velma follow any plans she'd made before?

"I didn't realize the house would be that crowded," Velma replied instead of telling the truth.

"You can always leave," her grandfather said as he stepped out of the shadows, returning from setting protective boundary spells. His glasses twinkled as the lenses caught lantern light. "Not that we're looking for you to go. I have a list of chores that need doing, and I know you have plenty of time to do them, unlike the others."

Her grandmother nodded in agreement. "You aren't a familiar face, so it's very helpful when talking with murder suspects."

"Those are two very enticing inducements." Velma knelt to rub away the loose dirt over the casket. "Will this be bad luck?" she wondered suddenly.

"You're asking that now?" her grandfather teased.

"Just curious."

There was a soft whisper of fabric as Velma's grandmother floated down into the hole, her magic outstretched, making it appear as if she had wings. Granny Rhodes landed right next to Velma. She adjusted the shawl at her shoulders and then lowered the lantern just a tad.

"It's always bad luck for the funeral home when someone hears we dug up a casket. It's happened three times, and only once was it by accident. Robert Thompson was—"

"Drugged to a point that he was unreactive to most tests," Velma finished, as this was a story often repeated to great laughter in livelier settings. "You should have known something was suspicious when there was a note to have no embalming done."

"Quite right," Grandfather called. "This man is different, though. He wasn't buried by us, and if he was alive, well, he's been underground long enough that we have a different problem."

Velma placed the tip of the shovel's blade at the casket's edge, popped it up, and then lifted the lid to the side.

Granny Rhodes let out a small whistle of surprise as the lid opened. "I should have taken up that bet, Benjy. All bone, no sign of any flesh."

"I never said it was otherwise, Hetty," Grandfather replied with a shrug. "Just stated the likely outcome."

"That's odd." Velma dropped the shovel to better look into the casket. "You said he was buried three months ago. He shouldn't be like this, even if he wasn't prepared properly. I would even say it's a different body."

"Why don't we check?" Velma's grandmother uncorked a small vial and waved her hand over the top. Vapors of silver smoke drifted over their heads and into the casket. The smoke rolled over the remains. It would have stayed silver if only one body had been in the casket, but it turned orange.

"Stars and shards," Velma swore. "A second body was in there! How could you do such a thing without being noticed?"

"You dig up the casket while the ground is still newly turned over," Grandfather replied.

"What about the sapphires?"

The lantern swung around, and a sapphire necklace bunched up like grapes glittered in the skeleton's hand.

Brushing aside some dirt, Velma knelt and tugged out her pendant, twisting it to form a magnifying lens. Bringing the lens over the jewels in the skeleton's hand, she covered as many angles as she could without touching anything. "Only one is real. The others are fake as the ones I found with the museum curator. They are part of the same set too, altered as they were with magic. Why didn't the curator catch this?"

"Because they see the gems as keys," Granny Rhodes said. "As long as it fits into the machine, no one thinks much of it."

Velma sat back on her heels, her mind whirling over these details. "What are we going to do? They're fake and the real ones were stolen a long time ago."

"The fake jewels weren't the only interesting thing in there," her grandmother said. "There's a ticket stamped a month ago for entry into the museum."

Velma glanced up at the grave marker that had been keeping her company this past hour.

"That can't be right," she said. "Nelson Palmer was buried three months ago. His body was replaced with a much older—and much deader—body. The ground wasn't recently disturbed. How is there a ticket from a month . . . Oh, this grave was dug up twice! Which means the jewels were also replaced twice, without knowing which one was real."

"Or," her grandfather said, "the jewels were buried for safekeeping. The real sapphire you identified, that's the master key."

"So more digging," Velma said.

"Literally and figuratively," her grandfather confirmed.

"Still, this is going to be helpful for the Magnolia Muses to know," Granny Rhodes added. "Now, let's put this all back."

Velma picked up the shovel and was just shutting the casket when her grandmother's words set in.

"Wait," Velma called. "That's it? I did all that work. Aren't we going to do anything more?"

"What else is there to do?" her grandfather asked. "We confirmed a key thing."

"Yes," Granny Rhodes agreed, "and we'll pass the news along and someone else will take care of it. When you get to our age, you like to be selective about which cases you work on."

"There's still more to do," Velma protested. "I want to see how it ends!"

"Well, you'll have to talk with the contact at the Magnolia Muses," her grandmother said. "We know Phyllis quite well and she may even let you assist her."

"I'll do more than that," Velma declared. "I'll solve this case!"

As her grandparents smiled, Velma knew right then she had been tricked.

They hadn't needed her to dig up this grave at all. It was a long, well-plotted ruse that led to a conclusion she would have rebuked if they had suggested it in a more straightforward manner. Because as much as they loved having her around, they were clearly growing weary of her moping around the funeral home.

Velma was far from moping now. Because in that moment, Velma couldn't care less about her grandparents' scheme. For the first time in weeks, a wind was blowing her into a new direction, and she couldn't wait to see where it took her.

CHAPTER 3

CHICAGO, ILLINOIS

The Chicago branch's office for the Magnolia Muses sat in a narrow building right in the heart of the newly christened Bronzeville. Downstairs had the most foot traffic, as the public features of the organization—legal aid, financial resources, community services, and more—were all done there. The second floor held classrooms and spaces for clinics and the third floor brimmed with staff offices. While it was reported that the fourth floor held private apartments, that was a lie. Instead of apartments, the fourth floor was for the investigation office, and for a variety of reasons this wasn't publicly disclosed.

Using her impromptu trip to Detroit as an excuse, Velma strolled into the office late enough to raise eyebrows, although there weren't many coworkers around to pass judgment on her. In fact, the floor was emptier than usual. Analyn Mamot and Gerald Lee were at their desks hard at work, but two other field operatives were out on assignment, while Brenda Sapolsky was on a well-deserved vacation. Although one temporarily empty desk seemed to be at risk of becoming permanently empty as Lionel was getting yelled at by their boss, Phyllis Gaines, for yet another screwup.

Velma tiptoed past Phyllis's door on the way to get her mail, hoping to avoid the edge of her boss's rough tongue. Velma thought she'd comfortably gone unnoticed when she heard, "Don't you sneak off so quickly, Velma."

Phyllis stood in the doorway as the berated Lionel slunk away. "You need to turn in your report to records. Inez Garcia was on dispatch this weekend, and told me about the call you went to see. I want to see two reports before the end of the day."

"Surely Charlotte's report means mine would be redundant," Velma protested.

"Two reports," Phyllis repeated, with no room to negotiate.

"I'll have them in by then," Velma said, and quickly departed for her office.

The space had more in common with a closet, but it had a door that could be shut and locked, and was her reward after crossing the six-year mark with the Muses. She had grown up knowing about the Muses, as several members of her family worked with or for them. However, when she first interviewed for a job, she was bluntly told she would only be accepted to keep good relations with the Rhodes family and not on her own merit. So Velma went to Paris and got a pilot's license. She smuggled bootleg magic and alcohol, played the piano for budding jazz legends, worked as a jeweler's assistant, bought a plane, and traveled to far-flung places. And then years later when she interviewed again, she didn't get a polite refusal.

Hanging her purse on a nearby hook, Velma took a seat and quickly wrote up the two requested reports, citing the incidents and noting both were a work in progress. With that thankless task complete, Velma sorted through any missives that needed to become her top priority. A quick study of the papers had her concluding that most tasks could either wait or be handed over to her coworkers. Although, an urgent request from Long Island caught her interest. Despite the Brooklyn office being well staffed and managed, this was sent to Chicago directly because it involved an enchanted necklace—and that was Velma's purview.

Jewelry, gemstones, and sometimes even just plain rocks were all lobbed in her direction no matter what part of the country they were found in, as Velma was the definitive expert in the organization, with enough practical experience to outshine the academic experts on staff. It was nice to know she had an area of expertise, but this usually meant extra work. This time, however, might be the first in a long while where she wasn't annoyed at the presumption. As she read the report, the description of the necklace and a note about odd behavior had her frowning. With the music box and pocket watch in mind, Velma found the section for the point of contact and picked up her desk phone.

Switching over to the external line, she fed the number to the operator, and after a few rings the phone clicked over.

"Homesteader Film Company," answered a young but tired-sounding woman. "To whom should I direct your call?"

"Someone contacted me about concerns regarding a necklace? Lissette, I believe?" Velma said with a quick glance at the report. With care, Velma tacked on the phrase shared with those seeking aid from the Muses. "She should know that she has found herself in the company of friends."

"Oh yes." The woman's voice lost its sheen of polish as it dropped to a rough whisper and she continued. "That was me. The necklace is being used in the movie and is doing strange things on set—mostly to the lead actress wearing it. My boss says it's just adding an effect to the film we wouldn't have gotten otherwise, so he won't get rid of it. The actress asked me to find help and I found your organization."

Velma pulled a writing pad toward her. "Where's the necklace now? I'd like to see it."

"It's on set in Long Island. I can give you the address. The crew will be there for the next week, but you mustn't let Ambrose see you."

Ambrose? With a start, Velma realized why the film company name sounded familiar. Ambrose T. Fowler was a film director making a name for himself these days putting out films with Black folks both in front and behind the camera. The company was centered in Metropolis, on the Illinois side of the border with Kentucky. She hadn't seen his films, but his star was shining too bright for Velma to not know who he was. Although this wasn't the first time someone from crew and cast on his films had made complaints that reached the Muses.

"Trust me, I'll be careful not to be spotted by him. Tell me about where I'm headed."

Lissette rattled off the address, but she didn't have more to say that wasn't already in the report. The woman was too jittery anyway—when she was interrupted by someone on the other side, she abruptly hung up on Velma.

Velma glanced at the phone and just shook her head as she jotted down her notes, limited as they were. With the requests sorted and set aside for the others in the office, Velma pulled out the newspaper she'd bought that morning. After being abruptly fired from the *Owl and Eagle*, these days she gave the paper only a passing glance for the baseball scores—and to keep track of the articles Dillon Harris was putting out, especially after running into him during one of her cases. The cover story was the arrest of Hounds McGee, and it continued onto pages two and three, describing how a perfume company was a front for McGee's empire of illegal tonics and potions. Dillon's article detailed the rising number of people growing deeply ill or blind from the alchemical waste dumped in the lower-income parts of the city. Velma grudgingly applauded the reporting. Having been in the business, she encountered far too many like McGee who had gotten away with doing worse. It was good to see that this piece of filth was going to have many unpleasant days ahead.

The only mention of the past weekend's air show was brief, with Velma highlighted as one of the key features. There was no note of the brawl and the chaos that had come around it. Was that cut for space or was this a ploy by Dillon to curry good favor before he inter-rogated her at a later time? He had brought up the apple orchard on purpose, and even went to great lengths to steer their conversation to the subject. But why? The apples were taken care of, and given the Hounds story, Dillon clearly had plenty to keep him occupied.

His dark, intensely focused eyes flashed before Velma, and she shoved the newspaper away. Dillon Harris wasn't anyone she had given much thought to when she'd been working at the *Owl and Eagle*, and there was no reason to start now.

Glancing through the paper once more just to quickly check the baseball scores from that weekend, Velma chucked the paper into the bin and went to visit Lois.

Lois Martel was currently the librarian who supported the inves-tigations team, a change she'd requested after growing weary of doing research work for legal aid. It had brought her from D.C. to Chicago, and she never complained about being bored again. The Muses had offices everywhere, but the investigations arm was regional, and the Chicago branch covered the largest swath of the country, which meant they were always busy, although Lois was more than equal to the task. The daughter of Haitian immigrants who'd fled the US occupation of the island, Lois was younger than Velma by a handful of years, but her no-nonsense air and constant grumblings made it seem otherwise.

Velma went first to the archives, where Lois was usually up to her elbows in papers. The back room of the library was a large space crammed with meticulously numbered boxes that held case files, newspaper clippings, photographs, journals, letters, telegrams, draw-ings, maps, and more. Copies of major documents, rare works on magical theory, and dangerous artifacts found a home in the archives as well.

While Lois herself wasn't spotted among the shelves, her new assistants were. Morris Broadleaf was grumbling about mnemonic devices as he filed away papers while Charity Peterson sobbed into a handkerchief. Velma's arrival sent the poor girl into deeper hysterics, and to spare them both from this awkward moment, Velma walked out of the room and headed for Lois's office.

Here she had more luck. Lois was at her desk flipping through the pages of an oversized ledger as she took notes.

"How's your day been?" Velma asked as she entered the room.

"Absolutely fantastic," Lois grumbled.

"I see you're in a good mood." Velma dropped into a plush arm-chair and reclined back as far as she could. "What did your assistants do today? I saw a young woman sobbing about the Dewey decimal system."

"As she should," Lois said sternly. "It has glaring flaws."

Velma studied her nails, noting how her friend was avoiding her gaze. "What's the truth?"

Lois sighed as she put aside the book she was working on. "Assistant Two broke the wirephoto machine, mislabeled some of the boxes that came in, lost an important archival report I had her file away, and put salt in my coffee."

"Now, you simply must fire her for that last bit," Velma said.

"I can't. Phyllis told me these are the last two assistants I'll get, as I had seven already this year. Which I think is a very hard line to take, as they were all let go with just cause!"

"Four assistants were dismissed for such crimes as shelving a book in the wrong section," Velma recounted, "two resigned because you never actually let them do the jobs they were hired to perform, and one quit after a lecture on the proper way to brew coffee."

"It's not so easy to be a mentor." Lois shrugged as she turned back to her work.

"I'm not sure you qualify as a mentor."

"Exactly! I just want to do my work and not waste time making sure my assistants aren't screwing things up. You'll understand once you have to train someone."

"That's why I stay on assignment," Velma remarked. "It makes it impossible." More serious now, she said, "Lois, if I put something in the archives, am I allowed to get it back when I need it again?"

Lois looked up, meeting Velma's gaze with a chilling and forbidding stare. "Nothing that enters the archives leaves."

"And if I said it's a matter of life and death?" Velma asked in a chipper tone.

"Still no." Lois pulled out a small calendar, marked something on the day's date, and then flipped back some months. "This is the fifth time you said that this year."

"It can't be that many times."

Lois suppressed a smile. "You don't want me to tell you how many it was last year." She dropped the calendar. "Why don't you just tell me about your current case, and we go from there?"

Velma launched into a summary of what had happened after the flight club's event, her trip to Detroit, and the report about the necklace out in Long Island having a possible connection. Velma hadn't brought the music box with her, but the pocket watch was enough to illustrate her story.

Lois nodded. "That *does* seem rather intriguing. Can I have a closer look at the watch?"

"Yes, but try not to touch it. I haven't proved it yet, but I'm pretty sure touching it with bare skin is a bad idea. My protective magics sprung up when I first picked it up."

"What you lack in smarts, you make up for in common sense."

"Gee, thanks."

Lois ignored Velma's sarcasm as she pulled on gloves and took the pocket watch into her hands. With care, Lois studied the watch from every angle, lingering over the strange symbol. "I don't recognize this mark. Luckily, I have a friend at Hayden College who studies this sort of thing. Can I keep this?"

"Maybe take a sketch. I'd like to see if I can get it fixed."

"And to keep it out of the archives," Lois added pointedly, although with good humor this time. "Because we're friends, I'll let this pass. Don't get caught."

"You bet I won't. Since this is the part where I ask for your help."

Lois sighed and picked up her pen and dipped it into the nearest inkwell. "What do you need, and is it something I'm actually able to give you?"

"It's all legit, I promise. I just need information about enchanted items. Preferably those of a mechanical nature, but I won't be too picky. I'm looking for incidents where people reported unusual behavior that stopped and started with no clear reason. Also, look for anyone known to sell, repair, or make enchanted objects. Is this enough for you to work with?"

"I believe so. I'll make contact and give you a list of places or people that might be the most useful. I assume the first on the list is the necklace on Long Island?"

Velma nodded. "I don't know how connected this necklace might be, but it's an enchanted object and the timing makes it impossible to ignore. Something's always thrown my way, isn't it?"

"That does seem to happen a lot to you," Lois remarked.

"What can I say? Trouble just loves me so."

Lois rolled her eyes. "Oh, I know. I read plenty of reports that detail it. Are you leaving for the day soon?" Lois asked, switching topics. "My brother is pestering me with questions about my job again, and I need you to pretend to be a coworker from the public library."

Velma groaned. "Why not tell him the truth about what you do?"

"My brother worries about me excessively," Lois said, "but he hardly visits me. Prepare your best lies for the evening. In turn, I'll buy you a drink from Checkers."

"Not much of a bribe, considering I don't have to buy drinks anywhere in town, Checkers least of all, after I hooked him up with a supplier that doesn't water down their liquor."

"A simple yes or no would suffice."

With extravagant flair, Velma declared, "Lois, you are my best friend. I'll gladly spend an evening lying to your brother if it makes you feel better."

"If lying doesn't work, we can talk about you being a pilot. That will certainly make good dinner party conversation."

"Or we can talk baseball," Velma said. "Everyone likes talking about baseball."

"My brother doesn't," Lois said as she began to grab her things. "Luckily, I have prepared a few details you need to memorize. It's only seven pages."

As they left the archives and headed down to the lobby, Lois rattled on about minutiae Velma was never going to remember. Making vaguely affirmative noises whenever Lois paused for confirmation, Velma busied herself with making a mental checklist for her upcoming flight. When Lois opened the door to the lobby, Velma was pulled out of her thoughts by the horrifying sight before her. She yanked Lois back into the stairwell, snapping the door shut.

"What's wrong?" Lois asked.

"Trouble!" In her brief glance of the lobby, she'd spotted Dillon Harris talking to Cornelius. The pair were adjacent to the front door and there was no way to avoid passing Dillon without resorting to several misguided but effective spells.

"Trouble," Lois echoed with concern. She pushed open the door to peer out. "It's just the reporter you had that silly feud with— Oh, I didn't know Cornelius was here today! He usually isn't here on Mondays."

Before Velma could stop her, Lois dashed out into the lobby, subtly smoothing out her skirt.

The two men sent greetings Lois's way, and a smile brightened Cornelius's features as his eyes fell on her.

Dillon waved at Velma, mockingly encouraging her to join them.

Velma had too much pride to slink away, so she walked over with the singled-minded determination to keep the conversation as brisk as possible.

"I covered for Randall in the clinic today," Cornelius said. "Although I might be here every day soon. His father died, and he's talking about moving back home to take care of his much younger siblings."

"How lucky," Lois said, then gulped, realizing how her words sounded. "For you, I mean. You said you liked coming here to do clinic hours."

"I enjoy the work the Magnolia Muses does," Cornelius said, "and I like coming here. You're here every day too, aren't you?"

"I work in the library," Lois said. "Fourth floor."

Velma cleared her throat loudly.

"I mean third floor, and it's a very small library. But very spacious."

"How can it be both at once?" Dillon asked pointedly.

Lois started stammering at the question, which perhaps explained why she felt the need to write out seven pages of extensive notes to keep her lies in order.

"What about your dental practice, Cornelius?" Velma said, taking the reins of the conversation. "Would that impact things?"

"I'm not looking to make a fortune." Cornelius shrugged.

"I don't care about money either," Lois added breathlessly.

"Then you two shall starve together once you get married," Dillon drawled.

Both Cornelius and Lois clammed up, turning away embarrassedly from the other. Velma glared at Dillon's cheeky grin, gripped by the desire to throttle him right there in the lobby.

Velma had several opinions about her closest friends in Chicago slowly edging toward romance—most of them being that it was a terrible idea. However, in the face of such mocking, suddenly Velma became the fiercest supporter of the would-be couple.

"What are you doing here, Harris?" Velma demanded. "If you want to interview the person in charge, this is not the main office."

"Just a follow-up interview with Cornelius about the brawl at the air show," Dillon said. "I would've gone to his office, but he said to meet him here. Didn't expect to see you, but I do love serendipity, as I was hoping to have a chance to speak with you again."

"Keep clinging to that hope," Velma said. She turned to her friends. "Let's head on out."

"Maybe you should talk to him," Lois encouraged her. "It might be important."

"It won't be," Velma said, even as she was curious about why Dillon was here. Even more so because he genuinely seemed surprised to see her at the office.

Her brief glance at him before she shut the stairwell door had been one of equal shock. That was rare. Dillon always popped up when she least expected, like mushrooms and half-remembered dreams. For her to surprise him was a nice change of pace.

Stepping aside for a semblance of privacy, Velma grudgingly asked Dillon, "What are you after? More quotes? I gave you plenty at the air show yesterday."

"Sadly no, " Dillon replied. He glanced around the lobby, his attention drifting to the various flyers and advertisements that covered the bulletin board. "You work here at this organization?"

A trickle of concern ran through Velma at his words. She had many reasons to dislike the reporter, but the chief reason she was tempted to cast a hex on him every time he popped up was that Velma owed Dillon a favor. Not a small favor either. A year ago Dillon had helped with a case of hers at a great personal cost. In the months since, however, Dillon made little to no mention regarding repayment. Knowing she owed him was like a pebble stuck in her boot, and she fretted about what he would demand. He was unlike anyone she knew, and Velma couldn't predict exactly what he'd ask for, especially if he knew the resources she had access to.

"I travel for the Muses representing their interests, couriering mail, collecting special packages, and transporting lawyers," Velma said promptly. "I'm sent because I can get to places faster with my plane."

She waited for follow-up questions—there were always follow-up questions with Dillon. This time, none came. Instead he paused.

"Then I suppose that's how you know Quincy Hodges?"

Velma paused at this name, but when she replied she made sure to keep her tone unruffled. "I dealt with Mr. Hodges previously, when I purchased a piano. Has something happened?"

"Nothing that I know of. Mail still comes around addressed to you about your column. Not so much these days, but the mail room keeps forgetting you aren't there anymore and leaves it in our mailbox—I mean my mailbox. It looked important, so I kept it."

From his jacket he pulled out a fat envelope, the sort Velma's older sister always called bad news. The letter swelled like a foreboding promise, and Velma would have happily not opened it, especially once she saw that the return address under Quincy's name was the false one used only for delicate and unusual situations.

"Don't worry. I didn't open it," Dillon assured her as he handed it over.

"You wanted to, I suppose."

"Of course. Who wouldn't! However, I don't open the mail of people I know unless given permission."

"That's who I am to you—someone you know?" Velma played at the seal, loosening it slowly to buy her a little time.

Dillon chuckled. "I doubt you consider us friends. *Acquaintances* seems too formal for someone willing to get down and dirty in the newsprint over a few paltry comments."

"How about rivals?" Velma suggested, slightly irked. "You got me fired because my column was more popular than your articles."

"Passing diversions will always attract more attention than a news story," Dillon said. "Now, are you going to open the envelope or not? Don't be a tease."

"It's nothing important. Hodges is probably trying to sell another piano."

"Then open it," Dillon said, undeterred. "I have no immediate plans and your friends have already abandoned you."

Velma looked over her shoulder. The corner in which she had last spotted Lois and Cornelius was vacant. So much for dinner with Lois's brother.

Scowling, Velma repeated, "This letter is nothing important."

"Then open it so we can move on with our lives."

She considered shoving it into her purse and walking away. If she did that, Dillon would investigate Quincy, if he hadn't planned to already. No one carried around letters just in case they met the intended recipient by chance. She might not be able to prevent Dillon from poking his nose in places where it didn't belong, but she could dampen his curiosity for now.

Ripping open the envelope, Velma pulled out pages from a crossword puzzle book that was padding for a small wooden carving of a horned owl.

"See, I told you it was nothing," Velma said, feeling Dillon's eyes on the envelope's contents. His disappointment in the lack of juicy details was palatable, and so crushing, that he probably didn't even hear her properly. "This is a gift to go with the piano. He sent this without knowing I wasn't at the newspaper anymore."

"When are you going to fix that? It's rather distracting to keep getting your mail."

"Just ignore it." Velma tucked the letter into her purse. "Now that your curiosity is sated and your errand complete, am I allowed to go home?"

He executed a low, exaggerated bow, his camera bag jingling. "Don't let me stop you, Miss Frye."

Velma headed out of the building, but she did not go home. Instead she went to Checkers. Because it was daylight, the nightclub bore its camouflage as a coffee shop. She sat down in a quiet corner booth, ordered a drink, and got out a pencil. She worked away at the crossword puzzles, easily filling the boxes with the right letters. Once they were completed, she used the hidden numbers carved into the owl figurine as a cipher key. She circled the letters across the seven puzzle pages, and the following message appeared:

TROUBLE AT THE WORLD FAIR

COME TO PHILADELPHIA TO TALK

BEWARE MR CLARITY

What had Quincy gotten himself into this time? Velma pondered. Her eldest cousin dealt in antiques—acquiring, assessing, and selling magical artifacts with great historical value—and until recently oversaw a very popular shop in Harlem. The shop had closed earlier that year and the last missive from home speculated that Quincy was seeking new work to better provide for his family. As he was her least favorite cousin, Velma had not given it much thought, but this missive made her wonder if she should have gotten more details. Velma had never quite gotten along with Quincy. Clashing personalities and a large age gap made it difficult long before they'd had a falling-out a few years back over the family's elemental pistols. An invention by a family friend, the pistols distilled potions via explosive propulsion so that ice shards, sleeping potions, flares, and more could be expelled like bullets. Gifted to Velma and her cousins when they each set out into the world, they had to promise to never sell or attempt to re-create the pistols. For Velma and the others, it was an easy promise . . . but not for Quincy. He thought they should have been sold. Not only that, as the eldest cousin, he thought he deserved them all. Through these series of arguments, he lost his set of pistols and they went to Velma. He took this as a major affront and laid his grievances at her feet using words and language that didn't bear repeating. These days, they were polite to each other when under their grandparents' roof, but once on the street outside, they were strangers. Yet now he asked for her help?

Velma was headed to Long Island anyway, so going by way of Philadelphia would actually be easier, as she was due a visit to her relatives. Judging by Quincy's enigmatic message, such a visit might even be needed.

CHAPTER 4

B efore Velma left Chicago, she had one last thing to take care of. The world's fair in that hidden message brought her to the area in which the International Exposition of Arcane Arts and Sciences was going to be held. Considered a precursor to the Century of Progress, which was to open in a couple of years, the arcane expo was broken out of the original plans for the world's fair because one of the buildings was to be the city's first arcane museum. The expo didn't officially open until August, and it was still very much in progress. A bribe to one of the workers on the site told her that a lot of the exhibits were still in storage, as last-minute repairs were being undertaken. A further tour of the grounds and quick glances at the five buildings set to hold the expo told her there wasn't anything of immediate concern.

Nor any sign of the trouble the letter hinted at.

Deciding to keep it in mind for now until she had further proof, she left Chicago hoping an interview with her cousin would bring better insights.

Arriving in Philadelphia with the sun to her back, Velma skimmed her plane across the McDowell farm with her fuel indicator very nearly on empty.

Her arrival had Jackson running out of the barn. He stopped short, though, and shook his head in mild annoyance seeing it was just her. She left the usual fee and extra for the family to watch her plane. For all his annoyance, Jackson tried to give the extra back, but Velma refused, as she'd arrived without warning and was borrowing his bicycle—a fact he learned as she hopped on it.

Evening was rapidly arriving as Velma pedaled to her grandparents' home, the only place she could get to in the dark without fail.

Well, that and the local cemetery.

She was quite proud of herself for that, because unlike some of her cousins who lived in Philadelphia for part of their lives, Velma and her sister came here only during the summers. Yet despite that, Juniper Street was a constant in Velma's life that had embedded itself in her mind and heart. Neither it nor its occupants were unchanging, but she always knew to expect a certain amount of chaos when she arrived—not just from her relatives, but from family friends like the Caldwells, who were often in residence. Her grandparents had operated the Mourning Dove funeral home since the 1870s, but more than just funerals and wakes had occurred within its walls. Various book clubs, charity organization meetings, civil rights meetings, family reunions, amateur theater, All Hallows' Eve parties, Easter teas, broomstick ceremonies, weddings, and much, *much* more had taken place in the various rooms—not to mention the many mysteries discussed and solved in dramatic fashion.

Knowing that dinner was likely well underway, Velma avoided ringing the front door and brought the bicycle around the back and through the garden. She had just put the bicycle away when a light blossomed over her head.

"Don't think you can sneak into my house without me knowing," called a voice from out of the darkness.

Velma laughed as she turned around and spotted a familiar figure standing outside the workshop. "You can't blame me for trying, can you, Granny?"

"One day you might surprise me. But today is not that day," her grandmother said.

Scattered starlight glowed over Henrietta Rhodes's head, illuminating her from her amused smile to the hairpins that gleamed with a magic all their own. Famous for her gift of storytelling as well as her dressmaking, she was the anchor of the family and remained steadfast despite any storm that battered around them. There was no better practitioner of celestial magic around, and the name Henrietta Rhodes still struck fear into the criminal elements in town and their descendants. Although to Velma, Henrietta would always be her dear and sweet Granny Rhodes.

Laughing, Velma strode over to hug her grandmother, breathing in the scents of good clean soap and lemon. "It's good to see you!"

Henrietta patted her back. "It's delightful when you visit, especially since your mother is convinced you have fallen off the globe." She pulled away, giving Velma a rather stern look. "Didn't I tell you to go to Bramble Crescent after your last visit? Your mother calls the house because she knows if you go anywhere, you'll end up here at some point."

"She calls here," Velma said, hoping to wiggle out of a lecture, "because you know everything."

"I do," her grandmother admitted, and her expression softened. "Or I try to, at least. I suppose telling Beatrice you're still alive will suffice."

Velma looked away in embarrassment as she let go of her grandmother. She did visit her parents as often as she could, but Velma had been dragging her heels about going back to Bramble Crescent for over a year since her last blowup with her sister. While Velma knew her father and mother were eager to see her again, Velma did not relish encountering her sister anytime soon, and the island was too damn small to avoid Carolyn completely.

"Did you run away from home?" asked a very youthful voice from the shadows.

Clutching a telescope to her chest, a young girl gazed up with avid curiosity. The daughter of one of her cousins, but which one, Velma couldn't recall until she saw the resemblance in the girl's features. This was Arista's daughter, and Velma hadn't seen the girl in several years since Arista lived in Minnesota, of all places.

"Not exactly," Velma remarked.

"Velma has run away from home more than a few times," Henrietta said. "Let me tell you a story about when—"

"Who else is here besides Gregory and his family?" Velma hastily interrupted. She loved her grandmother's stories, but depending on the tale, she didn't always like playing the starring role.

"Olivia is with us for the summer, as Arista thought it was time for her to start learning the family business. You won't see much of Francenia—the sleepaway camp she works for will be starting soon. Lysander has just moved out with his daughter after getting a new job at the post office out in Richmond. Lorene's grandson is taking a course at the college and lodging next door, so I doubt you'll see him. You just missed Emmett Caldwell, as he's got a job as a doorman at a fancy resort down in West Virginia. I'll tell you who's not here, though!" Henrietta continued with relish. "Emmeline was supposed to be here for the summer, but she's doing another film, and this time it's being made right in Paris."

"I know Emmy's happy about that," Velma said. Her cousin had moved to France eight years ago after being scouted to dance and sing at one of Paris's most famous venues. Emmy was now currently making appearances in movies. She wasn't starring, but they were decent roles that allowed her to act and were far better than the stereotyped options she had here in the States.

"What about Quincy?" Velma asked.

"He has not visited this summer," her grandmother replied, her eyes filled with quiet interest. "Nor am I expecting him anytime soon. You know he moved his family out of Harlem quite recently."

"Then he must be busy."

"Surely not busy enough, since you're looking for him." Henrietta's words were airy, but Velma heard a note of suspicion in her grandmother's voice all the same. "Why don't you get something to eat? Gregory's boys are cleaning up the kitchen, but there was something held back for you."

Velma got the covered plate and had barely sat down before the boys pestered her with questions about her plane and her travels, and of course gave her a hard time about the recent loss that her favorite team, the Third Street Hogs, took in their last game. At thirteen and fourteen, the pair were avid baseball fans, and Velma was probably their favorite cousin, as she'd gotten them signed baseballs from several players of varying notoriety.

Velma had just finished eating when she heard a whistle from the doorway.

Her grandfather stood there, urging with a slight nod for her to follow him into the hall. If Velma's grandmother knew everything, her grandfather understood how everything worked, as he'd been a blacksmith for many years. His curiosity and interest in all number of things were best seen in his eclectic book collection and the varying talents and skills among his children and grandchildren. Benjamin Rhodes was a pillar of the community as both a mediator and a dispenser of justice with unorthodox methods. Velma's most cherished memories of her grandfather were of sitting in his workshop with him as he taught her how to make rings, lockets, bracelets, and other pieces of jewelry.

At the sight of her grandfather, the boys went back to cleaning, and Velma took one last swallow of her food and slipped away to the peace and quiet of the hallway.

"What's the ratio of fuel you're running?" Benjamin asked.

"I got something new I'm trying, but I had to switch back to the old standard for this trip," Velma admitted as she followed him into the study.

He tutted. "That means you're mixing fuels up in your tank and I know you aren't flushing it out."

Velma shrugged. "You can give it a look if you like. I'll be here for a few days."

Her grandfather just shook his head. "Your mechanic didn't like my fixes the last time."

"I'll just tell him I did it."

"That solves nothing." He laughed. "It was a surprise to hear you were coming for a visit outside of your usual times. I suppose there's a reason?"

"I found an enchanted object. I thought—well, hoped—you could give it a look. It's a pocket watch, and there's a strange symbol carved on it."

"Curious," Benjamin said. That single word lingered around them as he turned over her words. "A strange symbol, you say?"

"I don't recognize it at all," Velma said.

"Even more curious." He was quiet for a moment. "Alexander studied symbols alongside his languages," he finally said, citing Velma's uncle. "You won't be able to talk to him easily. Alexander and Eleanora are traveling with Katherine in Libya. Katherine's last letter said something about some ruins in Leptis Magna. They might be traveling again soon. Alexander's translation work was taking too long, and delayed their trip to the Nile valley."

Her mother's older twin siblings had always traveled widely abroad for their respective fields of botany and linguistics ever since Aunt Kat's messy divorce. The trips had become longer since Aunt Nora had joined them. Aunt Nora was not an academic, but she loved to soak in the local culture of the area and drag Velma's uncle to all the tourist attractions.

"You have an address, don't you?" Velma insisted. "Can I send a wire to Uncle Alex?"

Her grandfather's expression didn't alter, but he looked upon her with even more interest. "We might be able to solve this mystery ourselves. Let me look at this pocket watch first before we go through all that trouble, shall we?"

While everything else in the house changed throughout the seasons, her grandparents' study did not. Three large bookshelves lined the room, and there was even one under the window. Her grandfather's piano sat proudly against the wall. More than a device to croon out delicate melodies and entertain family and friends, the piano was where he went to puzzle out the difficulties of the mysteries he worked on throughout the years, and he claimed more than one mystery had been solved as he tickled the keys. A basket of knitting supplies was in a corner, and several telescopes were lined up like ducks in a far corner. Maps of the city and outlying areas were spread across the wall by the desk, feathered with pushpins. Painted on the wall next to the door that led into her grandparents' bedroom was the Rhodes family tree. Far from static, each time change occurred within the family, whether it was a birth, marriage, or death, the tree shifted to include this information. The enchantment was uncannily accurate, which made her cousin Lysander, who learned through it that he had a daughter, call it both a curse and a boon.

Henrietta and Olivia were already in the study. Olivia knelt before the coffee table, shaking a pair of dice in a shallow bowl. Seated on the couch, Henrietta mended a small purple cloth that Velma remembered being used to illustrate a particular lesson about opportune moments of spellcasting. Benjamin settled opposite of them in the armchair, picking up the book he had left behind.

After casting a small spell that sent the piano bench sliding over to join them, Velma sat down and got the pocket watch out of her bag. "Grandpa, you don't have to look at it now. The morning will be fine."

Her grandfather waved off her words. "Doesn't matter. We're going to be up anyway waiting for Gregory and Zadie to get back."

"Murder or a wake?" Velma asked.

Olivia couldn't hide her laugh quick enough as Henrietta scowled. "We have a bet. He's saying it's unrelated, but I disagree."

"There've been two deaths that are very similar," Benjamin clarified. "Gregory's gone to check a few things that could connect it, while his wife is making the usual inquiries. If it weren't so far away, I'd have gone with them."

"We have to let the young people handle things, or they'll never know what they are capable of," Henrietta remarked.

Velma leaned forward with a slight grin. "Is this a hint you're not helping me much with this?"

"It all depends on what you brought us, my little magpie," her grandmother said.

Velma unwrapped her handkerchief from around the watch and held it out to her grandparents. She expected questions and mild curiosity. What Velma did not expect was the look of vast alarm exchanged between her grandparents. A look that had decades of nuance and understanding, and meant one thing only:

This is troubling.

Velma had already known this pocket watch could lead to great misfortune, but she had underestimated how much.

"You've seen this watch before?" Velma asked in a more professional tone as unease swelled inside her.

"Not the watch, but the symbol," Benjamin said.

"Earlier we found a man with a knife rammed in his stomach," Henrietta explained. "A suicide due to vast debts. At least, that's how it appeared, as there was nothing that indicated a struggle with an intruder. As we searched the room, however, we found an orrery. In a *hidden* room, I should add. The problem is, even though we concluded the orrery was involved, we couldn't figure out how. We brought it here to the house in case there was something we'd overlooked."

"An orrery?" Velma echoed. She vaguely remembered seeing a device like that in the study during her last visit earlier this spring, but she hadn't given it a closer look. Her grandmother had a great interest in astronomy, and an orrery was not out of place in the house. "I thought it was yours. I noticed it before but didn't think there was anything magical about it."

"Hopefully you will this time," Benjamin said. "It's down in the second cellar. Olivia will have to show you where it is as Zadie has been in one of her cleaning moods lately."

Olivia dutifully jumped up, eager to be of assistance.

They crossed over to the other side of the house and went down to the second cellar, which was used for storage only. The orrery Velma had glimpsed on her last visit was now set up on a table. Made of brass with an antique air, it displayed the sun and eight of the nine planets, although Velma shouldn't expect otherwise since Pluto had just been newly found. Each satellite sat on a thin metal rod, and the dangling lights in the cellar gleamed across the surface of the tiny planets.

The same mark from the pocket watch was prominently displayed on the side.

"I still don't understand what an orrery is," Olivia said. "I know it shows the planets, but I don't know what it actually does."

"It mainly demonstrates the motion of the solar system, and I think you can determine solar eclipses with them, but I could be wrong," Velma said.

"I guess that's interesting," Olivia said, although her tone implied the opposite.

"I'm surprised it's down here," Velma said as she continued her study.

Olivia took on a gossipy air. "It was in the front room before. Fletcher and Lewis were tossing a baseball around and nearly knocked it off the table. So it was moved."

"Because the boys broke something?"

"No." Olivia shook her head. "Because it *did* something. I didn't see it, but it got all the adults excited."

The boys must have hit something in their play that caused the orrery to react. Velma took a step closer to the device. The suggestion that the orrery had something to do with the mysterious death her grandparents had uncovered played on her mind as she peered at the miniature planets. One of the planets, Mars, was scuffed, and Velma tapped it lightly. The planet quivered for a moment and then it moved. The rest of the celestial bodies followed suit, spinning around in a mesmerizing dance. As the tiny planets twirled, a soft clicking sound began. Velma ignored it until a bluish glow radiated from the planets.

"Step back," Velma called to Olivia, but the suggestion was not needed. The girl was already on the bottommost cellar step, primed to run, and only still there because her curiosity had won out over pragmatism.

Velma reached out to stop the device. The bracelet on her wrist emitted a gentle pulse of magic and the Hydra star sigil slipped out.

The mythological creature rose overhead, glittering with stars, its necks craned toward the orrery below it.

With a flick of her hand, Velma directed it forward, and the Hydra's heads struck the eight planets. The orrery halted and the stand holding the sun lifted upward, revealing a small hatch. After a moment's thought, Velma reached over and flipped it open.

Out tumbled a pair of scissors.

Not any plain pair, though. They were gold, the blades etched with twisting ivy vines. The handles not only had the same symbol of the intricate circles but a name.

Clarice Sitwell.

Velma knew that name.

More than knew. She had grown up *knowing* that name. The cursed Sitwell family was famous on Bramble Crescent for all the tragedies that had preceded their departure, including Clarice Sitwell's suicide. Velma knew the name especially, as the house the family had lived in was her childhood home—her father's parents had bought the old Sitwell manor and turned it into an inn.

Originally built by Jeremiah Sitwell in 1812, by 1832 the manor was abandoned following a series of terrible events that had started with the death of Clarice Sitwell and concluded with a fire that nearly burned the home to the ground. The manor sat empty and decaying for many years, but not forgotten. Tragedy kept company with the ruined building: persistent rumors circulated that Jeremiah Sitwell had left spells that violently attacked anyone that attempted to get inside the house.

On an island full of magic, such rumors weren't hard to believe. The manor remained abandoned until 1867, when Vernon and Camille Newberry transformed the ruined home into Beacon Inn. Tourists filled the rooms just to see if the rumors about the house were true, but as Velma grew up, the tragedy faded with time. As for any ghouls or curses left behind, Velma and her sister had never found any proof of such things.

Apparently, they hadn't been looking hard enough.

If these scissors had belonged to that doomed woman, and had been tucked into the machine, and had the same symbol as the pocket watch and the music box that Velma had found . . . it meant only one thing.

A visit to Bramble Crescent was now in order, after she'd avoided the island for over a year.

Oh, how the stars were laughing at her now!

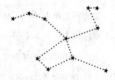

CHAPTER 5

These are well-crafted sewing scissors," her grandfather said as Velma sat in his workshop with him after breakfast the next morning. Suspended by his magic, the scissors slowly rotated before them so they could see the object from every angle. "Interesting that they were inside the orrery."

"Not my first place to keep something," Velma said. "There're no traces of blood."

"There wouldn't be—the man who last had the orrery wasn't stabbed with scissors."

"I was thinking of the person who had them before," Velma said.

Benjamin shook his head. "These aren't sharp enough to kill someone. To stab someone even in the neck would take too much force and damage the scissors. Look closely at the blades. There is no sign of wear. The owner never used them."

"Somehow they ended up hidden," Velma murmured.

"You say you're familiar with the name engraved on them?"

"*Clarice Sitwell newly made bride / wandered out into the unending tide / and she died died died,*" Velma recited.

"What's that?"

"It's a handclap game about the Sitwell family. All the kids on the island played it, especially once they realized Carolyn and I lived at Beacon Inn. There aren't any other Newberrys on the island, you see."

Her grandfather held out his hand and the scissors fell into his palm. With a slight shake of his head, he dropped them onto his workbench as he said, "That's the thing with small places—too many people knowing things they know nothing about."

"Well, in this case, *something* would be helpful." Velma sank onto the stool next to the table. "Clarice Sitwell died before the family left. As did her husband. I can't begin to figure out how these scissors and the orrery ended up here in Philadelphia. Her father-in-law, Jeremiah Sitwell, was a rather talented inventor. He made clocks and dabbled in other things from what I remember. He might have made all these things I've been finding."

"Items that left the island because the family sold them to pay their way," Benjamin suggested.

"It seems like it," Velma agreed. "There's no way to know for certain. This all happened in the 1830s. There isn't anyone alive to give an accurate account."

"There's always something. Stories pass from one generation to the other, after all. Your father might know something," Benjamin said with such care, it alerted Velma right away.

She leaned forward eagerly. "What do you know?"

"I suspect Rodney knows something he doesn't want to tell you, and he's done a good job of it because he hid it from us too." Benjamin didn't hide his annoyance at this feat. "It wasn't important then, but it seems it might be now."

"Perhaps these scissors can persuade him to go into any detail," Velma said.

"One would hope. Now, about this pocket watch. I'd like to make a thorough study of it before I make any repairs. When do you need it back? I have a few projects I'm working on." Her grandfather was officially retired, but his workbench was still covered with projects. He tinkered with anything as long as it wasn't glass or wand wood. He'd never had much luck with glass. As for wands, he claimed too many old prejudices to deal with. Although Wylda, another one of

Velma's cousins, was an expert wandmaker who lived in a remote part of Canada.

"The end of the week will be fine. You are doing me a favor, after all."

As he turned his attention elsewhere, Velma rolled up her sleeves and got to work on the music box. Because she already knew what it could do, she had no compunctions about taking it apart. Popping it open, Velma recognized all the pieces as being things typically found in music boxes—which was surprising given the quality of the music she had heard previously. As Velma poked and prodded, she found strange markings on the mechanisms. No, not just strange markings but star sigils. Velma traced her thumb along them. She'd never seen something like this before.

Making a note to ask Gregory for sketches—he seldom got the chance to draw these days, so it wouldn't be hard to convince him of this favor—Velma laid out the pieces of the music box and copied her observations into a notebook. As she finished making her notes, her grandfather asked rather abruptly:

"How does the rest of the rhyme go?"

She sat back, glancing at the music box across from her. "I only remember bits of it."

"Something is always better than nothing," Benjamin said.

Tapping her fingers along the wood, Velma remembered clapping and slapping her sister's hands as they sat in their bedroom while rain pounded against the window.

> At the house on the hill
> Bad luck and trouble done spilled
> One and two and two and one
> They came and got gone gone
> Mister and Missus by the moon moon moon

May come back soon soon soon
One and two and three
Three and two and one
Bad luck and trouble done spilled
Junior left first after getting his fill fill fill
Sally Sitwell was too late
Took too long and that was her fate fate fate

Velma kept tapping the table a bit more, humming to keep the beat. She knew she was missing words, but some of the important parts were still there:

Clarice Sitwell newly made bride
wandered out into the unending tide
and she died died died
Jeremiah Sitwell made it so
Will he come back we don't know know know

Velma stopped. "That's all I remember."

"Stars, that's rather gruesome, isn't it?" Fran lingered in the doorway. "They make children different on that island."

"Hardly," Velma scoffed before regarding her cousin. "You're here early this morning."

"You're here unexpectantly—but I'm glad."

"That happy to see me?"

"It means the odds of my brother and Zadie pulling me into the case they are working on has just gone down."

"Don't bet on those odds," Velma said. "I have a case of my own and I will only be here a few days."

"Then we need to talk soon. I have news about what really happened at the Saunders wedding—and guess what: you were right!"

"Francenia, what brings you by?" Benjamin interrupted.

"Just popped in to ask your help about something," Fran said. "And, Vi, can you do me a favor? When you're at the Caldwell store picking up fuel, can you grab a few things for me? I need some rope, a bucket, and a pronged hook for camp." Fran pulled a schematic from her pocket and placed it in front of their grandfather. "Grandpa, this is for the trap to protect Camp Artemis's boundaries from miscreants who want to harass us. We got fined for the protection spells we laid down last year. The head counselor says it's a political ploy, since the nearby white majority neighborhood doesn't want us there. The camp already has to pay this phony 'magic conjuration fee' to the town just to stay open. Which is why we're scrapping the herb garden this year." Fran sighed. "I was so hoping to teach my girls the proper way to grow moondancer flowers."

"You still could," Benjamin said. "They're Grade One magical."

Fran shook her head. "It's not worth it. It's a miracle we can keep the camp open at all."

Leaving Fran and their grandfather to figure out the best way to booby-trap the sleepaway camp's boundaries, Velma headed back outside.

The garden adjacent to the workshop was in full bloom with various flowers, some more enchanting than you might have thought at first glance. On the other side of the yard, Olivia sat on a bench playing cards with a boy around her age. Slung over his shoulder was a boxy hearing aid that made a rattling sound as he leaned forward to slap a card on the space between them.

It was a heated game, and they had an audience. On the rooftop, a cluster of juvenile crows watched the card game below with apparent interest. A few wings flapped up in annoyance when Velma blocked their view.

The birds moved to get a better view from the oak tree, and the small stormy cloud they made overhead caused Olivia to drop her cards with a small shriek as she tumbled to the grass in a sprawl of limbs. The subsequent squawking from the birds had the young girl quivering at each sound even though none of the crows would ever hurt her.

"Are you okay?" Velma asked with some concern.

"So many birds," Olivia squeaked, her hands covering her head. "Where did they come from!"

"They're always here," Velma said. "They won't hurt you. We look after them and they look after us, so there's no need to be scared."

The boy, still seated cross-legged on the bench, just shook his head and then signed, "She's only pretending because she was losing."

Velma signed right back, "How bad?"

The boy's grin was wide and toothy. "Very!"

Olivia's head lifted and she suddenly sat up, as if sensing they were talking about her. As her gaze fell on the boy, he quickly pretended to shuffle the cards.

"Did he tell you I was losing?" Olivia asked.

"No, not at all," Velma signed. She turned to the boy. "I don't think we've met before. I'm Velma, a cousin of Olivia's. And you are?"

"Emerson Dunmore. Miss Penelope is my fairy godmother."

Velma looked at him, certain she'd misinterpreted something. She was a bit rusty with her sign language skills, but not that rusty. "Don't you mean godmother?"

"No, fairy godmother," Emerson signed with a sly smile. "Miss Penelope is teaching me about all sorts of plants, when I'm not taking classes at the Needham School. The headmistress, Miss Lorene, gave me special permission."

"Oh yes!" Olivia cried, so excited that she switched back to spoken speech. "Aunt Penelope promises I can have lessons too. I'm interested in the poisonous plants, but my mother doesn't like the idea."

"Same as my mother," Emerson signed.

"Word of advice: don't tell your parents about anything you learn here." Velma winked at them. "That's what I did, and I turned out rather well!"

Velma headed into the kitchen, and she had just grabbed an apple when her grandmother summoned her into the study.

Seated at the desk, Henrietta tucked one of her elemental pistols into her purse before picking up her hat.

"You're headed to the general store, aren't you?" Henrietta asked as she adjusted the brim into place. "I have a list of things I'll need you to pick up while you're there. I would have Zadie do it, but since you're here . . ."

"It's no trouble. I won't be going to Long Island until later."

"Thank you so much. Penelope sent her new student to bring me to her place. She claims there's been a rather suspicious character stalking the community garden, so I'm going to make sure there is nothing to worry about. I don't think there is, though. I bet she just wants to gossip—she knows I'll leave the house if I get a whiff of trouble afoot! Penelope is my dearest friend, but even I get bored with all the botanical drama occurring in the circles she frequents. There're always barbs and curses, but never the interesting sort."

"Granny," Velma interrupted, "do you remember a rhyme that Carolyn and I used to do?"

"You must be more specific, my dear. There's been a great deal of rhymes, ring shouts, clapping games, skip ropes, and more done in this house."

"Yet, you remember all of them," Velma said.

A smug smile appeared on her grandmother's face. "I do my best. Tell me a piece you remember."

Velma did just that, repeating everything she'd told her grandfather, only to be interrupted midway through.

"That's not all of it," Henrietta said.

"I know. I only remember a piece."

"*Your* piece," her grandmother pointed out. "You know a part and your sister knows a part. This game of yours has call-and-response elements. You don't remember?"

"I was very little."

"And you ask me to remember!" she cried. "Stars above, child! Why don't you ask Carolyn about the missing piece?" A pointed look came with these words and Velma decided at once it was time to run her errands.

"I'm heading out," Velma said.

"Why don't you take Olivia with you?" her grandmother added as Velma passed through the doorway. Although worded as a question, it was a request with very little room to argue. Quite possibly, Velma suspected, it was the reason she'd been called into the room in the first place. "Also, if you have time today, could you show her some simple spell forms? Or how to use one of the elemental pistols? Penelope said she found a spare one the other day, and when she's done fixing it, she will put it aside for Olivia to have when she's old enough."

"I would love to, but doing a quick lesson might not be enough," Velma protested. "Why not let Gregory—"

"We have asked too much of Gregory and Zadie," Henrietta said with surprising firmness. "I'm not saying teach Olivia everything in a handful of days, but she's eager to learn. She's also starting to poke into things she shouldn't, and you know *quite* well about the perils of that."

Unable to argue this undeniable fact, Velma just replied, "I'll keep her busy, then."

As they headed for the general store, Olivia shoved her hands into her overall pockets as she and Velma walked. Fancy embroidery couldn't hide that the legs were slightly too short for her despite the hems being let out.

"How old are you now?" Velma asked.

"Eleven."

"I thought so," Velma said hastily. "You look about that age. You've gotten so tall."

They walked a bit more in uneasy silence.

"Do you know who I am without looking at the family tree?" Olivia asked.

The bluntness coaxed a chortle out of Velma. "You're named after Uncle Oliver, who was Arista's favorite out of the aunts and uncles. It was my suggestion after your parents couldn't decide on a name nearly a full week after you were born."

Olivia just nodded, saying nothing to ease the conversation.

"How do you like Philadelphia?" Velma asked desperately as they crossed the street.

"It's all right. I'm only here because my parents don't want me around."

"I doubt that," Velma said, already regretting her question. "Your father's a Pullman, so he's traveling a lot and they want you to be somewhere safe."

"I know that," Olivia huffed. "But he's *always* away, and while he's gone, Mama's also never around. She's dealing with spies the Pullman Company have around town who are trying to stop the Brother-hood from growing its collective bargaining power so the porters can get fair wages, reduced hours, and arrange a strike so we can get the fat cats to listen to the backbone of the company."

Velma laughed at the torrent of words that came out of the girl's mouth with the intonations of someone else. "You've been listening at doors when the union meets at your house, haven't you?"

Olivia's smile was as tenuous as it was sheepish. "I got caught listening in on the ladies' auxiliary meeting and my mother decided it was best I went away for the summer."

"Might be a good thing. You'll have fun here. Why, when I was your age—" Velma held out an arm, holding back her younger cousin, suddenly alert and wary. "Stay behind me."

Farther along the street loud voices and outcry tinged the air with a peculiar kind of fear.

The type of fear that only occurs when death shows up uninvited to the party.

"Do you think there was an accident?" Olivia asked.

"It seems likely with all the fuss. Shall we find out?" Velma asked before glancing at her cousin. Olivia would have seen dead bodies while at the funeral home, but there was a difference when it came to murder. Although Olivia had been here for a few weeks, Velma didn't know how acquainted Arista's daughter had become with the family business.

"I'll be fine," Olivia said quickly, seeming to sense that Velma was about to tell her to stay behind. "I've been helping Granny and Grandpa."

"Then keep your ears and eyes open and alert." Velma discreetly cast a spell along the street, sending a ripple of magic through the crowd to thin it out. The light drew people away, and the ones who weren't easily distracted were gently pushed aside with practiced ease as Velma got to the front of the crowd.

A woman lay face down on the cobblestones with a jagged piece of wood rammed into her back. A large splotch of dark and drying blood spoiled the delicate print of her dress. The flesh was cool under Velma's fingers, and she knew the woman was dead without even checking for a pulse. Not only was the body very stiff, bruising and discoloration of the woman's face and hands indicated death had occurred several hours earlier.

Given the pattern of foot traffic around her, Velma was tempted to say the woman had lain out nearly all morning unseen and undisturbed until now.

The fine light gray powder that appeared on the woman's clothes could explain that minor mystery. As Velma rubbed the powder between her fingers, she ran through a list of potential enchantments as well as anyone local who could have done such a thing. Both lists were quite long.

Looking up from the body, Velma expected to see Olivia staring down at the woman, but the girl peered up at the roof of a nearby shop.

The roof didn't look damaged, but before she could see what Olivia had spotted, a whistle blew.

Wyatt Jameson strode down the street. He worked at the city morgue, Velma recalled from the latest gossip, and his frown made him appear a decade older despite his having attended the same Sunday school classes with Velma every time she'd come to Philadelphia for the summer.

"You," Wyatt said to the young man who was clearly his assistant. "Let's get this woman off the street. Everyone, this is not a show—we need a clear path!"

His voice wasn't strong, but the flare of the Leo Minor star sigil he had cast with the flick of his fingers got the crowd moving in an orderly fashion. His assistant got a wheelbarrow from the shoe shop and ripped apart a burlap sack to cover the woman.

"And you," Wyatt said to Velma, "whatever you're thinking, know this is none of your business."

"I doubt it. Just look at her—" Velma began.

"There is nothing here of interest to you! Nor is it to you or your relatives. If a single Rhodes comes down to the morgue, there will be trouble on your heads!"

"Don't be so sure—you might need our help," Velma said. She pointed to the body, and the tenting done to the burlap due to the protruding stick. "It's pretty hard to accidently stake yourself in the back when you land face-first on the ground."

He sputtered and fussed for several moments as Velma egged him on. Not because the task delighted her, but because she spotted Olivia climbing up the side of a nearby building.

Silently applauding the girl's excellent instincts, Velma moved her right arm behind her back and discreetly tapped her bracelet. Unspooling a wind spell, Velma gave Olivia a little boost onto the roof.

"You . . . you," Wyatt went on, not quite coherent yet, "you poke your nose in places where it doesn't belong!"

"Only because I'm curious about so many things," Velma said. "I love to learn as much as I can, especially about strange accidents. Now, no need to be so formal. We're old friends, aren't we?"

"We are most certainly not." Wyatt's mouth twitched. "You've hardly spoken a word to me in twelve years!"

"Oh, that can't be true," Velma declared, knowing it was probably longer than that. She reached out to brush his shoulder, throwing him a smile to keep all his attention on her. "I'm in town for a bit. Why don't we go somewhere and talk about old times later?"

Wyatt huffed, "You're just trying to get into the morgue."

"Oh, now don't be silly," Velma said, patting his shoulder with a laugh, flicking a spell toward Olivia to soften the girl's landing back onto the ground. "Why would I want to talk to you in a morgue?"

"That's not what—"

"It's been a long time since we've seen each other. Things have changed."

Wyatt's scowl finally relented, and Velma knew she'd hooked him. "I heard you got married. You go by Frye now."

"Oh, that's all wrong! I just took a more exciting name to pin adventures on. Newberry is the name of a girl you bring to meet your folks. Frye is the name of someone you have a fun time with and then you hope your folks will like."

Wyatt blinked, clearly taking a moment to consider her words. His assistant, in the meantime, stood nearby, clearly uncomfortable about what she was saying *and* the dead body he was carting in the wheel-barrow.

In the background, Olivia scurried down the street with the bag she had clearly plucked off the roof clutched to her chest.

"You know where to find me," Velma said as she turned to leave, giving Wyatt a wink. "Unless you want me to look for you."

With a perfect turn that contained more of a flounce to draw the eye, Velma left him there, not bothering to wait for an answer.

Sometimes creating a distraction was simply too easy.

When Velma met up with Olivia at the street corner, the girl was busy going through the purloined purse. Before Velma could even ask how Olivia spotted the purse, her young cousin paused, freezing up in a particular way that Velma was familiar with.

"What have you found?" Velma asked.

Olivia held up a card. Or rather, two tarot cards pasted together to display the card faces. One side was a vase with a large sunflower while the other displayed moonflowers in a garden. For the uninformed it didn't make much sense, but Velma immediately knew what it was: a calling card, and one that needed no words to convey. Her grandparents had received such cards ever since they'd started solving mysteries in Philadelphia.

The dead woman had been looking for help, and she'd known exactly where to get it from.

She just didn't get it in time.

CHAPTER 6

I t even has traces of blood on it," Gregory said as he peered over his glasses to study the card. He handed it back to Velma. "Certainly is interesting."

"Just interesting?" Velma asked. "I thought you'd have more to say than that. Zadie already told me it's from the Vibrant Atelier tarot deck."

"Then that's all you're going to get from us. If you can't tell, we are rather busy." Gregory gestured around the main cellar.

The problem with looking into murders from the base of a funeral home is that other bodies often took precedence. As it was, each one of the four tables held a different dead body, all of whom had died in four different ways but had been found in the same locked room last night. While no one was saying *murder* quite yet, Velma had her guesses, but she wasn't sharing any of them. She had learned her lesson a long time ago about spouting theories related to cases in progress: speak up and you have to prove said theory.

Still, she would have liked *some* more feedback from Gregory. The youngest and only son of Uncle Alex and Aunt Nora, her dependable, earnest, and sometimes melancholic cousin was the obvious heir of the funeral home. Lanky like his father, Gregory had a dry wit and an ocean full of patience to deal with Velma and her shenanigans.

Just not today.

"You sound as if I'm trying to pass it to you?" Velma pouted.

"Aren't you doing exactly that?" Zadie asked as she cheerfully tied a heavy apron over her clothes. "You're dressing it up nicely, but you're about to request some assistance."

"I'm not asking for anything!" Velma said quickly, reminded of her grandmother's words about her cousin and his wife. "I didn't even bring the dead woman here."

"You better not," Gregory retorted as he picked up his sketchbook to draw the bodies before him. "We actually have a funeral planned later this week and we haven't gotten to it yet."

"Why not? You're usually very precise about these things."

"We're waiting on the body," Zadie chimed in helpfully. "Last we heard Oretha Lane is still alive."

"The woman's been comatose for a week," Gregory said with some exasperation. "Her son is convinced she's already passed, but I'm waiting for official confirmation."

"You didn't check yourself?" Velma clucked her tongue disapprovingly.

"Of course I checked!" Gregory rolled his eyes. "I just didn't jab her foot with the stick."

Velma's eyes trailed to the very long and thin rod that hung nearby. With a tip so sharp that it drew blood by brushing against it, the rod was a fail-safe to make sure the dead were truly dead. According to Velma's mother, the stick was first used during a case where one man faked his death three times.

"Thank the stars you didn't," Zadie said. "We would have lost the account."

"Only if she woke up," Gregory grumbled.

Velma waved the card once more at Gregory. "That means you have the time to help me."

"For the last time, Vi," Gregory exclaimed. "You know the rules: you find it, it's your case."

"Technically, Olivia did. She found Delia Moore's purse—that's the dead woman, by the way—thrown up on the roof. There wasn't much in there besides the card. A train ticket, a room key, a book from a library, a notebook, a half-empty perfume bottle, and her wallet."

"Just all the things you need to figure out who she is and why she was seeking help from the family," Gregory remarked. "So . . . why aren't you doing that?"

"I have another case," Velma said. "Besides, Olivia is old enough to solve a mystery on her own. You should have seen her jump up on the roof to get the purse. I didn't even have to give her any encouragement. She just needs help with the finer details."

"At least she wants to investigate." Gregory grunted.

"Now, Gregory, don't start this again," Zadie warned.

"What's the matter?" Velma asked.

"Olivia's the only one interested in mystery solving." Gregory sighed. "Our boys aren't even interested in puzzle solving despite my mother giving them several crossword puzzle books."

"I'm sure they'll change their minds when they are a bit older," Zadie added hopefully.

Velma could tell Gregory not so privately doubted it, and she couldn't help but agree. The boys had grown up here—if they had no interest in mystery solving after being in the heart of things, it wasn't going to change anytime soon.

"It might be for the best. My sister never liked mystery solving, and now she's running the inn after my father retired. It may be the same with Lewis and Fletcher."

"Stars," Zadie exclaimed, "do you think we'll be running the funeral home that long?"

This question wasn't for Velma, it was directed at Gregory with a sharpness that showed that this was another conversation they'd had before. The pair had met at the local art school, gotten married quickly, and started a family soon after. Because they stayed at Juniper Street, they slowly got involved in the funeral home and other activities, eventually taking over once Henrietta and Benjamin stepped back from the day-to-day work. For the past few years Velma assumed Gregory and his wife enjoyed running the funeral home, but she might have wanted them to do so since she had no plans to take over in their stead.

Gregory hastily cleared his throat. "After your visit to Long Island, how long will you be staying?"

"I'm not sure, my plans may change when I go see Quincy."

Gregory was stunned to silence while Zadie gasped. "You're *looking* for Quincy!" she said. "What did he do this time?"

"I just have questions for him," Velma said as she ignored the concern on their faces. "I know Quincy closed his shop and moved but nothing more."

"I can get you his address," Zadie said. "His wife sent us some old clothes that their sons had outgrown earlier this year."

"Was there a note that might have indicated any trouble or concern?"

"Only that she has too big a heart," Zadie said with uncharacteristic mordancy. "She sent the clothes, saying I'd know better than she about charity cases, which tells me things are going mighty fine with them."

"At least a few months ago," Gregory added darkly. "So what's changed?"

"I got a letter from him in the form of a crossword cipher," Velma said. "He gave me a warning of trouble and wanted to talk to me. I half expected him to be here at the house waiting for me, but given what Granny told me, your sister was more likely to come home from France than Quincy was to make a short visit."

"Maybe I should come with you. If Quincy is asking for your help—"

"He sent a letter to the newspaper office. Given the roundabout way he went to contact me, it must not be *that* urgent."

Velma met her cousin's eyes, aware that him asking to come with her to see Quincy was no small request. Quincy didn't get along with Gregory either, for a number of reasons, including Quincy saying some nasty things about how quickly Gregory and Zadie had gotten married.

"Because I trust you know what you're doing, I'm going to pretend to be convinced," Gregory said as he relented. "For now."

"Because Brooklyn is not the island he wants to go to," Zadie said airily. "Your sister and Edythe are running an artists' salon at the inn. We were invited but had to decline. Couldn't get away with all the dead bodies around."

"Edythe will host another if this is a success, and hopefully the funeral home will be less busy in the future," Velma said.

"People are always dying." Zadie shook her head. "That's not going to change anytime soon."

"Then you change the tune. Go on a holiday. This place won't fall apart in your absence. Just because everyone assumes you must do something doesn't mean you should."

"Is this advice or reflecting on your own choices?" Gregory asked.

"Now, why would I give an answer to such an obvious trap." Velma laughed as she sidestepped his question. "I'm just saying go on holiday, and the rest of us can cover for you. Fran and I did a rather decent job managing the funeral home that one week."

"What happened that week is a reason not to have a repeat performance," Gregory replied. As he glanced down at his wife he added with a wistful tone, "Although a week to draw something other than dead bodies would be nice. I can't remember when we last had a holiday."

"Think about it," Velma encouraged. "Now, what about Quincy's address?"

"Upstairs in my address book," Zadie said. "Don't do anything you regret."

"I can't promise that!" Velma called as she dashed up the cellar's stairs.

On the main floor, Olivia was seated in one of the hardback chairs in the dining room with her nose in a book. It was a very awkward place to sit and read, but it was by the cellar door, which had been opened just enough to let voices drift upstairs.

As Velma went to the front desk to grab the address book, Olivia easily abandoned her perch to follow Velma.

"Where are you going next?"

"I'm headed for Long Island," Velma said as she found Quincy's address. "And you can't come with me."

"Why are you going there? We need to find the murderer before the path goes cold."

"What makes you think there's a path to chase?" Velma asked.

Olivia held up her book, *The Cursed Sigil in the Railcar.* "That's what Athena Vance always does! There are clues at the site that can get lost if we delay."

"They were already lost," Velma explained. "Delia Moore didn't die there—what traces might have been at the scene were already stomped over by the crowd. Delia was dead for at least three hours before we found her. Also, it's not a case."

"But we found a dead body," Olivia protested.

"It's not important right now," Velma amended at the sight of the girl's confusion. "Not every mystery is worth pursuing. Sometimes you've got to choose what leads you follow and what you ignore. It's not always that easy." As Olivia drooped with disappointment, Velma added, "Chin up, kiddo. You're young and there're going to be plenty of mysteries to solve, especially the more you hang out here on Juniper Street."

CHAPTER 7

Velma landed her plane on the edges of a pickle farm in Long Island. An older couple, both liaisons with the Brooklyn Magnolia Muses office, waited for her with a bicycle and an autograph book. Velma signed the latter, and took the former to the film set.

At first she thought she might have missed it entirely. She was looking for a more defined set that had soundstages, looming lamps, and cameras. Instead the scene before her was akin to a traveling circus. Except there were no caged animals—just members of the crew moving lamps and other equipment between the tents.

"You would think that after Micheaux put out his film, there would be less pressure on the boss to wrap up this one," one of the crew members said. He had a rope around his shoulder, and the other carried a basket of potions. "The first talkie with an all-Negro cast is already out. What's wrong for settling with being second? Second is good."

"Second doesn't get remembered, according to the boss," the other replied.

"We're *already* second at everything else."

"We have to be first in something. That's why we're pushing. First one with magic effects can be historical. Even if we fail!"

"I doubt we're going to be the first. No filming is going on today. I heard it's because Delia locked herself in her dressing room. Want to take bets if she has been sipping too much of the shine?"

"Delia?" Velma exclaimed.

The pair spun her way.

"Yeah, Delia, star of this picture." The taller of the men cast a wary eye over Velma's neat blouse tucked into her wide-legged trousers. "Are you supposed to be here?"

"I'm a nurse." Velma straightened her spine and looked on with cool competence. "I'm here to help Delia, if you would be so kind as to point me in the right direction."

That was apparently enough to assuage their suspicions. Velma was led to a wagon, that with its faded paint and wind chimes looked to be a peddler's conveyance. A shimmer of magic ran along the door and shuttered windows, leaving Velma with a great deal of unease as she drew near.

Once the men were gone, Velma traced the arrow star sigil along the doorknob. Working the arrow like a needle undoing embroidery, she undid the spells until the door swung open. As Velma stepped into the wagon, she found that while the outside was rustic looking, inside it was Sleeping Beauty's boudoir, complete with frothy silk fabric hung from the ceiling. In the nest of sheets and blankets lay a young woman, so still that Velma bent over her to make sure she was still breathing. That was when Velma noticed the necklace in the woman's hand. The amethyst set in the center was stormy as nightmares and the deepest purple Velma had ever seen in the gemstone. The stone itself had been cut into an oval shape, the pendant being three finger widths wide.

Velma pulled out her handkerchief and took the necklace from the sleeping woman. Stitchwork on the handkerchief glowed a faint blue as Velma turned over the necklace and searched for the Sitwell mark. There was nothing on it. Nothing on the back, the sides, or even etched into the gemstone itself.

She had been so certain that Jeremiah Sitwell had made this! Yet even if it wasn't the object Velma was looking for, at least she was going to remove something harmful. As Velma considered how to report this, the actress stirred awake and then gave a gasp that would have been impressive if caught on film.

"What are you doing in here?" the woman declared, one hand flung to her chest. "I'll scream and get you taken away!"

"You'll do that to someone who just helped you?" Velma held out the necklace. "This was putting you into an enchanted sleep."

"I *want* such sleep. I have had the worst sort of nightmares lately, things you cannot imagine."

"I'm sure I can't," Velma drawled, "but this necklace does more than give you sleep. Used with great frequency, it'll leave you in a permanent dream state where you'll be unable to tell if you're awake or dreaming."

"Like Alice in Wonderland?" the woman asked almost desperately, believing Velma's fib.

"Yes," Velma blandly replied, figuring none of her lies mattered if she walked out with the necklace. "Just like that. I'm afraid that is why I must take it. Luckily, you have not used it often, Delia."

"Delia?" The woman blinked. She cleared her throat hastily. "That's right, that's my name."

"You don't sound certain," Velma remarked, letting her suspicions unfurl around her. This wasn't the effect of the spell, but something else. Velma narrowed her eyes until the woman squirmed.

The actress's shoulders slumped as she looked at her hands. "I'm not Delia. She paid me to pretend to be her today."

"An actress hired another actress to take her spot?" Velma asked.

"Times are hard. A lot of us take on as much work as we can," the woman said before proceeding to answer a question Velma hadn't even asked. "I'm part of the cast in a featured role for *She Comes Through in the End.*"

Velma hoped the actress was just a background player with a few spoken lines, because this woman wasn't fooling anyone.

"What's your name, then?"

"Mildred." Anxiously, the woman asked, "Am I in trouble? Because Miss Moore said I was just to stay here in the room and not go on set. Which was fine before, but the day's almost over and she's not back from Philadelphia yet."

The floor went out from underneath Velma. She'd suspected this, yes, but to hear it so plainly was still a bit of a shock.

Nothing was a coincidence, Velma reminded herself sternly as she asked, "Delia told you she went to Philadelphia?"

"If you're looking for her, I suppose that's your best bet. I don't know if that will help with the folks outside. I heard the director is quite particular. Do you think I could replace her if she doesn't ever show?"

"They might think you a thief," Velma said rather coldly.

"I'm not!" Mildred declared. "I got bored sitting in here, so I went looking around. That's how I found the necklace, and her other things."

Spread on the vanity's surface were the results of Mildred's search. While the actress had dived right for the makeup and jewelry, she'd left a notebook and other papers alone.

Velma flipped through the notebook first. Page after page was filled with names, with very little to say why such names deserved to take up space in the book. The names continued but then stopped rather abruptly, the last few pages ripped out.

Velma tapped those torn edges.

She didn't recall any loose pages on Delia Moore's body or belongings. If they were missing, Velma would find them, especially if they became important. Putting the notebook aside, she picked up the loose papers next. If Velma had any lingering doubts about there being more than one Delia Moore, they were banished at the sight of a flyer for a stage play that had recently ended its run. Although Delia was looking broodily off at a distance, Velma recognized at once the dead woman she'd found that morning.

The last thing of interest on the vanity was a small album propped up against the mirror. Dark brown with gold text, it was a blues record, "Sickle Moon Sways," performed by a singer that Velma had never heard of, recorded with a company she didn't know, Wise Records. As she turned it over, a note fell from it.

Thinking of days past in Ardenton. Your friend, Mr. Clarity, a hurried hand had scribbled—with a noose and skull and crossbones tucked into its center, right under the name.

Velma would have paused over *Mr. Clarity,* but this sinister addition was worthy of study for its own merits. A threatening letter was certainly something that would have encouraged Delia to seek help in Philadelphia. The note wasn't the only correspondence on this part of the desk. Below it were several unfinished letters.

The topmost letter was addressed to Giles Pacer. Although it could hardly be called a letter. Just a few stray lines, the awkward pleasantries of a former acquaintance that gave Velma very little concrete information.

The next letter was a bit longer and written to Laverna Addison. The letter was stiffly polite, with Delia saying that the costumer at the film she was working on had found something in a pawnshop that would interest Laverna. Tucked in the envelope was a photograph of a painted portrait of a Black woman stiffly seated in a chair, holding an open fan dotted with rosebuds. Her clothes were very old-fashioned, with the low collar and puffy sleeves pointing to antebellum times. The woman also wore the necklace that Velma held in her hand right at that very moment. No, not this necklace.

Something very similar in style, but not exact. Velma squinted at the photograph, spying the familiar Sitwell markings that the necklace she held lacked.

Impossible was the thought that rang in Velma's mind, but as she turned over the photograph, on the back Delia had written: *Clarice Sitwell—1829.*

Delia was looking for possessions owned by the Sitwell family! Did this Laverna person know something about them? Or more importantly, was Delia Moore's murder part of Velma's case after all? It seemed so. Picking up the next letter, Velma hoped this one might have something useful for her.

The final letter was addressed to Edythe Osbourne.

Velma sat back, all thoughts fleeing as ice water washed over her. This was one name she never wanted to see related to a case.

When Velma was deeply enmeshed in trafficking contraband magics and potions in California, Edythe had been one of the few people she'd considered a true friend. After turning her bootlegging money into riches with some well-placed bets at boxing matches, Velma left the whole business behind and brought Edythe with her to Bramble Crescent. There Velma had been delighted to learn that Edythe had met Velma's older sister at a library in D.C. during the war. Carolyn had been a student at Howard at the time and Edythe had been working in the personnel mustering division as a navy yeoman. Carolyn had told Velma scant details about the meeting, but given the fact that eighteen months later a romance had sprung up between Carolyn and Edythe, Velma managed to fill in the details.

Edythe wasn't just her friend now, she was family. If Edythe was involved in this . . .

Velma quashed those thoughts before they could go further. There was an explanation for everything. She was going to Bramble Crescent anyway. She'd ask then.

Try to think of it as a good thing, Velma told herself. Delia Moore was dead, so she couldn't answer questions, but Edythe might be able to tell Velma something.

Velma took the letters and the sinister notes and tucked them into her pocket.

Aware that Mildred was staring at her, Velma pulled out a few folded dollar bills from her wallet. "How much was Delia paying you to pose as her for the day?"

"Not that much."

"Good," Velma said. "I was never here, and if anyone asks, you don't know anything about me."

Mildred took the money, disappearing it with a rustle of fabric and a wide grin. "Who are you? I don't even know your name."

"I'm glad we understand each other. Now all you need to do is—"

"Fire!" a man's voice roared from outside. "Mage fire is burning!"

As Mildred shrieked, Velma snapped open the wagon's door. Actors and crew alike ran across the field as vibrant green flames stretched to the sky, choking the air with their unnatural smoke.

With protection spells and more at hand, ordinary fire rarely posed a threat if caught soon enough. But mage fire, or magically induced fire, was another matter. While sources varied, they were all very similar in the end: a fire that burned due to magical energies that could last as long as the spell was cast, allowing it to proceed with reckless abandon. People were right to run from it even as the green flames remained clustered at the corner of the set.

"Get the camera closer!" an intense man with a quivering mustache urged a more reluctant man. "We got to get this for the film. This is perfect!"

"Ambrose, there isn't a fire in the script!"

Ambrose pushed the man forward. "There is one now, once I get that footage!"

Velma watched as the director bullied his cameraman closer to the flame. There went the idea that the fire was on purpose.

Velma tapped the bracelet on her left arm, activating one of the star sigils engraved in the metal.

Drawing on the magic held in reserve, Velma flung her hand upward. A glittering crane dazzling with stardust flew up into the air. Daylight dimmed the majesty of the midnight-blue creature speckled with starlight, but it was only visible for a moment. The spell's wings fell upon the flames like a pot lid snapped closed over a cauldron. At first the green flames ate at Velma's magic, but then they yielded, quivered, and fell away. The flames vanished nearly at once, leaving only smoke drifting over the ground.

Ambrose T. Fowler's cry of despair was perhaps movie worthy itself, as the man dropped to the ground with further piteous moans. As Velma got a good chuckle from it, a bang cracked in the air behind her, and everyone, even the silly director, spun around to face it.

The little wagon that served as Delia Moore's dressing room had blown apart. Clothing, bedding, papers, and more were strewn across the ground. There was no mage fire here, although a wind was stirring things up.

Or Velma thought it was an ordinary wind, until she watched the papers spin in a definite corkscrew pattern away from the wagon.

"Bob, start filming," Ambrose declared, "and you, girl, get into frame!"

"Me?" Mildred asked as she stepped out of the gathered crowd.

"Yes, you. Are you in this picture or not? On my cue, you need to scream just like you did before!"

As Mildred took her unlikely spot in the film, Velma moved away from the crowd, trailing after the paper cyclone. It didn't go far, ending at the edge of the set. Velma ducked into the shadow of a nearby wooden structure and got out her compact mirror as a precaution. Angling it just so, instead of spotting a person eagerly stacking purloined papers, Velma saw half of a car speeding away, its bottom half hidden by a poorly done invisibility spell.

Or maybe not so poorly done, Velma mused, as the spell cloaking the license plate didn't unravel until the car was too far away from anyone at the movie set to see.

Grumbling, Velma stepped out around the structure, hoping whoever it was that had left in a hurry forgot a few things in their haste. Scattered in the grass was an empty potion vial that might have held the mage fire, a few stamped-out cigarettes—and a broken baseball bat that looked to be just the right size to match the other half found in Delia Moore's back that morning.

CHAPTER 8

While Brooklyn was just a stone's throw by plane, Velma would have arrived at Quincy's home in Weeksville faster if she'd taken any other mode of transport. There were very few reasonable spots in the dense neighborhood to land her plane, and she didn't want to land on a small beach and walk in. Her rattled nerves and sense of urgency had her making a risky landing in a small nearby park, squeezing just so between the trees.

Hopping out of her plane, Velma pressed on the star sigil faintly painted below the plane's name. Ursa Minor flared for a moment as the spell washed over the plane, rendering it invisible to the unknowing eye, with additional wards to keep people and animals from running into it.

The walk to Quincy's house was a short one, but long enough for Velma to collect her thoughts. The broken baseball bat she'd found was currently in her plane, waiting for further examination. It was proof linking the day's events together. At least, it would be if Wyatt Jameson kept that stick in Delia's back. Delia Moore's death was suspicious enough on its own, but this find made it clear it was murder.

The dead woman couldn't give her answers, but maybe Velma's cousin could.

Holding on to the sinister note, Velma knocked on Quincy's front door.

She cooled her heels on the front steps, waiting for what seemed far too long before an absolute stranger opened the door, a plate of half-eaten cake hovering next to her.

"Can I help you?" the woman asked merrily as she grabbed the plate back into her hands.

"I'm looking for Quincy Hodges?" Velma asked, uncertain if she was at the right place.

"Mr. Hodges is in the garden with everyone else," the woman said. "Follow me."

Without asking who Velma was or what business had brought her here, the woman led her through the house to the backyard, where a small garden party was underway.

Given his urgent note, Velma at the very least expected a somber sight before her. Perhaps her cousin's wife slightly weepy and a tense air about the place. Not children running around with toys, music crooning from a record player, a festive display of treats, and certainly not Quincy in the middle of telling a boisterous joke to his friends.

He did miss the punch line, though, when he looked up to see Velma standing in his backyard. As if a pin had been jabbed in his palm, he swiftly moved to intercept Velma.

"Mr. Hodges, looks like there's one more guest," the woman said.

"Thanks, Sue," Quincy said. "Make sure you tell my wife how much you're enjoying the cake. She's never baked with just honey before."

"It's very good, but then again I'm eating for two." The woman laughed. Quincy laughed as well, but his eyes didn't move away from Velma as he did.

"If anyone's looking for me, I'll be in my office. Just have some business that followed me home that I need to take care of." Quincy made similar excuses to his guests as he entered the house, his polite demeaner never shaking, until he shut his office door and rounded upon Velma with a furious scowl.

"You better have a good reason for showing up here—and it better be the death of someone we're both related to!"

"Why would you think that?" Velma asked.

"I can't fathom why you would show up here otherwise. How did you even get the address? Never mind, don't answer that. What do you want? I can't imagine you with your bootlegged millions needing any money?"

"I came here," Velma said, proud of how calm and steady her voice was, "because you wanted to talk to me." She held out the crossword puzzle letter. "This arrived for me in Chicago. You said there was danger at the world's fair and wanted to see me in Philadelphia. You weren't there, so I came looking for you."

Quincy huffed as he settled in his chair, idly steepling his hands together, his amusement as oily and slick as his smirk. "You thought it was from me? I never sent you anything or have had a need to. I can't believe you thought I did! I don't do ciphers, too easy to get the wrong conclusion drawn from them. I can't believe you thought otherwise!"

There was a mistake here, Velma realized as he continued to chortle, even if she wasn't sure if it was on her part. She couldn't focus on it. Quincy was having too much of a laugh at her expense, and she was regretting even dredging up a wary concern for him in the first place.

Quincy took after his father, with the sharp, weaselly features and slick mannerisms of a seasoned salesmen, which, given how hated his mother's former husband was, made it easy to dislike him. This reaction, making fun of her instead of wondering how such a letter ended up in her hands in the first place, was chief among the reasons Velma had disliked him for a long time before their big blowup.

"Glad to see your life isn't in danger," Velma spat. "I'll be leaving now, before I do something else you don't like—such as introducing myself as your cousin!"

Quincy stopped laughing at once. "I don't want trouble," he began sternly.

"I won't bring any. You won't see me again, if luck is on our side. Just tell it to me straight: You aren't dabbling in something dangerous, are you? I heard your business went under. These are desperate times and—"

"I'm doing well," Quincy interrupted loftily. "I've pivoted in a new direction."

It certainly did look like he was doing well. The glimpse she had of the house as she walked through said so. As did his office. Nicely decorated, the shelves held priceless books, several expensive trinkets, and lavish portraits of his wife and four children. Although an ornate cuckoo clock looked out of place given its slightly peeling, aged paint.

"Is that all?" Quincy asked, drawing Velma's attention back to him.

"No, we still have plenty to talk about."

The door opened, and one of Quincy's sons peered in. "Dad, where is— Oh," he said, spotting Velma. "Hello, Aunt Velma."

"What do you need, Junior?" Quincy asked.

"Mom needs help with the spells on the wine cabinet."

"I'll open it for her." Quincy got up from his chair. "Wait here, Velma. I'll be right back."

This party must be of some importance, because Quincy had just made a strategic mistake. If he wanted to hide something from her, he lost his chance right then. The moment he shut the door, Velma went to his desk. She opened drawers and moved papers about, seeking anything to support that what he told her wasn't true. She was also seeking anything that showed what he said *was* true after all. Whether it was truth or lies, Velma didn't know what to believe, and the only thing to do—besides shoving a truth potion down his throat—was to have his own words betray him.

Or numbers.

Flipping through the accounts book, she found a list of sales. There were twenty different items listed, with prices attached to them, dates of sale, sale location, and, most important, who they were sold to. While there were several names that could be businesses, a few stood out as private individuals. Velma copied this all down in her notebook. She was about to do some traveling anyway, and she could squeeze in time for a few extra trips.

Velma put everything back, and her gaze was fixed on the collection of vintage spellbooks residing on the shelves when the door opened. Quincy returned, his gaze sweeping about the space before resting upon her. He still looked foreboding, but there was a dash of some trepidation in his gaze that did not bode well. Velma's bag of tricks to handle reluctant contacts was useless against Quincy. There was too much history and too much connection for such tactics to work. Still she had to try.

"If you're still in the business of buying and selling objects," Velma said, "I found something I'd like you to take a look at."

As she reached in her pocket for a sketch of the pocket watch, he waved away her hand.

"Whatever you think I'm doing," Quincy continued, "I promise I haven't done anything. I can't sell the elemental pistols, since you stole what was rightfully mine."

Velma's jaw tightened at the memory of that vivid argument, and the only thing she could think about was getting out of this house before she punched him hard enough to knock that smirk off his face for good. "If that's true, then there's nothing more for us to talk about. I'll see myself out."

By the next morning, Delia Moore's body had ended up in the funeral home's cellar, delivered personally by Wyatt Jameson. He remained stubbornly certain it wasn't murder despite boatloads of evidence, but it didn't matter what he thought, only that he agreed in the end to bring the body over. He had no choice, really, because he didn't have anything that identified the woman as Delia Moore. To Wyatt, she was an unknown person, and there was a long-standing agreement with the city morgue to send such people to the Mourning Dove funeral home. Although that wasn't the only excuse for him to make his way to the house, with flowers alongside the corpse.

"We'll take over from here." Velma grabbed the bag of Delia's effects with one hand while ushering Wyatt out of the cellar with the other. The flowers had already been dumped on a nearby table, soon to be reincarnated as a funeral wreath.

"What about seeing you later?" Wyatt asked.

"Come around this weekend," Velma suggested cheerfully. "See you then!"

She shoved Wyatt out the cellar door, hastily closed and locked it, but couldn't easily shove aside Gregory's judging expression as he sat on a nearby stool.

"It was a bit of insurance," Velma said to her cousin. "I had to make sure the body came here for proper inspection eventually. Having her purse helped, of course, but a personal touch does wonders as well."

"Except your personal touches will lead me to make excuses after you vanish. Why do you always leave me to tidy up after you? I told you we are busy," Gregory said as he pulled aside the sheet to get his first look at Delia Moore.

"Yet, when you saw Wyatt arriving, you made your way down here," Velma said.

"I wanted to bring you the sketches you asked for of the music box," Gregory said dismissively.

"You're not a very good liar, you know."

"Fine," her cousin admitted with a sheepish grin. "I was curious. If Delia had arrived at the funeral home as planned, it would have been my case anyway. Any clue why she sought our help?"

Velma almost mentioned Edythe's name, but hesitated even with Gregory. She couldn't mention that piece without more information, but luckily, she had plenty of other items of interest to discuss instead.

"She was looking for a necklace with the same mark as the one I'm pursuing. My first thought is that someone doesn't want her to find the necklace—or similar items."

"Which might make your search complicated," Gregory pointed out.

"I'm used to complications," Velma assured him. Greogry's eyes were still worried, though. "Would you like a sketch of her? It might be helpful. I need to examine her anyway."

"Just a sketch of her face, and notes on any unusual injuries you spot."

As Gregory worked, Velma opened the bag of Delia's things and pulled out the broken shaft of wood. The tip was oxidated brown and Velma held on to it without her usual care. Wyatt's disregard for a murder scene meant any traces of information were dubious, and she had checked the stick she had recovered already and found it was wiped clean. The pieces did match, though, as she laid them along the table, neatly slotting together to form the baseball bat just like she'd thought. The smaller piece made up the first third of it, and was broken on an angle as if snapped over a knee or against a wall in haste.

"Other than the wound in her back, there aren't any signs of fighting that would have left injury," Gregory said as he handed over a quick sketch of Delia Moore's face to Velma. "Of course, traces of magical residue would be too confused by now, as Wyatt brought the body in through the use of several spells. We won't find anything useful, but I'll keep looking. How long should I hold the body?"

"Just a few days. I'll find out if there's next of kin to alert."

"What else can I do?" Gregory asked.

"I thought you said this was my case?"

"It is, but it seems to be getting complicated. There's something else you're not telling me." His words were mild, and expectant of her answer. "How did the visit with our favorite cousin go?"

"It seems that the note I received wasn't from him, or so he claims. Quincy was baffled at why I was there, and angry at me for upsetting his little garden party. I can't help but think the note is real. It warns about something terrible happening at the world's fair, and to be cautious about a person named Mr. Clarity. I know the latter has some merit. I found a threatening note sent to Delia Moore signed by Mr. Clarity."

"Who is your leading suspect in her death," Gregory concluded. He crossed his arms, going deep in thought. "He'll be hard to find. Mr. Clarity is likely a pseudonym. And the world's fair? Emmy said there's one going on in France, something celebrating colonization or some other nonsense. I'm going over to Fran's house, since Emmy's calling us today. Did you want me to ask my sister to look around the fair?"

"No need. There's an arcane exposition scheduled to open in Chicago at the end of August," Velma said. "I think that's more likely than the fair going on in France or the larger fair planned for '34."

"I forgot about the arcane exposition. My father mentioned he might attend when he and Mom return from their latest travels. It's right in your backyard. Is this good or bad luck?"

"It depends on how the next few weeks unfold."

After gathering the sketches from Gregory and taking her own glance at Delia's corpse, Velma left the cellar and headed for the workshop tucked into the backyard.

Her grandfather was at his workbench fiddling with one of the solar panels from the roof, while Velma's grandmother provided commentary as she sat in her customary chair polishing her pocket-sized telescope.

"Going to go stargazing soon, Granny?" Velma asked.

"No, just doing a little cleaning. I'm putting this aside for one of the children."

"Olivia?"

"No, not her. Although I wouldn't mind using it one more time before I put it up." Henrietta's eyes twinkled as she added, "I'd love to go in your plane again to see the stars, but I know this is a short visit."

"I'll return when the case is over. Although it might be a while." Velma sighed.

"That sigh doesn't sound promising."

"It's complicated. I found some new information on Long Island that made things more confusing. I also spoke with Quincy."

"He told you something useful?"

Velma thought of the notes she'd copied from his ledgers and how she trusted slips of papers more than his own words.

"In a way," Velma admitted. "I have several leads that I need to pursue. In fact, I should call it in to the Muses before it's too late. Grandpa, is the watch fixed?"

"Side table," Benjamin said without looking up.

The pocket watch rested on a handkerchief, the pair of scissors that had been in the orrery lying next to it. While nothing could be done for the fine scratches on it, the glass had been replaced, the watch itself polished, and the clock parts ticked merrily along. It was a thing of beauty, although Velma felt a shiver along her back as she held it.

"Looks good as new," she said to her grandfather.

"Glad to see you're happy with it. I suppose you don't want this piece?"

Benjamin placed a disc that could fit perfectly inside the pocket watch onto the bench's surface. The metal disc was punctured, and there were tiny scrapes that looked like star sigils.

"This was in the watch," Velma said as she held it up to the light. It brought to mind the same piece she'd found in the music box, although it was slightly different. "Do you think it played music?"

"There's no easy way to find out," Benjamin said. "A piece is missing from the watch that allowed it to play—might have been lost in the field where you found it."

"Can't you replicate it?" Velma glanced around the workshop, where out of the fires numerous tools both large and small had emerged.

"I can," her grandfather said, "but I don't think I should."

Henrietta nodded in grim agreement. "You said this watch sparked a brawl between two close friends, and you found a music box that did similar with sisters. It's best these things stay broken."

"What if I wanted to circumvent them, to neutralize future impacts?"

"Well then, that'll require you to stay another week. Three days for your grandfather to show you the mechanical side, and three more for me to show you how to circumvent it magically, and one day for you to piece it together. That's just putting off the inevitable."

"Which is realizing such knowledge won't be helpful at all, you mean," Velma added.

Velma's grandmother smiled with the wisdom that came from a lifetime of jumping into the heart of situations most tried to ignore. "You already have with you the tools to solve your problem. You just need to figure out which tools are the right ones."

"Or which ones you should forget," Benjamin added.

Accepting the advice, even if she didn't understand it, Velma nodded. "Thank you for your help. I know I stirred up a fuss for everyone."

Henrietta just laughed. "You are our granddaughter—we expect nothing less!"

With the pocket watch in hand, Velma returned to the house.

She picked up the phone at the front desk and settled into a chair to call the Muses office. At the last moment, Velma added the numbers to connect to Lois's private line.

"I told you, Morris, if you call me one more time, I will—"

"Calmly explain office etiquette because I can't fire anyone until next year," Velma interrupted.

"You keep being cheeky, Velma, and I'll have you reported for protocol violations!" Lois threatened.

"I'll just take you down with me," Velma said, knowing it was an empty threat. "I have a new name for you to search for: Jeremiah Sitwell. He's a strong candidate for making these items."

"What makes you think that?"

"I found a few things leading in that direction, including his signature on the pieces," Velma said. "He owned the manor that became my family's inn, but he and his family left Bramble Crescent in disgrace in the 1830s. It's likely he and his descendants sold the items as they traveled."

"You know this for certain?"

"If you mean proof, I'll have it soon. I'm headed home to Bramble Crescent to see what I can find."

"This is the first time you've been back in a while, isn't it?" Lois asked. "You should stay a few days and spend time with your family. Talk to your sister."

"Suggested by the woman who wants me to lie to her brother about being a librarian."

"Our circumstances are entirely different," Lois insisted. "I also need time to do my research, especially on this Jeremiah Sitwell."

"Hold on, that's just the first name I have for you. There are two more. Laverna Addison and Giles Pacer. They might be collectors of these objects."

"You're not certain?"

"I got their names from a dead woman's correspondence."

The line went quiet long enough that Velma was concerned before Lois continued. "Back up about ten paces and start again, Velma. Who is dead and why are you going through their correspondences? You're not working for your family's mystery-solving business—you're working for the Muses and there are rules in play!"

"It's part of the current case. Remember that necklace I got a tip about on Long Island? The woman who had it in her possession was impaled with a broken baseball bat yesterday. She was writing letters to Addison and Pacer but never sent them—and I believe they might be about the very same objects I'm looking for. In fact, I say the necklace fell into her hands *because* she failed to find the right one. She's not the only one looking. I think there might be someone who's been following her search and doesn't like it one bit. While I was on the film set, mage fire burned as cover for someone breaking into her dressing room. I think the same person had her killed. Someone going by the name Mr. Clarity."

"Velma, you're not investigating a murder, you know. You're searching for enchanted objects. Let the proper people handle that."

"I am the proper people," Velma said. "Also, it may help. If I'm right that Jeremiah Sitwell is the one who made these objects, then these are old objects. I need to find out why they are activated and sought after now, not to mention what's so important about them they resulted in a death."

"That's a tall order."

"One I can handle. Although, there's one more thing. I don't need you to look up information about this person, but just keep tabs on Quincy Hodges of Brooklyn, New York."

"How's he involved in all of this?"

"So far, there's only one tangible connection," Velma said, giving a partial truth. "Delia Moore and Quincy Hodges both received threats from Mr. Clarity. Beyond that, Hodges's connections to the case and the extent of it is something I'm eager to find out."

There was a small thump around the corner.

"I have to go," Velma said to Lois. "Talk to you soon."

Velma hung up and crossed over into the front room, where she found Olivia and Emerson playing cards. Or pretending to play cards, since the children held the cards backward and were hastily trying to correct that mistake as Velma stepped into the room.

A pair of broomsticks had been dropped in the corner, and the window was open so exceptionally wide that a breeze had knocked over a picture frame. Velma picked it up, checked for any broken glass, and faced the children.

"Olivia, it seems you were right after all. Delia Moore's death is important."

Olivia turned around, her face alight with glee. "Does it mean we get to investigate together?"

"I can't since I'm headed to Bramble Crescent. But you can investigate."

"Me?"

"Why not? I was solving mysteries around your age," Velma said. "Although, you need to not be so obvious at eavesdropping."

"Told you we were going to get caught," Emerson signed.

Olivia ignored her friend as she smiled. "You think I can do it by myself?"

"Of course, but have Emerson go along with you for company," Velma suggested. "If you find anything interesting about Delia Moore, or anything of importance, contact me. Just be careful—and if you get in trouble, ask for help."

"How will I know I'm in trouble if this is the first mystery I'm solving?"

"Don't worry." Velma patted her cousin's shoulder. "You'll know."

INTERLUDE

FOLLOWING HER LAST DELIVERY, VELMA GUIDED HER PLANE BACK INTO Sacramento, grateful as always that the lights of the city were bright enough to guide her even on a moonless night. As she made her approach, however, Velma realized that the light she'd spotted from a distance had been coming from the river this whole time. Up this high, the fire loomed, but the sight didn't worry her.

They were making another one of those steamboat moving pictures—Velma had heard this from William, who was doing a background bit as a boxer, a job that ironically made him more money than actually boxing in a ring. As far as Velma had heard, nothing in that picture was meant to catch on fire. Of course, she didn't know much about movies. Although that was set to change. Hollywood had relocated to Sacramento in search of potent potions to fuel special effects, and some directors didn't always care about what the potion did as long as it looked good on film.

Velma landed the biplane in the old farmhouse she used and headed for the Calendar Club. She played piano two nights a week in exchange for the owner turning his mechanical talents to her plane when she needed it. Velma used to play more, but that was before she'd started making bigger hauls with her deliveries. Whether it was alcohol or potions, Velma was the best person in the area to deliver the goods. Especially since, despite a few close calls, she'd never been caught or had to drop her cargo. Everyone in the business trusted her and she was paid very well for that trust.

No matter how much she made, Velma never counted her money after she received it. She just tucked her cut into a variety of tins hidden around her apartment, and only spent a small portion to place bets on boxing matches. She knew it was a lot of cash, given all the tins she had amassed. Velma was afraid if she knew how much she had in total, the outcome would lead to terrible things. She had come to California, to Sacramento, to prove something to herself and to the world. Whenever she left town, she was going to do it in style.

Velma approached the green-painted door, and gave the password to the man sitting outside. With a nod, a brick was pressed, and the wall split open to reveal the hidden entrance to the Calendar Club. The night was young, so music flowed around at a sedate pace, and there were quite a few tables free. Velma saw none of her friends at them. Shrugging off her disappointment, she approached the bar, ready to request her usual drink, when Moe slid a card across the counter stamped with violets.

"Left for you," the bartender said. "Didn't wait."

"Didn't or couldn't?"

Moe scarcely blinked. "I didn't ask."

She turned the card over. Yoshi had written one sentence: *Check on our friend.*

Velma forgot all about her drink, and shoved the card into her pocket as she headed right back out onto the streets. Yoshi's phrasing was vague, but Velma got the message all the same.

Edythe was in trouble, or would be in trouble soon.

Arriving at Edythe's apartment, she found Arturo Kingsley pacing on the landing between his apartment and Edythe's.

Edythe's next-door neighbor had left his home in Puerto Rico to engage in a full course of magic study and had been slowly drawn into the shadowy world of bootleg magic due to an insatiable curiosity, although he remained a scholar. Drinking with him led to several rather informative lectures. While he was always delighted to see Velma, tonight was for different reasons.

"You got the message!" Arturo cried. "Yoshi said he would be able to find you."

"How is she?" Velma asked, rooting around for a key.

"In a right state. The fire has her out of sorts."

"Why would it? She rarely goes down to the river."

"That's the Golden Lily's set. She supplied them the tonic, Ember Veil, just the other day. That fire has been burning since morning. Your friend, the boxer, told Edythe—I heard them through the wall."

"Why would William tell her that?" Velma exclaimed in outrage. "It would only upset her!"

"I think that was the point," Arturo said, and adjusted his glasses. "Someone in the crew dropped one bottle by accident."

Velma looked at the scholar in astonishment. "*One* bottle caused that fire!"

"By accident," Arturo repeated. "William is afraid the next time it won't be, though."

The door swung open. Edythe swayed in the doorway, clutching a bottle, tear tracks cutting through the soot and grime on her face.

"If they bomb another town, it'll be my fault!" she wailed.

Arturo's eyebrows rose at Edythe's words, but Velma shook her head for him to stay quiet.

"Now, don't be silly," Velma said as she ushered Edythe back inside, saying goodbye to Arturo as she shut the door behind her.

Edythe's apartment was more of a workshop these days. A very messy one, filled with ingredients, crates, and flasks spilling everywhere.

While the apartment was bad off, Edythe herself was even worse, diminished, and sunken in body and spirit, with bloodshot eyes, a gray pallor, and a painful sort of thinness that if she moved the wrong way, Edythe would shatter into tiny pieces.

Edythe had not been like this when Velma had last seen her, three days ago. But three days ago there wasn't a collection of empty bottles cluttering up the place.

Velma sat Edythe down in a chair and then fetched fresh water.

"Tell me what happened. Why is the fire your fault?"

"I made something for Johnstone." Edythe clutched the cup of water. "I didn't have the money to give him what he was due. In exchange, I took on a commission for a tonic. He gave me the ingredients and told me to make something out of it."

"I told you not to do that again," Velma said. "It's not a creative challenge when he does that. He always has an idea of what could happen with the ingredients, and it's never good."

"I know," Edythe whispered. "I couldn't stop myself. I needed a drink, and he had so many flasks, and it had been so long. . . . I wasn't thinking. The potion can't be duplicated. I didn't write it down."

"As if you could," Velma bristled.

Edythe flinched, and Velma instantly regretted her words. While Velma had not made the potion, this was her fault in every way.

Velma enjoyed the rush of danger that came with sampling the various tonics on the market and had bought that first flask of Siren's Wail from Johnstone. While Velma found the taste not to her liking, Edythe found that one sip was not enough. It turned out that Siren's Wail was the most intoxicating tonic out on the streets. It dulled the senses, bringing peace and serenity, things Edythe had been looking for since her family had disowned her. Like so many potions, the serenity Siren's Wail brought came at a price. Taking it left you impressionable to suggestions made by others, and over time the body craved it. You became so dependent on it that some people went into a state of shock after a long period of deprivation, to the point that most died, unable to get over the addiction. After Edythe had gone into that shock state, she vowed to not join the group that had succumbed. As far as Velma knew, Edythe was doing a good job of it. Or, rather, had been.

Johnstone was a dead man if he ever came into her sights again, Velma vowed.

Especially if Edythe truly got hurt this time around.

"You messed up, Edythe," Velma said, "but I can help you. I know you're trying to fix your mistake." She pointed to the bubbling cauldron in the corner of the room. "What's in there?"

"Counter-potion." Edythe looked up. "Should stop the flames. The remaining bottles . . . there were eighteen in total. I don't know if they've been sold yet."

They had probably been snatched up, but Velma said instead, "Worry about finishing the counter. I'll help you with it."

Edythe got up, slowly at first, but then staggered over to the cauldron to complete the work. Velma joined her, rolling up her sleeves and then dragging over a stool.

"If I put this in a flask, I can drop these from my plane," Velma asked.

"It might get you in trouble," Edythe said. "You have to fly close and you'll be seen."

"I'm okay with trouble," Velma said. "Once I'm done, I'm leaving town."

"Leaving town?" Edythe echoed, more than a bit startled.

"I've been thinking about it for a while. I made all the money I wanted to make and I'm craving new sights and new adventures."

"What about your friends here? What about William?"

"I'll leave him a note. I owe him that much for the fun times we had together." Velma shrugged. "But it's time to leave and I want you to come with me."

Edythe's head swung from side to side. "I can't. I shouldn't. I don't deserve that."

"This has nothing to do with you. I'm being selfish." Velma dipped a ladle into the cauldron and then pulled it out, watching as spider-web-thin strands of magic coated it. "It's not safe for you here, and I can't leave you behind knowing that I got you into this trouble in the first place. I told you we'd make so much money if you made the potions and I delivered them directly. I should have told you to keep writing poetry instead — your poems weren't that bad."

Edythe's head dropped and she stopped working. "I don't think I can do this."

"Do you want to put this behind you?" Velma asked.

Edythe nodded. She trembled as she did, but she did it all the same.

"Then you can do this. I'll help. It's what friends are for, right?"

CHAPTER 9

BRAMBLE CRESCENT, MASSACHUSETTS

The next day saw Velma flying over the small island that had been home for her formative years. A crescent shape like its name implied, it had the finest beaches, the sweetest blackberries, and was home to the best magical practitioners around. The southern tip was Wampanoag land, while the northern tip and central portion was Bramble Town. Dedicated island historians proudly stated that the town had been a free Black community since before the American Revolution. Activists talked about how it was a haven for those in need. Sailors recounted in awe the storms that swelled up in the neighboring waters. But for Velma it was simply the most beautiful place in the world.

Velma approached her family's inn with the sun to her back. She planned to arrive quietly, and it turned out this was great foresight. Several figures romped around the grounds surrounding the inn, but flying as she did from this angle, no one would see her plane fly past.

Although the inn was on a tidal island, there was no space for Velma to land her airplane. Not that she would. Given how the tides came in, it was best to park her precious plane on higher ground. Luckily, there was a small cliff that overlooked the inn. Here sat the barn she had built, for both safety and the vantage point, shortly after she bought her first plane.

Circling the barn now, Velma eyed the ground. Samson Tibbs lent his goats to keep the grass managed, but his schedule was irregular.

There were no goats today, and the grass was low, so Velma landed and parked her plane inside the barn without trouble.

With her bag slung over her shoulder, Velma considered the inn once more. A cozy multistory building, its outside was painted a cheery yellow, and the inn was framed by a garden and a towering oak tree. A path led from the inn connecting into town, but the path was subject to the whims of the tide. For about six hours before and after low tide, the path was exposed for easy crossing. Outside of that time it was covered with several feet of water, and required the use of a boat, broomstick, or other methods.

Some of the inn's guests enjoyed the isolation. Velma could understand that. Except, as she watched the water playfully lap up the path alongside it, all she could think about was being trapped with her sister, Edythe, uncomfortable questions, and the task ahead of her. Using the excuse of guests at the inn, Velma headed for her parents' house instead.

Velma took the long way around to avoid passing through the town square. She was a bit too well known. She had once flown a broomstick into Miss Wisteria's bakery, destroying half her merchandise and thus singlehandedly creating the 1911 Town Square Broom Ban. When word got around that she had become a pilot there was a law swiftly drawn up to keep her from flying her plane over the square as well. The mayor had insisted it was merely symbolic, but Velma never tested the proof of those words.

Velma's parents had a cottage on what was known as Candy Lane, because every home along the street was painted in bright, vivid colors like cotton-candy pink or robin's egg blue. Her parents' home was orange marmalade with a tidy garden out front and bird feeders dangling from the front porch. As her parents had moved there in 1926, the cottage was never home to Velma, but she had a fondness for the place, since she had bought the house for them with her bootlegging riches. Although they protested her giving such a gift, the protests didn't last long once her parents got a good look at the house.

Striding up to the porch, Velma was reaching for her key when the front door swung outward on its own volition.

As Velma froze on the doorstep, the door waggled back and forth, beckoning her as her father's voice floated down from the hallway.

"Carolyn, come back here and help me figure this out."

Velma left her bag by the door and slipped off her shoes to head into her father's studio.

Rodney Newberry stood over what had once been the kitchen table, staring down at the board game he was working on, his hands on his hips. Her father had played baseball on a rather famous team before taking over the family inn. Since Velma's older sister had become the innkeeper, he had retired to pursue his work with board games. His games had previously been something to keep Velma and her sister occupied but in recent years had become a new career.

"How would you cure the cursed king without killing him?" Rodney asked.

"Cleansing stones would be the best," Velma said.

Rodney's head shot up, his face filling with so much surprise, she knew it was genuine. "Stars above," he said faintly. "That is a good idea. I've been stuck on this for weeks."

"I don't even know what the game's about," Velma remarked as she stepped around to the table. A hexagonal board game rested in the center, with whittled wooden pieces and cards dotted with paint for proposed colors.

"Doesn't matter. The best ideas come from guesses."

"That might be one of the silliest things I've ever heard."

"Yet it seems true in this moment, so you can't say it's *too* silly."

"What is this game about?"

"Alliances," her father replied. "Players must work together or the gameplay becomes rather stagnant. The trick to winning is forming secret alliances that bring about unexpected results."

"What if no one plays along?" Velma said. "Sometimes it's best to go about things alone."

"Then the game is swiftly over, because if you don't work with people, there's no game at all." Rodney sat back and considered Velma carefully. "No one's called the house to complain about your airplane shattering the silence of the day. Did you sneak onto the island? That's impressive in broad daylight. Has something happened?"

"Nothing for you to be worried about," Velma replied. "How have things been?"

"Your mother and I are well if that's what you're asking. So is your sister, by the way. She and Edythe have their hands full with the inn. In fact, Edythe is hosting an artists' salon this week. Which is everything you could have learned from a single phone call."

"I have a case," Velma admitted, realizing it was futile to hide it any longer. She knew questions would crop up, but she had hoped to have a bit more time. "It starts with a pocket watch and ends with a connection to Jeremiah Sitwell."

Her father settled on a nearby chair, muted alarm spreading across his features. "What an odd case you must have if that old goat is involved."

"It is quite odd. I'm here hoping to find more information about him. I also wondered if you knew something," Velma added, thinking of her grandfather's veiled suggestion.

"You know as much as I do," Rodney replied. "Which are the same stories about dangerous magic that brought on the family ruin, including curses, tales of woe, and a ghostly wail heard on moonless nights."

"That can't be all. There are records, aren't there?"

"Not well kept. Anything you find won't be helpful."

Velma knew her father didn't like talking about the Sitwells, but she didn't realize how much he wanted to actively avoid the subject even for the basic facts. His evasions were also triggering the senses she had fine-tuned over the years from nervous contacts who dithered to avoid telling her the complete truth.

Before Velma could take a different tack, there was a sharp bang from the cellar. The table rattled hard enough that the wooden board game pieces nearly fell to the floor, and Rodney absently moved to grab a candlestick before it rolled off the side table.

"I didn't know Mom was home," Velma remarked.

"I convinced her to take a small holiday from the morgue before our trip. Your unexpected visit catches us in an opportune moment." Rodney gestured at the game board. "Edythe's contacts in New York have landed me a meeting to talk about my newest game. We're headed there for the pitch and to see an old friend of your mother's. If you had delayed your trip by a day or two, you would have missed us."

"You two are quite busy, then," Velma said.

"Life moves on even when you're not here to witness it," he replied mildly.

Velma took the chastisement in stride, she deserved it after all, and went with Rodney into the cellar.

They found Beatrice ushering smoke away with great vigor. With a heavy apron over her clothes, rubber gloves, and a pair of seemingly opaque goggles, she appeared very much like a figure from a moving picture . . . although hero or villain was up to interpretation. The town coroner on Bramble Crescent, Beatrice liked to claim she took the job to have access to a laboratory since Velma's father refused to have one in the inn. Although the truth was that, being the daughter of sleuths, she couldn't rest easily without knowing the truth behind the deaths on the island. Beatrice dabbled in alchemy and made potions with rather explosive results in her spare time, as evidenced by the current state of the cellar. Prohibition meant her mother's dabbling was technically illegal, but the letter of the law was focused on the selling and consumption of potions. Which meant it was a good thing her parents lived on Bramble Crescent, because anywhere else the neighbors would have ratted her out just for the somewhat frequent explosions.

"Beatrice," Rodney teased, "what have you done now?"

"It's not as bad as it looks! Open the window for me, will you, sweetheart?"

"Depends on what just blew up. We've had complaints, you know. From next door—"

"There's nothing to complain about—it's all harmless," Beatrice protested.

"Harmless or not you may just scare away our daughter after she finally showed up after all this time."

Beatrice removed her goggles. "What are you doing here, Velma?" her mother asked, both surprised and delighted. "Did someone die?"

"I'm here for a case," Velma said.

"Someone *is* dead, then." Beatrice shot her a grin. "I'd give you a hug, but I'm covered in various liquids." She thought for a second. "You just saved me a trip to Philadelphia. I'm sure your father's happy about that since it would have messed with his plans." Beatrice threw him a mocking glare.

"That's my cue to leave," Rodney said, popping open the window as he went. "Don't blow up anything else, my dear."

"I won't, at least not on purpose." Beatrice waved him off, smiling.

The smoke had cleared enough now that Velma could see the various flasks and bottles set up along the table. Some were still bubbling despite being removed from the heat, and there was of course the cauldron in the center of it all, ice coating its rim.

"What are you making?" Velma asked as she eyed the still smoking cauldron.

"Tweaking an ice-repellent spell. It was meant for the garden . . . but we can try it on your plane. Will you be here long enough for two experiments and a dry run?"

"I don't think so," Velma said. "I'm looking for information about the Sitwell family."

"Sitwell, Sitwell, Sitwell." Beatrice frowned as she turned over the name. "Wait, you can't mean the ones who owned the inn before your grandparents did? I knew the Magnolia Muses had changed a lot over the years, but they're now going after ghosts?"

"I found a few items made by Jeremiah Sitwell and I'm looking to find other hints about his work. If there was any place I'd find something, it'd be on the island."

"If there's anything to be found it will be at the inn. Make sure to talk to your sister about it. You are going to the inn, aren't you?"

"A bit later." Velma uncomfortably squirmed. "When she is asleep or off doing errands in town."

"My sweet violet," Beatrice said, "you won't find answers by avoiding your sister. You have plenty to talk about. Did you know Carolyn's considering remodeling the inn?"

"She's free to do what she wants with it—it's why she's in charge."

"Yes, but she values your input, which you need to deliver in person. And speaking of deliveries . . ." Beatrice clapped her hands and a nearby cabinet door opened to reveal a stack of dark tinted bottles.

Bottles of a slightly illicit nature.

Velma bit back a smile.

She had never had a chance to tell her parents about her bootlegging activities. Her mother had found out by accident when she discovered five bottles of dry wytchroot tonic from Havana tucked into Velma's suitcase. Instead of a lecture, Beatrice had only asked if Velma knew the best way to dispense of some potion byproduct. Which meant that even while Velma had left behind bootlegging and its assorted virtues and vices in California, she was still in the business of smuggling goods.

"I come back and you give me errands?" Velma pretended to grumble.

"There will be plenty more the longer you stay underfoot. Now, be a dear and go get the suitcase from the upstairs closet."

Velma packed up several bottles into the small suitcase. As she carried it upstairs, her father intercepted her in the hallway.

"Velma, if you want to find anything about the Sitwell family, look in the filing cabinet in the inn's office. My mother collected many things, some I never told you and your sister about. I didn't want you girls to know anything about that family," he said.

"I do know about them. There're so many stories about the cursed Sitwells."

"The stories about the curse of the Sitwell family were started by me."

Velma nearly gasped at this news. "You started the stories about the curse? Why?"

"I had the best reason. You and your sister. You were a few weeks old when outsiders came to the island looking for the Sitwell family. Thinking that *we* were that family, they laid grievances on our doorstep. I did my best to convince them there was no connection, but something terrible had happened and they didn't—or wouldn't—believe the true culprits were gone. Even if that wasn't us, we were a convenient source to take their frustrations out on. They broke into the inn and started up a great deal of mischief before we managed to send them away. We never found out what those people wanted, or what the Sitwell family did, but I didn't care. I just wanted it to be clear we had no connection. I started the rumors and spread the most fantastical tales around until the stories took on a life of their own."

Velma accepted this answer with a nod. "Did you invent the game they play on the island about the Sitwells? You know, the handclap game?"

Rodney shook his head. "That is the work of children and it was old long before I was born."

"Which means no one knows where it came from."

"I'm sure if you want to find its source, you can," her father said. "These secrets need to be brought into the light. It has been long enough."

CHAPTER 10

B y the time Velma made her way to Beacon Inn, she had missed the window to easily cross by foot. Water completely covered the path. Unlike most places, magic wasn't an option. Protective wards around the inn prevented even the simplest of spells from being performed. While it was possible to cast a spell that could make an ice bridge, the wards would make such a spell unstable, leaving the caster likely to fall into the water before they got past the midway point.

As Velma considered her options, one path forward immediately became clear when she spotted the boat tied up along the shore.

"You didn't call ahead," Carolyn said as she stopped her wheel-chair right next to Velma, her voice deceptively calm and almost as cheery as her lemon-colored dress.

"Wanted to surprise you," Velma said.

"Oh, you succeeded in that." Carolyn smiled. If Velma had hoped Carolyn's temper had cooled in the months since they'd argued, there was proof otherwise right there. For her smile was the one she gave guests who had just smeared jam on the antique lace tablecloth.

Carolyn was a year older, so they had both grown up with memories of having a sister, and to this day Velma couldn't think of one memory she had that didn't have Carolyn in the background until her older sister left the island to go to college. They were each other's secret keepers, partners for adventure, and the definition of inseparable.

Or at least they used to be.

Carolyn might have left first, but she always intended to return to the island with new stories from the world outside. Velma had run away from the island, and her return visits ever since were planned to be brief. The last time Velma was here was in the spring of last year, and she had argued with Carolyn at the end of it. It hadn't been about anything important—Carolyn had painted one of the guest rooms in a color Velma had loathed—but such an argument opened the door to the fight they were long overdue about Velma's responsibilities related to the inn and the promises she kept breaking.

"Mother called me," Carolyn said, glancing at the suitcase at Velma's side. "She said you were coming with the tonics she made. Good of you to help out for a change."

Without a word more, Carolyn waved a hand over one of the roses carved on her wheelchair. As the wooden rose opened, the suitcase flew into the rowboat bobbing in the water nearby. She stroked another rose carving, and the Sagittarius star sigil flashed above her hand and a ramp unfolded itself toward the shore, allowing Carolyn to roll right in. With an expert twist, she locked the wheels of her chair and settled in.

As Carolyn pulled up the oars, Velma hopped into the boat, fearful her sister would leave without her.

Velma had barely sat down before Carolyn tapped the boat's side, and the oars sprung to life to row them smoothly and easily across to the inn.

"How's Edythe?" Velma asked casually.

"My dearest is tucked away in her writing cottage," Carolyn said with equal parts amusement and annoyance. "She won't emerge until dinner, for the evening session of the salon."

"How is that going?"

"It's keeping us busy. We're in the middle of it right now, so whatever you're planning, you better not jeopardize it. Although it would be best if you'd tell me why you're here in the first place."

The rowboat shuddered to a stop midway between town and the inn.

"You couldn't wait to ask until we're back on dry land?" Velma scoffed.

"There are guests, and I don't want them to overhear," Carolyn replied loftily. Her eyes were sharp, though, as they focused on Velma. "It has to be something important to bring you here."

"Someone got stabbed in Detroit because of an enchanted music box," Velma said, deciding to go the most provocative route. "I believe the creator of the music box was Jeremiah Sitwell, given I found a few other things he made."

"The Cursed Sitwells?" Carolyn asked. When Velma nodded, Carolyn went on. "I can't believe it! How is that possible?"

"That's what I thought at first too, but I found a few things that connected them," Velma said rather vaguely. "Don't worry. I won't be here long enough to bother you."

"Too late." Carolyn tapped the boat's side and they chugged along to the inn.

Once the boat docked, Velma jumped out before it had even come to a complete stop, her ears stinging from the rebuke.

A tapestry of cheerful flowers greeted Velma as she approached the inn through the garden. There were two sides of the garden: the viewing portion, with ornamental flowers, scattered benches, and the large oak tree that had once held a swing she and Carolyn had played on as children. All paths fed right to the gazebo, the crown jewel of the garden. Covered in thick layers of ivy, it was the same cheerful yellow as the house, with a small telescope set up inside.

Memories of hiding out in the gazebo flooded Velma as she passed it, and she smiled when she spotted a bird perched on its roof. The intelligent eyes of a crow fell on her and the bird spread its wings in greeting. Velma nodded, appreciating the warm welcome.

On the other side of the garden, flowers gave way to rows of herbs, berry bushes, and the pumpkins biding their time for the harvest in the fall. As you went farther, you entered a maze whose center held more flowers and herbs, but of the magical kind. Edythe's writing cottage was tucked into this area as well, the excuse being that she could easily watch over and guard the magical plants, but this was also the only place she could hide away from the guests, as very few went deep in the garden.

The cottage, a tiny brick structure with wooden accents painted in a very precise shade of green, blended in with the garden. A small porch held a chair where Edythe let her and Carolyn's bathing suits dry after their morning swim. The cottage was the only place where no bird feeders were allowed to hang, but a sign was slung on the door that Carolyn had painted to read, *Quiet please—poet at work.*

Velma rapped obnoxiously on the door. "I'm here!"

"Go away!"

Velma continued to knock until the window shutters flew open and Edythe peered out.

"I said go away, Velma!"

"No need to be rude," Velma said as she came around to the window.

Tall and slender with widely spaced eyes and frizzy brown hair, Edythe had light brown skin and sharp features that favored her white father. She always looked slightly out of sorts, as if she'd suddenly awoken from a restless slumber. She opted for soft linen dresses with sleeves she could easily push out of the way, and often went around with an apron tied on just to stick her pens, her notebook, and scraps of papers she scribbled on. Her only jewelry was the oval locket around her neck, a twin to Carolyn's.

"You're not happy to see your dear sister-in-law?" Velma asked, trying not to think of the letter she'd found written by Delia Moore and the dire implications it would bring. It was hard to see how Edythe was connected to all of this as Edythe stood there, grumpy about being torn away from her desk.

"Not at all," Edythe said rather tartly. "You interrupted my creative flow. I will talk to you after tonight's session with the salon. Do not disturb the guests, either."

The window snapped shut, and the latch was drawn on the inside with an audible click.

Carolyn was by the gazebo waiting for Velma, a ghost of a smile on her lips. "I told you she was tucked away in there."

"She hasn't been this snippy in a while," Velma said as she picked up her suitcase.

"Her rival has gotten a poem into the second edition of *The Book of American Negro Poetry*. Such a feat has lit the proverbial fire underneath her, and she's determined to finally finish her book of poems. She just needs a few more."

"How many more?"

"I stopped asking that question weeks ago."

As she entered the inn through the kitchen, a wave of cooking fruit washed over Velma. It was jamming season, Velma recalled, although the stove was empty of any pots at the moment.

"How is this salon set up?" Velma asked. "How can Edythe be writing and running the salon at the same time?"

"The people here are mostly her friends and acquaintances, which is why we first invited Gregory and Zadie to join if they could. The level of work is not as much as with actual guests. There's a morning session and an evening session, leaving the afternoon free for creative pursuits. We provide breakfast and dinner, and they are free to come and go as they please. We have eight guests here currently, but because one of them is in the Cardinal room, the Dove room is open. That's the room you'll be staying in. It'll be easier for me. You weren't expected, so your bedroom isn't ready."

Carolyn stopped in front of a cabinet and twisted the drawer's handle counterclockwise. The cabinet receded into the floor to reveal a gently sloping path that descended into the speakeasy tucked in the inn's cellar. Visitors entered through an underwater passageway from town. The entrance in the kitchen was a legacy from the days when the inn had been a manor. Its further transformation was a joint plan between Velma and Edythe, with Carolyn humoring them, until it had become clear it was a viable idea. The space had needed little alteration. Just some tables, additional lights, and a door installed to cover what had been a pantry. Now, instead of cans and cannisters for storage, they kept bottles of liquor, jars of potions, bundles of dried herbs, Carolyn's enchanted jams, seed bags, and more.

Velma loaded up the shelves with their mother's tonic, quietly taking each bottle Carolyn passed over, falling into the routine of working in tandem. As she reached for the last one, she found it missing.

Carolyn was at the bar, waving the bottle at Velma. "Don't forget, one for drinking."

"To be certain of no troubles." Velma shut the pantry door before joining her sister.

Carolyn poured the tonic into the two glasses on the counter and then slid one forward to Velma. Velma took it and raised the glass in mock salute.

They always tasted the new stock together to make sure they knew what it was and what it did. Their mother was quite good when it came to brewing these things, but some tonics had unexpected effects, dredging up emotions of joy, sadness, or the musing over lost dreams as people sipped their drinks. There was once anger in the drink, and Carolyn had to keep that in the back, not daring to risk what could occur if she sold it.

The liquid that passed her lips today only relaxed both Velma's body and spirit as she sipped it in companiable silence with her sister.

"This is going to sell fast," Velma said.

"Too bad you can't be around to taste more."

"Carolyn . . . ," Velma began.

Her sister shook her head, cutting off Velma's excuses. "You have the plane and the time. There's no excuse I want to hear."

"I'm here now," Velma said weakly.

"You promised you'd help. That means being here to deal with guests, repairs, events, and not sneaking money into the coffers."

"I'm not secretly giving you money!" Velma protested.

Carolyn snorted and Velma was reminded of the wad of cash she'd added to the inn's coffers a few months after the Wall Street Crash.

"I'm not secretly giving it to you *again*," Velma amended. "If the inn isn't doing well—"

"The inn is doing well without you!" Carolyn declared stridently. "It would just do better with you here. The speakeasy is packed when you're pouring the drinks because you know what to recommend to anyone who comes up."

"I'm sorry I haven't come around more often," Velma said carefully, "but I'm here for a case."

"I suppose that's the only thing that could bring you back. Some important clue must be found here or you wouldn't show up otherwise."

"I told you, it's about the Sitwells."

"How do you know whatever you're working on is connected?"

"I found a few things," Velma offered. "A pair of scissors that once belonged to Clarice Sitwell."

"*Clarice Sitwell newly made bride / wandered out into the unending tide / and she died died died,*" Carolyn recited as if prompted. As what she said dawned on her, Carolyn shuddered with embarrassment and disgust.

Velma slapped the bar. "I knew I was right about the rhyme! Do you know the rest?"

Carolyn looked away. "No."

"Liar!"

"You're not here about the rhyme, and you're not even here to look through the old files. Both are phone calls. Both require giving us a warning. What is the real reason you showed up here like a summer storm that brings nothing but trouble?"

Velma meant to deny it, obfuscate, and spin some reasonable lie to get her sister to drop the matter. What came out of her mouth instead was: "I need to talk to Edythe, since she might be a murder suspect."

Velma slapped a hand over her mouth before she could say more.

Carolyn only sniffed. "I knew you were hiding something."

Velma lowered her hand as a realization struck her. "I watched you pour the tonic—how did you get the truth-telling element into it?"

"On the rim of the glass." Carolyn tapped it, smirking. "You must be preoccupied if you missed that. Don't worry—it's just Cassandra plant. It'll wear off in an hour or two."

"Not before you pester me with questions."

"My dear sister," Carolyn mocked, "you don't abruptly come here and not expect me to do anything! Now, to the matter at hand: Why do you think Edy might possibly be a murder suspect?"

Velma tried to fight the compulsion of the truth potion, but she lost in the end and the words tumbled out of her. "There's an unfinished letter addressed to Edythe, written by a woman who was recently found with a stick rammed into her back. This woman was looking for the items that may have been made by Jeremiah Sitwell. She had the calling card for our grandparents in hand. Two tarot cards pasted together from the Vibrant Atelier deck."

The smirk on Carolyn's face vanished so quickly, Velma was already deeply alarmed even before her sister began to speak. "That card," Carolyn whispered. "I gave it to Edythe as a joke. I told her if she ever got in trouble, she knew where to turn to. I never thought—"

"That she would pass it on to someone else," Velma finished.

"At least she had good reason to," Carolyn said. "This woman who died. How recent was it? Because I can tell you right now: Edythe has not left Bramble Crescent in the past couple of weeks."

"I didn't say I suspect her of murder, just that she *could* be a suspect."

"You're here to confirm details before you decide. What, you don't trust Edythe?'"

"There's a short list of people I *do* trust," Velma said.

Her sister sat back. She opened her mouth only to shut it. "I need to head upstairs to get dinner ready for the salon. You can get the key to your room yourself." Carolyn disappeared quickly without asking the question that hung around just waiting to be acknowledged.

Which was a good thing, because neither of them was going to like the answer.

The key to the Dove room was behind the front desk in the main hall, and Velma grabbed it easily, as it was the only key remaining on the painted display. A full house was an exciting prospect for the inn, given it was quietly struggling these days. Although the inn was not in disrepair. The main floor and its rooms were as well kept as Velma remembered, with fresh flowers in vases, neatly laid newspapers, and the faint scent of linen and the sea to make Beacon Inn a respite from ordinary worries.

Velma had loved growing up in the inn, even if she was always cleaning, tidying, or fetching items for guests. Many guests were strangers who stayed only a few nights and were never seen again. There also were regulars who came every summer season and had preferred rooms, favorite chairs, and recipes they always requested. Anticipating the needs of the guests was a talent Velma quickly developed. However, Velma often failed at keeping a polite smile when guests were unreasonably rude, which was why Carolyn became the face of hospitality. Velma excelled behind the scenes, making sure everything was in its place. Which was why, as she got the room key, Velma started organizing the papers on the desk, placing pens back into their proper places, and checking the guest book.

Scribbling in a fake name for the Dove room for the next few days, Velma checked the rest of the rooms. At first she was being nosy, but then she spotted a familiar name among the guests.

Laverna Addison was staying in the Sandpiper room.

Was this the same Laverna who Delia had written to?

Velma was inclined to say yes even without proof.

In fact, she was looking to see if Giles Pacer had checked in to one of the rooms as well when doors opened along the hall.

"Looks like we'll have one more for our little party!" a woman called.

Velma blamed the headache from the Cassandra plant for letting the guests sneak up so easily on her, for they were upon her before she could even think of vanishing. A trio had emerged from the smaller parlor. A painter, from the flecks of drying oils on his clothes. A sculptor, given the drying clay on her hands. And the third was probably a novelist, given the world-weary expression on his face.

"Are you part of the salon or a guest of the inn?" the painter asked.

"I'm a late arrival," Velma said. "I'm very excited about the salon, or what's left of it."

"It's all about having the space to develop your art," the sculptor declared, "and there's no better place to do it than here. I'm so glad we all took Edythe's suggestion. I can see why she's been able to create such wonderful poems since moving out here."

"You're friends with Edythe?" Velma said.

"Aren't we all?" the novelist drawled. He was older than the others by at least twenty years, but the painter and sculptor looked on with the amusement of tolerating a favorite gasbag of an uncle as he spoke. "Although I do appreciate your very judicious use of the word *friend*. Everyone claims friendship too easily—devalues it, I say."

"Spoken like a true misanthrope," the painter jeered.

As the men argued, the sculptor turned to Velma. "Most of us know each other, either from working together or hearing about the other's work. Half are writers and the others work in the visual arts. Where do you fall?"

"Performing arts. I'm Viola Heyward," Velma said as Carolyn came around the corner. "I am a pianist, so unfortunately I can't practice in my room."

"You'll have to fight with Madelyn for space in the drawing room," jeered the painter. "She's taken it over as her studio. I think she has plasters set atop the piano."

"I can work in the conservatory," the sculptor said quickly.

"No need to fight about space," Carolyn said as she joined them. "I can find room for you all. May I see you up to your room, Miss Heyward?"

As the artists departed, Velma flashed her sister a cheeky grin. "You don't need to be so helpful. I know the way."

"You clearly need looking after!" Carolyn declared. "I turn away for a moment and you invite yourself to the salon. Just because I'm using your bedroom as storage doesn't mean you have to go to extremes."

"I figure if I'm staying in the guest room, it'll draw less attention if they think I'm part of the salon just like them," Velma said.

Carolyn's outrage subsided, but only a small fraction. "Draw attention from doing *what?*"

"Don't worry about it," Velma said as she picked up her bag. "All this means is that I'll be here for a few days longer. Just like you wanted."

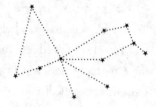

CHAPTER 11

Impulsive as it was to place herself as a guest of the salon, Velma didn't regret the decision. Being considered a fellow artist allowed the sculptor, Madelyn Sunday, to fill Velma in on all the details about the group gathered at the inn. Only slightly younger than Velma, Madelyn was clearly dying to have someone to gossip with. Velma endured Madelyn's scathing remarks about the patrons that a few of the others had, Madelyn's pondering if the marriage between the painter and his playwright wife was on the verge of dissolving, and her debating if including magic in art was a political act or not. Velma shifted through the details flung her way, and asked about the one person there was no gossip about.

"No one knows anything about Laverna Addison," Madelyn said as she sat at her pottery wheel, gently molding the clay. "The others think she got an invitation from Arthuro Kingsley. He knows all these people from being a librarian, and that's how the playwright Ernest Charles ended up here. I'm not so sure, though. We knew Ernest at least by reputation, but no one had ever heard of Laverna until she showed up."

"You didn't ask?"

"I'm curious, but not that curious. I'm here to work. I've just gotten back from a tour of Europe, studying sculpture and attending a seminar in Prague. I have to pay back my older brother, who wired me money when some of my plans fell through. He says I can take my time, but he's the only person in my family who believed I could be an artist. Most of them are farmers and they think art is for white folks and that we have to be practical. I want to prove—"

"It's very nice to have family who support you," Velma said politely, steering the conversation back to more relevant topics. "How has the salon been? How do the sessions work?"

"We pretty much do our own thing, and you're welcome to play the piano even if I'm in the room with you. I don't mind. I'm used to working with the clacking of— Ah, Laverna, you haven't met Miss Heyward yet!" Madelyn called out to the hallway.

The woman passing by stepped inside quite reluctantly. She carried a basket in her arms and still had on her sun hat. Right away Velma recognized the hat she'd seen out in the yard when she had first flown past the inn. Not much older than Velma's mother, Laverna wore worries in her features, and she had dark circles under her eyes. Her collared dress was stiff and cheaply made, and not well cared for given the uneven patches.

"Miss Heyward?" Laverna echoed.

"Viola Heyward, the pianist who will be in the last room," Madelyn said. "Isn't it exciting?"

"Now we have enough people to play a full game of Bowery Green," Laverna drawled. She paused, studying Velma. "Have we met before?"

"Maybe in passing," Velma said.

"Laverna is a dollmaker—you should see the dolls she has brought with her. They move all on their own!" Madelyn declared.

"With or without magic?" Velma asked.

"A bit of both," Laverna admitted. "My father was a toymaker like his mother and grandfather before him, and I suppose I'm carrying on the family tradition. It's nothing too special."

"She's being modest. They are very lovely," Madelyn said.

"Don't trust her word," Laverna said with a thin smile. "She's widely supportive of everyone's work, including the man who's writing the most depressing play in the world."

"May I see one of your dolls?" Velma asked.

"Not right now. I still have some work to do."

And just like that, Laverna Addison was gone, disappearing before Velma could get serious about her questions.

Dinner brought all the salon guests together, and Carolyn must have told Edythe about Velma's ruse, for her friend didn't slip up once addressing Velma as Viola Heyward.

The rest of the salon guests were much like Madelyn: pleasant for the most part, but background noise to Velma. They were important only for the lively conversation they brought. After dinner Velma was asked to play the piano, which she obliged if only to ward off any suspicions about her lie. Velma chose something simple to play at first but without even planning it, she fell into a complex medley. Her fingers danced along the keys and soon more than just music came rushing out of her. Music was magic, and magic was music, after all. As she played, she could see the illusions forming around her, tendrils of flowering vines that began to blossom into violets as dancers weaved between the flowers. The soundscape illusion left all the artists properly awed, and there were even tears in Carolyn's eyes that she hastily wiped away.

Edythe, however, just beamed as if she had invited Velma here to the salon in the first place. When Velma finished, the room emptied as the artists went to work on their crafts, until it was only her and Edythe left in the room.

Edythe shut the door and lit a candle.

A star sigil glowed in the wax, and traces of magic drifted around the room as Edythe turned to face Velma. "That should allow us to talk without being overheard. I suppose you want that. It's why you came here, after all."

"Carolyn said something?"

Edythe shook her head. "She didn't have to. I could tell when you showed up at my writing cottage this afternoon that you weren't just there to vex me. What news do you have?"

"It's about your friend Delia Moore."

Edythe didn't even react. "What did she tell you?" she asked.

"Delia didn't tell me anything. She never got a chance to. She's dead."

Edythe shut her eyes as she shuddered. "I had a feeling you were going to say that."

"You don't seem upset about it," Velma observed.

Edythe's eyes opened, heavy with a deep sadness. "I might have been expecting news like this. She was in a bad spot when she contacted me, but she had to be if she reached out to me after all these years."

"Why don't you explain that bit? We've been friends for a long time. I thought I knew all your other friends if only by name."

"Because Delia wasn't a friend."

Velma raised one delicate eyebrow as Edythe gave a strangled laugh. "She wasn't a former lover or anything you're thinking of! Delia poured drinks at the Calendar Club."

"I remember that place. It was nice."

"It got busted a few years back. Yoshi wrote to me about it," Edythe said absently. "Delia also worked for Johnstone."

Edythe looked away as she said the name of the man who had kept her addicted to Siren's Wail for the better part of three years. Velma wasn't one to relish deaths, but the day she'd learned that Johnstone had had a building dropped on him might have been one of the happiest days of her life.

"How did she work for him?" Velma asked.

"Delia was a courier. She picked up the tonics I made and dispersed them to the buyers. It's how we got to know each other. More importantly, how she got to know what I could do."

"Does Delia have any family you know of? She was found dead on the way to seek help from my grandparents, so her body is being held at the funeral home."

"You could reach out to them, but I think they had long cut connections," Edythe said. "Delia used to say her funeral would be sparsely attended."

"Would you attend?" Velma asked curiously.

"If only to have one friendly face for her last rites." Edythe hesitated before she continued. "We lost contact over the years, but when I was at the opening night of a friend's play two months ago, she was there. She made it a point to speak with me, but not to catch up on old times. Delia had found some coins that had some sort of potion residue on them. She wanted to see what I could get from the scraps and professed a curiosity about what might be on them. I could tell it was more than that, though. For all that Delia wanted to be an actor, she was a very poor liar. Especially when she was nervous. She was with someone at that play, which was why she didn't speak with me that long. I don't think it was someone friendly. She kept looking over her shoulder, although I had no idea who it was. I wish I'd looked closer, now that Delia is gone." Edythe took a deep breath. "I took the coins. When I got back home, I borrowed Beatrice's lab equipment and studied them. You know what I found? Nothing. Nothing I recognized, at least. I don't know what it was, but I could tell who had made them based on the technique. There was someone in California who specialized in glazes and coatings to place on buttons, bracelets, and brooches. I sent them to Yoshi to see what he could dig up. That's why I hadn't told you yet. I was waiting for his letter. If I'd told you sooner—"

"It might not have changed much," Velma assured her friend. "Delia was dealing with more than just coins."

"There is something else I need to tell you before I forget. The room you're in was supposed to be Delia's. She canceled abruptly last week. She didn't explain, but I thought it was because she couldn't get away from the movie she was filming. She said not to expect her and that she was sorry."

"How do you know Laverna Addison?" Velma asked. "All the other guests here are friends of yours or friends of friends of yours. But not her. It's blatant enough that the chatty sculptor was pestering me for details since I'm the only other unknown factor."

"I don't know her," Edythe said. "Delia had suggested I invite her. I wish I hadn't." Edythe scowled her own annoyance, causing her to overlook Velma's surprise. "Laverna is not participating at all in the salon! I expected that to some degree, given the creative process, but the salon is about our works inspiring everyone in their endeavors. We are a community of artists! That's how we produce our best work. I was very excited to have her here given her work with dolls. Carolyn thinks they're creepy, but I find them rather unique. Have you—"

"Edythe, don't you think it's odd Laverna is here when Delia's not?" Velma interrupted. "Especially if Delia wanted her invited in the first place? I wouldn't be surprised if Delia had planned to speak with Laverna privately using the salon as an excuse. The fact that Laverna stayed for this whole thing despite her lack of involvement is a major puzzle. Didn't you wonder why?"

Edythe looked a bit sheepish as she said, "Not really. Laverna paid the standard rate, while everyone else is only paying the off-season prices. I can't exactly question that—or her, for that matter."

"I can, though," Velma said.

The path back to town opened in the middle of the night when the tides receded, and Velma snuck across to get to her plane and radio headquarters.

Instead of dispatch picking up, Lois answered despite the late hour.

"I didn't expect to hear from you," Velma said as she leaned back, propping her feet on the dashboard. "Do you have so little to do that you're covering for dispatch?"

"Not exactly. I arranged for my radio to pick up your transmitter. I figured that would be best when I had key information to give to you. Didn't expect a trial run so soon. How's your visit been?"

"Enlightening. There is an artists' salon going on at the inn."

"And your sister?"

"Hasn't kicked me out yet. I don't quite have news for you about the case."

"Don't worry—I have some for you. I got a list of a few places you need to see in person, stretching from Boston to Sacramento. In total, fifty-two incidents and potential items."

"I'm going to pretend you didn't say that," Velma said. "That I'm dreaming this. Fifty-two places, stars above, Lois. I expected quite a few, but that is a lot."

"This is the list *after* I edited it down, to be within the last couple of years. The criteria you gave me matches many situations."

"Don't scare me even more," Velma muttered. Turning her gaze toward the twinkling sky, she felt the enormity of her task washing over her, leaving her teetering between excitement and trepidation. "There is so much I have to sift through to find the right items."

"You don't have to do it personally. We can recruit local agents, but—"

"I know what I'm looking for and what I'm not looking for," Velma interrupted. "Why don't you give me the list and I'll figure out my flight plan? Start with the most promising ones."

The first few cities Lois named were well-known places: Richmond, Indianapolis, Louisville, and Chattanooga. When she mentioned Minneapolis, Velma paused and flipped back a page in her notebook.

Instead of writing, she just listened as Lois named places Velma had already written down on another list—and not just big cities, but small towns like Vado, New Mexico, and Briony Canyon, California.

"Lois," Velma cut in, "Lois, stop, just stop. I'm afraid I've got to apologize to you. I don't need your list. I already have it."

"You already— I spent hours on this! What are you talking about? How could you—"

"That's the thing: I didn't realize I had it until now. There's something I haven't told you yet because I was trying to figure out how it all connected. Well, I think I have my answer."

"Don't hold me in suspense," Lois said rather dryly.

"Do you remember when Dillon Harris showed up at the office? He had a letter for me that had arrived at the newspaper. It was from Quincy Hodges, my cousin," Velma said frankly. "Quincy buys and sells rare and antique items with a special focus on the arcane. His letter warned of trouble and a threat made by some person called Mr. Clarity. I saw my cousin yesterday, and he claims he never sent the letter. I was certain he was lying to me, so I searched his desk and found a ledger of items he's sold. The places where the sales occurred match what you just told me now. Not perfectly, but close enough."

"Have you confirmed that they are the right ones you're looking for? What have you found out about Jeremiah Sitwell?"

"Nothing much so far. Like I said, there's an artists' salon going on at the inn, and I promised not to upset too many things. Also, Laverna Addison is here."

"The same one you asked me to look into?"

"Yes, she's a dollmaker, and was invited by Delia Moore."

"What? How did Delia get invited to the salon in the first place?"

"She knew Edythe back from her old brewing days."

The silence over the line rolled in like a deadly fog, and Lois's tone was brittle as she replied: "I can understand you not telling me about your cousin. It's a question mark. But this. Edythe *knows* Delia. A woman who has died. Regardless of your connection to her, Edythe's history—"

"That's why I didn't mention it. I had to confirm with Edythe first. I can't just accuse my old friend of murder without knowing the full details, or report her to the Muses just because she knew someone a long time ago."

"This is getting too personal. First the items are connected to the original owner of your home, you find two of them by chance, and now not just one but two members of your family have a connection to this. Velma, do you know how this looks on the outside?"

"Like I'm the perfect person to solve this," Velma said, forcing every bit of persuasion she could at her friend. Because she needed Lois's support, not just for the resources but for the certainty Velma was going about this the right way. "I got this, Lois. Plus, I know you'll tell me if I fly too close to the sun."

"I'll tell you the moment your wings begin to melt," Lois retorted. Her heavy sigh filled the plane's cabin, and Velma could almost see her friend sitting with her head in her hands over the latest headache Velma had brought her. Lois was by nature someone who went by the book, and a large portion of their friendship was mostly dealing with how often Velma threw that book away as circumstances demanded. Which was probably why, despite it being the middle of the night, Lois had answered the radio hail.

"Tell me the items your cousin sold. I'll focus my research on those places and figure out the logistics."

"Not by yourself? You'll have your assistants help, won't you?"

"If they can manage it," Lois scoffed.

There were twenty items that Quincy had sold, and by listing them out to Lois, Velma truly got a chance to understand what she had written down in haste yesterday, such as the fact that seven of the items were all sold to one individual. Brayton Strickland had bought a jewelry box, two music boxes, a pocket watch, a stereoscope, a gyroscope, and a mantel clock. The pocket watch and the music box mentions gave her pause, of course, but Velma puzzled over the gyroscope, as it didn't seem to fit in with the assortment of items. Even the stereoscope, which was more of a toy, seemed a better fit than that.

As for the rest, Velma took particular note of the buyers who had spent many pretty pennies to get certain items in hand:

LOCKET AND BRACELET (SET)	MINNEAPOLIS	EGGERT MOUNDS
SPINNING TOP, DANCE TOY	BOSTON, MASS	HOLSTEAD CO & ASSOC
TINTED GLASSES	DALLAS, TEX	MARIE DREW
TEA SET	LEWIS COUNTY, WASHINGTON	INGRID WEYMAN
CHESS SET (TRADE)	ODESSA, TEX	SMITHFIELD PAWNSHOP

Velma absently circled Sacramento in her own notes. She was going there anyway to see if information about those strange coins Edythe mentioned could be had. Chattanooga got a special note from Velma as well, for Brayton Strickland seemed to be based in that area. Five of the sales had been made there, although the first two had been in Minneapolis.

Velma again hesitated at that city. Arista lived there. Perhaps her cousin could make inquiries for Velma. But that required a call, and probably lying to Arista about how she had brought Olivia to a murder scene. While Arista knew that Olivia was likely to get involved in mystery solving, she probably didn't expect it to be like this.

After concluding her call with Lois, Velma made her way back to the inn and entered through the kitchen. Quietly making her way without any lights, Velma was just deciding if she was going to use one of the hidden staircases to get back upstairs when she heard muffled voices.

This was not entirely unusual given the salon. When Velma had snuck out earlier, the only person still awake was the misanthropic novelist whose room was the Cardinal bedroom on the main floor. A light had been on in his room and he had been muttering to himself as pen scratched against paper. Now that light was off, and voices came from the other side of the floor.

It was just the other guests, she told herself. Yet, Velma's breath quickened all the same as she turned in that direction.

The voices led her to the library, where Laverna sat in the dimly lit room with a book open before her and one of her dolls atop the table.

Velma could see at once why Carolyn had proclaimed the dolls creepy. The doll was more like a marionette, and had very human-like features and proportions. With ivory-white skin and raven black hair, the doll was dressed like a ballerina. From the doorway, Velma watched as the doll slowly pirouetted, its head and fixed eyes locked on Velma. Standing in the doorway, Velma realized the voices she'd heard weren't people talking, but a song emitting from the doll while Laverna softly sang along.

"Did I wake you when I left my room?" Laverna said, stopping when she noticed Velma. The older woman's question was polite, but it was as polite as someone inquiring about a broken arm, when they could clearly see the bone protruding flesh.

"I get restless at night," Velma said. "I wanted to go for a walk, but I didn't want to get locked out. I'd figured I get a book instead."

"That's a good idea. You'll get locked out here. One of the others, I think it was the painter, got locked out the first night until dawn. It was rather humorous, since he wore such a horrid nightgown," Laverna said.

"It must have been," Velma said, unsure where Laverna was going with this.

"Anyway, I got restless myself. It came to me suddenly on how to fix her." Laverna placed a hand above the ballerina. The doll's glass eyes flared, and it stopped moving. "I remembered something I'd read earlier." Laverna gestured to the book in front of her. "Very clever stuff, you know. I figured it was easier to work down here than in my room. I suppose sound echoes anyway. I'm finished for now."

"It's a very nice doll," Velma managed to say. "One of yours?"

"Yes, but I didn't create it. My great-grandfather made it, but it broke many years ago. I made some adjustments so it could dance again. It was attached to a music box once, but I broke it free."

"Now she dances on her own."

"More or less."

Laverna gathered the doll and book, then drew a small star sigil to cast a light that bobbed before her.

"Good night," Laverna said.

Velma echoed the same. She lingered in the room, pretending to grab a book off the shelf.

Once Laverna's footsteps could be heard on the staircase, Velma cast a spell about the library to check for traces of residual magic.

A dusting of sea-green residue gleamed along the window frame as expected, given the wards. However, on the table was a bright yellow circle that shone as brilliantly as the sun in the exact spot the doll had been dancing in.

CHAPTER 12

The salon ended two days later without further incident. Velma kept a close eye on Laverna for the remainder of the time, but the woman did not sneak about in the middle of the night again or do anything worthy of Velma's discreet surveillance. Laverna merely participated in the salon and worked on a set of dolls dressed like clowns. When the others departed on the ferry back to the mainland she was with them, without a hint of any intention to linger on the island.

With the guests gone, Velma was free to toss aside the ruse and do a more thorough search about the Sitwells. That search, as it turned out, took her into town. Velma had checked the inn's filing cabinets one night and found that while her Newberry grandparents had meticulously collected everything of value related to the Sitwell family, it was not currently in the drawers. There was a note in her father's handwriting from fifteen years ago mentioning all the materials were on loan to Seraphina Mills.

Given it was so long ago, Velma liked to think he had forgotten. She doubted that was true, but she liked to think so. Luckily, Seraphina still lived on the island, so at a decent hour and carrying a couple of jars of Carolyn's best jams, Velma strolled over to the eminent historian's home.

By now the entire island knew Velma was back, and Velma's errand was delayed multiple times by everyone in town, it seemed. Louisa Hatter and her cousin thanked Velma for the generous donation to the Bat Conservation Center. Mr. Lyon asked about investing in the new game that Velma's father was working on. Her old classmate, Decker Sevenwaters, jokingly gave back the ten dollars he owed her, saying it wasn't his fault it was a year late. The deputy mayor sternly teased her about flying her plane over town. Mr. Brown and Younger Brown asked Velma if the speakeasy under the inn would be open tonight. And Paloma Tull decided to ruin Velma's day.

The innkeeper at the Candlewyck blocked Velma's path with a sickly sweet smile as she pushed her impressionable children forward.

"Are you back for good?" Paloma asked. "I hope so. Carolyn's going to need all the help she can get as not many tourists are coming to the island these days. And if I'm having trouble, I know Beacon Inn surely is."

Eyeing the children, who were watching her with wide brown eyes, Velma replied as civilly as she could. "Things are quite wonderful. Carolyn and Edythe are running an artists' salon, with some of the finest playwrights and artists from Harlem. Although I'm sure you heard about it. Like you heard about Carolyn's lemon-blackberry jam."

Paloma's smile became rather forced. The rivalry between the inns was positively Shakespearean and had been going strong since the days their grandparents ran things. No one knew why it started, but any chance of the feud fading away vanished when Paloma stole Carolyn's recipe and tried to pass it off as her own. It wasn't even the first time Paloma, or her brothers, copied the inn. Back when Edythe was still newly arrived on the island, she stayed at the rival inn and found that the Candlewyck had copied the tablecloths, wicker chairs, rugs, and even the cutlery.

"I haven't heard anything about what's going on at Beacon Inn," Paloma said loftily. "I've been quite busy. The inn is fully occupied, and of course there's my husband to manage, and my dear children to look after." As Velma rolled her eyes at such obvious bragging, Paloma added, "There's also been a slew of recent thefts at the Candlewyck, as well as stray magics left lying about. My brother was nearly hexed the other day when he removed them."

"It's probably pranks," Velma said, and then realized Paloma was looking at her sharply. "Are you blaming me? I've only been back here a few days."

"Yes, after being gone for over a year," Paloma said. "Then you slinked back so quietly, as if you had done something to be ashamed about. Again." Paloma flashed a bright smile. "I'd love to chat longer, but I must dash. Talk to you soon!"

"Or not," Velma muttered as Paloma and her children strode off.

"That girl deserves a good hex to set her straight," murmured a familiar voice.

Seraphina Mills, with her groceries floating next to her, peered up at Velma from behind thick, round spectacles. Wizened, with a firm grip on her cane, Seraphina was even tinier than Velma remembered, but her voice was just as firm as it had been at Peter's funeral.

"Hello, Mrs. Mills," Velma greeted Peter's great-aunt. "Do you have time to talk? I'm looking for information about Jeremiah Sitwell and you're probably the only one who knows anything of value."

"I know a few things," Seraphina admitted. "Although, why would I tell you?"

"It's a matter of life and death?" Velma offered.

Seraphina clucked her tongue. "You're always so dramatic, just like your mother. Come along, child, I suppose it's time I return all those old books and papers."

Led into a tiny cottage that was here when the town was first founded, Velma sat with a glass of blackberry sweet tea at a small round table dabbled in sunlight. The jams she had brought as a peace offering were placed on a nearby counter. As Seraphina's groceries flitted about the room putting themselves into the cabinets, the old woman brought over a small crate.

"I was writing a book about your Sitwells when Peter took ill," Seraphina said. "He always liked the stories, and I think you became friends because he wanted to figure out if Clarice Sitwell drowned or not."

"I remember first seeing him by the rocks that rimmed our little island," Velma said. "My father was terrified that Peter was going to fall into the water since the current is quite strong. We never did prove one way or another what happened to Clarice."

"I'm surprised you never did." Seraphina tapped her cane and her chair moved around so she could take her seat. "Isn't the other side of your family full of sleuths? I remember the first time I met Mrs. Rhodes. Quite the formidable lady, she quickly figured out the trouble with a missing will. I should have asked her about Clarice back then."

"Some mysteries can't be solved," Velma replied.

"What a pity. I would desperately like to know," Seraphina said. "When I moved here ages ago, I was intrigued by what happened that autumn evening in 1832. Most of what people told me was speculation. But there was one thing everyone agreed on. A great lightning storm had sprouted up directly over the manor, with all its might focused upon the home. The night sky was bright and brilliant with light that looked like hands clawing at the sky, but the manor was hidden by clouds of thick fog. Then a howl like a banshee wail filled the air, shattering windows in the homes nearest to the manor.

When the fog vanished the manor was left in ruins. Nearly everyone I spoke to said that this was cosmic retribution for the arcane experiments Jeremiah Sitwell had done to the vexation and concern of his neighbors, and I agree."

"That wasn't in your book," Velma said.

"Of course not, it was too fanciable. My book was meant to be the history of the entire island, not just one family who brought more trouble than was decent. That was why I planned that new book. I wanted to beat away the myths to reveal the truth." Seraphina pushed the crate forward. "However, I never wrote it, but the materials here should prove interesting to you. Although, why are you curious? You never had much use for history."

"History appears to have some use for me," Velma said. "Thank you for this."

"I was long overdue returning these boxes. Tell your parents hello for me."

As Velma picked up the crate, Seraphina continued quietly. "If I led you to think I blamed you for Peter's death, I'm sorry for that. I should not have allowed my grief to hurt you or burden you with guilt. I am glad to see you again. You were my favorite student, after all, and you are flourishing exactly as I hoped you would."

Velma stood still at these words, and for the first time she looked over at the empty chair across from her. In the sunbeams, Peter wildly gestured with a spoon as he explained he was going to sail around the world after they graduated, and he forgave her for not wanting to come along.

"I know," Velma replied, and turned to leave.

Velma hitched a ride back home in Decker's wagon, as she had caught him heading south. With the crate tucked next to her, she thumbed through the aged papers. There were tax documents and old newspaper clippings, and photographs of the ruined manor. There were a few letters written by Jeremiah Sitwell and his wife that had been sent to people in town, mostly invitations to dinners and parties and a very drawn-out argument over clocks ringing at all hours. There were no other personal papers beyond that, besides a letter of introduction for a lady's maid. The last thing in the crate was an oilskin packet. As she unwrapped it, a small commonplace book fell into Velma's hand. The moment Velma lifted the cover, she knew she had found the one thing that would make this trip worthwhile.

According to the pages, the book belonged to Clarice Sitwell.

It was not a journal that neatly outlined Clarice's thoughts, hopes, and wishes. Instead, contained within the pages was an eclectic assortment of fancies focused on the topic of celestial magic. Clarice had been Jeremiah's assistant, which is how she'd come to the house in the first place, a position she kept even after she'd married his son. Many of the entries concerned machinery and devices and made note of experiment dates. These dates often had marks next to them denoting failure. For many months it seemed Jeremiah Sitwell had labored on a machine that Clarice described only as *proof of the inherent majesty of magic.*

The dates of the experiments ended abruptly, with no sign of the machine showing any success. The last entry was a few days before the date roughly recounted as the day the manor was destroyed, and Clarice's writing expressed a fear of Jeremiah's plans for the machine and if she could summon an *impossible courage.*

Cosmic retribution for the arcane experiments performed was what Seraphina had said about the destruction of the manor. What if it hadn't been a storm, and instead an experiment gone wrong by Jeremiah Sitwell himself?

It was a tantalizing idea, even if there was no way to prove it.

Continuing with her search, Velma flipped through the last pages of the commonplace book, which contained a map of the original house. Velma studied it for a long time, noting the differences from the house in its modern state, but the bones of the house, as well as several passageways, had remained unchanged.

Or so Velma had thought.

As children, Velma and her sister had been in and out of every nook and cranny in the inn. They left no cabinet unexplored or any closet uninspected, through a desire to uncover the inn's hidden passageways. They even found places that their father, who had also grown up in the house, had never discovered. Part of it was due to an insatiable curiosity and getting trapped by the tide, but another part was that Carolyn was not allowed outside as she recovered from polio. They made the inn the backdrop of every adventure of their childhood and had seen every bit of it . . . even the places they were not allowed in.

They knew the inn backward and forward, so why did the map show a passageway in the library that Velma had never seen before?

The book slipped in her hand.

The library!

Laverna had been in the library the other night. Was it possible— could it be possible she knew about the passageway?

"What's wrong, Newberry?" Decker called, as Velma jumped off the wagon with the book in hand.

"I have to take care of something. Can you bring this crate around to the inn later?"

"Sure." Decker shrugged. "For a stiff drink and you showing off your plane to the tribe's children."

"Deal!" Velma called.

Velma dashed back to the inn as if she had sprouted wings, and hurried through the main hall and into the library. She pulled a book about celestial mechanics off the shelf so the lever would release and allow the bookshelf to swing forward. Standing in the cramped storage room, Velma was peering at the dusty crates of old books and decorations when Carolyn entered.

"What are you doing?" Carolyn asked, somewhat alarmed.

"I'm trying to prove that there is a passageway here."

"If you didn't find another opening when you were stuck in there for five hours, you're not going to find it now. It's just a storage space."

"First, I wasn't stuck—you locked me in as a prank. Second, I found an old map that suggests there was a passageway when the Sitwells lived here."

"It likely got destroyed when they ruined the rest of the house. It's also not where I found the new secret passageway."

Velma blinked, but Carolyn just smiled as if knowing how thunderstruck Velma was. "If you don't believe me, I guess I'll just have to show you."

Carolyn brought Velma to the storeroom tucked into the back of the kitchen. Primarily used for long-term food storage, it was a narrow space that left little to the imagination. Although, at the far end of the storeroom was a wooden door that Velma would swear until she turned blue that she had never seen before.

"I found it last summer when I was putting up my jams," Carolyn explained. "I dropped a jar, and when it splattered along the wall, it revealed the spells hiding the door."

"You didn't go in?"

"I would have, but then there's this." Carolyn placed her hand on the doorknob.

Like words emerging from invisible ink, several star sigils in vivid orange light stretched forebodingly across the door.

"I don't mess with these sorts of things," Carolyn said as she let go. "I leave them to you."

"Of course you do," Velma remarked. "But you left it for so long. . . . Is this what Mom meant about renovating?"

Carolyn nodded. "I told them when I first found it. I would have told you if you'd come home for the lantern festival."

A weeklong festival that celebrated the end of summer, the lantern festival coincided with the Perseids. There was a parade, a craft show, a puppet show, and a festival dance, but the sisters' favorite thing had always been flying lanterns from the Old Brambles Lighthouse. They had done it since they were children, and the tradition had remained unbroken, as Velma returned to the island every year . . .

Except for last year.

Instead of responding with an excuse or an apology, Velma pressed a hand against the door, focusing on the enchantments left behind. These were well-crafted spells, but they were clearly fading if this door was revealed like this. At their full strength she would have had to expend some effort to remove them, but now it was significantly easier. Turning her wrist around as if she held on to an invisible dial, she twisted it slowly to rip apart the enchantments before her.

Once the door was clear of any magic, Velma reached for the doorknob and pulled the door open to a passageway consumed by shadows.

"You first," Carolyn encouraged.

"You found the door."

"You opened it. If it's something dangerous, you can handle it," Carolyn added with cheerful confidence.

Velma snapped her fingers so a light floated above her hand. "Glad you think that."

While there was a slight incline, the tunnel gently sloped under the house. The stone at her feet was worn and powdery in places, with a rough finish. Her flickering light revealed cracks along the wall, and there was enough discoloration in the stone that Velma knew it was original to the house.

The tunnel ended at another door. This one was not locked, but Velma had to expend some effort to pull it open.

Dust and musty air greeted them, but thankfully no ghouls or curses. If there were any, the increased illumination banished them completely. Velma was immediately reminded of the workshop back in Philadelphia, except there was more space and fewer tools lying around, and the bookshelves held only boxes and crates.

"So the inn had one more secret for us," Velma whispered. "This must have belonged to Jeremiah Sitwell. Did Dad know about this?"

"No idea. He wouldn't even come down to look, and neither would Edy. She thinks it's a curse," Carolyn said. "Mom checked the door, though, because none of us understand how it could have been hidden so long."

"I'm more curious about why we can now. It can't just be time decaying the old spells; most decay within a few years of the caster's death if not sooner. This was decades ago, though."

"Why don't you worry about what was so important in this room to merit the spells in the first place?" Carolyn headed directly to the large table tucked into a corner, but Velma stopped in front of the far wall, enticed by the way in which the light ran along it. The wallpaper was smooth and seamless despite its age, until it rippled where part of the wall jutted out. Running her hand along the edge, Velma pulled on it. With a small shudder, the wall slid to the right as if on wheels, revealing a set of schematics and designs for all manner of things. Some were easily recognizable, like early cars and planes, but others boggled the mind.

"Carolyn, come see what I found!"

"No, see what *I* found," Carolyn called from the other side of the room. "It's more interesting."

"I doubt it," Velma said, only to be proven wrong from first glance.

Spread across a table lay several dusty items in the process of being put together: toys, a gyroscope, a vintage astrolabe, an anemometer, and a few smaller things Velma didn't recognize right away. No matter what the objects were, they all had the Sitwell mark with its oddly arranged circles engraved into the wood or metal.

As Velma checked the objects, she could see more places along the workbench. Places that appeared empty at first glance, but the more she looked, the more she realized the dust was thicker in some places.

Something else had been here, possibly several things, and they were missing. That was a problem. The reason why pointed to a larger and more pressing issue.

Someone had been able to find this place, get through the layers of protections and locks, to enter the innermost part of the house. Places where magic only let in family.

As her gaze fell on a cuckoo clock, the answer came to Velma with a chill.

Because she had just seen the cuckoo clock's twin.

"Has Quincy been to the inn recently?"

"Why would you ask about . . . Oh." Carolyn's eyes widened in alarm, for she knew their cousin well enough to know why Velma had asked in the first place. "Quincy had business in Boston just before last Christmas, and stopped by the inn. Things were busy at the time, and I paid even less attention to him than usual. I noticed he was missing for part of the day, but I thought he went into town and didn't give it much thought."

"Why would you think he'd find a secret workshop at the end of a secret tunnel we never knew about, and steal several items from us?" Velma quipped.

"You really don't think Quincy did something like that?"

"What if I told you I have proof?" Velma said as she took out her notebook. "I found this in a ledger of his recent sales. When I started mapping out incidents across the country centering around magical items, I saw them echoed in this list. I haven't confirmed they're matches, but this can't be a coincidence."

She held out the list to her sister. As Carolyn studied the notes, Velma waited for the protests that these speculations weren't enough evidence to prove or disprove anything. However, Velma had underestimated her sister, and even perhaps overestimated the rift between them.

"No, it isn't a coincidence," Carolyn said. "I remember him walking around the inn with this astrolabe."

Carolyn went over to the table and picked up the astrolabe. It had less dust on it compared to the others. "I thought he had purchased it as a present for Granny, and I was curious about where he had gotten it from. I asked questions about it, maybe too many questions, so he must have put it back. Maybe I should have stayed quiet, and we would have found him out sooner."

"That wouldn't have stopped him," Velma said.

"Honestly, while Quincy was here, I cared more about making sure he didn't walk out with my elemental pistols," Carolyn admitted. "He thinks because I have no use for them, I wouldn't notice."

"Maybe that's why he came to the inn in the first place, only to find a bigger prize. I bet he doesn't even realize what he's taken or the sequence of events he's started."

"When are you leaving?" Carolyn asked.

For the first time since Velma arrived, the anger that lingered in her sister's eyes was not present. Just a sadness that was somehow even worse to witness.

"Soon, but I could stay a few days more," Velma said. "I could take time to sort these lists. There might be news from Philadelphia, Gregory promised to call. I suppose I could even go back to see Quincy again if I can get him to be honest with me this time—"

"You have leads to follow and can't delay," Carolyn interrupted. "Besides, you found out what you needed."

Had she?

Velma could spend days poking around the house, but she wasn't going to find anything bigger than what she had on hand. Other things could fill in the details, but nothing she was certain that would outshine the potential discoveries in her travels.

"I'll give you the information to connect with my friend at the Muses," Velma said. "If anything else happens, Lois will pass the news along."

CHAPTER 13

When traveling across the country, Velma for the most part followed the airmail routes, using the arrows that glittered across fields at night in the empty pockets of the countryside. She had her maps and charts, of course, but following those arrows helped when she ended up in unfamiliar territory, as she'd only made the trip west by plane a few times, and usually to a single destination with no detours.

Her travels this time around would be different. Instead of a trip from A to Z with minor stops, Velma planned for the trip to be a series of pit stops as she hopscotched across the country.

Because she was more familiar with the East Coast, Velma began with a leisurely trip checking the extra items and incidents Lois had found between Boston and Miami.

The stops were far from promising.

All these places had some mention of enchanted objects that caused some unusual behavior in people, but all the objects were very much like the sleeping necklace Velma had found on Long Island. Obviously enchanted, but not enchanted in the way she was looking for, nor did any have the Sitwell mark.

This was good, since it meant the items weren't causing havoc. This also confirmed that Quincy's list was what she should be following to cross-reference with the list Lois had given her.

Which was why, as Velma flew into Chattanooga, she had a buzzing feeling in her belly, a sensation to be on guard and ready for whatever came next. She was in the city to visit not a site of a magical incident but to speak with Brayton Strickland, who had bought several items from Quincy. Lois hadn't found much information about Strickland by the time Velma landed, but within a few hours, Velma didn't need it.

If there was one thing Velma had learned over the years out in the world, it was that names had power. Particularly names that made everyone look twice over their shoulder, lower their voices, and then speak in code. Brayton Strickland's name had an impact the moment Velma started asking around, from the local contacts she had, to the generous family who let her leave her plane at their farm, to the folks at the boardinghouse she was staying at, to the unscrupulous fellow she spoke with as she twirled a drink while jazz played on in the background.

Strickland was the sort of man everyone knew, just to make sure you didn't cross him at a bad hour. Everyone she spoke to had something to say. He was the King of Sin in Chattanooga. He'd once cursed a man who looked at him funny. He was behind the Christmas Eve mass poisoning of '29. He was the reason the wand ban in town was overlooked. He sold music that could make a grown man strangle his mother for some coin. He was always at the baseball games played in town, no matter who was playing.

As luck would have it, there was a game set just the day after Velma arrived in town.

Velma arrived at the field in a crisp striped suit, with added polish to her jewelry and an alluring smile on her lips. She wanted to cause a stir and, so far, she had. Eyes tracked, heads turned, and more than one female companion irritably snapped her fingers to regain her man's attention.

Velma pretended to ignore it all as she headed for the stands. She wasn't going to look for Brayton Strickland—she was going to have him find her.

At the foot of the bleachers, Velma paused as she added another coat of lipstick. She angled her compact mirror to watch as people passed by. She wasn't standing there long before the crowd split apart, vanishing into the background as a man stalked toward her.

"Now, don't tell me some fellow got you out here waiting?"

Given all the rumors about him, he was younger than she'd anticipated, only a few odd years older than she was. While someone else would have called him handsome, his eyes were too hard and calculating for Velma to consider him so. Although they had never met, she *knew* him. She knew people like him. People like him owned things for pleasure, and what they owned didn't matter, be it objects, riches, or even people. Especially people. Looking up into his face, Velma could believe the rumors that he'd purposely poisoned a supply of tonics just to make sure everyone in town knew he was the only person they were allowed to buy from.

Which meant, even if he'd bought items from Quincy without knowing what they could do, his interest in enchanted items in general was not going to be good for anyone.

"I came here for the game—just waiting for everyone else to settle down first," Velma said.

"Arrived too early?" he asked.

"I like to make an entrance."

"Well, you certainly have. I'm Brayton Strickland, and if you want the best view of the game, I'll show it to you and more."

Velma favored him with a sultry smile, wielding it as she would any spell at her disposal. "I trust you can."

Brayton took Velma into the stands, and she knew he was a true baseball fan. His chosen seats were right above the first-base line, high enough to see the field and close enough to hear some of the chatter in the dugout. While they weren't given a wide berth, there was a surprisingly great amount of space between them and their nearest neighbors.

That was pretty much all Velma noticed as they sat there on the bleachers. She wasn't even that aware of the field, as all her attention and focus was on the viper sitting next to her.

"So, who's the lucky fellow who brought a gal like you to town?"

"How do you know we've just never crossed paths before?"

"I know you aren't from around here, you're something special!"

"What a trite line." Velma laughed.

"It's true, though. You have the shine of someone who's been far and wide. More than that"—his hand trailed over her arm, fingers nearly gliding along to her bracelet—"I'm sure I've seen you before."

"If you tell me it was in your dreams, I walk away," Velma said, forcing a teasing note as she carefully shifted her arm to the side. Her skin was already crawling at his closeness. Him touching her bracelet would only trigger the spells she had in there, and she might not be able to stop them from striking him.

"I'm not a liar. Those eyes, that mouth, I know I've seen your face before. Are you in pictures?"

"Not at all."

His gaze enveloped Velma to a point of near suffocation. "You should be."

Stars, he was trying to place where he'd seen her before.

Could he have seen a photograph of her and her plane in a newspaper somewhere? Or maybe not the newspaper at all? Given his line of work, they might have crossed paths before, but she thought she would remember such a forceful personality. The only place recently she might have been too distracted to have noticed him would have been at Quincy's garden party. He couldn't have been there, could he?

"I'm not in pictures," Velma said, hoping to distract Brayton. "Although I'm trying to get into music. I used to sing at this little club north of here. The band walked when pay was late for three weeks straight."

Brayton chuckled with complete understanding. "So you were waiting for someone after all," he said. "You were waiting for me."

"Whatever do you mean?" she said with faux innocence as she batted her eyes.

"You want to sing somewhere, give me a date, give me a song, and give me your best smile," Brayton said.

There were several things she'd rather do, including sticking her hand in a boiling pot of oil, but Velma forced a coy smile across her face. "I'm not sure about that, but there are other things I would rather speak about instead."

"What else is there that interests you?" Brayton asked. "Did you want to record an album? I can't help you there, I'm afraid, not anymore."

"I'm interested in buying enchanted items, and I hear you're the man for it."

Brayton sat back, his interest cooling. "Depends on what you heard."

"It depends on what *you* have," Velma gently pushed, knowing she was making a small gamble as she did. She knew his sort very well. His sort believed themselves cleverer and smarter than the rest. The best way she found to handle them was to feed that idea even more. Velma usually relied on a few smiles and glances, playing up her natural good looks and charm. But she didn't even want to encourage that here. Brayton was dangerous behind that veneer of charm. Besides, a direct approach would be best, as the truth—or at least a portion of it—was better than false pretenses.

Velma took out a small sketch of the music box she'd found in

Detroit. "I'm interested in a music box that when played, people's emotions are heightened to a point that they act in unexpected ways."

Brayton's eyes narrowed as he quickly looked over the sketch. "Now, why would I have anything like that?"

"Because I hear you're a man who knows his magic," Velma said. "That you're a collector of rare enchanted objects. Such things I wish to have in my possession."

"Maybe you should get your hearing checked."

"Oh, my hearing is *just* fine."

"Then hear this clearly," he said so chillingly, Velma wished for the smothering flirtations from moments before. "Any collector is not going to part willingly, unless for a price."

"Cost is no object."

"Oh, the price I'm asking for goes beyond that." His voice was soft as he spoke with an undertow that would drag her to her doom if she wasn't careful. "It might not be one you can pay."

"I have the means," Velma insisted.

"I doubt it. If I were you, I'd forget all about the music box."

"But—"

"It's not for sale."

He didn't say goodbye, just stood up and walked along the bleachers without a word.

It took all her self-control to let him walk away. She had fumbled. Her simple questions had not only been stonewalled, he'd deflected them. He'd told her nothing, and worst of all she'd put him on guard. Even if Velma had planned to snoop around his nightclub, she couldn't now since he might be anticipating such an act.

She hadn't messed up this bad since she'd been fresh in the field.

"Well, well, look who showed up. I was getting bored out here, and here you are. Isn't that lucky?"

Dillon Harris stood on the bleachers behind her. He carried his jacket over his shoulder, revealing a blue shirt with thin vertical stripes. As always Dillon had his camera bag slung over his other shoulder, but he carried his hat as if fearful a gust of wind would send it flying away. He grinned, far too pleased at taking her by surprise.

"You and I have a very different definition of *lucky*," Velma retorted.

"I doubt that. In fact, I like to think it's very similar. We just have different measures for luck. For you, it's perhaps related to how the right word or smile can get the answers you need. For me, it's our frequent meetings."

"How so?"

Instead of answering right away, Dillon plopped right down in Brayton Strickland's vacated seat. He got comfortable, propping his hat on his head.

"I'm on the hunt for a story. There always seems to be one when you're around. So, lucky."

He had a grin on his face as if he'd just discovered man could fly without brooms or planes. Velma wanted nothing more than to shove him off the bleachers.

"I'm just here to watch the game," Velma replied, hoping he'd take the hint.

He didn't, and stretched his legs out onto the bleachers in front of him. "That may be true, but I don't know why you came all the way to *Chattanooga* when your beloved Third Street Hogs are playing the Augusta Coachmen this weekend on their home turf."

Dillon's words gave her pause—for there was no easy way to spin this around—but it was only a misstep in this dance of theirs.

"Business took me out of town," Velma said.

"What kind of business?"

"Personal," she said smoothly, arching her eyebrows in a knowing fashion. "*Very* personal."

She expected her words to ruffle his feathers and knock that smug smile off his face. Instead he cheerly replied: "I suppose you're visiting family. I hope your cousin is doing well."

Below in the field there was a crack of baseball meeting bat, followed by the crowd roaring in delight. Dillon hooted and hollered alongside the crowd, but Velma sat back, digesting his last words. How could he have possibly found out Quincy was her cousin? Velma had changed her name when she'd gotten into bootlegging. There were no public records that could possibly allow him to connect such things. He was a good reporter, but was he *that* good?

"My cousin?" Velma asked.

"Yes, your cousin," he echoed mockingly. "Aunt, uncle, brother, or whoever you're going to claim is near death and needs you to nurse them back to good health. Don't even bother feeding me a lie about why you're in town—I know it's a cover. You're in Chattanooga for a reason. You might as well tell me, because the truth doesn't stay hidden for long."

"You caught me!" Velma declared as relief flooded through her as she realized Dillon had just thrown out a wild guess to provoke a reaction. "I'm here gathering information about a potential Pullman strike. I'm passing on messages as a courier to get everyone unified."

"That's very noble," he said. "Rather risky. But very noble. *If* it was true."

"You think I'm lying?"

"I wouldn't level such a nasty accusation to your face, but there is a ring of falsehood I can't help but note. I must hand it to you, though: you're very creative. It's why I bother asking in the first place. I always enjoy our little chats. Even the times you left me locked in a railroad car, stranded on top of a dam about to break, or dangling off a cliff."

"I'd hardly call those *chats.*"

"Meetings, then. Encounters. Moments of serendipity. Whatever you call them, they're always quite interesting and I always look forward to seeing you."

"I wouldn't—" Velma caught herself, surprisingly flustered at how easily the words had rolled off his tongue. "I wouldn't say the same."

"Come now, Miss Frye, don't be coy. We always seem to meet under unusual circumstances."

"A baseball game isn't all that unusual."

"Not even depending on the company with whom you're viewing it?"

Beneath the brim of his hat, Dillon's eyes sharpened, and his body language lost its relaxed air. And his next words were far less cordial.

"I don't insult your intelligence, so please don't insult mine," Dillon said. "I don't know why you're here, but if you have business with Strickland, I'd advise you to stay away from him. He's up to no good."

"That is something the whole town can tell you," Velma said.

"For good reason. I know you've gone toe-to-toe with mobsters back home, but Strickland's cooking up something you don't want to get a whiff of."

"Your warning is not needed. Unless there is something you know that I haven't found yet?"

Like the flash of gold in a pan, his grin was back. "Now, I would never claim that."

"Now who's insulting whom? I know you well enough that you don't go anywhere without your nose twitching about for a story. Brayton Strickland is a big story."

"Brayton Strickland is a familiar story that has different players and aims but the same beginning, middle, and end. I'm not interested in what Strickland is up to today."

"I can't believe that's true!" Velma declared. "You're always chomping at the bit to report wrongdoing, scandal, and anything you feel obligated to share. You're pestering me about why I'm here. I don't see you offering explanations for your presence."

Dillon's grin was broader and wider this time. "I'm on holiday."

Velma had barely started her huffing and puffing about *that* blatant lie, when a cry came across the crowd.

At first Velma thought it was baseball related, but everyone was looking skyward and not at the field at all. Vibrant red letters began to fill the sky above their heads: *Judgment Comes to All! Heed This Warning!*

CHAPTER 14

The bleachers around them gave a mighty shudder, the metal moaning and groaning. Outcry seemed to grow even louder as a few half dozen blasts of magic failed to stop the metal from collapsing. In fact, they appeared to hasten its demise.

"Looks like we're abandoning ship," Dillon said, leaning forward to snap pictures of the crowd streaming toward the ground.

"Which means abandoning it now!" Velma grabbed his arm, pulling him away to the stairs.

Dillon just shook her off as he stubbornly snapped another photograph. "Running now means we get squashed in the stampede!"

"This is not an illusion!"

"Nor is getting stomped on." Dillon still seemed unbothered by the chaos unfolding around them. "The *Titanic* took hours to sink. The only real peril was the freezing temperature, lack of boats, and poor planning."

"And people trying to save fools who don't have a lick of sense!" Velma stomped off, leaving him behind to fend for himself. "Stay here and get squashed like an ant—I don't care!"

The bleachers rattled again, and Velma slipped, forgetting that she wasn't wearing her usual heeled boots.

Dillon caught her before she fell. "Careful." They ended up thrown against the rail, shoulder to shoulder, him pressed against her as he supported her. Grinning, Dillon added as he snapped another picture, "Thanks, I got the perfect shot."

"Let go of me!" Velma shoved him away, ready to escape him and the bleachers, but a quiet wail from behind them stopped her in her tracks.

Velma and Dillon turned to see a little girl clinging to a rail as the bleachers continued to rattle. A few rows above them, a man who could only be the girl's father lay sprawled across the bleachers, his head bleeding from a deep cut, a broomstick snapped in half at his side.

"They went up instead of down," Dillon observed. "Smart, but very unlucky."

Whistling at the girl, Dillon turned over his hand so a tiny star-speckled rabbit appeared. "Hey there, bumblebee, keep an eye on me."

The girl laughed as the rabbit bounced from his hand to his shoulder to his head.

With the girl distracted, Velma climbed over the metal seating and grabbed the girl's father, carefully pulling him out. As she steadied the unconscious man against her, Dillon appeared on the other side. Together they carried the man off the bleachers while the little girl hurried ahead, chasing the rabbit to the ground. Other spectators appeared to lend a hand, taking father and daughter to get medical attention.

Even as the bleachers finally collapsed to the ground, most of the crowd's attention was still skyward.

The skywriting above their heads had changed to add one final parting line.

"'Heed Members of Rational Clarity,'" Velma read, and then added more softly to herself as something clicked into place. "MR Clarity." It wasn't a person the note had warned against, but a group. A group that was going to further complicate an already complex situation.

"Looks like someone wanted to make a statement," Dillon said. He held on to his camera, but he didn't move to take a picture like Velma thought he would. Instead he only stared up at the sky. "Have you heard about this group?"

Velma shook her head. "I don't know anything useful."

"All the more reason to find out," Dillon declared. "I have a feeling this isn't their first time around the sun."

Without a word more, he walked over to the nearest person and started asking questions.

As authorities from town swarmed the field to figure out what had happened—and more important, who to blame—Velma considered performing a vanishing spell before more unwanted attention fell upon her. Yet, seeing that Dillon was getting answers instead of confusion about what Members of Rational Clarity was, she found herself lingering on the fringes of his conversations.

According to several people, Members of Rational Clarity was known in the general area, and the event they had just witnessed was not the first time the group had made a statement.

"Things have been happening for a while," a balding older man eagerly told Dillon. "The first time was on Walnut Street Bridge. Folks over here who remember don't cross it even if it means going well out of their way to get to the south side. They've lynched folk off that bridge. I was too young to know what happened, but I avoid crossing it too unless I got no choice. Earlier this year, Rational Clarity rattled that bridge to make all the cars and folk float in the air. It wasn't for too long, but what a sight!"

"I didn't hear anything about this," Velma said, drawn in by the man's vivid recounting.

"You wouldn't. The white folks on the south side kept it real quiet—we're not supposed to have that sort of magic, after all," the old man said dismissively. "It wasn't that many cars. Since then there hasn't been much, just a few odd magical happenings. No one knows what they want. Maybe it's just for attention. This is the first thing in a while, in fact."

"Does it concern you that these things are happening here? Why not on the other side of the river if this group truly wants to make an impact?" Dillon asked.

The man shook his head. "This is for us. I look at this message and see a reminder of our power and ability to shape the world as we see fit."

He must have seen something very different in those bloodred letters in the sky, for Velma could only see high-minded ideals at odds with their methods.

"That's a neat theory," Dillon said as the old man went to rejoin his friends. "Too optimistic for my taste."

"This doesn't encourage you to take action?" Velma remarked, just to gauge his reaction.

"Nobody who's hoping to help makes destruction their top priority," Dillon said without any of his usual quips. There was a firmly shut door at the end of his sentence, and it was not a door Velma wanted to open. Still, she was drawn to wonder what was behind it. Because whatever was behind that door showed up in his articles in varying strengths.

"I was looking for you!" A young man sporting a baseball uniform strode over in a rush. Handsome, tall, and strapping, there was something familiar about him that had Velma puzzled, until he stood next to Dillon. Brothers, Velma realized with a start, with more similarities than differences at first glance. Dillon was smaller than his brother, but not lesser by any means.

"I should have known you were out looking for a story, Dill. You got me worried after you said—"

"I said," Dillon declared with a return of his usual exuberance, "that I would be here watching the game until something more interesting came my way—and she did. May I introduce Miss Velma Frye, aviatrix, one-time columnist at my paper, and an intrepid traveler? Miss Frye, my brother Fitzhugh. I suppose he's somewhat of a decent ballplayer."

"Pleasure to meet you, Miss Frye," Fitzhugh said, immediately pulling off his cap.

"Looks like someone in your family has manners," Velma declared as she flashed the younger Harris a playful smile. "You play a good game."

"Miss Frye," Fitzhugh said, still smiling politely, "we were losing well before chaos unleased itself from Tartarus."

Velma managed a laugh. "Oh, I guess I wasn't paying as much attention as I thought!"

"No worries—you weren't alone. Dill, I came to tell you that you were right. There was a deal struck between the managers about how the game should go, down to the very scores of the innings."

"I told you your manager was as trustworthy as a broken latch on a windy day," Dillon said.

Dillon's brother just shook his head. "It's not his fault. From what he was saying, it was the only way to play here. We need to play to make a season, or it'll be a wash like last year. Although, it doesn't seem that important right now." He cast his eyes about worriedly at the ruined bleachers and field. "I don't like the look of this. Do you know what's going on?"

"Is that why you came over here, little brother?" Dillon said. "You got two eyes and two ears that work well enough."

Fitzhugh scoffed. "That means you don't know!"

"To be determined," Dillon remarked.

"The team's getting ready to hit the road soon. Our shortstop has a baby on the way and is awfully nervous to make sure he's back before the babe arrives. You won't be able to ask all your questions about what happened here."

"Then go on without me," Dillon said.

Fitzhugh hesitated. "Are you sure, Dill?"

"I'm on holiday," Dillon replied. "I'm beholden to no schedule except my whims. Get back to your team. I'll give you a ring soon enough."

Fitzhugh continued to weakly protest, while Dillon kept brushing him off. There was something going on—Fitzhugh's nervousness seemed only to increase with each passing moment as he looked around the field opposite of where the team's bus would be.

"Your brother is doing an interview with me," Velma smoothly lied. "A feature on aviation he's been pestering me about for ages, and I decided to make his dreams come true. I am not on holiday like he is, though, and have a schedule to keep, so the interview is en route to my next destination. I'll drop him off at a nearby town and make sure he calls you. Or"—Velma winked—"I'll give you a call to make sure you know your brother is in safe hands."

Overwhelmed, Fitzhugh could only look over at Dillon.

"It's like she said," Dillon drawled with a decidedly casual air. "Go on, Fitz—you don't want to be left behind because three's a crowd."

As if on cue, one of Fitzhugh's teammates called out to him, urging him to get back to the bus.

"Nice to meet you, Miss Frye, and thank you." Fitzhugh shook Velma's hand and dashed off with one last goodbye to his brother.

The moment Fitzhugh was out of earshot, Velma turned to Dillon, brewing suspicions reaching their boiling point. "So it finally happened. You got run out of Chicago for one of your articles!"

"I wasn't run out," Dillon said patiently. "I was advised by my editor that I should visit one of my siblings or, failing that, make up a sibling to visit for a few weeks. Hounds McGee is not a fan of my work. I wish he would have sent a letter instead of blowing up my car."

He shrugged as if it made his words less horrifying.

"Your car?" Velma echoed at his nonchalance.

"Thoroughly destroyed, I'm afraid. Luckily, I wasn't around when it happened. I'm on holiday, as I said. Hitched a ride out of town with my brother since touring baseball teams don't stay put for long. I thought I was going to write a few articles about their season, but this"—he swirled a finger around to include the field, the sky, and Velma all at once—"intrigues me much more. I simply must find out what's going on."

"Look forward to staying intrigued," Velma retorted, her sympathy not enough to edge out the surge of annoyance at his implied intentions. "You're not learning anything more."

"What about the feature on aviation and your glorious exploits as a pilot?"

"That was to make sure you didn't drag an entire baseball team into your troubles. Your brother looks like a good kid."

"He is, and you lied to him, spinning such falsehoods that it will crush his spirit when he realizes the truth. Why did you do it?"

"You were looking for an excuse to part ways. You wouldn't jump on a bus with only your camera if you weren't desperate, but you also weren't concerned at all about the bus leaving without you."

"Right and wrong," Dillon said enigmatically. "Why would I rush to leave when I have more interesting things to tend to? There's a story here, and it starts with why you're in Chattanooga. Just be honest: I already know you're not telling the truth. Does this have something to do with the letter that arrived at the newspaper the other day?"

Velma shouldn't have been impressed that he'd made the connection. This was to be expected of the most annoying reporter in the world. No, she was impressed that he'd held that card close to his chest until he could drop it at a moment when Velma had few choices but to admit the truth.

"There is a connection," Velma said. "I am following up on information and it's taking me on a little trip. I'm headed to California next."

"What are the odds? I'm headed there too!" Dillon declared with unconvincing surprise. "Would you mind giving me a ride?"

"I'm not going to—"

"It'll be a great *favor* if you did."

His words stopped her in her tracks, and outrage filled Velma with such speed, she nearly bit her tongue to keep in check her less favorable comments about Dillon's character.

Of all the times, of all the places, this was when he finally called in that blasted favor!

"You are asking for a favor?" Velma said, nearly spitting acid with each word.

"Yes." Dillon grinned, unaware that numerous eyewitnesses were the only thing preventing his quick and untimely death. "Payment is due: you owe me, Miss Frye, and I'm here to collect. I sense a story brewing, and I want a front-row seat to it. I'm coming along with you and will see this through to the end, whether it's California or elsewhere."

"Why under all the stars above would I agree to that?"

"Because you gave me your word." Dillon withdrew from his camera bag a slender, twisting coil of metal in the form of a lemniscate. The star sigil engraved on it, Libra, burned bright in his hands, granting the infinity symbol an eerie glow. Velma had created the metal piece herself, and it bound her to him. While breaking the promise wouldn't bring harm, the knowledge that she had gone against her word would remain.

The favor he was asking for wasn't that bad, she tried to convince herself. He could have asked for worse. He could *still* ask for worse if she refused. There was space enough on her plane for him, and if he got on her nerves, she supposed she could always stick the enchanted sleep necklace on him.

Dillon twirled the lemniscate between his fingers. "'A favor to be returned, asking only what is reasonable and fair,' is what you said. I find that the terms of my proposal meet those qualifications."

"You would!" Velma snapped.

"The terms are reasonable," Dillon continued, undeterred. "I'm asking for no more than what you're doing already."

"What if there's no story?" Velma asked. "What if you travel with me and whatever I'm looking for leads to something you can't publish in any paper?"

"I already have something I'm working on." Dillon gestured to the fading messages from Members of Rational Clarity. "I got a tip about this group some months ago regarding their activities. They're supposed to uplift the race, but a lot of their activities are disruptive acts of magic that jeopardize coalitions with a great deal of ugly rhetoric thrown in. Previous incidents have been out west, particularly in California, but a few have been scattered around the country. I already heard about the incident at the Walnut Street Bridge—that's why I skipped town with my brother. I knew the team would play here in Chattanooga, and I saw it as a chance to sniff out information from less official sources."

"So you do have a story," Velma said, knowing good and well she couldn't refuse now. Yet again, their investigations had brought them together, but for once his work would be useful to her. This was the third time she'd come across the group's name, and she needed to find out who they were and how they might impact her work. If Dillon was already investigating Members of Rational Clarity, there was no need to duplicate his efforts. Having him around might even be useful.

"I suppose you can travel with me," Velma said finally.

The favor in his hand flared once more and the magic left it, leaving nothing but dull metal behind.

"Now, was that so hard?" Dillon declared as he tucked the lemniscate back into his camera bag. "You honestly act as if I were asking you to help me avoid a mobster who wanted me dead for exposing his operations."

For civility's sake, she let that comment pass. "Are you ready to leave immediately?"

"I am. Just need to make a phone call first."

"You can do that when I head back to my hotel." Velma glanced down at her now ruined suit. "I have to change and get my luggage."

"What do you think about a quick stop in St. Louis?" Dillon pondered in a tone that promised trouble.

"I'm not stopping there for long. I have an itinerary."

"Don't worry—if things go as planned, we won't have to stop at all. First, a question: What are your feelings about doing something vaguely illegal?"

CHAPTER 15

St. Louis, Missouri

D illon's plan involved grabbing a mailbag tossed from a moving train high enough to be snatched midair as Velma's plane flew past.

"When you're fleeing for your life, you have to pick what truly matters to you," Dillon said as they made their way back to Velma's plane. "And that was my camera. My typewriter and I had to part ways. My words are up here." He pointed to his temple. "Given everything that has occurred, it seems I'm going to need my typewriter after all. She may be a temperamental beast, but I have tamed her well and no replacement will do. You can fly low enough to grab a mailbag from the air?"

"Don't insult me!" Velma swung her bag over her shoulder. "I'm just surprised your brother agreed to help with this. He's a rail mail clerk, he might get in trouble."

"Beaumont owes me a favor as well," Dillon said. "He had already gone and collected my things when I skipped town. I'm just moving up when I was supposed to meet up with him."

"It's good that your siblings are eager to help in your hour of need. Although why not hide in a mail sack and get to California that way?"

"For the convenience, of course. Why catch a ride on the rails when I can go by plane? Haven't you been proclaiming the wonders of flight? Now here's your chance to show what the big deal is. Where is your plane, by the way?"

She reached out her hand and pulled at the invisibility spell over her plane, dramatically revealing it in all its glory.

Dillon gazed upon it with clear delight. "That explains why there are never accounts of your plane outside of towns! That's not just a very good invisibility spell—you got it set up so people won't run into it by accident. Quite clever casting."

Velma scowled to hide how pleased she was at the compliment. He was just rattling and rambling as always. It meant nothing.

She cleared her throat and fixed him with a stern stare. "Before we set out, let's make a few things clear. There are several rules, and the most important one is stay out of my way."

"You forget—I've seen you fly," Dillon said. "I wouldn't dream of interfering. I don't have a care in the world with you flying this bird."

He ducked inside the plane's cabin and Velma paused at the door to collect herself.

She had taken family and friends numerous times over the years in both the biplane that she had first bought and this plane. Even the people who didn't express a fear of flying were quick to make jokes about the odds of needing some spell to stay in the air. Dillon's breezy comments were just flippant words, but it was nice to hear for a change someone speaking with no qualms at all.

While Dillon had Velma flying for St. Louis the next morning, they did not enter the city limits. Instead Dillon directed her to an isolated train platform on the way to the city. Velma kept an eye out for the train as she flew in a gentle loop above the platform, her spells keeping them out of sight. The mail crane was extended, and a somewhat limp mailbag was held between the poles, but Dillon told her to ignore it.

"It's a drop-off," Dillon said, "not a pickup. Use the crane as a marker to gauge your distance. Beau will launch the mailbag filled with my belongings upward for me to catch. I just need to return the bag to him later."

Velma watched as Dillon moved about the cabin, doubts bubbling up as he nearly grabbed the wrong latch.

"And if you miss?" Velma asked.

"I won't. Beau has pretty good aim. He won't hit your plane."

"I'm more concerned about you falling out."

"Are you worried about me?" Dillon teased. "Haven't you caught someone falling in midair before?"

"I have," Velma said, and added under her breath, "although I might miss this time."

Dillon opened the plane's door with the ease of someone who had been in her plane more than a handful of times. It was with that same ease that he leaned out, one hand gripping the door handle.

A train whistled below them, speeding along toward the city. Velma descended at once to get into place.

As the train roared past, a mail hook came out of the train car, grabbing the swaying mailbag.

As this occurred, a few cars down, a second mailbag flew up into the air like a reverse shooting star, haloed as it was with a faint blue aura. Dillon plucked it right out of the air and fell back into the plane, clutching it to his chest.

He hadn't even shut the door before Velma flew back up and left the train behind.

"You got it?" she asked.

"Oh yes." He opened the bag and pulled out a typewriter case swaddled in a horse blanket. "Hello, darling." He pressed a kiss to the case. "Did you miss me? I'm sorry I had to leave you behind. Won't ever do it again."

"Ridiculous," Velma muttered as he went on like that for some time, but a smile tugged along her lips all the same. "I hope it wasn't just a typewriter he sent you."

"I got clothes, money, extra film rolls, and all the essentials, so no need to break from your schedule for a shopping trip. Although I must say, it's a very interesting schedule based on this map."

He grabbed the folded-up paper before she could snatch it from sight. "Your next stop is in Arkadelphia. That's a bit off the beaten track. Why are you headed there?"

"You don't need to know."

"I can find out," Dillon said. "I can find out every gory detail of your business. But I'd rather you told me yourself."

Telling him the truth of her business was not part of the deal. Nowhere in this favor of his was she required to tell him anything at all. Yet Dillon had already noticed the map she had marked with her destinations, and that was unlikely to be the only thing his sharp eyes had caught. Velma was collecting items and talking to people, and like the persistent shadow he was, Dillon would be there to witness it all and would swiftly figure out what was going on. The only way to avoid that meant not making the stops at all—which defeated the purpose of her travels.

Velma took the pocket watch out of her bag and placed it on the dashboard.

"It all started with this. On the day of the brawl at the airfield, I found this pocket watch. It's the first of similar objects that have sparked unusual incidents. The Magnolia Muses have sent me to investigate these objects and the incidents around them."

Instead of being satisfied with this, Dillon protested. "The Muses don't do anything like that! Can't you tell me the truth for once?"

"I am telling the truth. You saw me there at the office in Chicago. I work on the top floor for a branch of the organization that quietly handles magical oddities, dangerous curses, and other mishaps. It's not widely known—we work hard to make sure it stays that way. Which you've made increasingly difficult. It seemed that whenever I was investigating something, you somehow got a whiff of the same—or some ancillary—part of the trail. This time is no different, like that letter you gave me that my cousin sent."

For the first time, Dillon appeared truly startled. "Your *cousin?*"

"Quincy Hodges is my cousin," Velma confirmed. "He found a few enchanted items and sold them. I'm tracking down the people he sold the items to, like Brayton Strickland, as I found that the places where Quincy sold them underwent some sort of unusual magical incident soon after." She would have said more, but Dillon wasn't hearing a word she was saying.

"Quincy Hodges is your cousin. I thought—" Dillon abruptly stopped talking.

"Thought what?" Velma asked. As he remained stubbornly and unusually silent, Velma couldn't help but tease. "Don't tell me you thought he was an old boyfriend?"

His continued silence had her chuckling.

"You did, didn't you? Stars above, the very idea of having such personal mail sent to the paper. I probably would have been fired earlier for doing something like that!"

"How is the letter part of things?" Dillon said in a transparent attempt to shift subjects.

"My cousin's note was a warning about trouble at the world's fair—which I believe to be the arcane expo. Quincy wrote that he hoped to speak with me at a relative's house. He also told me to be wary of Members of Rational Clarity."

"So you do know something about MRC," Dillon said.

"MRC?" Velma echoed.

"It's for the sake of brevity. I'm not saying Members of Rational Clarity every single time—it's ridiculous. I thought you might have encountered the name before from your reaction to the message in the sky."

"I wasn't lying about that," Velma replied. "I truly don't know anything about the group. I've just seen it twice before. First in Quincy's note, and second in a threatening letter sent to a woman who was recently murdered."

"Most people would say killed or died," Dillon said as his notebook and pen made an appearance. "Why do you say murder?"

"There's nothing accidental about someone stabbed with a broken baseball bat."

"You saw the body?"

"I found the body," Velma admitted. "This woman, Delia Moore, was looking for the same items I am seeking. Which are also the same items that my cousin sold recently to Brayton Strickland and others—and, well, it's complicated and a lot to explain."

"We've got some time." Dillon gestured toward the sky. "Just start from the beginning, and I'll catch up."

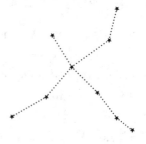

CHAPTER 16

T he whole lot was meant for a penny sale at Second Chapel AME," Marie Drew declared as she set out the collection of jewelry, masquerade masks, binoculars, opera glasses, and a pair of green-tinted glasses before Velma and Dillon. "One of the girls helping me put on the glasses. She shrieked loud enough to shatter windows, and kept talking about the horrid sights she saw. Even after she took the glasses off, she continued to see them."

"How long did it last afterward?" Velma asked.

"And was she the only person who saw something?" Dillon added.

Velma fought the urge to glare at him from across the room.

They had been traveling for a few days together, following up on leads in Arkadelphia, Tulsa, and Lake Charles. He hadn't embarrassed her or hindered her so far, but he was prone to wandering around a room or a site, taking pictures. When his picture taking wasn't distracting the contacts, his incessant questions further interrupted her process. While Velma could tolerate it before on the other stops, this interview in Dallas was the first time she had come face-to-face with a Sitwell artifact. It wasn't enough to look at the green-tinted glasses. She needed to claim them. If Dillon asked the wrong question, he was going to make that task very complicated.

"Two others wore them," Marie went on. "Another woman who's part of the committee and my neighbor's son, who was too curious for his own good. Neither said they saw much, but the boy has had

nightmares since. Which is why I suppose how word got around. . . .
Say, who told you about this in the first place?"

"Anonymous tip to the newspaper," Dillon lied smoothly. "Can
we talk to them?"

"You would only upset them. Poor Bonnie has been prescribed
additional tonics for her nervous condition. Mrs. Edwards insists it
was a trick of the light. Asking around further is just going to make
things worse. There are already rumors being whispered that people
should avoid the sale because I have dangerous items. Which is ridiculous, as I have only what I collected from the community."

"Not these glasses," Dillon pointed out. "You bought them specifically to add objects of interest."

The woman stiffened, anger crowding her features at his words.
"Are you calling me a liar?"

"You're misrepresenting—"

"He means only that we were informed you got the tinted glasses
from elsewhere," Velma cut in, leveling a glare at Dillon.

"I bought them from a traveling gentleman," Marie admitted, the
words leaving her as easy as butter melting on a cold counter. "He
was at the same estate sale I was. I had bought some quizzing glasses.
They are the perfect size for a project I'm working on. He wanted
them and brokered a deal in which I got several pairs of tinted glasses
for them."

"Several pairs?" Dillon echoed, seizing upon this fact. "Where are
they?"

"Broken," she said uncomfortably.

"Is that why they weren't reported, or is it because those other
pairs gave visions of good fortune that didn't leave people screaming?
Meaning, you saw no reason to alert anyone?" Dillon pressed.

Marie shifted uncomfortably. "I don't know what you're talking
about."

"I'd like to see all the tinted glasses," Velma said, building on the foundation Dillon had set for her. "*All* of them. Because while these glasses might show auspicious visions, the magic in them can be as twisted as the one that showed nightmares. In fact, they may lead you to greater peril. Is that something that you want to risk?"

Not much later, Velma departed with five pairs of tinted glasses: the green pair that showed nightmares, three pairs with blue-tinted glass that was cracked beyond repair, and a pair of rose-tinted glasses that promised pleasant visions. Each pair had the Sitwell mark on the nose bridge.

"Now, that was a nice touch, warning that the visions would harm her reputation," Dillon remarked as they headed for the plane. "Would have tried it myself, but it was much more effective coming from you."

"Which is why I'm the one who asks the questions," Velma said. "Never do that again!"

"*Never* is a very strong word," Dillon said quite blandly.

"You're not here to ask questions."

"My questions got the glasses in the end, including the ones she didn't want to give up," Dillon pointed out. "You were handling her with too much care. Just because she wasn't doing anything dangerous doesn't mean you should give her the lead to dance around. That gives more time to add confusing tales."

"The only confusing thing is your questions. I have a set method for this that you keep upending. If you can't stay quiet, you need to find something else to occupy yourself with while I'm making these visits."

"And have you accidentally leave me behind when an interview goes very badly like in Arkadelphia? I think not, Miss Frye. I won't make it that easy for you to get rid of me."

"Tell me something I don't know," Velma grumbled.

She had almost left him behind in Arkadelphia, but not on purpose. For reasons she didn't care to know, he had taken to sleeping in the cargo hold of her plane even when arrangements had been made for room and board. When Velma left to go speak to a man about a cuckoo clock, Dillon had been curled up under a blanket, sleeping. She'd thought he was still in the hold, until she was getting ready to head off and looked back to find him being chased by a very angry farmer.

The flight out of Dallas was silent for the most part, with only the echoes of Dillon's typewriter keys clacking in the cargo hold.

He was right and they both knew it. Dillon's questions *had* gotten more answers out of Marie. Velma had been reluctant, focused on getting the glasses, as they were the first real item she had found so far. If she was reluctant then, maybe she had also been in previous encounters as well. Because this wasn't just about finding the items. The more she learned about them, the more she'd get answers: about a murder, vague threats, her relatives, and secrets regarding her family home.

Rain splattered on the window. At first it was light, but then it began to pound demandingly against the glass. Velma glanced at the ground below, studying the landscape. When she saw a clearing well away from any human settlements, she made her decision.

Dillon peered between the seats. "We're landing?"

"Going to wait out the storm," Velma said. "It got too strong too quickly. The last time I took the chance, the wind nearly ripped off my wings."

Once on the ground, Velma turned everything off, though she left her plane ready for a quick takeoff if needed. Given how the rain was battering the glass and metal, she doubted trouble from human sources would be a concern.

Velma pulled out a storm lantern from a compartment below her seat and pressed her fingers along the enchantments carved into the metal so that light greatly illuminated the cabin. Velma spread her map across the seat and started making notes in her flight log.

"You should sleep," Dillon called from the back of the plane.

"I can't sleep with that banging going on."

"You should take the chance to rest while we're grounded. It's the wise thing to do."

"Haven't you heard I'm far from wise?" Velma said.

"Don't tell me you've never slept in your plane before?"

"I have many times."

"Don't believe you," he said in a singsong tone with his typewriter as his accompanist. Soon the sound of typing was amplified, until she couldn't even hear herself think.

Velma twisted around to peer over the back of the seat. "You made your point. Stop that noise!"

With a smirk, Dillon twirled a finger, returning the typing noise back to its normal volume. He sat on one crate, his feet propped on another. Papers floated around his head, and the chameleon star sigil hovered over his shoulder, providing light. For someone who had disparaged planes and their usefulness, he had gotten quite comfortable in the cargo hold. In fact, he had not complained at all about their traveling so far, other than some turbulence that had gotten his typewriter out of alignment. It wasn't that Velma wanted him afflicted with airsickness or nausea, but seeing him take so well to flight was distressing for reasons she didn't want to think about too hard. Much like the smile he shot at her.

"Is that the article about Members of Rational Clarity?" Velma asked.

"Part of it," Dillon replied. "I've been tracking work done to improve magic rights, and it seems WONDR is becoming the leading group in the fight for magic rights as other organizations have turned their attention elsewhere since the passing of the Wand Act."

"The teachers' union?" Velma asked, flabbergasted, as she recognized the name of the group behind a mass boycott of the *Amberstone Spellbook*. The text included spells that were well known for usage in lynchings, and WONDR's boycott had made headlines all over for its eventual success. Velma was slightly aggrieved that the group had needed to act alone because leadership at the Magnolia Muses hadn't wanted to get involved.

"According to the bulletin I got, WONDR is changing their focus, expanding membership more broadly, and perhaps even changing what the letters in their name means," Dillon said. "What interests me is that while WONDR has a few local groups they are working with, MRC is nowhere to be found."

"That just means they want to strike out on their own."

"That doesn't make any sense. It's best to pool resources if you have the same goals. It's kind of like how you're wasting your money on inns when you have a pretty snazzy plane to sleep in."

"It's my money to waste," Velma said. "It's only been one inn so far. I know enough people that we can bunk down at their homes with no costs other than to help with some chores."

"That's not the issue," he grumbled. "I didn't think about the logistics when I asked to travel with you."

That was obvious from the first night he curled up in the cargo hold, but it amused Velma to think such an old-fashioned issue was troubling him.

"I'm a very modern gal," Velma informed him, "so I have no qualms. But if it's awkward for you to travel with me, maybe we should part ways in Sacramento?"

"I just thought you slept in your plane while traveling," Dillon said, sidestepping her words as always.

"I have landed and gotten my forty winks when caught in a storm like this. There have also been a few times when I camped out in my plane because I knew it was more dangerous to be seen flying. Invisibility spells while flying were tricky for me to learn at first. I forced myself to learn them when I was trapped for two days in Oregon after I landed in the wrong town to pick up fuel."

"Surely you haven't only slept out when it was dangerous," Dillon remarked.

"There were a few times," Velma reminisced. "I went camping in a desert once, for some stargazing. And one time I went to a jelly and jam festival with my sister. We'd gotten lost along the way, which meant we had to—" Velma swallowed hard, unable to continue.

The typing stopped. "Do what?"

"I had forgotten how much fun we had on the trip," Velma continued, pushing past a bubble of regret. "We had bad maps and got lost for so long that I nearly ran out of fuel, but we had so much fun. It feels like that trip happened a long time ago."

"Whatever you argued about, it's not important," Dillon said.

"How—"

"I have ten brothers and sisters. Do you think I get along with all of them? Even with the ones I do get along with, I have quarreled with rather badly and dragged my heels on making apologies."

"You don't have advice on how to make amends?"

"Would you take it?"

"Probably not," Velma admitted, although she added softly, almost to herself, "Though it depends."

"Depends on what?" he asked. "That I don't ask too many questions or poke holes in your obvious lies?"

"Both," Velma returned, and considered him again, not trusting his seemingly innocent expression. "And if the advice is of any value."

She wasn't entirely joking, but he laughed all the same. "Value is in the eye of the beholder."

Velma laid back on the seat as the typewriter keys sung in harmony with the rain, pondering his words as she was lulled to sleep. The rhythmic typing somehow soothed her, as if she knew that still hearing it meant trouble wasn't bearing down upon them.

The next eleven stops they made on the way to California passed without much fanfare. Velma gathered four more Sitwell objects: a spinning top, a desk clock, a stereoscope, and another music box, plus a handful of other enchanted objects. Most were given over freely, as people were glad to be rid of them, while others required a hefty dose of persuasion. All were tied to strange incidents, but they had been minor events that had caused only disturbances and hadn't resulted in major harm or even death.

Dillon still asked his questions but never took over the interviews, letting Velma lead the dialogue. In the larger towns, he often went off on his own, seeking information about Members of Rational Clarity. He never strayed far, though, and was nearly always waiting for her at a nearby street corner, scribbling away in his notebook. His efforts didn't always yield pertinent news, but he always had an interesting story to tell of his day's adventures. His company proved especially useful when he played decoy a handful of times, not to mention his rather robust knowledge about enchanted tea sets played a key role in securing those items.

"All I did was point out the obvious signs that they were given a faulty set," Dillon remarked as he placed a teacup atop a crate. As his camera flashed, he continued. "The design on the rim, the lip, the curve of the handle—all are key details that make it easy to spot a fake."

"Details you knew quite well," Velma said as she crossed the cargo hold to get one of the smaller crates. She opened it and began rearranging the contents to make space for the tea sets. They had gotten one with the Sitwell mark on it, but also two bonus sets that were enchanted as well. "Did you learn all of this for a story?"

"Not exactly," Dillon said. "I worked as a personal archivist for an old biddy in upstate New York, photographing her collection of one hundred and eight tea sets. I also verified that the enchanted ones were properly registered. When she died she let me have three sets: one to sell, one to keep, and one to curry favor with."

"Here I thought you'd always been a reporter."

"I had to lie low for a time because I was in a spot of trouble."

"Not the first time you've been run out of town?" Velma asked.

"Of course not. I'm an old hand at this." Dillon winked. He put away his camera and picked up the teacup. "It's so strange that this has the mark on it. The ones in the center of the incidents that first caught your attention were all mechanical. It's like the glasses. It doesn't fit."

"It does fit," Velma insisted. "Quincy sold this set. Don't forget, the incident that brought us here involves a cup breaking and everyone losing the ability to speak for three hours."

"There are five different spells that do that," Dillon said. "How do you know it's the cups? It makes more sense if you drank from it. What if it's something else?"

"You're being ridiculous."

"Shall we find out?" Dillon held the cup by its handle and raised it to a height that would ensure it would break if dropped.

"Go ahead. You not being able to talk for a clip would be a boon," Velma said. "And if breaking it does something worse, I'm leaving you behind. We're a good day's walk from Seattle, by the way. Is proving me wrong worth that risk?"

"It is when you shut your ears to anyone else's opinion," Dillon retorted. But he replaced the cup gently into the case before he stalked to the front cabin.

Velma carefully wrapped and stowed away the tea set, drawing out each action to let him fume for a bit. She hadn't said anything that wasn't true; it wasn't her fault he saw insult in her words.

Dillon was bent over his notebook when Velma joined him in the front. He ignored her as she turned on her plane.

"I also spoke with the owner before we left," Velma said once they were aloft and headed away from the town. "She told me that the broken cup had a bootleg tonic in it. She didn't want to say anything because she was afraid of being reported. She thought you were a prohibition agent with all your questions."

"You can never ask too many questions!"

"They were quite nervous about something even before we started talking to them. I think someone might have threatened them. The cups could be stolen for all we know."

"Are you looking for a fight?" Dillon asked suspiciously.

Velma shrugged. "It's been uneventful."

Dillon flipped to the back of his notebook. "Of the twenty stops we've made, five included you threatening someone with your magic and two included you actually using your spells. You snuck into an attic or cellar four times, locked someone in a barn once, started a brawl in the middle of a nightclub one and a half times, and used me as a decoy four times without asking first. You call this uneventful? Some of this isn't even related to finding the Sitwell objects."

"It's what traveling with me is like," Velma said airily. "My cases bring me all over but I don't focus solely on them as there might be trouble brewing elsewhere. Who knows what could happen if I didn't?"

"That would be far more convincing if you didn't always choose the extreme option."

"I don't tell you how to do your job, don't tell me how to do mine."

"Actually you do," he said, rather coolly.

"Now that's unfair—" Velma began, only to be interrupted when a flash of magic skimmed across the front of the plane. The phoenix star sigil exploded into a fireball. Velma jerked her plane out of the way, hissing as the lashes of flame veered far too close to marring her paint job.

"Look over there! There's two of them!" Dillon called as he pointed to a pair of broomstick riders. One was a woman. She was farther away and laden with a heavy pack, gasping in clear fright. The other was close enough to be their attacker. The young man bobbed between them as if choosing what path to pursue.

"They're not working together," Velma said.

"Think it's related to our visit or something else?" Dillon asked.

The young man darted for their plane, diving to strike. Velma veered away once more, but his spellwork buzzed a little too close to her starboard wing for Velma's liking.

"Doesn't matter with this fool in the air," Velma muttered.

"He can outfly you?" Dillon asked.

"Outmaneuver, maybe. Take more risks most certainly, but outfly me? Never with a plane, broomstick, or feathered wings on my shoes!"

"Of course not." Dillon jotted down a note in his book. "One count of air-to-air combat."

"I see you have jokes," Velma said as she opened the hatch above their heads. "Hang on."

Velma brought her plane around in a clear challenge to the man and then sped past him. Like she'd hoped, he pursued her, his broom coming dangerously close to her plane more than once.

"Does he not have any sense?" Dillon called as the man didn't get clipped on the propeller only because Velma veered her plane away in time.

"If he did, he wouldn't even be attempting this."

Once they were over a clearing, Velma pressed a small purple button and waited until her ring flashed with a similar violet shade.

"Hold on to this for me," Velma said as she pushed the controls toward Dillon.

Dillon grabbed them on reflex, not even realizing what was occurring at first. "You're asking me to fly your plane!"

"Well, there's no one else, is there?" Velma replied as she stood up. "Keep it steady."

As Dillon protested further, Velma flew up through the hatch. The boost from her magic lifted her like a seed in the wind, and she landed gently on the roof. With Sagittarius at her side, Velma directed the spell to fire a glittery arrow right at the man's pesky little wand. The shaft of wood split apart, sending tiny pieces fluttering in the wind. With a howl, he charged right at her.

Velma jumped and landed nimbly on his broomstick. Before he could even react, she booted him off. He fell onto her plane, and she jumped down as well, with the broom in hand. With surprising speed, he was on his feet and swinging a fist at her. Velma brought the broomstick up in time to block the blow, which snapped it in half.

"You broke it!" the man cried.

"Technically you did," Velma replied.

She tossed the broken broomstick out of the way just as he swung at her again. She ducked a few of his punches, and her fist had satisfactorily collided with his jaw when the plane lurched underneath them. Pitched backward, Velma caught herself from going over the edge with a well-placed spell of compressed air. The man wasn't so lucky. He went over like a sack of grain.

Velma tapped her ring on her left hand, and the Net constellation etched on the wing flared to life. At Velma's guidance, a thin net woven with strands of starlight snatched up the young man before he could make it even closer to the ground.

Velma called down to the open hatch. "Dillon, I said keep it steady!"

"You're not making it easy!" Dillon hollered back at her.

Velma jumped down to the wing and walked along it to where the young man dangled in the net spell. As Velma debated letting him swing for a bit longer, the young woman who had been chased drew as near to the plane as she dared. At this distance, Velma recognized the young woman as the daughter of the owners of the tea sets. She had been quiet and nervous while Velma had spoken to her parents and hastily left to run an errand before Velma could turn her attention to her. "Thank you, miss," the woman said. "He was going to hurt my folks. He's the one that broke that teacup, and he's been blackmailing us for weeks since. He was going to make me do a job for him."

Velma nodded. "And you refused. I'd like to hear more once we're back on the ground."

Velma got the blackmailer into her cargo hold with a few spells looped around him to prevent trouble. Out of breath and with a touch of magic strain, Velma collapsed into the front seat and looked over at Dillon. He held the controls in a death grip and was breathing as if he had been the one to jump out of the plane. Reaching over, Velma patted his hand and then gently loosened his grip, taking back the controls.

"You did well," Velma said as he moved back to the passenger side. "Keeping it steady is the most important task." When only uncharacteristic silence answered, she added, "Are you going to add this to your tally? I just revealed the secret to my trick. My plane has autopilot rigged up. I turn it on every time I do my wing-walking trick. We were never going to crash as long as you didn't wrench things out of alignment."

"You told me to hold on!" Dillon cried.

"Would you have been able to sit still otherwise?"

"No," Dillon admitted ruefully, "I guess not."

"Now you know for the next time."

Dillon vehemently shook his head. "This is never going to happen again!"

"Don't be so sure as long as you're traveling with me."

"Because just about anything's possible," Dillon muttered, but he wore a faint smile all the same as he made a tally in his notebook.

CHAPTER 17

SACRAMENTO, CALIFORNIA

W hile Velma was able to leave her plane at a nearby airfield, the farm about a mile down the road where she usually borrowed transport from was under new management. Since the last time she had been in California, Old Mickey's son and his family had moved in and had peculiar ideas about how to do things. They were perfectly happy to assist Velma, but for Mickey's granddaughter that assistance came with a price.

In order to borrow the farm's truck, Dillon paid Nettie five dollars. Arriving at this price was the result of a haggling session that went on long enough Velma was offered refreshment. In the end, Dillon and Nettie shook hands and the terms of agreement were settled: they could have the truck for the length of time they were in town—as long as they filled up the tank first.

"The girl's got moxie," Velma remarked as Dillon drove them into town.

"She knew we couldn't say no! I bet she didn't charge a king's ransom because she knew I'd walk to town instead. You should have asked about broomsticks—they would have been cheaper. Though she'd probably try to rob us on them too!"

Stifling a laugh at his complaints, Velma explained, "Sacramento doesn't allow broom flying within the city limits. The fine you'd pay for it wouldn't be worth it."

Although Velma had visited Sacramento a few times since she'd departed, the last time had been in '27, and the differences she saw now were stunning. She was from Chicago, so she was used to grit and grime, but Sacramento had more of both now. Stars knew that Sacramento was hardly virtuous, even in the past, but in her memories, the city had remained gleaming with shiny promise, even though she knew better than most it was all a façade.

Still, it was unsettling to walk through the West End and see her favorite shops shuttered, pass the peeling posters of bygone days, and witness the streets filled with so many people with numb expressions of despair.

Luckily, the Garden Theater was just as she remembered it. It was owned by an old friend of hers, Yoshihiro Miyakawa, who had inherited the place from an uncle when he'd left town to open a restaurant in San Francisco. The first person in his family to be born in the United States instead of Japan, Yoshi had always had big dreams and the ambitions to follow up with them, and he was never one to pass up an opportunity. His theater was a staple in this part of town, both for its entertainment and key services to the community. Downstairs was the theater, leaving upstairs as a venue for jazz, boxing matches, and traditional Japanese sports. Although a sizable number of folks came solely for the covert magic market whose wares were as diverse as the clients who frequented it.

The theater's door was locked and barred with signs posted in four different languages about being closed to the public, but that the match between Eduardo Díaz and Daniel Moy would still go on. She recognized Moy, the American-born Chinese Mexican boxer who was just making his debut the last time Velma had been in town.

"Nice place," Dillon said as he parked along the street. "What incident are we looking into here?"

"Just me—there's no 'we' going on," Velma said. "I'm checking in on some old friends. I'm sure you can find something elsewhere that draws your attention. Didn't you have your own reasons to be in California?"

"You're being mysterious again," Dillon said, once more avoiding her question. "Which disappoints me because I thought we were making good progress in getting you to trust me."

Velma rolled her eyes. "Just accept I'm a mystery you're never going to solve."

"Velma, is that you?"

With pleasure, Velma greeted Yoshi's sister, Fumiko, and then introduced Dillon. The young woman stood in the doorway, a stack of posters in hand. Though far from the little girl Velma remembered, Fumiko still held something impressionable and innocent in her round face and bright eyes.

"Stars above, it's so good to see you!" she cried happily as she let Velma inside.

"I'm only here for a short trip. Is your brother around?"

"I'm not sure he'll see you. There was a terrible brawl in the movie theater and it's going to shut us down."

"A brawl," Dillon drew out the words. "How very *interesting*. Tell me more about what happened."

Unaware of the brewing tension between the pair, Fumiko answered, "I wasn't there until afterward. My brother would know something more, but he won't talk to me about it."

"Then we can find something more," Velma said.

They headed upstairs to a multipurpose room that, depending on the hour of the day, served as a meeting hall, boxing ring, clinic, or classroom. At this hour it was empty, its tables and chairs stacked neatly to the side.

Fumiko knocked on a wall panel where a hidden door led to the Unseen Market. "Velma is here."

Floorboards creaked on the other side and the door opened.

"Velma, it's been a while," Yoshi said.

"Well, it's been— Stars above, what happened to you?" Velma cried as she got her first good look at her friend.

His right eye looked like it was pulsing, a clash of vivid dark purple, dirty yellow, and sickly green circling the socket. The eye itself was fine, if only strained a bit from squinting. It was quite a terrible black eye, and it distracted from the bandages wrapped along Yoshi's arm and neck from other cuts and bruises.

"Don't look at me like I'm dying. I just broke up a fight the other day. Is it not getting better?"

"You look like death warmed over," Dillon put in.

Yoshi's good eye darted over to Dillon. "A friend of yours?"

Dillon thrust out his hand. "Dillon Harris, reporter for the *Owl and Eagle Dispatch*. You got injured breaking up the brawl in the movie theater. How long did it take to subdue the crowd?"

"Not too long—and how would you know that?" Yoshi said with a stern glance at his sister.

Fumiko lifted her chin. "If anyone can help figure out why it happened, it's Velma."

"Yes, she can help with anything, but not with that eye," Dillon said. "Couldn't you find a healing poultice with all that stash back there?"

Yoshi's polite smile froze and his hand clenched reflexively, although he didn't snap the door shut to hide the Unseen Market.

The back room was filled with tall shelves packed with neatly stacked jars, vials, small boxes, and pouches filled with various magical goods and potions. There was a large assortment of herbs and other potion-making materials. This being a market, there were more specific items as well, like washi paper, candles of different sizes, inks, bells, strings of varying weight, many types of clay, and a rainbow of gemstones. Some were clearly marked to show which arcane discipline they went with, while others were not so clear to Velma.

"It's just a bruise—it'll heal without magic," Yoshi said.

"Tell me about the brawl downstairs," Velma said. "What started it? Gambling? Heated tempers due to romantic mishaps?"

"I wish," Yoshi said. "I wish that very much, because then I would understand why it happened. I put on a film, and the next thing I know there's fighting and magic being tossed around. I was afraid of a stampede. It was a very big crowd that night since it was a penny entrance."

"Penny entrance? Is that to fill the seats?" Dillon asked.

Fumiko nodded. "It was my idea. On those nights, we play some silent reels with a record to accompany them. We used a new one that night—"

Yoshi shushed her. "I don't know why the fighting started. Maybe people didn't like the film."

"Or maybe the record player is the root of the trouble," Velma pointed out. "I've been tracking incidents like this. What happened at the theater was not by chance. Nor will it be the only time, if I don't get a look at the record player. Shall you show it to me?"

At first Yoshi said nothing, and then his expression changed, shifting from alarm to as still as an arctic breeze. He shoved his sister into the back room and slammed the door shut.

Fumiko banged on the door, but her muffled cries receded into the distance as Yoshi turned to them with an unblinking stare.

"You don't want to do that," Yoshi said.

"Don't want to do what?" Velma asked. A sliver of alarm had her taking a step back, shifting her weight slightly to gain better footing.

"Asking questions that don't need answering," Yoshi said, and then withdrew a topaz amulet. The gemstone flashed as he spun it about, and although Velma was anticipating action, she was still too slow to fully block the burst of magic directed at her.

She raised her left arm just in time, and the crackling magic rebounded against the enchanted metal, veering away from her. All very good, until she remembered she wasn't alone.

She turned, alarm coursing through her—but Dillon was fine.

Dillon cupped his hand, grabbing the magic and encasing it in a spell of his own so it was like a tightly packed sphere. Calmly holding it, Dillon flipped it around before tossing the sphere back at Yoshi.

The spell struck the wall, rattling the tables. One of the tables knocked into Yoshi's left side and he buckled to the floor. It was a blow that would have knocked most off their feet for a few moments, but Yoshi got up almost immediately. He careened onto his feet, still spinning his amulet, the gemstone in its center flashing malevolently.

"Yoshi, don't do this," Velma said. She had drawn upon her own spells, but clutched them desperately in hopes to not release them. "Don't make me hurt you."

"You have to," Yoshi said, and tendrils of magic flew from the amulet's core.

The tendrils grabbed Dillon by the arm and flung him across the room. He hit the wall hard and bounced, crashing into the stacked chairs. Velma leapt forward as she removed one of her earrings. She pressed hard enough along the metal to snap it in half, and a puff of smoke burst from it. A decoy of herself appeared, facing and taunting Yoshi.

As the decoy made a distraction, Velma reached over to help Dillon, but instead of her pulling him up, he pulled her down with a quick tug.

Sharply edged shards of compressed magic imbedded themselves in the wall right behind where her head had been moments ago.

It had flown right through her decoy!

"That was supposed to work," Velma said numbly as the shards boomeranged back to Yoshi's amulet to be charged up again.

"The decoy's not working on him." Dillon picked up his glasses, shoving them back on. "You said this was your friend?"

"One of my best."

"I don't think he knows that anymore," Dillon remarked. "You not hitting back is not helping matters."

"I can't risk hurting my friend!"

"Then you have less time than you think."

Velma protested until she saw the incoming magic reflected in Dillon's lenses.

Velma spun, and the spells coiled in her bracelet unfurled to reveal a peacock. Its tail feathers snapped open, protecting them from the renewed onslaught.

Yoshi struck at the star-speckled barrier, his gestures becoming erratic as he tried to force his way through. His hands clawed at the magic, attempting to rip it apart.

He was moving too quickly for Velma to knock him into sleep. If she didn't stop him soon, he was going to bring the building down on all their heads.

"He's holding something," Dillon said, his voice sharp enough to snap Velma's attention to him. "It's something he hasn't tried to throw at you yet."

Yoshi's hand had been clenched the whole time, but for obvious reasons Velma had been too distracted to notice.

"What could that be?" Velma wondered aloud as she looked through the feathery barrier into Yoshi's face. His body was rigid and tense, his mouth set in a hard, unyielding line—except his eyes.

His eyes were frightened, alarmed, and desperately seeking hers.

He didn't want to fight her—something was compelling him.

Something she couldn't see. Something different from what she'd faced before.

But not anything she couldn't handle.

Velma charged through the barrier of her own magic, ignoring how the spells tickled across her skin.

A direct approach was the only way. Subtle approaches weren't working and only delayed what she knew she had to do in the end.

"I'm very sorry about this," Velma said. She drew back her arm and struck a blow squarely under Yoshi's chin. It knocked him back enough that she could grab him. She locked him into a headlock with one arm, and while she grappled with him, she twisted his other arm. Gritting her teeth, she pressed her nails into the flesh of his wrist and didn't stop pressing until his fist opened.

Instead of a gemstone or a stubby wand, a coin fell to the floor.

As it rolled along past her foot, the initial shock faded and Velma recalled with a start why she had put Sacramento on her list in the first place. She had traveled all this way to ask Yoshi about the coins that Delia Moore had given Edythe. This was just hardly how she'd expected the conversation about them to go.

"I suppose you found out what the coins do after all?" Velma said.

Yoshi nodded vigorously, tapping her to get her to let go.

Velma did, but remained on guard just in case.

Yoshi collapsed to the floor, well away from the coin. He coughed, trying to get his breath before he started to explain. "I asked too many questions about the dimes. Then this coin got placed on me."

Dillon walked over. "What got placed on you?"

"A coin—don't touch it," Velma said. "It controls your mind."

"A coin did all that." Dillon whistled. "If I hadn't seen it in action just now, I'd never have believed it."

"Why would someone want to do that to you?" Velma asked.

Yoshi gave a hollow chuckle. "I run an underground market of magical goods and items. Who wouldn't want to have control over me, especially when I refuse to bend to others' demands?"

The wall panel snapped open as Fumiko stormed out. Her bristling anger stopped short at the ruin in the room.

"It's like the night in the theater," Fumiko said, gasping. "Except no music."

"I don't think the music was the cause," Dillon remarked.

"Yes and no." Velma got out a handkerchief and picked up the coin.

Yoshi flinched and even Dillon looked wary. Her handkerchief, embroidered with protection spells, contained the coin's foul enchantments. The coin was a silver dollar minted in 1921, although to her eye the design didn't seem to be accurate. The lettering was slightly off and Lady Liberty faced the opposite direction.

"Who's making these coins?" Velma asked Yoshi.

"Malcolm Gladstone. I don't know if you've ever come across him before."

"Can't say I have, but we'll be acquainted shortly."

"I wouldn't look for him," Yoshi advised.

Velma gestured around at the disturbed contents of the room. "I can handle a little trouble."

"It's not that. He's a pawn. He just makes the glaze. He's replicating work that was already done before, directed by someone else. I don't know who's behind it, but I got the record player from them. I can't remember who it was. I don't know if it was the coin's magic or some other spell at work. I know I was instructed to use the record player and given details on when to use it."

"Do you still have it?" Velma asked.

Yoshi paused, shuffling through his scattered memories, but his sister spoke up.

"We still have it—it's in pieces. You told me to hide it away," Fumiko said.

"I don't remember that," Yoshi said.

"This coin probably doesn't have as strong of a hold as it seems," Dillon said. "It controlled you, but you could resist in certain areas. It's why your attacks toward Velma were relentless but not brutal. How you immediately put your sister away from danger. Why you managed to keep the damaged record player, even if you were compelled to get rid of it."

"That's good?" Yoshi asked, confused.

"It might mean the coin isn't as powerful as I thought," Velma said. "Let's see the record player."

Fumiko had hidden the record player under the floorboards in the storage room tucked into a hatbox lined with magic-resistant materials.

It wasn't much to look at. The record player was in pieces, more parts than machine, although a few were large enough to be of interest. Velma picked up what could have been part of the lid. Stamped on the sliver of wood was a name and slogan: *Wise Records, the sound of new music.*

"Wise Records," Velma echoed, feeling as if she had seen this name before.

"Where's the record to go with it?" Dillon asked Fumiko. "I assume it got broken as well?"

"Not as badly as I thought. It got scratched, though. It won't play."

"Might be for the best," Dillon said.

"I agree," Yoshi added grimly as his sister twirled a small topaz pendant of her own. The stone turned clear as quartz and a gentle wind lifted a basket off the topmost shelf and into her hands.

"This is the record we were given to play," Fumiko said.

Dillon grabbed the badly scratched record, turning it over, but

Velma didn't look at it even as he angled it in her direction. Velma's eyes had locked on the other record sitting in the basket, and she knew where she had seen the name Wise Records before.

Velma had held this very same record in Delia Moore's dressing room. She had put it aside that day and now, as Velma held it, she reconsidered that simple act with regret.

"Do you know anything about Wise Records?" Velma asked Dillon.

"Not much," he said. "If it's a record company with a wide distribution, my younger sister might be able to help. She's amassed a large collection."

"Ask her if she has any albums from Wise Records. I need to confirm something. I've seen a record just like this before."

"How recently?"

Velma didn't answer right away. She had flipped the record over to look for additional information. According to the label, the record had been pressed in 1920, and its listed performer, Posy Newman, was accompanied by the Strickland Jazz Parade.

CHAPTER 18

Before they followed up on Malcolm Gladstone, Dillon dashed to a phone to call a few contacts about Wise Records. As he made himself cozy in a phone booth, Velma reclined in the farm truck as she read Dillon's notes about Brayton Strickland. The pages written in Dillon's meticulous hand detailed Strickland's band from the formation, dissolution, and rumored activities that involved a grisly murder. Strickland was never officially charged because he was a man of power and influence, even back in 1927. Dillon had not written anything explicit about Wise Records, only that Strickland and his band had worked with a few artists on their records over the years.

"So that's what you meant by being interested in his past," Velma said when Dillon returned. "I thought it was something else, but this is not a surprise. Strickland hinted at this when I spoke to him."

"Like many things, a minor detail is turning out to be relevant. I don't know if there's more out there or not." Dillon threw his hat onto the seat with slight disgust.

Velma shut the notebook and sat up. "You didn't find out anything about the company?"

"I found plenty," Dillon began. "Wise Records has been out of business since '22. Went belly-up like a beached whale due to financial issues. They were red-hot in their first years, and produced records for big-time singers like Shirleen Hines."

"I know her. I think I have her latest record," Velma said. "I had no idea she started at Wise."

"Probably for good reason. The people I was talking to didn't utter a peep about how Wise went bust. I assume there was a scandal, a horrendously bad one."

"No details?" she teased. "Or you didn't have enough time?"

"I had time to ask, but no one was willing to play ball. I did find out who founded it. Giles Pacer and Edwin Addison."

Both of those names rang alarm bells in Velma's mind, but one did just a tad bit more.

"Addison?" Velma echoed. "Could he be related to *Laverna* Addison?"

"Very likely. I need to see what public records I can get on that. Edwin Addison is dead, though. Part of the company's downturn seems to be related to his demise: after his death the company shut down within a month. It seems Pacer was the face of the company and recruited musicians, but Wise wouldn't have existed without Edwin's talents. He perished in an accident at the factory. It's a very peculiar sort of accident. No one can agree if it was outside sabotage or equipment failure, but the grounds are magic scarred and there are a lot of superstitions about the place. I have the address for the factory site—it's not far from here—but I'm not sure if it's worth a visit. The factory was razed to the ground recently."

"How recently?"

"About three months ago." He paused. "It's in Briony Canyon, by the way."

"That's one of the places I was meant to visit," Velma said as Dillon waited patiently, her map of destinations flashing before her eyes. "Three months ago is when an incident was reported there. Was the factory destroyed around then?"

Dillon nodded. "Coincidence, I think not."

"It might be worth a visit, but you don't have to join me," Velma said carefully. "It doesn't have anything to do with your article."

"I hope not, because writing about a man enchanted by a coin will strain credibility," Dillon said. Off Velma's surprised expression, he added, "I'd change names, of course. You can't blame me for writing about it—it's intriguing."

"No, it's that after what happened, you're still coming along?" Velma asked, genuinely surprised. "As I said, this has nothing to do with your article."

"It might not, but it's curious." An impish grin took ahold of Dillon's features as he continued. "Or are you trying to make sure I hang around? Because I've gathered information much quicker than calling the Muses, and without further delaying your travels."

Velma winced at his blunt, but accurate, words. "There is some benefit to having you around," she admitted.

"You also don't want Lois to know I'm traveling with you," he added casually.

She sighed, not even bothering to deny it. She had called Lois only when she thought Dillon was asleep, but clearly she had been mistaken.

"Was it that obvious I was contacting her at the Muses?" Velma asked.

"Your friend is a bad liar. Plus, she already admitted you worked together."

"Lois is a trained librarian, though. My travels have been based on her research and she has access to resources in our network that you don't."

"Which is a very good thing on her part, but she can't provide the connections. I don't want to brag," Dillon said as he dramatically drew out his words, "but I happen to be quite excellent at finding connections between disparate information."

"Trust me, I know firsthand. It's how we ended up running into each other on my previous cases. Unless you were following me."

"What, chasing after you like a lovesick puppy?" Dillon scoffed as he turned the truck on. "You wish. We just both get ourselves tangled up in things most sensible people would avoid."

"Nobody has ever called me sensible."

Dillon chortled. "Same here!"

The address Yoshi had given Velma took them to the other side of town. Instead of driving all the way in, they left the truck behind and walked the last few blocks. It hadn't changed much over the years, but Velma didn't remember a printshop. According to Yoshi, Malcolm Gladstone kept rooms above it. Yoshi wasn't sure if Gladstone lived or simply worked there. The location was convenient for his work: the street was a bustling place that would make it easy for Gladstone to send and receive packages frequently. Although today it seemed busier than usual.

A small crowd was gathered out in the street around a candy shop. It took only getting within earshot to know there had been a raid by a pair of MD agents. Both were young Black men; one shoved a bulky bag of items into the car, while the other confronted the candy shop owner.

"You are being charged with possession of illegal arcane herbs," the young agent called over the rumbling voices of the crowd, "indecent levels of magic performed in a private business, and the intent to sell and distribute illegal tonics. We found all these on your property, following a spike of 276 VF units."

"That doesn't even make sense!" heckled an old man in the crowd. "You're just spouting off numbers."

"The Bass family has done nothing wrong," a woman called. "You leave them alone."

"You should be ashamed of yourself, Freddie! They only hired you to commit raids against your own people. White folks don't want us to use our magic—why help them?"

"Enough!" the other MD agent called as his partner hesitated. "We'll take you all in too if you don't settle down!"

"Please," begged the candy store owner, "I don't know how any of this happened. I got nothing magical in my shop, I swear to it!"

"Are these Magical Detection agents doing a raid?" Dillon whispered to Velma. "I've never seen one happen in the daytime like this."

"They must be bored," Velma said. "I suppose somebody in town is quite desperate to 'clean up' this neighborhood. Funny, the MDs only come knocking on decent folks' doors."

"They don't look like they're paid enough to do raids like this," Dillon observed, "or pick on a tiny shop like this."

"Which is why this isn't a raid—it's a setup." Velma glanced through the crowd of onlookers. Right in the thickest knot she spotted a middle-aged woman and her young son. The woman appeared agitated but not sympathetic over the scene unfolding before her.

"I'll be right back," Velma said. She walked past the crowd but didn't join it. She stood on the other end of the street until she was in sight of the MD agents' car, then gave it a nudge with her magic.

It rolled slowly at first, jerking enough to catch the eye of a child. As the boy laughed, it caught more attention and the MD agents spun around.

"Who's doing that? Stop it!" The man with the list attempted to halt the car, but the moment he flung his magic outward toward the vehicle, it sped up and then winked out of sight.

"If it gets stolen, we'll be canned!" the other agent cried, and both men ran along the street, not knowing that they had already run past their invisible car.

Jeering rose up in the crowd, and amid it, Velma approached the candy shop owner.

"You should take this time to thoroughly check your shop for anything incriminating," Velma said. "Those fools can't take you in without hard evidence, and whatever they collected just vanished. If you do have trouble in the future"—she pulled out a card and handed it to him—"call this number and explain."

"Did you . . . ?" the shop owner wondered.

Velma smiled. "Not so loud. I'm only here on a short visit."

"I didn't do anything they said." The man took the card, shoving it into the apron he wore over his clothes. "I don't know where any of the magic came from."

"I believe you," Velma assured him. "Make sure to check your locks—you'll likely find an issue with them."

In the emptying streets, Dillon spoke with the woman Velma had noted earlier. Velma's lurking suspicions only grew despite the woman tearfully twisting a handkerchief, especially since her son was nowhere to be found.

Dillon, notebook in hand, nodded as he listened to the woman. While pretending to turn the page in his notebook, he pointed to the printshop with his pen.

Velma went around the back. Ignoring the rickety fire escape, she flicked a wind spell at her feet and gently floated up to the second floor, landing silently next to the boy, who was anxiously trying to unlock the door to the second-story apartment.

His panic meant that he didn't see the glimmer of starlight along the door until it was too late—but that was fine. Velma had already taken care of it. As the protective wards lashed out toward him like angry clawing hands, Velma sliced through the magic almost lazily, to the boy's startled surprise.

"You need to be more careful," she said to the boy. "Don't run," she added, even as the boy threw himself down the fire escape. Velma twirled a finger and the boy drifted back, dangling from an invisible hook. "I thought you wanted to see what's inside?" she asked. "I certainly do, since you and your mother don't want the Sniffers to see."

"We got nothing to do with it," the boy said. "Honest, I swear!"

"Then stick with me," Velma said, dropping the boy back to his feet. "This won't take long."

Having banished the former protective magic, Velma got the door open easily. While she brought the boy along to make sure he didn't run off, she almost had him stay outside. The air reeked of ink and oil, with an acrid undercurrent.

Chemical, she realized, glancing at a long table with all the flasks and tubes any half-decent chemist would have. Something had burned in this room recently, but enough time had passed to let it recede.

A small tray of coins sat on the table as well. Velma hoped to find this, although she couldn't tell if they were enchanted like the one Yoshi had or not. There were stacks of paper all about—as to be expected above a printshop. Soot-stained curtains hung from the lone window in the room, and in the middle of the space was a small round table with a twisted piece of melted metal sitting atop it. Velma thought it had previously been some sort of machine, given some of the half-melted parts she spied, but she didn't have a clue what it was.

"Is this what exploded this morning that had you blackmailing your neighbor?" Velma asked.

Instead of the boy, his mother answered.

"It wasn't personal. I was going to vouch to get him released. A bottle or two of Meadow Memories will get you fined, but this foul experiment was going to put me in the dampest, coldest cell around."

"Meet Susan Thompson," Dillon said as he lurked in a corner, his eyes locked on the woman despite his light tone. "She rented this space to Malcolm Gladstone about a year ago, and she's gotten far more trouble than what it's worth for the rent. Gladstone not only used the shop as a site of illegal sales, he also was stealing from her printers."

"You didn't report him?" Velma asked.

"At first I didn't mind. He brewed little tonics, things I can't get easily," Susan admitted. "I knew what he was and what he did, but he paid the first of every month, and that's all I cared about until he started experimenting." Susan waved a hand around the space. "I heard music, I heard loud bangs, and we smelled all sorts of things drifting from this room. My spells on the shop kept it contained, and being a printshop could excuse most of the noise. Then this started." Her eyes went to the melted magic in the middle of the room. "Is it dangerous?"

Of course it is! Velma wanted to cry. Everything the woman had just described on top of the few things Velma had observed screamed *dangerous*. But that wasn't what the woman was asking with her desperate, pleading eyes.

"Regardless of what it is," Dillon said, "you should leave this place before Gladstone returns. I'd advise you to leave even if he never returns, since your neighbors are probably aware of your peculiar situation—or they will be shortly."

"You," Susan sputtered, looking at Dillon and then at Velma, who matched his expressionless gaze with one of her own. "You can't be serious? This is my business! It's all I have!"

"Is your life worth it?" Velma said. "Because Malcolm Gladstone just nearly killed you, your son, and everyone on this street. And if it's not because of what he's tinkering with, it will be the other things he's involved in that will have people seeking revenge. Don't make you and your son a target. If you're any good at this business, you can start over somewhere else easily." Velma pulled out another card, identical to the one she'd given the candy store owner. "Call this number and explain, and you'll have help."

Susan swallowed her protests. "Thank you."

"Don't thank me yet," Velma said. "Start packing."

Mother and son scampered out of the room, leaving Velma and Dillon alone to stare at the twisted remains of the experiment gone wrong.

"Are you calling this in?" Dillon asked her. "Or is this a call to Yoshi and other old bootlegging contacts?"

"I don't know if Yoshi— Oh," Velma said as she realized. "I guess you figured out I did some bootlegging when I used to live here."

"I'm not sure 'figured out' is the right phrase," Dillon remarked. "More like I didn't ignore the obviously glaring signs the moment we got into Sacramento. Although I suspected it for a while, between your cargo hold having several cleverly hidden compartments and the fact that I haven't been able to get a decent drink or tonic back home since I started slandering your good name in the paper. I'm guessing you transported liquor?"

Velma nodded. "I primarily couriered potions, tonics, and liquor over the Mexico border, although I did some from Canada a few times. A bulk of my work was local delivery. Once I made enough money, I quit. I do keep in contact with people. The owner of Checkers is an old friend. Old friends are helpful for things like this."

"If you can trust them. You believe Yoshi gave you a good tip?" Dillon asked as he looked around. "He didn't mention this machine."

"This might be new or unrelated," Velma said. "Could you take some photographs?"

He laughed. "Do wolves bay at the sight of a full moon?"

With his camera Dillon walked around the small table, taking pictures. When he finished, he went to document the rest of the workshop. As he did, Velma returned her attention to the remnants of the machine.

She had thought the coins to be the most alarming find in the room. This half-melted machine was something much worse. She wasn't sure telling Yoshi was the best idea. She scarcely knew what to make of any of this and doubted he would know more than she.

What she did know was that Gladstone had left a mess. Aside from the papers scattered about, some badly singed too, she found half of an invitation to an auction in Los Angeles and promptly overlooked it in favor of handwritten notes with a series of equations scribbled upon them. Those pages were also badly burned, and the ink was smudged enough that she could hardly read a word. She squinted all the same until a box crashed to the floor.

Velma spun around, only to realize Dillon had knocked it over on purpose.

"What are you doing?" Velma cried, only for Dillon to wave a poster in her face. Velma pushed it aside, not bothering to read it. "This place is a powder keg! You could have stirred up—"

"Plenty has already been stirred up." Dillon held up the poster again, then pointed to the large text and read aloud: "'Come witness the true will of magic'—this is one of the key phrases from the MRC. Phrases like this appear on all the other printed materials. All these posters and flyers, they're for the MRC."

"The shop owner did say Gladstone was stealing from the printshop." Velma looked over at the boxes Dillon had been exploring. There were dozens of stacks ready to be sent. While the posters weren't marked to explicitly say Members of Rational Clarity, Velma trusted that after all the research Dillon had done he easily recognized the group's rhetoric.

"If Gladstone's part of it, I have another reason to track him down," Velma said.

"He might be hard to find."

"I don't think so." Velma held out the invitation she had found on the floor. "There are several copies—looks like he forged some with the printer."

"It's an auction," Dillon said. "In Los Angeles, held at Giles Pacer's home."

"Giles Pacer?" Velma nearly snatched it back. "I didn't see that on there!"

"It's the part that burned off. I recognized the address because I got Giles Pacer's information when I was making my calls earlier."

"Then we know where we're going next. I'd planned to talk with him soon, now that I know he cofounded Wise Records. I don't know what Gladstone is planning, but if it's any sort of mischief, I might be able to use that to get Pacer to talk to me."

"I don't think he will talk to you."

"He will," Velma said. "I'm very persuasive."

Dillon shook his head. "I'm not doubting that, but even you might find it challenging. Giles Pacer is dead."

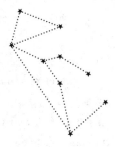

CHAPTER 19

D illon claimed he'd had a good reason for holding back that tidbit about Giles Pacer when he'd first told her about Wise Records. Only one contact had told him this news, and it was a contact he seldom trusted.

"I wanted to confirm the news before I mentioned it. I figured Gladstone was more important," Dillon said as Velma stomped out of the workshop. "I didn't deceive you on purpose!"

"You neglected several details, which is nearly the same thing!" Velma spun around on the fire escape, and Dillon stumbled back. "You could have framed it as a rumor. Half my work is dealing with rumors! I have traveled hundreds of miles due to a whisper I heard in a crowded room. Let me decide what information is valuable or not. Or else this is where we part ways."

Dillon leaned forward, playfully wagging a finger in her face. "Then I shall let you know every single inkling that comes to pass."

"Don't make fun of me!"

"I'm afraid I must," Dillon replied merrily. "If I cannot make light of the things I take great pleasure in, what is the point of living? No one has told me: tell me every rumor the moment it has first sprung up! You will not regret this."

"I believe I already do," Velma muttered, somewhat thrown at such a resolution but not overly displeased. "Let's go find a newspaper or two."

The first newspaper they found carried a notice on page two about the death of the founder and president of the Pacific Western Life Insurance Company. The story continued onto page four, where the reporter recounted scant details of the robbery and the head injury that had left the president dead at the scene. Brief biographical details followed, highlighting Pacer's insurance company, work in the music business, and devotion to the community in Los Angeles through several charities he'd sponsored.

"'Due to specifications in his will, no funeral services will occur,'" Dillon read as he and Velma sat in the farm truck, the newspapers spread around. "'Giles Pacer will be cremated privately, and his entire estate will be auctioned off to the public to raise money for the church he had been a devout member of for the past ten years.' Well then, isn't that convenient? The man we're interested in talking to just got himself killed within weeks of Delia Moore's murder."

As Velma put aside the newspaper she held, she knew there was no way she was getting rid of Dillon now. Stars above, *she* wouldn't leave if the situation were reversed. Pacer's untimely death was suspicious, curious, intriguing, and everything else you could probably toss at it, before you included everything else they had found out that day.

"I guess our plans have just been changed," Velma remarked.

After exchanging the farm truck for Velma's plane, they flew south.

Velma had a friend who owned and operated a dude ranch on the outskirts of Los Angeles. While Marjorie wasn't that good of a friend to let her stay a few days without paying room and board, Velma knew she had a safe place to leave her plane.

The ranch was self-sufficient, balancing both the needs of commerce and leisure. Paying guests and orphans got equal care and attention, as did the many farm animals on the grounds. A central site of recreation for the Black folks of the city and surrounding area, the ranch provided horse stables, a broom-racing track, a tennis court, a swimming pool, and a multipurpose building that had seen everything from balls to scientific lectures. Marjorie even claimed the Nifty Dude Ranch was featured as a main setting in three films, including a Western that touted an all-Black-and-Native cast.

"Really," Dillon said. "What's the film's name?"

"Do you think I'm lying?" Marjorie challenged, with a hint of a threat in her husky voice. A widow three times over before she'd turned forty, Marjorie was the person who had gotten Velma into bootlegging in the first place and had shown her that you didn't always have to use magic to enchant and bewitch others.

"Dillon is a reporter," Velma explained. "He just likes to know all the facts, to his peril."

"I've also never heard of this ranch before, I'm quite curious." Dillon said in a vain attempt to charm the older woman.

"You must have never been west of the Rio Grande if you haven't. Why don't we change that?"

Marjorie gladly regaled Dillon with the ranch's history, leading them away from the small barn that housed Velma's plane to the guest residences. While more of the little houses were closed than usual, a few were currently occupied, with some of the guests sitting out on the porches, including a man currently attempting to whittle wood while at times veering very close to slicing off his fingers instead.

Marjorie opened a door to a cabin with a pot of violets out front. With a flick of her fingers, the lights turned on to reveal several tastefully decorated rooms with violets, both the flower and the color, as the main accent. "Everything should be as it was when you were last here. The only thing new is a phone line in the cabin so you don't have to walk down to the main house. Meals are taken at the house, since there only a few people here. It helps with the children's table manners. Although I'm not sure how long you plan to stay."

"We should stay here a whole week since we paid for it," Dillon grumbled.

"The only charity I run is for children, Mr. Harris," Marjorie said. "Although if you were to write an extensive portrait of Nifty Dude Ranch detailing its history, current endeavors, and prospects for the future, we could negotiate the subject of payment. Only if you're interested, of course."

Dillon's eyes brightened. "What do you think of a series of articles about your ranch? One article for each night we stay?"

"To cover each night?" Marjorie retorted. "Words are cheap!"

"He's a very good writer," Velma put in. "His investigations put away criminals, people trust his opinion on local politics and events, and his write-ups about my air shows are part of the reason there's a dedicated following for the High Flyers."

Marjorie gave no indication that Velma's words altered her opinion, although Dillon appeared seemingly struck by Velma's endorsement. *Shocked* might be a better word, Velma considered as she avoided his eyes. He was a good writer and a better reporter. For all their tangled history, Velma would never deny that.

"Three articles," Marjorie said. "A history, an overview of the offerings here, and a promotional piece for an upcoming event. In exchange you'll pay half price for the rooms, no charge to borrow my car, and I need to see the articles before publication."

"Deal," Dillon said. "I should warn you, though: I don't write fluff. If I write about your ranch, it'll be the whole story, including warts and buried skeletons."

Marjorie cackled. "So you have heard about the ranch before! I must get rid of the rumors about me and my three dead husbands."

"I can help with that," Dillon added eagerly. "I'll clear your name if you promise we'll stay here for free."

Marjorie threw her head back in a bout of raucous laughter. "I like you, young man! I hope you last longer than Velma's last boyfriend! How is William doing? Is he still boxing?"

The air suddenly tensed around Velma, and her face turned slightly warm. "I haven't spoken to him in years. And you're mistaken, Marjorie. Dillon and I are just traveling in the same direction."

"We're just working together for an article," Dillon added.

Marjorie silenced their rambling explanations with a tap to her nose and a wink. "Let's pretend you are a couple—this cabin has only one bedroom, and I can't in good conscience let you stay if the details are complicated. I'll have to insist you rent out another cabin, at full price, and consider any previous deal null and void."

Marjorie had let far more scandalous things occur on the ranch than an unmarried pair sharing a cabin, so Velma knew that the threat was just her having fun at their expense. Given how Marjorie smirked in Velma's direction as she continued to tease them, this was perhaps the true price of their stay, as Marjorie would choose a good laugh over coins whenever she could.

Before Dillon could say something he would regret, Velma forcibly asked, "Marge, when I called earlier, you said you were familiar with Giles Pacer?"

"Who isn't?" Marjorie sat in an armchair, elegantly draping one leg over the other. "He was very well known in the city. I knew him personally—rather well, I might say." Her lips quirked in a mischievous smile before continuing. "I'm the architect who designed his house. It was such a shock when I heard the news about his head being bashed in by a burglar. Although rumors say he was running numbers, others think it was just some scheme with illegal magic. I know the latter is not true at all."

"Was it truly a burglary gone wrong?" Velma asked.

"It seems to be. I also heard that Giles was last seen in public arguing with a man. It could have been over anything, though. Not enough to kill, I don't think."

You'd be surprised, Velma thought, *how many simple arguments lead to murder.*

"You designed Pacer's home," Dillon asked. "You're an architect?"

"I dabble these days. I used to have a small firm, but I had to close it. I still design, but it's only for projects I find of particular interest. The house I made for Giles is one of my favorites. I took a very modern approach to blending pieces of the Mediterranean and French Regency styles. Not fully one of each, but the flavor of both is there. Pacer allowed me to do as I wished, and when my projections came in higher than budgeted, he made it work. His only insistence was that his piano would be able to move easily throughout the house."

"Did you put any secrets in the house?" Velma asked, fervently hoping there would be a hidden entrance she could utilize.

"Like a secret staircase or door? No, no, I tried. I wanted to—many of my other clients often request such features. Giles didn't want it." Marjorie's brows came together as she attempted to recall the conversation. "He said he didn't want an extra door to guard. I thought it an odd passing remark, but now that he's dead, I can't help but wonder if he had a reason for such caution."

As Velma and Dillon had arrived the night before the auction, they had time to prep and prepare. Dillon went to work on his article while Velma updated Lois about where she was . . . and found excuses about how she was able to gather a wealth of information all on her own without Lois's help. Luckily, Lois had news of her own to impart to Velma.

"You need to go to Denver next. Jasper—you remember Jasper, don't you, your old partner? He's called in something just now. Not only are you the closest one in the field, it seems it might be related to your search. It's not urgent enough for you to go there directly, but he says not to delay."

"What happened in Denver?" Velma asked.

"There's been a fire. Jasper found something he wanted other eyes on. You'll have time for it, won't you?"

"I was going to go to Las Vegas, but I can return if needed. Is there anything you can tell me about Giles Pacer?"

"You already know the most current information. I've been working to confirm that Laverna Addison is the only daughter of Edwin and Clara Addison. It's a little tricky. I have a record of a birth in a small town that I can't find. I'm not sure if it's because these records come from a time when the state was still a territory or because I had my assistant pull the information—although I think it's the latter."

"Don't fire anyone," Velma cautioned. "I can follow up on the details."

"You . . . are offering to deal with paperwork?" Lois asked suspiciously.

"This could be very crucial information," Velma said, sticking with the truth in hopes her friend would back down.

It worked. Lois grunted in agreement. "I'll share with you what I found. You might be able to go there yourself to confirm. It's in Colorado too, a town called Ardenton."

"I'll take a look."

When Velma left the kitchen, there was no sign of Dillon in the main room other than his typewriter set up on a table. He had already laid out extra blankets and a pillow on the couch, thoughtfully avoiding a slightly awkward conversation in the aftermath of Marjorie's teasing.

Spotting a blanket shoved around the cracks on the bedroom door, Velma knocked. "You know the bathroom doesn't have any windows," she called.

"It also has no space."

"Are you developing the photographs? I want to see."

"Do you? Come in quickly, then."

Velma entered the dimly lit room and found herself greeted by photographs suspended in the air by Dillon's magic.

He stood near a table, in the middle of processing film. Her entry had stalled his work but he started up again once the door shut. He had pushed up his sleeves to work, and Velma found herself watching the subtle movements of his arms as he developed the photographs, so much so that she didn't even notice at first what the images were until Dillon commented on the melted machine in Malcolm Gladstone's workshop.

"You won't find anything interesting here," Dillon said. "Look at the ones drying over my shoulder instead."

"Am I making you nervous?" Velma asked as she hastily looked away.

"I'm not used to having someone lurking about. Also, the pictures from the baseball game turned out better than I'd hoped. I even got a picture of what caused the bleachers to collapse."

Velma found the photograph right away, as it hovered at eye level to make sure it wouldn't be missed. It was hard to say when exactly during the chaos of the collapsing bleachers he had snapped the image—it might have even been by accident given the lack of a central focal point. If it was by accident, then it was as if the stars had aligned for that very moment. The image was of a phonograph on the edge of the field. As the record spun, swirls of magic formed the letters of the parting message that had filled the sky above the field.

Who would have thought a record player would be a tool of chaos wielded by a magical anarchist group? Then again, Velma had seen far stranger things.

"A record player started this?"

"Not on its own," Dillon said. "Look at the photo to the left."

In this one, a man stood almost out of frame as he adjusted the record player. Although caught in profile, there was enough of his face for Velma to recognize him.

"Brayton Strickland," Velma cried, truly flabbergasted. "He's part of Members of Rational Clarity? How is that possible?"

"A myriad of reasons." Dillon shrugged. "He might believe in the cause, or he might be doing a grift—it's hard to say. These images aren't solid proof, but it raises interesting questions that I hope to find answers to while we're here in Los Angeles. Besides tracking down Malcolm Gladstone, I'd like to see if I can connect Strickland to MRC. That would be quite the coup."

"You can look, but we won't be here for long," Velma said. "Denver is next after the auction. It's an urgent call from headquarters."

Dillon turned to face her, holding the photograph he'd just pulled out of the developing fluid. "How urgent?" he asked. "I have a friend who was going to help me with my research."

"Urgent enough that I need to go there as soon as I can. We could return," Velma offered, "or we split up for the day. I go to the auction by myself and you do your research."

"That sounds like you're trying to get rid of me," Dillon pointed out.

"There's no reason to now," Velma assured him. "I want to know about this Rational Clarity group as much as you do. It's easier if you do the asking around."

"Less work for you," Dillon said, but his tone was warm with his usual bemusement. "Is that the only reason you're keeping me around?"

"You ask good questions, and I suppose you are good company," Velma said, sweetening the pot before she added, "and I was hoping you could find a small town named Ardenton."

"No wonder you're being nice to me—you want something!"

"I only asked because Lois looked and couldn't find it. If you don't think you'll have better luck . . ." She let her words trail off into a tempting challenge, but there was no need for such a ploy. Dillon was already nodding.

"I never said I couldn't," he said. "And it's not luck. It's skill and perseverance. I'll find the town along with everything else. Won't take me long at all. I'll probably be done before the auction even begins."

Velma laughed at the outrageous boast. "Don't rush to try to meet me. It'll be easier for me to sneak into the auction on my own."

"I'm sure it will be." Dillon's grin was more mischievous than usual as he asked, "I suppose you'll walk in there as hired help for the day, won't you?"

"I never sneak into places. The best way to go unnoticed is to loudly announce yourself!"

CHAPTER 20

The following afternoon, Velma arrived in the West Adams neighborhood that Giles Pacer had once called home. While there were a few lovely houses lining the street, Pacer's sprawling mansion was easily the crown jewel. Framed perfectly by an ivy-cloaked wall that partially shielded the house from the street, the building loomed in a quiet display of wealth and influence.

Between the crowd and the expensive cars rolling by, it was easy for Velma to fall into step and pretend she was part of some group's party. Small clusters of folks lingered in the garden, and Velma saw more silk, pearls, and genuine gemstones than she had seen in a long time. She also spotted several fake diamonds and emeralds in rings and necklaces, but that was to be expected. The auction had attracted wealth, and to be part of it you had to make it clear you belonged. Velma had no worries there. Adorned in her favorite scarlet fringed dress, with earrings that resembled tiny chandeliers, her usual bracelets, and a feathered headband that belonged to Marjorie, Velma knew no one would question her presence at the auction.

She also knew, as she gave a friendly wink to the attendant at the door, that he was going to be hardly bothered to ask about any invitation she should have.

"I need a little help," she simpered as she fixed her eyes on the man. "I heard about this auction, but I'm not sure what to do?"

"It's just an auction, miss." From a nearby basket, he pulled out a church fan, except instead of painted Scripture quotes or doves, the number 42 was drawn. "There's a select number of items for the silent auction—you just leave your bids in the book next to them. The main auction in the drawing room will hold the more interesting pieces."

"When would that be?"

He pointed to a chalkboard with the list of numbers for various collections and the time each auction would occur.

"If you want my advice . . . ," he began.

Velma batted her eyes at the man. "I would so *love* to have it."

A silly smile crossed his face, and he stood up straighter as if to improve the impression of his rather slight frame.

"Don't be fooled by the impressive-looking things. Small packages hold wonders. Such as myself."

"Do they really?"

"Yes! Sure, the piano, his collection of Alexandre Dumas first editions, and even the sword rumored to have been used by Toussaint Louverture are all very valuable. There are a few things, like a snuff box, a chess set, and a jewelry box, that seem to be gathering some interest."

Velma hid her surprise with a flip of her fan. "Interesting, but I don't see them on the board?"

"They wouldn't be, not by name. They are in lot number twenty-three." The man was clearly enjoying the attention she was seemingly lavishing on him, and was compelled to keep it longer, for he added in a rush, "I worked for Mr. Pacer, he was a good man, but he was obsessed with these things. He got the snuff box just before he died. The chess set and jewelry box, oddly enough, came afterward. The estate almost didn't let the lot be sold, but the will stated it must."

"Who manages the estate? Is it you?"

He continued to make himself ridiculous over this perceived flattery. "Not me. I'm—"

There was a pointed cough some distance away as an older woman dressed in the same uniform as the attendant looked right at him.

"Or maybe later," he said hastily. "I have to go attend to other matters." He barely stepped away before the woman shoved a tray of drinks into his hands and pointed in a direction that would lead him far away from Velma.

According to the chalkboard, the bids on lot number twenty-three wouldn't happen for another hour or so, which left Velma with plenty of time to fill. She grabbed a drink from a passing attendant and began to inspect the rooms. Each one was arranged by theme, and the most prevalent theme of all was that Giles Pacer had been a man with a deep interest in music. The piano that Marjorie had mentioned was an elegant ebony beauty with a long, sleek build with ivory keys that begged to have fingers dance upon them, drawing out tunes. Beyond the piano were several other instruments in varying states of use, quite a few record players, and a whole cabinet filled with sheet music. A few were on display in a special case to allow for easy viewing. Some were popular pieces by W. C. Handy while others were obscure blues and ragtime pieces that were unknown even to Velma.

"Of course he kept this!" The loud and distraught voice brought Velma's attention to the only other person in the music section.

She looked to be Velma's age, but the severe cut of her dark gray dress and her hair pulled tightly into a bun put a decade on her. Ink spotted her hands, and a pair of glasses dangled from a thin silver chain around her neck. Her features pointed to a melting pot of different backgrounds, but her skin was as dark brown as Velma's.

Instead of sheet music, the woman focused on a violin and a cello, as well as a barrel stuffed with violin bows next to them. Spying the framed photograph positioned nearby, Velma pointed to it.

"Did Mr. Pacer play in this band?" Velma asked.

"No, he sponsored it because he had been quite a fan," the woman said. She blinked hastily with some regret. "I mean, that's what I heard."

"I'm Velma," she said to put the woman at ease. "Velma Frye. I work at a music shop."

"Not in Los Angeles," the woman declared with a touch of defensiveness. "I've never heard of you before."

"True, the shop is out east," Velma said breezily, with increased interest at what was making this woman so jumpy. "Do you own a shop in town, then?"

"Yes, the Porter Music Shop, inherited from my father," the woman said, and a bit awkwardly she added, "I'm Portia Milburn. I did business with Mr. Pacer for many years."

"Including selling instruments to him?"

"As well as other things." Portia's eyes went back to the barrel of stringed bows.

"Custom work?" Velma asked.

"Yes, but it was a long time ago," Portia said.

"I hope he didn't ask you to hide wands alongside instruments," Velma remarked calmly.

Air hissed between Portia's lips and she clutched the chain at her neck. "How did— You couldn't—" Portia swallowed hard. "You're in the trade too?"

Velma tried not to chuckle at the accusation. Given the woman's manner and the rumors around Giles Pacer, wands weren't too far-fetched.

"I had a friend who got me to sell some, thinking I could hide them in the shop," Velma said, quickly stitching together a lie. "All it did was get me in trouble again and again. I'm just a point of contact. I know it's risky. The Wand Act allows for ownership, but selling is a bit murky. Are things better out here?"

"Not much. I don't sell wands at all. I just sell instruments, and not even much these days. Giles, Mr. Pacer, I mean, was my biggest customer."

"Sounds like you knew him well," Velma said. "I'm sorry for your loss."

"I am too," Portia said. "He was a good and honest man, despite the usual flaws."

She stepped away, and Velma took one last look around the room before stepping into the hallway. Not far from the door's entrance, she stopped and flipped open her compact mirror. Pretending to check her makeup, she watched as Portia slipped back into the room and plunged her hands into the barrel with the bows.

Stealing from a dead man whose dying wish was to auction off his things to charity wasn't good luck, but if there truly were wands in there, it might spare an unknowing bidder the trouble of a raid by prohibition agents.

Leaving Portia to do her good deed, Velma moved on to the next room. In contrast, this room was quite packed with people drawn to a collection of stage costumes and props, from Shakespearean stylings to medieval finery. Unlike in the previous room, the book here had many silent bids marked. Velma was tempted for a moment to join in as her gaze lingered on a chunky peridot-studded bracelet.

"You're Velma Frye!" a voice announced into the room.

Because it wasn't announced with outrage, Velma turned with slight interest to a young woman with a gleeful air that made her seem much younger. She was dressed in the black-and-white attendant uniform, and nearly dropped the tray of drinks in her hands as she stared up at Velma. "She's a pilot!" the girl said to the other guests, who were staring in their direction. "A famous pilot, one of the best in the country!"

"How nice," an old man said before ushering his wife out of the room.

"I'm Emily Brooks," the server said with wide, frantic eyes. "It's a pleasure to meet you, Miss Frye. Well, for real, this time!"

"We've met?" Velma asked, cursing her minor celebrity.

"Not actually. It just feels like I know you so well. I've read every article about you. I want to be a pilot—I was thinking of joining the Bessie Coleman Aero Club."

"Well, that sounds like a good idea. The club has some fine people and—" Velma took a hasty step back as Emily clutched her tray and moved forward to block Velma's way.

"Did you fly here from Chicago? I would love to see your plane. They say you have a magpie painted on its side?"

"I painted it myself. If you'll excuse me—"

"The auction isn't starting yet," Emily said, "at least not anything you'd be interested in. Just the old man's clothes."

"You work here?" Velma asked.

"Just for the day. I'm trying to save as much as I can for pilot lessons."

Velma forced a smile, trying to think of a way out of this conversation that wouldn't risk her cover more than it already had been. "Why are you interested in becoming a pilot?"

"Ever since I saw the movie *The Flying Ace*, and it's just left me wild over the idea. I wasn't allowed to fly my broom—my parents thought it was improper. But with planes, I know it's possible!"

"A movie did all that," Velma said. "Well, I guess they can do good things."

Before Emily could ask for an autograph, Velma placed her empty glass on the tray and moved swiftly back into the hallway.

The main auctions for the various lots were still ongoing, but the hallway was filled with people wandering between the rooms, making it hard to move around. Yet despite the tight fit, no one was going up the stairs for some reason. If there was an attendant standing guard keeping people from going up to the private rooms, Velma might have overlooked this. The more she watched people approach the stairs, however, the more she noticed them abruptly turn in opposite directions, as if they had suddenly changed their minds.

When someone *did* step on the stairs, the person jumped off, blinked, and then moved away.

Abandoning her plans to circulate the downstairs rooms, Velma twisted her bracelet around. Pulling at the spell she had carved into the metal, she manipulated it as she approached the stairs. No one stopped or said anything to Velma as she climbed the first step. Which was even more curious. She shouldn't have been the first person to notice the spell, yet it appeared that she was. Velma felt the pressure of magic at first as she breached it, but it was no trouble for her to shift it around.

Upstairs was deserted, despite the silent auction clearly being set up here as well. The closest room from the stairs held baseball keepsakes, very valuable keepsakes, in fact, given the teams and players featured, but when Velma opened the silent auction book to check, there were very few bids. This was matched in the book in the next room. Instead of pondering over this oddity, Velma went into each of the remaining rooms, finding nothing of interest until she entered a small private study.

Despite all of Giles Pacer's possessions being on display in the house, this was the first time Velma felt as if she were crossing into personal territory. It might have been the whiff of cigar smoke and sweet caramel candies. Or it could be the threadbare sweater tossed on the back of an armchair or the dime novel left on the corner of the desk with a pencil acting as a bookmark.

Still, none of this was enough to stop Velma from rooting through his desk.

The smaller drawers held nothing of interest, but the large file drawer was locked. Velma bent down and removed her earrings. She bent them slightly and they expanded into a pair of slender lock-picks. With a twist of her wrist, the lock popped open and the drawer came free.

Inside was a handful of records, and Velma had flipped past two before she found an album with Delia Moore and the Strickland Jazz Parade.

While this was noteworthy, the Wise Records logo got Velma's complete attention. Although the logo was similar to what she had seen before, on the album that Velma held in her hands now was an updated version that included interlocking circles: the Sitwell symbol.

As she stared at the record, the pieces fell into place.

The record player used at the Garden Theater was from Wise Records. Delia Moore had had a record made by that company. Brayton Strickland had accompanied Delia on the record. Delia was looking into an object made by Jeremiah Sitwell. In addition to Edythe, Delia had contacted two more people before her death, Giles Pacer and Laverna Addison.

Giles Pacer was dead, but Laverna Addison was still alive as far as Velma knew and could answer if her father was indeed Edwin Addison.

Or more importantly, if his grandfather had been Jeremiah Sitwell.

The Sitwell family had disappeared after leaving Bramble Crescent. Changing their name to separate themselves from the tragic history was no surprise. The only surprise was that the family would return in this fashion.

Wise Records' connection was no coincidence. Nor was the fact that Laverna Addison had been at the inn and stayed for the salon even after Delia hadn't shown up.

Even now Velma could see that creepy doll turning around in a circle. Laverna's interest might be a personal legacy. She might have been looking for the items left behind in the secret workshop. If Laverna knew about the secret workshop, what else might she know?

Mulling over these thoughts, Velma went deeper into the drawer, where she found an unmarked envelope stuffed with papers.

The topmost was a note from Delia Moore: *They believe the machine will show the inherent majesty of magic. You must get rid of Edwin Addison's notes. I don't know what they will do and I cannot stop them.* The second page was sheet music with oddly familiar lyrics:

At the house on the hill
Bad luck and trouble done spilled
One and two and two and one
The family of wicked fates
Leave them alone or it will be late late late

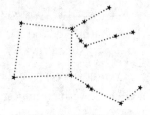

CHAPTER 21

Some of the words were different, but Velma recognized pieces of the handclap game about the Sitwell family. The fact that someone had heard it and turned it into a song was bewildering . . . second only to the context in which it was being shared.

Someone was looking for a machine. What was meant by "the inherent majesty of magic"? It seemed familiar although why was this song the key?

One thing at a time, she told herself.

Velma shoved the papers back into the envelope and stuck it into her purse. Closing the drawer, Velma continued her search. She had barely started up again when light ran along the length of the bracelet on her left arm. Velma looked up just in time to see a ring of magic swirling around her, effectively trapping her in place. The source of such a spell was an older man standing in the doorway, his face brimming with a coursing fear that Velma lacked.

Velma drew the first star sigil she could think of. Canis Minor bounded out, and the star-speckled dog ran right toward the boundary, tearing it to shreds with its paws.

The man turned and ran, only to have his path blocked by Libra. Taking the form of a woman speckled with starlight, the spell held a glittering sword to the man's throat.

"I'd like to talk," Velma said rather cheerfully. "I think you'll find you'll prefer that to your other options."

"I got nothing interesting to say," the old man sputtered.

With his shabby, worn suit, he didn't look like he was about to place a bid on any of the items downstairs. Yet Velma didn't quite peg him as a thief, either. A shock of gray cut through his hair and beard, and the numerous scars across his broad hands set him apart from the rich folks sauntering about downstairs. True, he didn't belong in this world, but he didn't look that keen to belong in the first place.

"I beg to differ. You attacked me, so I get to ask you questions."

"I just don't like seeing people kicking up the bones of the dead," he countered. "You shouldn't be here."

"Neither should you, it seems," Velma said, unbothered. "It was your spells keeping everyone from coming up here, wasn't it? What were you hoping to find?"

"None of your business."

"Spoken like someone who has something to hide."

"Spoken like someone who already figured out what to take."

"*I'm* not a thief."

The man snorted.

"I'm a reporter," Velma lied easily. "I heard that Giles Pacer was seeking to purchase enchanted items. I think his death around the procurement of one of them is a bit too timely."

"You're not wrong."

Surprised by how readily he'd given up that information, Velma tried not to let it show in her voice. "There was foul play involved."

"I'm not sure I would call it that," the man said. "Giles reached out to me last week, asking for my help. I turned him down, but I wished I hadn't." The man pulled himself together, glaring at the star sigil still threatening him. "I will tell you more if you're so curious, but only if you remove this."

Velma considered him for a moment, as well as her ability to summon other spells in case he decided to run. With a nod, she dispelled both Canis Minor and Libra and said to him:

"Let's talk, then. Were you friends, Mr. . . ."

"Kenneth Poole," he said. "I was not friends with Giles. I used to manage the factory he ran."

"A factory?" Velma echoed, pretending ignorance to keep the man talking. "I thought he was in insurance."

"He owned and ran Wise Records many years ago. I oversaw the factory that pressed the records. At least, I did until the explosion happened." His eyes grew dark with the memory. "I barely got my people out in time. As far as anyone knows, some sort of potion ended up in the furnace. That was the story so we wouldn't get too much attention. That wasn't the truth. It was sabotage."

"From the competition?" Velma asked.

"For all the usual reasons," Kenneth said. "Wise Records wasn't the first Negro-owned recording company, but we were successful. When you have any success, no matter how small, white folks want to squash you into nothing. No, it was no mistake what happened in the end. I should have seen it coming—things always go this way."

His attention fell to the small drawer Velma had not opened yet.

"What is in there?" Kenneth asked.

Velma pulled open the drawer and the first thing her hand fell on was a wand case.

The wand itself was unremarkable. Dark wood with an intricately decorated handle and a fleur-de-lis at the base.

If she was disappointed, it was nothing compared to Kenneth.

The old man's face had collapsed into a mess of anxiety.

"What were you looking for?" Velma asked.

"Something he should have never kept."

"What exactly would that be?" she asked.

Kenneth looked at her warily, but as he opened his mouth to speak, a loud bang rattled the house to its very foundations.

Velma leapt, ready to fend off an attack. The old man had toppled to the ground, however, his hands clenched over his ears as he cried out in alarm.

If it wasn't him, it had come from somewhere else—like where the main auction was being held.

Velma hurried out of the room to head back downstairs and was immediately pulled into the chaos that filled the hallway. It didn't appear to be a fire, but the frantic voices around her indicated a possible magical peril. At this point it didn't matter. Panic had set in and classic mob behavior was underway. As people surged around her, Velma spotted some attendants trying to keep people away from the far end of the hall. Using the crowd's chaos to her advantage, Velma pushed one man into the other, and let the heightened emotions do the rest of the work for her. As the men began to loudly accuse each other, the attendants moved away from their posts to break up the fight.

At the first moment she could, Velma snuck into a nearby closet, holding the door firmly shut as she waited out the chaos on the other side.

Her instinct was a good one. No sooner had she shut the door, an attendant bellowed, "Everyone out of the house! The auction is suspended for now. Please wait outside in the garden until it's safe to return!"

This message got repeated several times, and Velma listened for footsteps and other noises to retreat.

"What is going on out there?" Velma whispered to herself.

"Hopefully nothing too terrible."

Velma recognized the answering voice, even before a light illuminated the small space.

Dillon sat on a crate, a notebook in hand as he smiled at her. "I would suggest you get your own closet, but that'll get us both in trouble."

"When did you— You're supposed to be—" Velma sputtered, somehow still surprised he had made his way to the manor after all.

His answering grin seemed to know the course of her thoughts. "Couldn't let you have all the fun. I'll tell you what I found later, but first let's get on to eavesdropping before we miss the good parts."

Velma tapped out the Aries star sigil on the door, drawing the lines and vertices with care to craft an invisibility spell, then pulled the door open just wide enough to peer out into the hallway.

With the hallway empty, she could see that the storeroom door had not been destroyed. Instead it was covered with intricate star sigils that angrily warned off any further attempts of entry. Only one attendant had remained behind to act as a guard, the flight enthusiast Velma had spoken with earlier, Emily Brooks. The young woman stepped away from the door and then looked down the hallway before she signaled someone to approach.

Velma had a short list of people she expected to see. Namely the two people she'd had long conversations with, Portia and Kenneth. Next were some workers at the event who had looked too closely at the items. Even the elusive Malcolm Gladstone was someone she'd expected, even if she had no idea what he looked like.

Laverna Addison was never even a possibility.

Laverna said something to Emily and then went inside, leaving Emily to guard the door.

The young woman, for her part, appeared to have some regrets. Her gaze traced the hall with no small amount of anxiety as she kept watch.

When Laverna reemerged with a hand over her now bulging pocket, Emily jumped a bit, clearly ready to protest.

Before Emily could utter a word, Laverna drew the arrow star sigil into the air and flung it right at the girl.

The moment the spell hit the girl's chest, Emily's eyes rolled back and she collapsed onto the floor.

Without even looking back, Laverna walked down the hall, drawing another star sigil. Her magic rippled around, whisking her out of sight as if she had never been there in the first place.

"I didn't expect that," Dillon whispered.

He had moved from the back corner of the closet to stand right next to Velma. So close, she was startled she hadn't noticed sooner. But she didn't move away.

"I figured this place would be tempting for thieves, but these were not the key players I'd expected," Velma replied.

Emily stirred on the ground, moaning weakly, and Velma pushed opened the door, dropping the concealment enchantments. "Shall we find out what other surprises are in store for us?"

As they stood in the hallway, Dillon pulled at the lapel of his suit jacket as he tapped something in his pocket. There was a flash of light, and she had to wonder if there was a tiny camera hidden in there.

"Nice suit," Velma said, when he noticed her looking.

Dillon straightened up and grinned. "I aim to impress."

Emily groaned then, and Velma knelt next to the hapless young woman. After checking for any obvious head wounds, Velma snapped her fingers and cast a proper spell that sent Emily more gracefully into the arms of enchanted sleep.

"Did you want to see what the thief was after?" Dillon asked. "Go ahead and look. I'll make sure the staff won't interrupt you."

"What will you do? Distract people with pointless questions?"

Dillon shrugged as he drew a star sigil, letting the wisps of magic flow around his hand to form an orb the approximate size of a baseball. "Something like that."

Casting aside her doubts for now, Velma slipped inside the room. Tables were weighted down with boxes and crates filled with meticulously marked items. It wasn't too hard to find lot number twenty-three, placed as it was prominently in the room. Although the crate had been riffled through, it was not empty. Left inside was a snuff box, a chessboard that was missing half its pieces, and a collection of dented tin. Nothing of value.

Or that was what Velma thought until her bracelet lit up as it passed over a corner of the box. She ran her hands along the crevices until she felt something cold and long. With care, Velma pulled out a hatpin that her grandmother would have gladly adorned her hats with. It was certainly not Velma's style. Still, it was striking. The embellishment had a flat, round shape and looked like the sun during the middle of a solar eclipse. Black kyanite ringed with a thin band of copper made the stone's center, and the smoothness of the stone gave it a slightly ethereal effect. Although the stone looked very much enchanted, it was cool to touch and perfectly ordinary. The most intriguing part was the familiar mark, the intricate circles etched on the back of the pin.

The hatpin joined the papers she had hidden away in her purse, and she put everything back before returning to the hallway.

Dillon, as promised, was guarding the door. A misty swirl of his magic blanketed the end of the hallway. Poor Emily Brooks was no longer lying snoring on the floor, but the boldly drawn star sigils on the closet door pointed to where she was currently tucked away.

"What did the thief take?" Dillon asked.

"Objects from lot twenty-three, but not everything. I can't believe how she orchestrated all of this. She must have paid that girl for assistance, and I bet she's behind the explosion."

"She's a clever thief, then."

"What if I told you that was Laverna Addison?"

Dillon just scowled. "Then I have one fewer question for you. There's enough time to go through all the details later. We need to get out of here without raising suspicions."

That was going to be difficult.

There were windows in the hall, yes, but they opened out into the courtyard, where people would certainly notice someone making a hasty escape. As for walking out, it couldn't be done without drawing more attention.

"What do you propose?" Velma asked. "Another spell?"

"Not at all." The magic he had cast around them vanished, and he winked at her. "Just trust me."

Those words didn't fill her with much confidence, but there was no time to protest. The moment Dillon's magic was gone, footsteps hurried their way. Soon all the workers at the event had gathered in front of them, as they were no longer distracted by the spell.

"You! What are you doing here?" cried a woman who was clearly in charge. She strode forth, directing a pair of men next to her. "Detain them until the police arrive!"

"You can't." Dillon held out a card with a confidence that said all forms of attack would not strike him down this day. "We're from a newspaper in Chicago, here to report about the events of the auction. In the aftermath of the explosion, we stayed behind to gain a better idea of the source of the disturbance and potential impacts. Now, I can't say we will delay writing about all these intriguing events, but if you violate our rights, I can promise a rather blistering article that will ensure more attention than you—or anyone else tied to this auction, including some of your prestigious guests—would like."

"Is that a threat?" the woman asked, even as the others behind her looked on worriedly.

"A promise," Dillon said easily.

"One we don't wish to occur," Velma added. "However, if the situation calls for it . . ."

"I say let them go," a young woman said.

"He's definitely a reporter," a man added. "He was asking questions earlier about the event."

"It's not worth it," another man said.

"I'm not getting paid enough for this," muttered someone in the back.

There were more whispers and hushed replies, until the woman in charge clapped her hands together. "You can leave, if you wish," she declared, each word dragged from her with great reluctance. "First let us see your pockets, and her purse."

She was so busy looking for the extraordinary that the scraps of paper and hatpin tucked in Velma's purse went unnoticed by the woman despite her scrutinizing eyes, and the pair was dismissed with a grim nod.

"What do you think?" Dillon asked as they headed along the street, away from the confusion that engulfed the grounds around the manor.

"I'm impressed," Velma found herself admitting. "That was much easier than what I had in mind."

"Power of the press," Dillon said. "Pen being mightier than the sword and all that. Aren't you glad I showed up after all?"

"I can always count on you to pop up when needed." Velma couldn't help but laugh. "Did your research turn up anything?"

"I found out plenty," Dillon said, "I'll start with the most important bits, I discovered the reason why Lois had trouble digging up information on Ardenton. According to many sources, it doesn't exist anymore. At least one person said the town was cursed out of existence."

An entire town cursed out of existence was not the strangest thing Velma had heard so far. Through her travels she had seen as many wonders as she had disturbing sights. To her the question wasn't how it was possible, but why it had occurred in the first place.

Magic was only a tool. A method in which a practitioner's will was interpreted and realized. To remove something from existence required the human touch.

"My contact confirmed Ardenton's existence up until 1905," Dillon said as they drove back to the Nifty Dude Ranch. "A prosperous town, it appeared in the 1900 census with ninety percent of the population marking Negro, but by the 1910 census, there was no record of the town at all. Services that involved Ardenton were no longer there, the post office doesn't even acknowledge it, and there were no more birth or death records. It all seems to abruptly end in 1905. Illness seems to be the main reason, as three-fourths of the population were afflicted with varying degrees of *veneficium pneumoniae*. The first reports came in 1901. Dozens died from it, mostly the elderly and the ill. A full quarter of the town's population died from the disease over the four following years, which led to superstition and mass exodus."

"What a terrible way to go," Velma murmured. Commonly known as magic sickness, *veneficium pneumoniae* was a very quick-acting illness that nearly always arose when corrupted magic was used. With death a common outcome, the other most distressing aspect of the disease was that it permanently impaired a person's ability to draw on magical energies in the world around them. This was by far the biggest number Velma had ever heard—and it was only what Dillon was able to find. The true number was likely much higher.

"It is such a terrible thing," Dillon echoed, "but that's the aftermath. From the few accounts I found, something occurred before all the illness, widely believed to be the cause. It's speculation mostly and quite unbelievable."

"Nothing you can say will shock me."

"Okay, then," Dillon said, "this was what I was told. A violent storm appeared over the business district in town out of nowhere on a cloudless day. It was a most unusual lightning storm centralized over a cluster of buildings. The lightning that flared in the sky was said to look like hands clawing to rip apart the heavens. With each clash, the streets were soon hidden by clouds of thick fog, and a howl like a banshee's filled the air, then a blast radiated, engulfing half the street and setting most of the buildings on fire. The storm itself vanished in a blink of an eye, and nothing like the sort was ever seen since then. Unbelievable, right?"

"No, not unbelievable—very believable. Terrifyingly believable," Velma whispered.

Dillon had just repeated a description she had heard before about the destruction of the Sitwell manor. But if the exact same thing had happened at Ardenton—the same place where Edwin and Laverna had been born . . .

The machine will show the inherent majesty of magic.

Inherent majesty of magic was Clarice Sitwell's description of the machine that Jeremiah Sitwell had experimented with.

Maybe there *was* a machine after all! A machine had destroyed the Sitwell manor and then done the same in Ardenton many years later.

A machine that Jeremiah Sitwell had made with all his ambition to do something with magic no one had done before.

And someone was looking for it.

Not just looking for it—someone knew all about it, according to the note Delia Moore had sent to Giles Pacer. What did Delia mean about Edwin Addison's notes? Did Addison write down how he re-created this machine? And if Pacer had Addison's notes following his cofounder's death, how long did he have them, when did someone else get them, and what was being done with them now?

Thinking of the melted metal in Malcolm Gladstone's workshop, Velma felt a chill settle on her neck.

Was Gladstone attempting to re-create this machine? Yoshi claimed that the man was a pawn, so if Gladstone wasn't making it for himself, who was he working for? And what did he plan to do?

"Are you all right, Velma? What's wrong?"

Dillon's use of her first name brought Velma out of her swaying thoughts. She must have looked a right state, because he appeared every bit as alarmed as she felt, and he didn't even know what she knew.

Should she tell him? They were headed to Ardenton. While she had only had her suspicions, she was certain enough of what they might find. However, to tell meant explaining how she knew these things and why, which would only raise questions she didn't have answers for yet.

"I'm fine," Velma said finally. "It's just been very eventful these past few days. I need to rest up. We have a long flight before us."

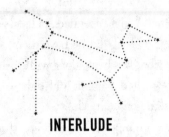

INTERLUDE

VELMA LIFTED THE TRAY OF DRINKS HIGHER AS SHE WALKED THROUGH THE narrow gaps between tables. The boisterous laughter that filled the train compartment came not just from the alcohol flowing freely, but also from the card games at hand. A few of the other servers discreetly coughed, but the fumes from the bubbling tonics didn't bother Velma after all her time in smoky juke joints. While the heads of several crime syndicates were here tonight, including the seconds-in-command, the Magnolia Muses' attention on this train revolved around a package rumored to be aboard.

When she reached the bar at the other end of the compartment, Velma dropped the tray of empty glasses and got Jasper's attention.

"I slipped Alton Clayton the drink," Velma said. "You owe me five dollars."

"We don't take bets on missions." Jasper's tone took on a lecturing note, and Velma had to fight the urge to make a pithy remark. As a seasoned field agent, Jasper took his role of mentor very seriously, and over the past two years they'd worked together, Velma had been held captive to enough lectures to know how to wriggle out of them with ease.

"I saw Cecelia Pike seated at the table."

"The heiress who owns the statuette?" Jasper said. "She's here?"

"Unwillingly," Velma said. "She looked like she wanted to claw Clayton's eyes out. But she's hoping to win the card game against him. She won't, because they're all cheats—and I rigged their cards to prolong the game."

Jasper sighed. "I thought we agreed to do this quietly."

Velma tried not to smile. Over the years, she'd developed a reputation for achieving success through rather explosive efforts. It wasn't on purpose. Sometimes to get a job done, you needed to make sure an entire city block knew you'd neutralized a threat.

"It'll be quiet since you're here keeping an eye on the situation," Velma told Jasper, although he continued to look skeptical. "I'm going after the package. I'll see you at the rendezvous point."

Velma worked her way through the train, moving too quickly for anyone to call out to her. After she passed through the kitchen, she pulled off her apron and cap, and adjusted the vest she wore over her clothes, hoping her plain black dress would not draw too much attention. Velma and Jasper had cased the train earlier, and thought the caboose might be an option, given how much of the gathering was kept away from it.

This theory seemed to be holding true, for once Velma left behind the crowded train cars, she found a pair of guards standing by the door to the next compartment, which shimmered with magic.

"You're headed the wrong way," a guard said to a very drunk passenger.

"I'm exactly where I need to be," hiccupped the drunk.

As the argument went on, Velma saw her chance. Pulling at her bracelet, she tapped into the magic stored in the gemstones and let it loose.

Her magic lashed out, shattering the lamps and plunging the corridor into darkness. Amid the cries of alarm, Velma surged forward to cross the barrier into the latter half of the train.

Ignoring how the barrier sealed shut behind her for now, Velma headed to the last car, spying a door that was locked and warded tight. She removed her earrings and had just bent them to form lock-picks when she heard footsteps behind her.

"Well, now, this is getting interesting."

The drunk man she'd spotted before stood behind her now, although his intoxication had clearly been an act given the lucidity in his gaze. Velma prepared to knock him out, but instead of a gun or even magic leveled at her, he had . . . a pencil in his hand?

"Who are you?" Velma asked.

"Dillon Harris," he said. "I work for a local newspaper. I caught wind of the missing heiress and connected her to the visiting crime lord, and eventually a priceless statuette. I've been chasing this story for a long time, and if you beat me to it, I'm going to have some very strong words about it. Unless you found something I haven't, which I doubt."

"What are you talking about?" Velma asked, flabbergasted at everything he'd just said. "I don't work for a newspaper."

"A likely story," Dillon remarked.

Resisting the urge to argue with him, Velma snapped her fingers and sent a sleeping spell right at him.

Velma turned back to the door and threw it open. The summer night was surprisingly cool, although that might have just been the rushing wind flying past her as the train hurtled at full speed along the track. She paused, staring at the rails, before she jumped over to the caboose.

Velma wasn't expecting the door to be unlocked, but she was a bit disappointed to see that a lattice of magic wrapping the door in a vise.

"Look at those layers. Somebody spent some money to get a prac-titioner to do this!"

The reporter stood behind her, staring at the door as well.

She had missed him with that spell, and she never missed!

Did he deflect it?

How was this scrawny fellow capable of such a feat?

As if knowing he was being judged, the reporter grinned and held up a key.

"I estimate you've got very little time before they notice you're up to something."

Velma grunted and waved a hand over the wards, and the spells ripped apart. "If you're looking for the heiress, you came in the wrong direction."

Dillon winked. "I smell a bigger story."

Velma reached to grab the key, but quicker than she had expected of him, the reporter moved past her grasp and unlocked the door.

"Ladies first," he said.

Velma gladly pushed her way through, summoning the Virgo star sigil. A maiden made of stars stepped out into the air next to Velma and walked among the crates, as if she were on promenade at a ball. The spell stopped and pointed to a very small box that was the perfect size for the statuette.

Just as Velma went over to retrieve it, another box some distance away throbbed an angry red.

There was only one thing it could be.

Velma grabbed the small box and pushed her free hand onto the reporter's chest.

"What's wrong?" Dillon asked as Velma shoved him out of the caboose.

"Bomb!"

He had enough sense to shut his mouth. Dillon flung himself out the door first, and then reached back and grabbed Velma, tossing her in an almost orchestrated move to the other train car.

There was no time to shut the door, but there was just enough to cast up a protective shield.

As the bomb went off in the caboose, it rattled against the shield, absorbing the resulting energy from the blast.

As one problem was solved, another swiftly rose to take its place.

Flames crackled along the caboose. While they were ordinary flames, the heat kissing against her skin promised trouble.

As Velma gathered the box into her arms, Dillon aimed a spell at the flaming caboose.

"That's like tossing a bucket of water on a grease fire," Velma said as she rubbed her bracelet. "That's not going to help at all, and will probably make it worse."

"Not aiming for the car."

Before she could ask what he meant, he flung a glittering arrow made of stars to the coupling. It snapped, and the caboose broke off to be left behind as the train roared on. Chances were that the caboose wouldn't be lonely for long. Its cackling flames were likely already calling alarms for several miles around.

"This has been an excellent evening," Velma said, "but I'm afraid this is where we part ways."

The reporter laughed. "How are you going to manage that? Guards block your way back to the front, the train is going at full speed, and it's not like there's a river nearby for you to jump in."

"Water is not a soft landing," Velma said absently as she cradled the box in her arm. She beamed at Dillon, glad to know that the evening was ending on a high note. "Good luck with your article."

Then Velma *did* jump off, casting a wind spell to fling herself several feet into the air. Once she was high enough, she pulled at the vest she wore over her dress, and the fabric opened into a parachute. As she floated away into the night, Velma waved at Dillon.

When Jasper met her later at the recon point with the abducted heiress, sightly mussed and quite annoyed, Velma still had the memory of the utterly amused—and slightly enchanted—expression on the reporter's face.

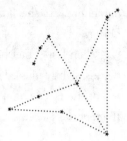

CHAPTER 22
DENVER, COLORADO

A rriving in Denver the next afternoon, Velma landed outside the city limits at a location remote enough that she could safely leave her plane behind.

Dillon had walked into town ahead of her. He was on the hunt for more information about Ardenton and needed to mail an article to his editor. While these tasks were not anything he wouldn't have done anyway, Dillon was diplomatically staying out of the way in case Jasper might report the walking protocol violation Dillon was. However, upon meeting Jasper at the appointed time, it was clear he had bigger things on his mind. He stood on the corner like a sentinel holding watch. While his expression revealed nothing, relief flooded his eyes at seeing Velma.

"Right on time, just as you said," Jasper remarked with his trademark grimness. "The situation has changed slightly since I last contacted the Muses."

"In a good way or bad way?"

"Both, it may be."

Jasper's move to Denver had been to stay closer to his aging parents, and made him the sole investigator at the local Magnolia Muses office in town. Denver had a small but vibrant Black population that had grown around the rail yard. Working here brought some unique challenges given the area's history, but Jasper was more than capable of handling anything flung his way.

"I'm working as a fireman at the town's only Negro station. It's a good way to get on the ground floor of all the incidents that happen in town. Earlier this week a boardinghouse caught on fire. We got most of the people away before it collapsed, but one man did not make it. While a few things survived the fire, a mirror made it through without a scratch. That mirror is the reason I called it in. Lois said this might interest you."

"Oh, it certainly does. Where's the mirror now?"

"I had it brought into the station."

"And the dead man?"

"Walter Cripes. He worked at the rail yard. Was pretty involved with the AME church in town but had few friends, since he'd just moved here. His room was the one with the mirror. I managed to have Walter Cripes and the items recovered from his room placed at the station as well. Separate rooms, of course."

"Why is the body there and not at the coroner's office?"

"Concerns about magical aftereffects."

"What effects?"

"It took nearly six hours to stop him from hovering in the air, and another hour to stop the glowing. Yet his death has been declared an accident. Not that the police would care to investigate things further either way, but it seems a bit far-fetched to think this was purely accidental. I did send a message to see if we could contact his family for a funeral. I'm using that to delay things too. How do you feel about pretending to be a relative?"

"That makes things complicated, but I'll do my best. If you can get me in and out without being seen, though, that'd be better."

Jasper took Velma through the back of the station, and pointed out the two storage rooms in use. He unlocked both doors, then headed upstairs to make sure no one would come down to bother her.

The first room held the mirror, and it was larger than she'd expected. Propped up against the wall, it was nearly as tall as the doorway and was untouched from dust, age, or even ash. Velma avoided looking directly in the glass, whispers of her grandmother's stories about how the souls of the recently deceased and the unwary found themselves trapped in mirrors. Along the frame, star sigils had been carved into the metal. They were likely the reason the mirror had survived the fire in the first place. As Velma traced the symbols, wondering what skill allowed this to happen, she noticed a mark at the top of the frame that wasn't a star sigil at all.

It was, of course, the same mark she had been searching for all throughout her travels.

Jeremiah Sitwell had made this. Or maybe one of his descendants had.

Even though a man had died not far from this mirror, Velma's bracelets weren't showing any signs of warning as she stood in front of it. Her feelings of unease came more from superstition than anything from the mirror itself. This mirror was creepy and intimidating, but it wasn't dangerous.

Jasper had implied that the mirror had been the source of the fire, but looking at it now, Velma didn't think it had been. It had merely survived because of the protective magic carved into the frame.

So why did Walter Cripes end up floating in the air?

With that question and more in mind, Velma hastened to go into the next room.

Wintery mountain air blew into her face with such force, Velma found herself wishing she had kept on her flight jacket. She did her best to ignore the chill as she carefully pulled back the sheet over Walter Cripes. Still dressed in the clothes he'd died in, his plain and rough attire held nothing more interesting than the ashes that remained on him. The smell, though—that was a different story. Yes, he and his clothes reeked of smoke, but there was also something else, something slightly bitter. Velma leaned forward and took a deep whiff. The name of the herb was on the tip of her tongue, but she couldn't name it right then. She got out a pencil, though, and jotted her impressions on the page.

Because he had been found floating, Velma knew his body would be covered with magical traces. There might be something else a bit more mundane on him, though. She moved his limbs, seeing nothing unusual. Then she spotted a mark near his neck, half hidden by his collar.

A wound from the building collapsing due to fire, or something else? Like someone attacking him? Jasper hadn't mentioned anything that pointed to someone taking advantage of the chaos. However, the number of situations in which an explosion of magic was a cover for murder or other violence was quite high. While it was likely Walter Cripes was just an innocent bystander who'd had the worst sort of luck, he could still have some connection to the Sitwell-Addison family.

Velma was just re-covering him with the sheet when Jasper knocked on the door.

"What did you find?" he asked.

"Nothing that will help you," Velma admitted. "The arrangements to bury him can be made. I'll send you the money to make sure he gets a proper homegoing. That mirror, though. What do you know about it?"

"The owners say it came with the house. They bought it some years ago, back in 1904."

"They're lying."

"I'm sure they were," Jasper said. "The boardinghouse wasn't exactly legal . . . just allowed to do its business as long as they don't cause trouble. Are you saying you know where the mirror came from?"

"I suspect it's from Ardenton."

"Ardenton!" Jasper's face animated with alarm and, for the first time, genuine fear. "You can't be serious."

"You've heard of this place?"

"I've heard more than I care to. It's a town—or used to be a town—a few hours from here," Jasper said. "It's an abandoned town halfway to nowhere, and so cursed, they say if you take anything from there, even the tiniest of pebbles, bad luck follows you. Sometimes not even returning the item fixes it. I went there myself a while ago. I haven't found evidence of a curse, but something happened in that town. You go to Ardenton, you better make sure your boots are free of dust when you leave."

"How very interesting," Velma said finally, "and good to know."

"Velma," Jasper demanded abruptly, "are you planning to go to the town?"

"Why would you ask that?" she said innocently.

His eyes narrowed. "Because I know you."

"I'm following a lead, and it's taking me there."

"Wouldn't you rather see the boardinghouse?" Jasper suggested. "There might be something of interest there."

"Why didn't we go there first, then?" Velma asked curiously.

"I thought it might be too dangerous, but if you're eager to go to a cursed town, danger is clearly not a problem."

Deciding that going to the boardinghouse might temper his concerns, Velma nodded. "Then I will look around. Any idea what caused the fire? Was it an accident, or the work of a group like, I don't know, Members of Rational Clarity?"

At first, from his lack of reaction, she thought Jasper had no idea what she was talking about. Then she saw his face, which, while remaining as expressionless as before, had suddenly lost a certain spark.

The same spark Yoshi had lost.

It was only in the space of mere moments that she noticed this, but it was more than enough time to prepare before he attacked her.

Velma crossed her arms in front of her, connecting her bracelets. Upon contact, a small shield spread out before her, taking on the weight of Jasper's blast of raw magic.

Velma jerked her arms forward, thrusting his magic away. It rocked him backward a small distance, but he stood his ground.

Unblinking eyes locked onto her face as Jasper manipulated his magic to create a very solid-looking staff. Grasping it, he lunged, swinging it at her head.

Velma ducked as the staff shattered the glass on the shelves above her. Shards rained down upon her head, and she barely got her hands up in time to keep the worst from falling. She winced as glass bit into her skin, but there was scarcely any time to do more—Jasper swung for her head once again.

This time Velma rolled out of the way, heading for the table where the dead man lay.

Ducking around it, Velma caught her breath, twisting around her bracelet and loosening the magic within it.

Despite the current situation, this was good.

Jasper may have been under the influence of another blasted coin, but he was far more in control. He was being forced to attack her, but his code name with the Muses was Marksman. Projectiles were his specialty as a field agent. If he had enough agency to change weapons, Velma had a chance. It meant Jasper was able to push back, just like Yoshi had retained enough sense of self to put his sister out of harm's way when he had been under the coin's influence.

"Fight it, Jasper," Velma said as her bracelet clicked into place. "If you force your will on it, you'll overcome it!"

The staff wavered, but then Jasper darted forward.

He wasn't clutching a coin like Yoshi, which meant she couldn't just knock it out of his hand. This required a little more creative thinking.

Looking down at the dead man on the table, she said, "Sorry about this."

Velma kicked the table over and poor Walter Cripes went flying across the room.

Jasper moved out of the way, and as he did Velma tossed her bracelet, pulling out a string of golden light from it. Holding on to one end, she lassoed it around Jasper like a spider capturing its prey.

He struggled and writhed but didn't break free.

With a hand on her bracelet, Velma danced her fingers along the metal. Jasper lifted into the air and slowly turned upside down. Clenching her hand into a fist, she shook him. Keys and other items fell from his pockets and there was a small metallic ding as a coin hit the wood.

Jasper went limp within his bonds at once, and Velma carefully lowered him back to the ground. She should have knocked him unconscious, for he looked at her wearily. "Must you always go to extremes?"

"When the need arises. Your old age is getting to you, friend. You picked up a coin that drew you into its influence."

Jasper's eyes went to the floor, his chin tightening. "It was in the room with the mirror. I didn't think it was dangerous. I suppose you know about it, then? Something else you've been tracking? Related to the group you mentioned," he suggested.

"Members of Rational Clarity," Velma repeated, watching him closely.

He was out from under the influence now, so he didn't do much more than nod. Velma let loose the magic that encased him.

Jasper collapsed onto the floor and sat there for a moment before he gathered up his words. "I heard some rumors, but I thought it didn't have anything to do with me."

"Things are more related than you think," Velma said as she picked up the coin with a handkerchief. "That's why I'm going to Ardenton."

"I have no course to stop you," he said. "Just don't go alone."

"I don't plan to."

CHAPTER 23

Velma climbed into her plane without Dillon noticing, intent as he was on organizing his notes. This lack of notice didn't last for long. She fumbled and dropped a jar of healing salve. It bounced on the seat and ended up landing near him.

Almost immediately Dillon looked up, his eyes first glancing at the jar and then at her. "What happened?" Dillon asked.

"Nothing," Velma said, ducking her hands out of sight.

Dillon grabbed her left hand, turning over the bruised and bleeding skin. "Yes, this looks like nothing to me."

Velma yanked her hand back. "I'll be fine in a moment."

"Try several minutes," Dillon said as he retrieved the jar of salve.

"Aren't you going to ask me to explain?"

"You obviously hit somebody. I'm sure they're worse off than you."

"Yes, Jasper is."

Dillon's eyebrows rose as he opened the jar. "Were these his own actions or the influence of another coin?"

"A coin. How did you know?"

"If my former mentor and friend attacked me, I'd be more upset. Then again, I'm used to such things. Hands out," he said.

"I can do it," she protested, but he had already dipped his fingers into the jar.

"I don't bite," Dillon teased, waggling the healing salve smeared on his fingertips at her. "Some people even say I'm a delight."

Velma held her hands out, knowing that arguing with him wasn't going to change anything.

"I'm just used to doing this by myself."

"Well, this time, at least, you don't have to," Dillon said as he dabbed at the cuts on Velma's hands. Dillon held her hands carefully as he applied the healing medicine in thin, precise layers. His touch lingered on her skin, especially as he studied her hands, looking for any spot he might have overlooked. The salve was cold, but it was not the reason she shivered under that surprisingly intimate gaze.

"They're only minor cuts," Velma protested feebly.

"Ignoring the pain won't make it go away," Dillon replied, so soberly that Velma was startled, until he flashed his usual grin at her. "If you can't manage, I'll have to fly this bird. Neither of us wants that, especially me."

"You think after such a short time you can fly my plane?"

"I've learned quite a few things." Dillon shrugged. "Mostly that I was wrong about my initial impressions."

"About planes, prospects of aviation, or daredevil pilots?" Velma asked.

"All of the above," he admitted.

"I should have made a bet," Velma declared gleefully. "I could have won you over months ago if I'd gotten you up in my plane!"

"Maybe you should have," Dillon said as he let go of her hands. Looking at her directly, he added, "There are many wondrous sights up here above the clouds."

Velma had a dozen reasons to dislike Dillon Harris. He saw through her lies. He never passed up a chance to tease her. He didn't mince words and wasn't shy with his opinions. He was the direct opposite of the men she'd dated in the past: too talkative, too much of an attentive listener, and too eager to plunge into trouble. She had all those reasons and more, and yet she only needed one reason to like him and that outweighed everything else.

"All done." Dillon screwed the lid back onto the jar. "This stuff is rather potent. You should be healed up soon."

"Then we can be on our way," Velma said absently even as she wished they could stay here just a bit longer.

Once Velma's hands had finished healing, it was on to Ardenton. Jasper had not given Velma a map as he insisted she'd know the town when she saw it. The vague words had only frustrated her until she saw exactly what he meant.

Her first view of the town was a blight in an otherwise fertile area. It was a perfect circle as far as the eye could see—a too eerily perfect circle formed as if punched into the ground.

Which meant at least some of the rumors were true.

As she flew over it, Velma gripped the controls tight. Which was why, when the plane's engine suddenly cut off, she was already halfway prepared.

Panic bloomed like flames in a corner of her mind for a moment before she firmly stomped it down and let cool reasoning take over.

This was not a mechanical problem, but a magical problem. To solve it required skills that drew on both.

Ignoring the wail of her instruments going haywire, Velma jerked the controls back. She pulled the nose of her plane upward, leveling it enough to glide.

That gave her a few seconds as all the physics stuff she barely remembered came into effect.

"Hang on," Velma called as she slammed a fist against the hidden panel next to her and pulled out an elemental pistol. Because there were three kept in there, Velma spared a fraction of a moment to make sure the spot of gold paint was on the bottom, before she flipped it over.

With her left hand still holding on to the plane's controls, she fired the lightning pistol at the console.

Dillon's startled cry was lost as lightning zipped through the plane and it shuddered, shaking the very world around them.

Instruments squealed again, but the sound receded. Or maybe the sound of blood thumping in her ears dulled it. With the boost of power, the plane sped on. As she passed over the town again, she saw the glimmer outside her window that she'd missed before, and this time Velma wrenched the controls to the right. Her plane nearly rolled over, but the engine remained on.

Knowing that she couldn't cross Ardenton without catastrophe, Velma made for the ground, landing as near to the town as she dared.

"Well, that certainly confirms the curse," Dillon said once they'd stopped moving.

His words were strained under a panic bubbling up behind his eyes, and there was ink spotted on his hands from accidently snapping his pen in half. He rambled as he cleaned up the ink. Velma let him have a moment to regroup, because she needed one too—she hadn't known that firing the pistol would work when the idea had popped into her mind.

"Do you think the town impacted your plane?" Dillon asked.

"All I know is that whatever is down there, it doesn't want anyone to come near."

They both looked out toward the town.

"Maybe we shouldn't go in," Velma mused.

"Maybe we shouldn't," Dillon agreed, even as he took out his camera. "But you'd always wonder if you didn't, wouldn't you?"

Now, there was an argument she couldn't help but agree with.

"Let's go. I want to see if the stories are true," Velma said.

"You still doubt them?"

"It's kind of my job to doubt things until I have more proof."

"Mine too." He grinned.

The sun had ducked behind the clouds, bringing a sudden chill to what had otherwise been a heady summer day. From a distance, all appeared well in Ardenton, but up close was a different story. The outlying fields were barren and parched. And the buildings that rimmed the town were sun-bleached and faded. Boxes and bags had been tossed to the ground, their contents spilling out from the houses and into the street. Not just valuable silverware and jewelry, but plates, clothing, and even books. Although the items changed throughout the town, the mess did not. No matter where she looked, Velma found only disarray and no indication that anyone who had called this place home had ever returned.

As they turned a corner, a faded sign declared to all:

DO NOT TAKE ANYTHING FROM HERE!

"I appreciate the warning," Dillon said, "but why is this not at the edge of the blight?"

"Because it's a warning for fools like us. If the devastation before wasn't enough to convince us, maybe this will."

The more they walked, the greater the stillness grew. Stillness that was unbroken except for them, the only living creatures around. No bugs. No birds. Not even plants. As far as Velma could tell, there was not a single weed pushing itself through the dirt. The only signs of life were the traces of the people who had once been there. Fallen baskets scattered in the street, tools left stranded on the ground, a wagon stripped of its parts left in the middle of the road and a shoe so tiny that it could only fit on the foot of a child.

"I wouldn't worry too much about that." Dillon held his camera, but it wasn't pointed in any direction. In fact, he clutched it so tight, Velma worried he might break it. "People took things and then brought them back when they realized it was bad luck. Look at how much is within throwing distance."

"I suppose you're right."

"I *am* right," Dillon said. "Let's keep going. There's still more to see ahead."

The road took them to the town's center, where a well stood. Unlike the rest of the town, it appeared untouched, with a rusty pail sitting on the rim of the well.

Velma peered down into the well, drawing the swan star sigil in the air next to her. With a single nod, the star-speckled swan dove into the well's depths. The bird didn't travel for long before the light flickered out like a candle.

"Tell me you meant for the spell to do that," Dillon remarked.

"Of course not," Velma said. "It's odd that the spell fell apart down there instead of up here."

A muscle jumped in Dillon's face. "*That's* what you find odd!"

Ignoring him, Velma pushed the bucket resting nearby into the well. Counting seconds, Velma watched the metal gears rapidly spin until a small splash could be heard from the bottom of the well.

"At least that means you're not going to jump down there," Dillon said.

"Don't be silly. I'm not going to get mud on my good boots." Velma cranked the bucket back up, gripping the handle with both hands. Dillon didn't move to help, but he did cast a spell, to be on the safe side, the lurking star-speckled scorpion appearing ready to grab at whatever might come out of the well.

The only thing that came up was the bucket.

Although, a closer look at it nearly had Velma dropping it once again, this time by accident. A plant with broad, shiny leaves was caught along the bucket's rim.

"In a town without any life left in it, how did this plant manage to thrive tucked away at the bottom of a well?" Dillon asked.

"I think whatever happened up here didn't reach below ground," Velma said.

Dillon nodded as he took a photograph. "It persevered despite everything."

From the well, they took their time walking the streets. Passing by more buildings. While seeing the homes in disarray was upsetting, it was the shops that did it for her. The quaint streets of Ardenton reminded her too much of Bramble Crescent. Ardenton was not on an island, but it was off on its own, so families had relied upon each other for everything. The shops reflected this too. Along the street were signs for a shoemaker, a wandmaker, a music shop, a bakery, a toy shop . . .

" 'Addison Novelties and Toys,' " Velma said, staring up at the lopsided sign.

It dangled off the roof, partially obscuring the neighboring shop's sign. The building itself was a shell, as there was nothing left of the interior. A hole was in the shop's floor as if a bomb had exploded right inside the store. Nearly everything had turned to rubble, and the few items that remained were half melted. The nearby shops were similarly decimated, with blown-out windows and collapsed walls that remained as fallen after nearly thirty years.

While the entire town had set her teeth on edge, standing here in this spot, Velma felt all those feelings compound into something greater. Something overwhelming, something that threatened to pull her into the abyss.

"I guess the stories are true. This is where the storm sprouted up." Dillon bent down and poked his pencil at the ground.

"I wouldn't do that," Velma said.

"My pencil is not going to cause any trouble," Dillon said, still poking about.

"It's caused me plenty of trouble."

"Touché," he said with a smile, then turned back to the dirt. "However, this is hardly dangerous—say, what do we have here?"

His poking around revealed a fountain pen. It was shiny, and its somewhat molted appearance reminded Velma of serpentine. Velma cared little about pens, but she was still impressed by the craftsmanship of it, despite the metal nib being dull and lightly scratched. Dillon picked it up and angled it so she could see the underside of the pen and the Sitwell mark on it.

"This certainly confirms a connection," Dillon said.

"Put it back," Velma hissed.

"You don't really believe in a curse."

"Someone is here! Look closer. There's hardly any debris on it. Someone just dropped it!"

No sooner had Velma spoken, a bolt of pure magic smashed hard into the ground before them.

Velma didn't even think—she grabbed Dillon's shirt collar and hauled him backward even as he snapped a picture with his camera.

"Now is not the time for photographs!" Velma cried.

"That's why you'll never be a great reporter like I am—there's always time for such things," Dillon said. He might had said more, but his demeanor shifted entirely as his gaze locked onto something in the distance.

A shadowy figure emerged, obscured in smoke and fumes of magic. The fading light made it hard to tell if this was a person instead of some guardian spirit of magic, but for once Velma had zero inclination to find out.

"I think it's time for us to leave," Velma said.

"Agreed."

Dillon bolted down the abandoned streets, charging ahead with surprising speed.

Velma followed a few paces slower. She ran her fingers along her bracelet, activating every spell she had, and sent a menagerie of animals at the figure behind them.

Magic lashed back at her, whizzing past too close for her to avoid. Before Velma could even move to defend herself, Dillon rammed into her, knocking her to the ground.

The collision of spellwork over their heads rattled the empty homes, and then green licking flames sprouted up before them, blocking the way forward.

"Mage fire!" Velma exclaimed. "Don't go near it!"

"That's a problem when we've got someone chasing us," Dillon said.

Velma looked back at the looming shape in the distance and saw the chances of escape decreasing. "You should go on ahead."

"That voids our agreement."

"What?"

"The stipulation of the favor," Dillon said. "I travel with you all the way. And no abandoning."

"This is not— This is different!"

"Yes, because I came along here to help," Dillon said as he drew the crow star sigil next to him. "So let me."

The star-speckled bird swirled around in his hands. Instead of lobbing such magic toward the danger they were fleeing or toward the danger blocking their way, he flung it at their feet.

The ground launched them skyward, as if they were on an elevator moving too quickly to make any reasonable stops. They got over the growing green flames, but kept going upward into the sky, until suddenly they were falling. Velma held on to Dillon as they landed on the roof of a nearby house. His magic had slowed them down, so instead of crashing, they slid along the rooftop before dropping gently to the ground.

With the distance they needed to cross cut almost in half, they made it back to Velma's plane in no time at all.

Amid all the excitement, her plane remained hidden from sight. As they got closer, Velma clapped her hands, pulling away the spells that hid it, and flung open the doors.

"Come on!" Velma urged as she shoved Dillon inside. "Help me get this bird in the air!"

She pointed to the correct sequence of levers and buttons, furiously working to get everything moving. Once the engines were running, she threw the plane into motion, skipping over the rest of her usual preflight rituals.

As the plane lifted into the air, her instruments began to squeal, warning of approaching hostile magic.

One last blast of magic shot past them. The skies exploded into fireworks, dazzling swirls, and pulses of magic, that for all their beauty would be catastrophic if they brushed against her plane.

Velma threw the plane into a steep vertical climb. She risked flying through the clouds above, heading through the seemingly endless fluffy white mass head-on. Instantly her vision darkened as nothing but gray splashed against her windshield. In that moment, her heart skipped, as she feared she'd made the wrong choice. The moment passed and they burst through the clouds.

No magic from their pursuer could reach them up here, and as Velma glanced out the window she spotted no attempts to even try. Velma lessened her grip on the controls as she leveled her plane and found she could breathe easily once more.

"You're going to be the death of me, flygirl," Dillon said.

Velma nearly whipped her head around to him. "How can you say that when you're the one who picked up the pen? I bet you kept it. If we have bad luck from here on out, I know who to blame."

When he said nothing, Velma's irritation simmered further to the surface. "What, no snappy comment?" Velma moved to shift gears, and it was only then she saw the blood smeared all over the controls.

She glanced at her hand, staring at the red stain across her palm. Not her blood.

"Don't faint on me," Dillon said. "I don't think I can fly this plane on my own."

Dillon was propped up in the corner of the cockpit. One hand pressed firmly on his other arm, barely concealing the gaping wound. His complexion had dulled, and perspiration had broken out on his forehead, even though at this altitude he should have been shivering. "It looks worse than it is."

"People have said that before, and they were dead within hours," Velma snapped.

She banged her fist against the compartment where she kept her maps and gear and pulled out the last dusty potion bottle inside.

"Drink this. It's a few years old, so it won't be as potent, but it should stop the bleeding."

"Why do you have it, then?" Dillon asked.

"Peace of mind," Velma said. "Dillon, drink it or I'll shove it down your throat!"

He picked up the bottle and popped the cork. By just the faint smell she knew it wasn't as strong, but it would work well enough.

It had to.

Dillon downed the expired healing potion and slumped back. "That's disgusting!"

"If you live, don't complain," Velma said.

Common sense told her to go back to Denver. Jasper might not be equipped to handle magical wounds like this, but he was bound to know someone who did. She turned on the radio, hailing Jasper, hoping he'd pick up.

The line crackled to life.

"Is that you, Velma?" Jasper said.

"Yes, it's me—"

"Wherever you are, stay there! There's been another fire, just like the one before. It started in a pawnshop, but it spread along the street. I have it handled, but you can't come here. Someone's looking for you. No name, but a description of your plane has gone around. Someone has blamed—"

Jasper's voice distorted as if his words were stretched through a wire, and then a sharp noise crackled across the radio and she lost him.

Velma pressed at the button, calling for him to no avail, but gave up, deciding that things were worse than she thought on his end.

Desperately, Velma hailed Lois next.

Before Velma could even begin explaining, "Royal Garden Blues" filled the air, and Velma shut off the radio at once. When Lois had that record play, it meant only one thing: their communications, tenuously built and crafted with a heavy dose of magic, were compromised.

Stars and shards, this was truly the worst time for it! She could only spare a thought that whatever was going on in Denver—and Chicago—was related to this attack.

Of all the times for this to happen, why now?

Dillon had slumped over in his seat. His chest rose and fell rhythmically, the potion finally taking effect. She should be relieved, but she knew it was temporary. When it wore off, she couldn't do more than the basics.

Should she go back to Los Angeles? Should she try pushing for Chicago? Or even Philadelphia? Could she get there in time? Did she have enough fuel?

Was there someone closer? She cast her mind to her mental map of the United States. Thinking where it was safe and where some of her friends would be. New Orleans was too far. Portland, where Hazel was with the Chinese Flying School, was out of the question. Same with Vancouver.

Kansas City, she realized. Her friend Nan Kingfisher was there, doing a parachuting show as part of her tour through the Midwest. While it was far, Velma could fly through the night and get there before the potion's effects faded.

She could make it.

She had no choice.

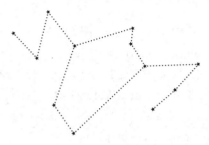

CHAPTER 24

T he first sign of trouble was an unfamiliar rattle that came from the bowels of the plane. Unexpected sounds were never a good thing when you were flying. So when she heard the pop, followed by a clanking sound, Velma had already braced herself before the plane started to drop.

Instead of trying to recover, which she was pretty sure was a lost cause at this point, she turned off the engines and guided the plane as best she could to the ground.

It was not a crash.

She was right side up and nothing was on fire, nor did her plane go through, in, over, or under anything. But they hit the ground harder than she'd have liked, and everything that wasn't tied down rattled about.

She checked on Dillon first. He was still slumped against the window, seemingly unbothered by their sudden descent. Pulling off the blanket she'd tucked around him, she inspected the bandage. She had stopped only once after leaving Ardenton, and that was to tie on a tourniquet, recalling her lectures about medical aid when magic wasn't enough. His blood had seeped slightly through it, but the bandage wasn't fully saturated. She dropped his arm, and nearly hit her head on the top of the cabin when she spotted one of Dillon's eyes open and staring right at her.

"How long have you been awake?" Velma squeaked.

"When we crashed," Dillon remarked. He sounded very much himself, although slightly sluggish. "I had thought of how things could get worse. I'm glad to see I'm not wrong."

"You must be feeling better if you can say things like that," Velma said as she folded up the horse blanket. "And it wasn't a crash, just a very hard landing."

"You're the expert," Dillon said. "Where's my camera?"

Surprised that it wasn't the first thing out of his mouth, Velma lifted the console panel. His camera sat nestled among her things, as Velma had placed it there when she'd had a moment to spare. She was glad she had when she saw how Dillon relaxed against the seat.

"I thought I left it behind. It could be the only way to figure out who attacked us. Did you see who it was?"

"No," Velma said. "That wasn't the most pressing question then. Or even now, to be honest."

Dillon looked over at her skeptically. "You don't care about the person who tried to blast us with magic and then blow up your plane?"

"There are other problems to tackle first."

"I suppose you're right," Dillon conceded. "Do you know where we are?"

"Hopefully close to Kansas City. We are at best two hours short of the city limits, although I'm being slightly generous."

Velma peered out into the field. She saw nothing, not even the dots of houses or an impression of a road. "Let's hope we got pretty close," Dillon replied. "Are we stuck here? How's that radio of yours?"

Velma blew out a breath, gladly turning to the task at hand. "Got to give it a look. We landed hard, and I know something is broken, but I don't know exactly what, or if it's multiple things. Or, worse, something I can't fix with the tools I have with me." Velma reached into the back to get her tool bag. "I need you to keep watch."

From her tool bag she retrieved the ice pistol and handed it to him. "Use this. It expels chunks of ice when fired, and the harder you press, the wider range of ice will spray out."

He turned it over in his hand, glancing from the dot of blue paint on the side to the swishing potion installed in the back of the pistol.

"Is this related to the one you shot the plane with?"

"I have a few of them. They're family heirlooms."

"All I got passed down were old clothes. Who exactly are you, Miss Velma Frye?"

"Someone who is about to fix a plane the best she can," Velma said. "How's your arm?"

"Aching, but I can ignore it for a time."

Velma nodded, as this was the best they could hope for given the situation. "Just don't strain yourself. No matter what happens next."

"Stars willing," he said.

The stars were willing indeed, for when Velma went under her plane, she found that the damages were all things well within her ability to patch, tighten, seal, or mend with twine. There was cosmetic damage, and some things that had gotten bent that shouldn't have, but the *Fowl Weather* would fly again and fly soon.

Dillon sat on the port wing as she worked. He kept up a running commentary about baseball, because even when they'd been feuding at the newspaper office, it had been the one topic they could hash out with only minor disagreement.

"I was hoping one of your trips would take us to New Orleans. I wanted to see how well Armstrong's Raggedy Nine played."

"It wouldn't be a good game," Velma said. "None of those teams headed by bandleaders are. It's just convenient because there are usually enough players to make up a team."

"I know it won't be good, but it's memorable. Jazz bands battling onstage and on baseball fields. Makes a nice story, and one people will gladly read. I learned that when I used to write about my own games at my hometown paper."

"Must have been a small town to cover sandlot games."

"I played semipro ball for a few years," Dillon said. "I wasn't the best hitter, but I was a great center fielder—I don't want to brag, but I can get a baseball where it needs to go, no matter the distance."

"If you were that good, then why is your brother the one playing professionally?"

"I gave him my gear when I quit. My talents were needed elsewhere."

"Of course they were," Velma remarked. "Who did you play for back then?"

"St. Petersburg's Silver Rays. I came all the way from Roslyn Keys to make the team."

Velma popped up out from under her plane, startled because she knew that name from old reports at the Muses, about how a theft of a wand ended with a small town facing mob violence. A pair of students had stolen a wand and were practicing casting spells with it. The wand had exploded, killing a young white girl and injuring her friend Randall Brant, who happened to be Black. He was arrested for theft and, before the trial was over, was turned into a monster.

"You're from Roslyn Keys? Were you still living there when . . ."

Velma stumbled, not sure how to finish asking the question, if she wanted to dredge up such a history. But he had deliberately mentioned the town's name.

"Roslyn Keys was home," Dillon said simply. "I covered news about the trial and when the verdict came out, I rushed to get back home. I knew that while the jury found Randall guilty, other opinions wanted blood. A mob marched on the town before the sun had even set. My mother refused to leave, so we stayed. The next morning, when we saw what was left of the town, she was the first to say we should take what we could and leave. I never went back. The town is gone and to rebuild is too costly."

"Yet," Velma said softly, "you went to Ardenton after hearing those rumors. If I'd known—"

"They're nothing alike," Dillon said. "I can make sense of the sequence of events that ended swallowing up my hometown. I won't ever understand it, but there are pieces that give some form of explanation. Ardenton is nothing like that. I could feel that dead town watching my every move. What people say happened and what *really* happened there are so clearly different. That's why I went—I want to find out the truth. It's our job to make sure to find it and spread it as far as possible."

"Our job?"

"Yes—you and I. Our jobs aren't all that different, if you think about it."

"Except you do whatever you can to achieve your end," Velma said.

"So do you," he began. Before he could finish his thought, he sat up abruptly, shifting the ice pistol in his hand. "We have company."

Distantly, Velma could see several rust-spotted cars headed in their direction. Dirt was kicked up in plumes as the cars crossed the field, unmistakably headed toward Velma and Dillon's location.

"Stars and shards," Velma muttered.

"Tell me you fixed everything," Dillon said.

"I did, but we won't get up in the air in time. Unless you stall them with the power of the press."

Dillon's mouth twitched into an attempted smile, but there was no mirth. "I'm not sure if it'll work this time."

The cars rolled to a stop a short distance away—but just outside the range of any spell Velma could cast in haste. The three cars were parked side by side in a half circle. Velma reached into her bag and pulled out the heaviest and biggest wrench she had.

Magic would win the day, but she'd try intimidation first to buy time.

Dillon got up, half concealing the ice pistol under his injured arm.

Velma thought of telling him to get inside. All it took was one look at his perfectly composed features to know that wasn't going to happen.

Slowly, the car doors opened one by one.

A middle-aged Black man stepped out first, closely followed by three young men and women who resembled him close enough to be kin. They lowered their shotguns and put away potion flasks as they smiled at Velma and Dillon. Seeing smiles on friendly faces sent relief sweeping through Velma so strongly that she had to steady herself along her plane to keep upright.

"Now, I've seen a lot of things in my time," declared the leader with a broad grin, "but this takes it all! You folks own this plane, don't you?"

"It's mine," Velma said. "We had a little trouble, but I got it mostly taken care of."

"You need a place to stay for the night?" the man asked.

"You can park your plane on my land if you like!" someone else called.

Velma was hardly going to refuse. Not to mention, she didn't have much of a choice, but that wasn't a bad thing. As it turned out, her plane had landed a handful of miles from Quindaro, a small all-Black town filled with hardy people in the middle of unforgiving land. The town was the sort of place that wasn't on any map, and you only knew about it if you were in the area. It wasn't far from Kansas City, but there was no need to press on further. The townsfolk were more than eager to help.

Velma didn't always put her complete trust in well-meaning strangers she'd just met, but the town had a doctor and her plane was repaired enough that if they needed to leave in a hurry, they could. Dillon was sent ahead to the doctor's house to get his wounds looked after, while Velma oversaw the towing of her plane to town. There was no one here who could fix it, but they could help get some parts she might need. Fuel would be easier, although it might cost her. But money was the last thing Velma was worried about.

"I wouldn't advise leaving right away," Dr. Haywood said as she examined Velma later. "You need to stay put after your little ordeal."

"We shouldn't stay here for long," Velma protested.

"Given who my brother worried might be in that plane, I don't have much to complain about," Dr. Haywood remarked. "Plus, it's good for the town to have a little excitement. It's not often we get a pilot here, let alone see a plane flying past. Although you're in quite a state. Shallow scrapes, bruises, jammed fingers, and injured ribs on top of exhaustion, stress, and I'm sure a healthy concern if someone looks too closely at your plane's cargo."

"You won't find alcohol or tonics in my plane," Velma said steadily. "I'm not being followed. He got injured and I foolishly pushed on, trying to reach a friend of mine to help."

"Well, luckily you have help here," the doctor replied. Although she didn't outwardly acknowledge Velma's words, her tone was less brusque as she coated healing salve onto Velma's various cuts and bruises. "You'll be healed up in a few hours. And your husband—"

Velma coughed hard enough for the doctor to place a stethoscope to her back.

"How is he?" Velma said once she regained her composure.

"Severely exhausted and dehydrated, but otherwise quite fine." Her chin pointed to a plate with small but jagged crystalized shards stained with blood. The plate was surrounded by several protective wards. "I pulled that out of his arm. Your little potion, expired as it was, helped combat the jinx. It may have saved his life."

"That's a relief," Velma said after a few moments.

The doctor sealed up the jar of salve. "I'd loved to learn more about that potion you gave him. It did the work of five separate elixirs I have."

"It's a family recipe."

"Then I'd like to know what you can tell me. It's my price."

"Only that? I might not know much."

"You can haggle with me later. But you need to rest first. Go take a bath and I'll have a tray waiting for you in your room."

The doctor had put them up in a hastily made guest room. Dillon was asleep, gently snoring in the double bed, propped up so he wouldn't lie on his injured arm. Although Velma knew the doctor did a good job, she checked the bandage anyway, fretting about latent magic in the wound. She'd just happened to have the potion with her. If she hadn't, would things have turned out so well?

"You are going to heal up perfectly without even a scar," Velma said as Dillon snored on, "because this is a minor injury, and no one asked you to do something so foolish. You could have died. I already lost someone before, and I don't want you added to that list."

A tray awaited Velma on the nearby table, and while the smells didn't entice her at first, with her first bite she remembered how many hours it had been since her last meal. Ravenous, she made quick work of the plate, and she was nearly done when she realized she'd made a mistake. As she swallowed, Velma could taste the faintly peppery herb known as Dream Powder.

The food must have been liberally coated with it, for it hit her hard enough that Velma could barely get up from the table, her eyelids already growing heavy.

Her last thought as she fell upon the armchair was that the good doctor would get along quite well with her sister.

When Velma woke, she was sprawled on the other side of the double bed, a blanket thrown over her. She woke mostly from having grown hot under the blanket, but it was the pitter-patter of rain on the windowpane that fully pulled her away from slumber, as she mistook it for typewriter keys.

There was no typing, however. Instead of attempting to work on an article with his injured arm in a sling, Dillon sat up with a book. From the angle she lay at, Velma couldn't fully see the title, but she saw Melvin Winterberry was the author. Several books by the same author were stacked on the small nightstand, alongside a pile of Velma's jewelry, including her bracelets.

"About time you woke up," Dillon said.

"How long was I out?" Velma asked, eyeing the books with particular concern.

"You slept a full day and a half. That's what sleeping powder does," he added as Velma shuddered. "Don't feel bad. I got doused too."

"You needed it." Velma sat up, tossing off the blanket. "I didn't. I've got too much to do. I need to check—" Velma winced as she pulled at one of her mending wounds. "I can't believe the doctor did this."

"Can't trust doctors—they don't know anything, do they? At least that's what I tell my brother, who likes to gloat about his medical practice."

"Maybe we could have gone to see your brother for medical assistance instead?" Velma suggested.

Dillon lowered his book with a snort. "We would have gotten worse treatment. I only get along with three of my siblings, and he's not on the list for reasons best left unsaid."

"You only get along with three out of ten siblings?" Velma chuckled as she rolled over to her side to peer up at him. "Can't say I'm surprised. So it's Fitzhugh, Beaumont, and . . . ?"

"My youngest sister. Lynn is more opinionated than me, if you can imagine it."

"I can't," Velma said. "Is she a writer too?"

"No, but she did say my rather unorthodox approach to life and career made it easy for her to do the same. Which is funny because I got where I am completely by accident."

"Are you rethinking your life choices?"

"I am rethinking the wisdom of starting a minor feud with someone just because she got a column on day one at the newspaper."

"I knew you made that rude remark about Uriel's flight on purpose!"

"I'm a very petty person."

"I didn't steal a column from you; it was created just for me."

"That's not the whole reason. You claimed to not remember me from our encounter on the train," Dillon admitted with a shrug. "There were also your subsequent lies when we kept running into each other in increasingly dubious settings over the past year. I figured if there was one thing you weren't going to lie about it was planes, and I was right."

"You could have just ignored me."

Their eyes met as Dillon replied, "No, that's entirely impossible."

Unsure of what to say that, or even if she could say anything to such words, Velma desperately pointed to the camera bag on the nearby table. "You said your camera might have evidence of who attacked us. Can I see the pictures?"

Dillon said nothing about her abrupt change of subject and simply replied, "I have to develop them, but I'm a little short-handed at the moment." He gestured to his sling.

"I'll help," Velma said, eager to keep busy in any way she could. Velma pulled his camera out and as she glanced at it, she paused. "There's a couple of shots left on this roll."

"Clear them off, then." Dillon shrugged.

"You want me to take pictures?" Velma asked, rather surprised.

"Why not? It's not like I'm thrusting the controls of an airplane into your hands."

"You're never going to let that go, are you?" Velma said as she removed the lens cap.

"Never!"

As he replied, Velma pressed the shutter button in quick succession, capturing him on film.

"I didn't say take a picture of me!" Dillon protested, though without any real heat.

"Think of it as revenge or a souvenir from our travels."

Velma managed to convince the doctor's children to let her borrow a few bowls and towels. When she returned, Dillon had started transforming the space into a makeshift darkroom, and she helped to place blankets just so, blocking any light.

Dillon carried with him vials of developing solution, which he instructed her to pour into the bowls. The most nerve-racking part was getting his camera open. Velma could feel Dillon watching her as she fumbled to retrieve the film. If he was worried she'd drop it or do damage, he said nothing, just calmly walked her through the developing process.

The photographs she just took of Dillon were first, and then they worked backward to Ardenton. Velma studied each image of the doomed town the moment it first came into view. They didn't show

Velma anything she hadn't seen already, but there was one photograph she looked at the longest. Snapped off by Dillon as she'd dragged him away, it was a low-angled shot of the person who attacked them. Velma couldn't make out any features, but she saw enough to be confident it wasn't some sort of ghoul.

After the photographs of Ardenton came the pictures from the auction at Giles Pacer's home. These came from a tiny camera that Velma had spotted on the lapel of Dillon's jacket. Despite the small size, the images came out remarkably clear. The last photographs were slightly warped around the edges, giving them a dreamlike quality, like the one taken of Velma in the aftermath of the auction. Caught turning to look warily over her shoulder, Velma was the only thing in focus, the world around her soft and blurred.

The other photographs on the roll were much clearer, which was why, when Brayton Strickland's face first appeared, there was no mistaking who it was. He was photographed in the garden, in conversation with someone just out of frame.

"Strickland was there?" Velma said, plucking the photograph out. "I wonder if he knows Malcolm Gladstone?"

"I don't even know if Gladstone was at the auction at all. I wasn't there long enough to ask. Too many people and no easy way to ask about a stranger with an uncertain connection."

"I didn't ask either. I was more focused on the auction."

Strickland wasn't the only familiar face that showed up in the photographs. In the very next photograph, Marie Drew, the one-time collector of tinted glasses, stood in the hallway not far away from the music shop owner Portia Milburn. In fact, as Velma looked at the photo, they appeared to be close enough that it wasn't by chance Dillon had gotten a picture of them together.

It was not a combination Velma would have ever dreamed of seeing, and it unleashed a torrent of questions. Marie had lied to them in their brief interview, but Velma had dismissed any concern, viewing Marie as harmless. As for her conversation with Portia, it had been brief, but the woman was smuggling wands. What would bring such a pair together?

These weren't the only questions that arose to pester her. As Velma pulled more photographs out of the basin, each image added to her list. Whether it was an image of Kenneth Poole arguing with a door attendant, old records on display in the house, or even the chaos that cut short the auction.

"They were all at the auction," Velma whispered. "Strickland, Marie, and Laverna. I met this man, Kenneth Poole, who surprised me while I was going through Pacer's desk. I also spoke with her—"

"Posy Newman," Dillon said as he pointed to the picture of Portia.

"No, her name is Portia and she owns a music shop. Or," Velma considered how often she gave fake names to others, "that's what she told me. Although, that name sounds familiar."

"Because Posy Newman is the singer on the record we found in Sacramento. I can prove it's the same person," Dillon said. "It should be this photograph or the next one. I visited the newspaper archives earlier—it's why I had this particular camera with me in the first place."

The next photograph Velma removed was an album advertisement from ten years ago featuring Portia Milburn, Laverna Addison, Brayton Strickland, and Delia Moore.

Velma looked up, staring at Dillon. "If you didn't have this photograph, I would have never believed you!"

"If I didn't see it myself, I wouldn't either," Dillon said with relish. "It seems they all worked at Wise Records at some point." I even spotted an article that gives songwriting credit to an M. Drew, which must be

Marie. This explains a few things, but does it explain everything? We don't know why after all these years they've banded together now, and I don't think it's to pay their respects to Giles Pacer."

"They were there about the machine that destroyed the manor," Velma whispered.

"I'm confused," Dillon said carefully. "I think there's something you haven't told me yet."

Velma met his gaze, seeing only patience in his eyes. Patience and grace for her to answer honestly, for he had already pieced most of it together.

The truth was much less complicated than any lie she could spin right now. More than that, after everything they'd been through, to lie now would be the greatest betrayal of his trust.

"My name is Violet Newberry. I grew up on Bramble Crescent in the inn that was built over the ruins of Sitwell manor. The items we are looking for were stolen by Quincy from a hidden room buried underneath the inn that is very likely Jeremiah's workshop," Velma said. "When did you figure that out?"

"From the way you approached things, I knew you had some connection. It felt personal. I even thought you were related to Jeremiah Sitwell for a moment. My research on the man led me to Bramble Crescent and Beacon Inn. I spoke with Carolyn Rose, and she told me less than what I hoped to find, which is to say, nothing. She just gave me some platitudes and suggested I didn't know what I was talking about."

"I'm surprised she even spoke to you if you led with those questions. You never mentioned you were researching Sitwell."

"I was curious why, of all the things you asked me to look up, you never asked about him. Turned out there was a reason why: you knew all about him already."

"Not everything. I'm still learning more about him, it seems. The story of the storm that began Ardenton's woes is very similar to the story we tell on the island about the night the Sitwell family left. I always thought it was a storm, but I only just realized the storm might have been magical backlash from a machine Jeremiah made. I believe that Edwin Addison re-created his grandfather's work, and it went even worse. For whatever reason, he kept the notes about the incident and left them behind when he died. Giles Pacer had them, and Delia Moore wrote to him warning him to get rid of them, but she was too late. The notes had already passed into the hands of someone else eager to re-create the machine. Luckily the attempts have failed so far."

"Shards and stars," Dillon said as he put together the last of the pieces. "That experiment we found. Do you think Malcolm Gladstone was trying to re-create it?"

"Or someone hired him to do it."

Dillon nodded grimly. "My question is, why would someone want such a machine?"

"To prove 'the inherent majesty of magic.' That's what Delia's note quoted." As Velma began to explain about Clarice Sitwell's notes, Dillon jumped so quickly that it was as if someone had dropped a brick on his foot. He all but flung himself to the corner of the room where his bag was and grabbed his notebook. Too agitated to speak, he thrust it under her nose, pointing to a key passage:

Recruitment for Members of Rational Clarity (MRC) occurs mainly through civic and social groups, building on connections. But posters and literature emphasize their key goals and objectives, which is to impress upon the might and inherent majesty of celestial magic, and the way they are going about it is counterproductive for long-term relations.

"Shards and stars," Velma whispered.

Every puzzle piece she had just gathered was as important as she'd thought. Only, the pieces came together in a different arrangement, revealing a pattern that for the first time was starting to make sense.

If she were to belong to an anarchist organization, why would she look for small items to sow chaos when a single machine could make a statement on a scale that would achieve every goal she dreamed up?

"They're going to use the machine at the arcane expo," Velma whispered. "I have to go find— I have to go—"

"You don't even know where to begin looking," Dillon cut in. "And even if you do know where to look, would you be able to get there in time? Your plane is pretty banged up. Can you trust it to do any fancy flying you might need? Plus, the arcane expo won't open for a few weeks. You have time—use it wisely."

"Meaning get my plane repaired," Velma said by way of agreement. "What sensible words."

"Not sensible. Selfish." Dillon tugged at his sling. "I don't want you to use the excuse of a little injury to get rid of me. I said I wanted to see this through, and we're not quite there, are we?"

"No, we are not," Velma agreed, recognizing the undercurrent of another promise tucked in his words. "There's plenty left to do."

V elma arrived midafternoon in Chicago as Cornelius was giving a flying lesson. She knew he was giving lessons, because when she flew up next to his two-seater fixed wing, the plane quivered like a bird and nearly dropped right out of the sky.

She would have stayed in range for an assist if Cornelius hadn't signaled for her to stand down.

Velma pulled away and landed. Although she delayed getting out until the other plane was on the ground. Cornelius all but jumped out of his plane, and strode for Velma's, swearing up a storm.

"Bad flight?" Velma asked, with amusement at seeing her mild-mannered friend so out of sorts.

"I saw my life flash before my eyes three times! This was worse than Harold King!"

Velma leaned over to look at the hapless student, who was kicking stones despondently.

"Is he going to fly again?"

"Not if I have my way," Cornelius said rather grimly. "How's your plane holding up? Looks like you've had some interesting times," he added as he stared at the marks of her recent travels across the *Fowl Weather*.

"She's a little battered, but I'm still flying."

"Your mechanic's going to be happy."

"He'll be the only one," Lois remarked.

To Velma's surprise, Lois walked out of the airplane hangar, hastily shoving a set of books into her bag.

"What are you doing here?" Velma asked.

"That's *my* question, since I thought you were dead! I've been trying to contact you for *days*, ever since Jasper said he lost contact with you!"

"I got in a spot of trouble and my radio got damaged. I landed in Kansas in a very small town—"

"There are such things as phones! You are just two days shy of being declared missing. I almost called your family, because I'm pretty sure they could find you!"

"I'm sorry I worried you. I was trying to adhere to blackout protocol after getting the communication-compromise signal."

"That happened because the communications relay went down. A few people from the Atlanta office got exposed while on a case."

"What happened?" Velma said before remembering Cornelius was right there. "I mean—"

"It's fine. I told him everything," Lois said. Her expression softened slightly as she peered up at Cornelius. "He said I was too worried about you filming stunts in a movie."

"That's the best lie you could arrive at?" Velma asked.

"It's been a very tense few days," Cornelius said blandly. "I took her flying earlier and she was hardly panicked at all. I was so proud until she said she didn't have the capacity for fear at the moment."

"I can't believe I missed that," Velma said with true regret. Although she did not regret if her absence had finally brought her friends together. Lois and Cornelius weren't holding hands, but there seemed to have been a shift in the air around them, leaving only the first tender blooms of new romance.

"What sort of trouble did you encounter, anyway?" Lois asked.

As if on cue, Dillon gingerly climbed out of the cabin with care to not disturb his healing arm.

Lois's surprised turned to amusement. There was even mischief twinkling in her eyes as she continued. "I see trouble has found you once again. Was he traveling with you the entire time?"

"Our paths crossed because of an article Dillon is writing," Velma stiffly remarked.

"That's always the case," Lois replied, but despite her obvious curiosity, she said nothing more as Dillon joined them.

"Do you need a ride back home?" Cornelius asked. "I'm just about finished."

"Go on without me," Dillon said. "I have to call my editor to find out if it's safe for me to be back in town."

"He had to flee with only his camera because a gangster didn't like his latest article," Velma explained to her bewildered friends.

"Well, I suppose those sorts of things happen," Lois remarked.

"You should be careful about what you write," Cornelius added.

"So I'm told," Dillon said. He nodded at Velma. "Thanks for the assist. It was very interesting traveling together. I'll let you know how the article turns out. It won't be printed soon. I might need to get a few finer details."

While Dillon wasn't going to say much in front of Lois, he had left behind in the plane all the photographs related to Velma's case, plus his notes on Members of Rational Clarity. He left no additional note on why he would leave them in her hands, but there was a slightly creased photograph of her looking pensive as she held the pocket watch she'd found on this very field—and that seemed to be reason enough.

Velma's mailbox at work was bursting with notes when she returned to the office the following day. Velma sighed, feeling a headache coming. She had a great deal of paperwork awaiting her given the processing required for the objects she had recovered. The prospect of even more paperwork getting shoved at her made her want to turn back and go home. A feeling that increased as Velma's boss came around the corner, coffee mug in hand.

"Step into my office," Phyllis said as she greeted Velma. "We need to talk."

That this was what Phyllis chose to do first thing this morning did not bode well. Velma tried to rein in her imagination as she took a seat and waited for the bad news.

"I'm glad you're back in Chicago. I assume you heard about the communications failure?" Phyllis began. "Well, this is not widely known, but information was leaked. We don't know the quality, but we were one of the four offices hit. All field agents are to return for the time being."

"I have good timing, then."

"Yes," Phyllis said. "All I need now is your update and final briefing."

"Final briefing?" Velma echoed.

Her boss's expression did not change. "I assumed that's why you've returned. You've been at this for a while, and taking up significant resources. Aren't you finished?"

Velma swallowed hard but then straightened up. "I'm not finished. In some ways I've just begun. And I've worked on cases that lasted longer than this."

"I've been advised to tell you that this case needs to be wrapped up. Your actions in California have caused some alarm about the free range our agents have."

"I didn't do anything in California to cause alarm."

"What about the cards you gave out to the two people charged by Magical Detection?"

"One was falsely accused," Velma said, "and the other is implicated by— Wait, did you turn them over to the Sniffers? I gave them the cards so they could get help! I promised they would."

"It's not your role to judge if they need help—others hold that happy power," Phyllis said. "We work in partnership with Magical Detection as determined by our leadership in situations like this."

"That was the wrong call to make. The Sniffers will only make things worse."

"Magical Detection," Phyllis corrected firmly, "has priority in this area."

"They shouldn't! We're supposed to be helping people! It's why I joined."

"And that's why I've let you stay in the field. You often see things unfold and act on it right away. Charlotte Allen tells me without the actions you took in Minnesota last year, the Frank McKinley case would have never been resolved in a favorable fashion."

"Why not let me continue as I am, then?"

Phyllis's mask cracked slightly, revealing barely suppressed frustrations. "You're not the only one I have had this conversation with. Lionel did something similar."

"I'm in good company, then!"

"That you are. It doesn't help that your investigation ties to Members of Rational Clarity. Leadership has declared that for all their magical hijinks, this is not under our domain."

"Are you kidding! How can we not be involved with this? After all I've seen in Denver alone—"

"You are to submit a report and pass the work on to the Enforcers of Arcane Relations."

"We can't. It's not right . . . ," Velma began. Seeing her boss's face, and the forming rebuke, Velma nearly panicked. Phyllis never passed things on to EAR if she could help it. This was not good. Velma knew she had a good case on hand, with strong suspects for murder, theft, and mayhem. She just didn't have the proof to hand over right then. She had conversations, she had a few objects and photographs, plus the words of a reporter.

Then again, who said Phyllis needed proof?

Phyllis had all but said she disapproved of how things were being handled. With a few well-placed words, Velma could easily convince her boss to let her continue. Phyllis cared more about a job done well than following rules, after all. It was why, despite Velma's history of explosive results, Phyllis just covered for her and never asked for anything more than a report.

Velma took a deep breath and did what she did best: improvise.

"I have a plan in motion to handle this," Velma said, projecting calm and confidence. "While things appear quiet, this will not be true for long. In my travels I have uncovered traces of these actions, and the suspects involved. They are seeking a deadly machine of untold power, and I have reason to believe the International Exposition of Arcane Arts and Sciences is a key target. They haven't found the machine yet, but they are getting close. I have been tracking members of the group, going to the places where they have been meeting up."

"Such as the auction in Los Angeles?" Phyllis asked.

"It was a major meeting place for them. To prevent them from acting on a plot at the expo, I need more time. I don't need resources from the Muses. I have it handled. I just need permission from you to continue, because I'm on the verge of wrapping this up. If I step back now, they will enact their plans unhindered—you know as well as I do that our counterparts at EAR are not equipped to handle this task."

Phyllis looked at Velma long and hard, each moment stretching out into an eternity before her boss finally said: "I want your final report within a month, Frye. No extra resources. No extra time. I want that machine in the archives or confirmation of its destruction."

"I'll have it sooner," Velma said, and hurried out of the office before Phyllis could change her mind.

Or Velma changed hers, for that matter.

For all her bluster, Velma didn't have much of a plan to bring a decisive end to things. In fact, she had no plan, no idea, other than trying to read through all of Dillon's notes about Members of Rational Clarity. She needed to see if there was any hint about the group's methods to help her follow their tracks to the fabled Sitwell machine. The only strong lead was Malcolm Gladstone, who was a ghost for all she knew. He might even be dead, succumbing to the same bad luck as Delia Moore or Giles Pacer. Unless he was their murderer, of course.

Velma didn't think so. Yoshi had said Gladstone was a pawn. Although being a pawn didn't always mean you weren't powerful.

Regardless, she couldn't find out either way for a while. Velma was grounded for the foreseeable future. Her mechanic had already taken a good look at her plane and told her she wasn't going anywhere for at least a week. When she said she didn't have time to waste, Lester upped the estimate to twelve days.

That wasn't long in the grand scheme of things, but it could be costly.

In a week, who knew what could happen?

Velma planned to keep an eye on the arcane expo, of course. First she wanted to locate the elusive Malcolm Gladstone, and speak with Brayton Strickland, Laverna Addison, and the others she'd had rather intriguing encounters with during her travels. They were scattered across the country, up to who knew what mischief. But she needed to talk to them again. She needed to determine what plans they were putting together.

It would be so much easier if, instead of chasing after them, she could trap them in a room somewhere . . .

The idea appeared to her almost like a vision.

Yes, she *could* gather them in a room together.

Her family's inn was the beginning of the case—why not make it the end?

Getting them all to the inn was a bold swing. It would bring them onto her home turf, but it could also invite trouble into a place she held dear. Yet this was the best option, and the more she thought about it, the more she knew it was the only way to gather them together without drawing too much attention.

Someone had killed three people, and attempted to kill her—it was past time to find out why.

Lois waited outside Velma's office, with a stack of papers and a slightly worried expression.

"I heard Phyllis had stern words about your case," Lois said as she followed Velma inside her office. "But you're unscathed."

"Phyllis wasn't that mad at me."

"Are you done with your case?"

"I've gotten approval to finish up. Phyllis gave me a month, but I think I can get it done sooner."

"If anyone can, it'd be you. How many objects did you find throughout your travels?"

"Sixteen. They are in for processing, save of course the ones too big for my plane. I need to put in orders for pickups on those. Although it's still not all of them."

"Are you planning another trip across the country, then?"

"There are a few people I spoke with who I need to talk to again, and this time I'm gathering them at my family's inn."

"That's very risky."

"I have a plan for that."

Lois snorted, but Velma insisted, "I do. I'm going to invite them and ensure their attendance by appealing to their worst nature."

"They won't come if you sign your name," Lois pointed out.

"I'll sign as Delia Moore," Velma said. "They know her. And she's dead, so she can't mess up my plans."

"If you're sending letters, you need to move quickly. Dispatch can help you pass along the ones farthest away. Do you need addresses for the people you're contacting?"

"I will. Please try to get them as discreetly as possible."

"You know I will." Lois paused. "This is all you're going to get from me, as I've been assigned a few urgent cases. So I guess the information you get from Dillon Harris will have to be enough."

"It will be," Velma began, until she caught the smirk on Lois's face.

"It's a protocol violation," her friend said, not even pretending to be stern about it, "a very extreme one, considering you brought a civilian with you on this case and had him provide information. It'll be hard to overlook, but I think I can manage."

"Can you?" Velma asked, only slightly surprised that Lois had figured it out.

Lois beamed at her. "Easily, but I want to hear everything first!"

Once Lois sent along the addresses, Velma spent the rest of the day writing the letters and then sending them to the the key suspects: Laverna Addison, Brayton Strickland, Kenneth Poole, Portia Milburn, and Marie Drew. Using the ruse of a dinner party, each invitation was personalized to best intrigue the recipient, drawing on what Velma knew about them. She held one invitation in reserve, the one meant for Malcolm Gladstone. Lois was unable to find him, despite the resources at her disposal. It wasn't too surprising, given Velma had more direct contacts with the man and had still failed to find him. Perhaps it was for the best. Malcolm Gladstone had disappeared all on his own, and very likely for good reason.

Despite all this planning, Velma had neglected one very important detail.

She had yet to inform her sister about using the inn as the site for what was sure to be a very interesting night. Velma put it off for as long as she could, but that evening when she returned to her house, she called the inn.

"Carolyn, it's me," Velma said when her sister answered the phone. "Do you have any guests booked about two weeks from now?"

"Why do you ask?"

"I need to have the inn for a weekend to host a dinner party. Not for fun," Velma rushed on, knowing that, at this very moment, Carolyn had lifted her eyes to the sky in pure exasperation. "It's for my case. I believe I can bring it all together, but only if I do it there."

"With my help?" Carolyn asked.

"Yes." A dozen reasons flooded Velma's mind, but there was only one reason Carolyn would heed. "I need your help. I don't know if I can pull this off otherwise."

A long silence followed before Carolyn spoke again. "You said two weeks from now. I'll make sure things are ready by then. How many guests should I prepare for?"

"You'll do it?" Velma said, uncertain she had heard right. "I haven't explained what's going to happen—"

"It's a dinner party. I know how to set up such things. As for the rest, I leave it up to you. How many guests? Or should I say suspects?"

"I have five written down. One of them was at the salon Edythe hosted."

"Laverna Addison," Carolyn supplied.

"How did you know?" Velma asked.

"Her creepy dolls. She left them behind, and we found them in places where no guests should have been!"

CHAPTER 26

Although Velma said Carolyn didn't need to send any of the dolls to her, they arrived on Velma's desk not even two days later with the speed of a falling star. Inside the box lay several dolls in pieces, all of which had been cleanly cleaved in half with a sharp edge, including their heads.

Carolyn always did hate clowns, Velma surmised as she picked up half of the ghoulishly grinning harlequin jester. Carolyn had given a rather dramatic telling of spotting a doll climbing the hedges in the maze in the garden. At the sight, Carolyn grabbed the axe and chased after the doll. She chopped it to bits and would have chopped down all the hedges if Edythe hadn't stopped her. They then went on a hunt around the inn and found two other dolls, one in the attic and the other atop the bookcase in the library. Those dolls were dormant, but the sight of them had been just as alarming.

Carolyn's impulse to turn the dolls into firewood revealed that the harlequins had mechanical equipment inside their wooden bodies, which Edythe and Carolyn thought were radios. While Carolyn was afraid of them being some sort of listening ear, Velma thought the sensors had more in common with a seismoscope. Especially since the doll found in the library contained a tiny slip of paper riddled with lines with peaks and valleys that seemed to track the magical activity in the inn.

When Velma called to inform her sister of this, Carolyn cared only about Velma transforming the dolls into ash.

"This tells us something more interesting," Velma protested.

"Yes, that this Laverna Addison is bad news," Carolyn retorted. "Burn the dolls. If you bring them back with you, I will never talk to you again!"

Laverna Addison was indeed bad news, and Velma's top suspect for the murder of Delia Moore and the various conspiracies. Which was why, despite Carolyn's fervent wishes, Velma had to leave the dolls as they were for now.

"You have more for the archives?" Morris Broadleaf said when Velma brought down the box.

"I do," she said, barely glancing over at Lois's assistant.

Velma had been down here every day this week, bringing in the items she was handing over to the Muses for safekeeping. She had kept a few on hand, such as the pocket watch, hatpin, fountain pen, sheet music, and scissors, as some were still useful for the investigation and might even play a role in the dinner party. As for the larger items, like the mirror in Denver and the orrery that had been in her grandparents' possession, they had arrived two days ago and been brought into the archives.

Velma sighed as she glanced at the form. "I should have to fill out only one form for all of this—it's for the same case."

"We must account for every item on its own," Morris declared. "Otherwise, items will be lost, never to be found again."

"I think that's the goal of some of this," Velma said.

She picked up the box, only for him to grab the other end.

Velma nearly slapped his hands, but her stern glare was enough to get Morris to relent.

"Part of the protocol is visual confirmation," Morris said.

Lois never asked for that, Velma nearly muttered. But her friend was occupied with other work, leaving Velma at the mercy of the overeager assistant.

When Velma lifted the lid, the young man cringed at the creepy cut-up dolls. She shut the box with a satisfactory smile.

"Confirmed," Morris gulped. "I will put this up with the others you have brought for case 4345."

"Don't rush on my account," Velma called as the assistant entered the archives, the box held gingerly under his arm.

Velma had wanted another glance at all the items she recovered in her travels, which was why she'd brought the dolls here in the first place. With the assistant barring her way, it didn't seem likely she'd get that chance.

Which was just as well. Velma had quite a few tasks remaining before she left Chicago. Her mechanic had called that morning to say the repairs were finished, and it looked like she might be able to leave sooner than she had originally planned. With her bags packed and ready to go, Velma made one last tour of the grounds of the arcane exposition. It would open the following Monday. Compared to her visit weeks ago, the grounds were bustling, with signs, statues, and signposts leading to the buildings. There was even a sculpture garden, which reminded Velma of the rough works she had seen at the art salon. As Velma continued to look at the elephant sculpture, its trunk raised to the sky, she realized she had seen this exact one, created by a sculptor who'd had plenty to say when Velma had asked questions.

A camera flashed behind her, and Velma turned on instinct.

As her fluttering heart hoped, Dillon was on the other side of the camera, with the same smile he always had upon seeing her.

Chicago really was a small place. She'd taken pains to avoid crossing his path these past few weeks, and yet, as always, he just showed up when she least expected it.

As she lifted a hand to wave, she realized with a start he wasn't alone.

Madelyn Sunday was with him, and maybe it was because the younger woman was standing right next to Dillon, but Velma was able to notice right away that her features were a softer version of her brother's.

No wonder Madelyn had instantly latched herself to Velma at the salon! The younger woman had known exactly who Velma was and she'd had great fun with that knowledge.

"What luck, what serendipity, what a twist of fate to have brought us here!" Dillon declared as he took another photograph of Velma in front of the sculptures as he and Madelyn approached.

"You're covering the arcane expo for the newspaper?" Velma asked. "I thought you didn't do fluff pieces."

"My editor said I needed to keep me out of trouble. Although I got it on good authority there's a chance something interesting might occur here," he added with a wink. "Also, my sister is display-ing some of her sculptures. She just got the acceptance notice at the very last minute. Which makes the entire European tour I paid for worthwhile in the end."

"You only paid for the boat fare," Madelyn said, "and my hotel that one week when it turned out the person who posted about the apartment was a liar. I paid for everything else."

"What about an artists' salon on Bramble Crescent?" Velma asked.

"I paid for that," Madelyn said easily. "It's nice to see you again—is it Violet, Viola, or Velma?"

"I answer to all three," Velma swiftly replied. "Since you didn't mention anything at the salon."

"I figured a famous pilot would want to go incognito." Madelyn shrugged. "I also figured anyone who could give my brother a run for his money wasn't half bad. Dill's been bored ever since you left the newspaper, but I think—"

"Lynn, one of your sculptures is about to fall over," Dillon interrupted. "If you keep running your mouth, I hate to imagine what could occur."

Madelyn mimed buttoning her lips. She strolled over to the sculpture garden and pointedly turned away from them.

"What a small world this is," Velma said. "I should have known she was your sister. She talked far too much. Did you send her there on purpose?"

"Yes, but not why you think. Lynn's been mopey ever since coming back from Europe. I'd encourage her to join a circus if it would make her happy."

"There was also the Hounds McGee article," Velma pointed out. "How is that?"

"Perfectly fine. Apparently he has bigger enemies than me, so I'm not going to be bothered for a while. Were you worried about me?" he gently teased.

"Just wanted to know if you needed to get out of town posthaste. I figured when I didn't hear a thing, there was no news."

"No, no news, not until today. It's why I'm glad to run into you like this," Dillon said with a look over his shoulder. "Lois told me you were either at the expo or the airfield. I need to speak with you quite urgently."

He waved a hand over the air next to him, and Olivia appeared.

"Olivia!" Velma cried, thunderstruck at the sight of her younger cousin.

With her knapsack bursting at the seams and a broomstick in hand, Olivia had all the looks of a runaway to her, although without the usual reasons.

"So she does belong to you," Dillon said.

"She's my cousin's daughter," Velma explained. "Olivia, don't tell me you flew all the way here from Philadelphia!"

"No, I got a train ticket," Olivia said as she squirmed, clearly wishing she was still invisible. "You said if I found anything interesting, I should contact you."

"You couldn't call me instead?" Velma asked.

Olivia shook her head. "It's very important."

"Not enough to bother other people," Velma said. "I'm sure Mr. Harris has plenty of things to do."

"I'm happy to be bothered," Dillon said. "She came to the newspaper office looking for you. I figured it was related to the letter you received before."

Velma looked sharply at Olivia, recalling the crossword cipher. There were a bunch of crossword puzzle books at the house on Juniper Street, and Olivia was learning all about the family business.

"You sent the warning pretending to be your uncle?" Velma said. "Why didn't you say anything?"

"Because Uncle Quincy is in trouble, but I couldn't tell anyone. I know everybody doesn't like him, so they wouldn't focus on what really was going on."

"Yet you contacted me."

"Mother told me what you did last year," Olivia said. "She says it doesn't matter what it is, you'll help within reason. Uncle Quincy needs help because he's in business with bad people, the same ones who killed Delia Moore."

"The same ones," Velma whispered. "How do you know?"

"I think we should talk about this elsewhere?" Dillon suggested quietly, casting a wary look about the fairgrounds. "My car's nearby. We can head to my apartment or somewhere else if you prefer?"

"Your apartment," Velma said, glancing over toward Madelyn, who was not hiding the fact that she had been intently listening the entire time. "And your sister?"

"I am going to meet up with Fitzhugh," Madelyn answered instead. "You go on without me."

Olivia spent the car ride detailing Quincy's visit to Minneapolis earlier that year. As it turned out, it was eavesdropping on her uncle that got her sent to Philadelphia. He had noticed her and mentioned the snooping to her mother, who believed his version of events.

"She was looking for an excuse to send me away. I got followed the other day by some people who are against the union." Olivia said as they entered Dillon's apartment. "When you talked to Uncle Quincy, I'd hoped you'd get the truth out of him."

"I failed then, but I won't this time around." Velma promised.

Dillon's apartment was a decent size, made slightly smaller by the pottery wheel in the main room and other items that pointed to the presence of his siblings in the space.

Dillon brought Velma and Olivia into the small room that was his office when it wasn't also a darkroom. Photographs hung on the wall, and there were pages of what must have been an article he was working on pinned on a nearby board. His desk held his typewriter and a stack of notebooks, plus a collection of records untidily stacked in a box. Dillon let Olivia sit at the desk chair as she recounted the most sensitive aspects of her story.

"After you left, Emerson and I followed up on the addresses that Delia Moore had for various places in New York City. Most of the people were nothing special. A hairdresser, a fruit seller, a dressmaker, and a few friends. But one address brought us to a meeting hall—actually, it looked just like that one." Olivia pointed to one of the photographs behind Velma.

Dillon got up right away and plucked down a photograph of a nondescript building. As he held it out to Olivia, Velma could see an address in Queens written on the back and the words MRC *meetinghouse*. "This building?" Dillon asked.

Olivia nodded. "I remember the gargoyle on top of the roof. It looked like it was watching as people entered. I got too distracted, so it was Emerson who saw Uncle Quincy first. He had a box with him. Because of the gargoyle, he couldn't bring it inside."

"Wards to keep it out of the building," Velma surmised.

"He had to put it in a closet," Olivia said. "He argued quite a bit with the doorman until he started attracting attention. Then another man came out and they had a quick conversation. Emerson created a distraction and I was able to get inside. I looked to see what was in the box. Once I saw what was in there, I had to take it."

From her knapsack, Olivia pulled out a shoebox. Inside the box were a pair of elemental pistols. They were Velma's twin cousins' pistols. A matching set, with diamond shapes carved into the handles. They were supposed to be locked in the cellar of Fran's home back in Philadelphia. Why they were not was the second question buzzing in Velma's mind. The first was why they were broken. The cannister, where potions could be inserted, had been changed. Instead of a round flask that could hold sloshing potions, a narrower glass fixture had been welded onto the back, and although it was cracked open, fragments of wood remained inside. Wood that crackled with enough magic to let her know it might just be wand wood.

"I'm so glad you took them," Velma said as she trembled with both outrage and horror at these abominations.

"He's not supposed to have these, right?" Olivia asked.

"Not at all. He stole them," Velma said. "Worse, he's altered them. He might still have the other ones. The twins had three apiece. Four are missing. Did you tell anyone?"

"I told Granny and Grandpa," Olivia said. "They said not to tell Uncle Gregory or the others because they'd get upset. They did say that *you* needed to know as soon as possible, since you can take care of it."

"Take care of what?" Velma muttered, mostly to herself. With a sigh, she placed the abominations away. "Wait, if you told them and they said to tell me, you didn't sneak away—you were sent!"

Olivia nodded. "Granny said this was the hands-on part of my lessons."

Her grandmother was very keen on Velma instructing Olivia in the ways of magic and mystery, but surely this wasn't what Henrietta had in mind? Probably yes, Velma determined grimly, recalling how her own previous magic lessons had gone. Henrietta Rhodes was an advocate of learning through experience, the more unorthodox the better.

"Who was the man your uncle spoke to?" Dillon asked. "Did you hear a name?"

"Not his name," Olivia replied. "But they mentioned someone else: Malcolm Gladstone. He was traveling, coming back from a place called Ardenton."

"Ardenton!" Velma exclaimed.

"Now, I didn't see that coming," Dillon remarked.

"If he's traveling, then he was there—he attacked us!"

"That would explain some of the magic lobbed our way." Dillon absently tapped his healed injury. "The question is, did he expect trouble or was he just overly prepared?"

"Like he knew we would be there?" Velma asked. "The Muses communications were compromised. But if he or someone he's working with has access, that's an even bigger mess. And—" Velma stopped, struck by a thought as she looked around Dillon's office. "Where are the photographs from the auction?"

Dillon got up once more and pulled out photographs to hold before Olivia. When Olivia pointed to Brayton Strickland as the man she had seen with her uncle, Velma wasn't surprised at all.

Strickland, Quincy, and the elusive Malcolm Gladstone were all working together. If it wasn't on the machine that destroyed the Sitwell manor, then it might be these pistols, and either way, this was far from good news. Illuminating news, but far from good.

"They didn't see you?" Velma asked.

"No, I don't think so."

"Good, because your ability to lurk about might be useful for the dinner party."

"You said I was bad at eavesdropping."

"You're bad at eavesdropping on *me*."

"There's a dinner party?" Dillon remarked with exaggerated outrage. "I didn't hear about this."

Until this afternoon, Velma had not planned to let him know, but now she knew without a doubt that she wanted him there.

"Don't worry—you're invited." Velma pulled out the extra invitation. "The rest of the guest list shouldn't surprise you. I invited Brayton Strickland, Marie Drew, Kenneth Poole, Laverna Addison, and Portia Milburn to my family's inn."

Dillon nodded. "To put an end to where it all began. Very poetic."

"Laverna has been there before under false pretenses. I don't know if any of the others have. Or to what extent they know about anything, really. I'm taking a chance they will show."

"You are confident they will?" Dillon asked.

"I wrote the invitations to ensure they would attend," Velma said. "I signed them as Delia Moore."

"Clever. When do we leave?"

"First thing tomorrow," Velma said. "That's enough time for you?"

Dillon just grinned. "If you said leave right now, all I'd ask for is a moment to grab my camera!"

INTERLUDE

St. Paul, Minnesota

August 1930

VELMA HELD ON TO THE RECEIVER AS SHE KEPT HER GAZE ON THE MOVIE theater. "You do know that this isn't exactly what I do. Someone else would be better for this."

"There is no one better." Arista's voice was crisp as it came through the phone. "Even more so, I trust you. I would put my daughter's life in your hands."

"That's sounds less like flattery and more like you're trying to sway my opinion," Velma said. "Why do you need me to deliver a message? You're just across the river."

"I can't risk it. We are being watched."

Velma tried not to roll her eyes. Arista and her husband were deeply involved in the Pullman's union, with Clem being a major leader. While it was risky work, Arista often exaggerated things. The latest drama was about this recently fired porter who Velma was supposed to meet. Arista was being annoyingly coy over the details despite insisting Velma drop everything to travel to Minnesota.

"Why don't you tell me what this is about?" Velma asked. "You wouldn't ask me here otherwise."

"I don't know the truth," Arista admitted. "He sent his family to stay with us, and his wife has expressed her worries about why."

"You could have led with that," Velma said. "If he sent his wife and kids away, it means he's planning something excessively foolish, dangerous, or quite possibly both."

Down the street by the movie theater, a man appeared from around the back carrying a tool bag and matching the description Arista had given her of Frank McKinley.

"I see him," Velma said. "Talk to you soon, Ari."

Velma left the phone booth and followed Frank McKinley at a distance. She didn't have a hard time of it. He kept his eyes lowered as he walked as fast as he could without drawing too much attention. Although he would have been just as well off if he had run. From the moment he set out, a car was not far behind.

Velma sped up, coming abreast of Frank, and hooked her arm around his.

Frank started, "Who—"

"Just talk to me," Velma said. "Don't look around, or behind. You're being followed."

"Why should I trust you?"

"Clem Simmons says you're invited to dinner next Sunday and that his wife wants you to bring music."

"You're not with the union," Frank protested.

"Correct, I'm here to help you."

"No." Frank pulled away from her. "No one else is getting involved!"

Then he did something truly foolish: he ran.

He ducked into a nearby alley, turning over bins and other rubbish to keep Velma from following.

She sighed. Why did they always run?

Velma slapped the brick wall. The hare star sigil exploded from her fingertips and charged forward, expelling bricks from the wall to form a narrow walkway. Velma ran along them and quickly closed the gap between her and Frank. She leapt from the last brick and somersaulted in the air to land before him.

"I'm trying to help you!" Velma called as he stumbled back in surprise.

"No one can help," Frank said, panting. "You'll get hurt."

"You certainly will if you go it alone," Velma said.

These words especially seemed to ring true, for that was when gunfire rang out. A bullet shattered a nearby bottle, piercing the brick next to them.

Velma swore and dragged Frank behind her. She lifted her left arm and expanded the protections on her bracelet. A halo of golden light pulsed from the metal, and the hail of bullets not only rebounded against her bracelet, they flew back to their owner.

She looked over to find Frank's eyes bulging as he stared at her.

"If you're going to run, make sure you're not running into danger first," Velma said.

"You're here to help?" Frank stammered.

"Thank you for finally realizing that. Don't run from me again."

Frank's nod was all the answer she needed. Velma urged him forward out into the street just as an unfamiliar car barreled to a stop in front of them. Its door sprung open.

"Get in!" Dillon Harris called. "Or your day's about to take a turn for the worse."

For the seventh time that year, Dillon had showed up unexpectedly during one of her cases—but this was the first time she had ever been glad to see him.

Pressing a hand on Frank's shoulder, Velma pushed him into the passenger seat. "Don't worry, he's with me." Velma slammed the door shut and got in the back.

She'd barely got in when Dillon took off along the street.

"You're here to help too?" Frank asked.

"Of course I am," Dillon said, somehow managing to carry on the conversation as if they were at a dinner party instead of driving haphazardly down the street. "I want to help with the documents you have in that bag."

Frank clutched the tool bag. "You know about the medical reports?"

"I know that Dr. Richard Patton handed over papers to you the day before he was killed in a mugging. I assume you dragging your heels on delivery is why you aren't dead yet."

"The intended contact is dead," Frank said. "But I couldn't get rid of the reports. They are about an experiment done on poor share-croppers. Or rather, an experiment where they don't treat patients because they want to see how *veneficium pneumoniae* progresses without treatment. I can't just ignore it, but I don't know what to do."

"I do," Dillon said. "Give me the documents—I'll publish them. I'm a reporter."

"You can hash out the details later." Velma glanced over her shoulder once more to see if they were being followed. "Frank needs to get to safety."

"What he needs to do is get out of town," Dillon said.

"How will I manage that?" Frank's voice broke. "I can't even cross the street without being followed. How can I get anywhere?"

"She has a plane," Dillon said.

Frank turned to stare at Velma, a wordless question in his eyes.

"I can't take everything you have in this life with me," Velma said, "but I can take your most precious things with you."

"But, but—" Frank sputtered.

"Don't argue with her," Dillon said. "She's already made up her mind. Which direction do I head in?"

"East—we need to get his family." Velma drew the crow star sigil, sending it ahead to her elder cousin. "Then we get to my plane. You're not coming with us."

"Wouldn't want to get aboard anyway," Dillon said.

"I mean you can't come with us. They're going to keep following this car and you'll have to play decoy. I know it's a lot to ask and—"

"Luckily, I got a full tank, and experience doing this sort of thing," Dillon said easily.

"You also can't publish an article using the reports," Velma finished.

"What? There is no story without them. You can't ask that, not with a story like this! My family are sharecroppers and this could have happened to them."

"I'm sorry, but there's no other way." Velma pulled off her bracelet. As she heated spots with her magic, the bracelet became flexible enough that she could twist it into an infinity symbol. The star sigils etched on it glowed as she imbued it with a different and stronger magic. "I promise someone else will take care of it. Please, don't publish the article, and in return you can ask a favor of me—anything that is reasonable and fair."

"A favor is not— Oh dear," Dillon said mildly as he spotted their pursuers plowing through cars in their way. He spun the car around in the opposite direction, whisking them out of sight. "Fine, you owe me a favor. What's the rest of the plan?" Dillon asked.

Velma handed over the lemniscate and readied her next spell. "I'll tell you on the way."

CHAPTER 27

D espite the pressing events in their near future, taking the scenic route was worth it, if only to hear the delighted gasp from Olivia as the plane appeared over Bramble Crescent in all its glory in the early-afternoon light.

"It really is shaped like a crescent moon!" Olivia cried.

"You thought it wouldn't be?" Velma chuckled.

"Sometimes things are given ironic names," Olivia said rather seriously.

"I share your skepticism," Dillon said. "I thought it would be an exaggeration."

Although he sat back in the cargo hold with his typewriter, the fervent clacking of keys had ceased sometime ago. He now leaned over the seat to watch as Velma flew across the island, skipping past the beaches, the eponymous brambles, and the cheerfully colorful homes spread over it. With Dillon right behind her shoulder, Velma couldn't help but show off her home. She flew around the old light-house, passed over Redbird Park where a tea party was in progress, soared over Mr. Jackson's apiary, and skimmed over town square, to the delight of many and to the outrage of a few.

"That's the inn right there." Velma pointed as she turned her plane about so Olivia could better see.

"I didn't know it was on its own island." Olivia bit her lip as she leaned back in her seat. "How are we going to get across the water?"

"When the tide goes out, a path emerges linking the inn back to town. When it's out, we have about six hours to freely cross, and a little more if you don't mind walking across a sliver of the path. We're pretty good at keeping track of the tides, but for the guests who forget, we have a boat. My sister-in-law swims across if she's desperate, but I've never done it. I just don't like to get my hair wet."

Instead of laughing, Olivia stared balefully at the water and then shuddered. "I don't like it!"

"Well, it's the only way," Velma said. "Cheer up. You have your broomstick. You can always fly over—"

"Olivia," Dillon interrupted, "how would you leave an island without a boat? Brooms aren't an option."

Olivia wrinkled her nose before saying, "I would create a bubble of air and walk under the waves. That way I wouldn't be seen."

"That sounds like a great deal of work," Dillon said.

The girl scowled as she twisted around to look at him. "What would you do?"

"Freeze the water to walk across, of course. Why bother waiting for the tide?" Dillon said, pitching his voice toward Velma. "The distance is not a mile. You can sustain an ice bridge that far."

"It's about a quarter of a mile," Velma said, "but it's not the water that's the problem. The seabed has old enchantments that disrupt such things. Trust me on this. My sister and I thoroughly tested it over the years. It's possible, but it's not worth the effort. I've only managed it once, and I had to run."

Velma landed and parked her plane in her barn. With her bag slung over her shoulder, Velma walked toward the edge of the small cliff that overlooked the inn. Wind rushed past her, plucking at her blouse and trousers as she gazed at the horizon.

Velma smiled all the same, because this was home. No matter how long she had been away or if other places held her heart.

She was home.

"Oh no," Dillon called. "I think she's going to jump!"

"Jump?" Olivia peered around, holding her broomstick. "I thought we were going to walk through town?"

"Why would we need to do that?" Velma said. "This path winds away from the inn, and I prefer a direct route."

"But—"

"This is Bramble Crescent," Velma said, running a hand along her bracelet. "It's unlike any place you've ever been."

Velma stepped off the cliff, and a flurry of birds burst around her. They surrounded her, gentle wings stirring up winds to slow her descent. With a flick of her hand, water streamed upward, freezing and hardening to become steps that Velma walked upon in a moving spiral to the ground.

"Oh! That's what you did." Olivia flew on her broomstick next to Velma, watching the flowing magic. The girl darted close to the spellwork, peering at it in awe. "This is much more interesting. Dillon said you had a parachute."

"Not with me today."

Olivia glanced back at the cliff. "How is he going to get down?"

Her answer arrived as soon as the words were out of her mouth: Dillon stood on his suitcase, the luggage glimmering with magic as he surfed the air. Although he clutched his camera bag and typewriter case tightly, there was a euphoric expression on his face as he circled Velma and Olivia. An expression Velma had seen on many visitors to the island when they realized exactly what it meant to be here. Bramble Crescent had rules regarding magic, but the rules here were not the same as elsewhere.

Here magic was truly limited by your capacity to embrace all you could imagine.

"Race you to the inn!" he called.

"No, just to the ground below us," Velma said. "Your little trick will sputter out halfway to the island. Your broomstick will be fine— you can go ahead safely," Velma added to her cousin.

"That's all right," Olivia said. "I think there was someone waiting for us down there. Is that Aunt Att?"

Although the gray hair was probably the reason why Olivia had thought it was Beatrice, it was not Velma's mother waiting for them. Sitting on the bench next to the sign that pointed to Beacon Inn was Miss Essie and her vividly painted orange-and-green cart.

This was the problem when Velma arrived on the island with some fanfare: everybody knew how to find her.

They landed in front of Miss Essie. Velma and Olivia more gracefully, Dillon less so as he stumbled to keep his full weight off his suitcase.

"How good of you, Violet, to let us know when you're in town," Miss Essie said.

"How good of you," Velma echoed in return as she strode up to the wagon, "to make sure you didn't miss seeing me this time around."

For two weeks every summer, Miss Essie traveled all over the island with her wagon rolling next to her to sell the paper lanterns she spent the rest of the year making. Every home had one of Miss Essie's lanterns, and it was said that those who did not entered winter with bad luck.

"I see you're ready for the lantern festival," Velma said to Miss Essie. "Although you still have quite a few left to sell."

"I've been saving them for you, since the island's favorite pilot had other places to be." Miss Essie tapped a nearby lantern. "I wanted to make sure you didn't forget this year."

"Can I buy one?" Olivia's eyes were fixed on a lantern with a hummingbird painted on it.

"Yes, you can," Miss Essie said sweetly, and then gave Velma a shrewd look.

Miss Essie charged Olivia a penny for the lantern, and Velma coughed up three dollars for two more lanterns. When Miss Essie's gaze fell on him, Dillon quickly picked up a striped lantern.

"Think of it as making up for last year," Miss Essie said when Velma asked what she'd do with the pair.

"With interest," Velma grumbled. She took the lanterns and left before the old woman could convince her to purchase even more.

Luckily, by the time they'd completed their purchases, the tide had gone out, revealing the path.

"What are you going to wish for?" Velma asked her cousin as they headed for the inn.

"Don't know yet," Olivia said. "What could I wish for that I can't find here? This place is amazing!"

As they got closer to the inn, Edythe stepped out onto the front porch, her apron laden with pens and notebooks.

"I expected you a bit sooner. I thought when you jumped off the cliff it was to avoid going through town?" Edythe called cheerfully.

"Miss Essie cornered us." Velma held up the lanterns. "I think she was madder than Carolyn about me not coming to the festival last year."

"They are lovely lanterns too. I'll put them up for you— Oh," Edythe said, noticing Olivia. "Who's this?"

"Olivia," Velma said. "Arista's daughter."

"That can't be!" Edythe cried. "You've grown up so much since I saw you last! Wait, why is she here?"

"I'm mentoring. This is Olivia's first time helping to solve a murder. She did legwork for me that I couldn't do back in Philadelphia regarding Delia's death."

"You, a mentor," Edythe said, amused. "Well, I suppose there are worse people to learn from. She's here for this dinner party, then?"

"We need all the help we can get," Velma said, clearing her throat and gesturing to Dillon. "Which is why one of the guests is more of a decoy."

"Dillon Harris, reporter at the *Owl and Eagle Dispatch*," Dillon said as he dropped his suitcase onto the porch.

"Your partner," Edythe remarked. There was a short pause in which Velma froze uncomfortably, and then her friend continued with a hint of mischief in her dry words. "With the Magnolia Muses. About time you had a new one. I always hated how you went off on your own. Nice to meet you, Dillon. Although I wish we could meet under less unusual circumstances. I'm Edythe Osbourne."

"We don't work together for the Muses," Dillon replied blandly, "but I disagree slightly. I have a feeling these are quite the *usual* circumstances."

A smile stole across Edythe's face. "You're not wrong there. I'll show you to your rooms. Olivia, you'll be up in the innkeeper suite with us. As for Dillon, you'll be in—"

"In Bluebird." Carolyn appeared on the porch so suddenly that even Velma, who knew of the somewhat hidden door on the side, jumped in surprise. Although sitting in her wheelchair didn't allow her to loom over Dillon, Carolyn's lofty air more than made up for it, and she directed simmering disdain toward him. "The Bluebird room will suit him. It's below our suite, and opposite of Dove, since

Velma will be playing the role of guest again. It's best to keep you apart, to support this fiction you're creating."

Dillon matched Carolyn's gaze with a steady grin. "Nice to meet you. I'm—"

"I know exactly who you are. You're that reporter who called my sister a liar, a fraud, and a terrible pilot who was using fancy tricks to distract people. I believe you got her fired too."

"I thought his name was familiar," Edythe whispered.

"That's a misunderstanding . . . ," Dillon began, unbothered by these accusations.

"You also talk too much," Carolyn shot back.

"Well, you have me there," Dillon admitted. "I like to think it all balances out in the end."

"He didn't get me fired." Velma stepped in before Carolyn's words could turn venomous. "The newspaper was going through changes, and I didn't have time for the column anymore. Dillon is my guest, but also here to help with the event—I wouldn't have gotten as far without his help."

Don't be rude to him, Velma added unsaid, only for Carolyn to look away.

"I hope you're prepared to do what's required," Carolyn said to Dillon with a marginally less hostile tone.

"I have just one question," Dillon said. "Why are the rooms named for birds but the inn isn't named after any bird?"

As Carolyn's eyes narrowed dangerously, Edythe quickly clapped her hands. The inn's door flew open and Dillon's and Olivia's bags flew inside. "I'll show you to your room, Dillon. And you too, Olivia."

They shuffled away, leaving Carolyn and Velma facing each other across the porch. The intensity in Carolyn's gaze had not wavered, for her hostility toward Dillon was meant for Velma.

"Before you step inside, I'm going to hear all the details of your case, in order, chronologically and alphabetically if needed."

"I can't do both."

"Then let's start with the simplest thing. Why would you put together a dinner party when the guests could be implicated in murder?"

Velma sat down on one of the wicker chairs on the porch, bringing her eye to eye with her sister.

"They are all looking for objects made by Jeremiah Sitwell. At least one of them is focused on finding a deadly machine made by him. A machine that I think explains how the manor was destroyed in the first place."

"It was destroyed by a storm," Carolyn said.

"Didn't you look through the commonplace book I left behind? There's a list of experiments. Based on that I believe it wasn't a storm at all but the machine and the experiments Jeremiah Sitwell was undertaking."

"There is no machine," Carolyn insisted. "I've been all over the inn lately after finding those creepy dolls. There is nothing."

"I know," Velma said, "but it's what they believe that matters."

"I wonder how they got their information," Carolyn said bitterly. "There are only stories, most of which were made up by our own father."

"There are a few things that weren't," Velma said softly. "*Clarice Sitwell newly made bride / wandered out into the unending tide.*"

"*And she died died died,*" Carolyn recited back. Her mouth twisted in an odd smirk this time, acknowledging how that rhyme would never be forgotten by either of them.

"Dad never made up that rhyme. He said it was old even when he was a kid, which meant the children who lived here when the Sitwells left the island made it up. They witnessed things and put it in a rhyme."

"Or heard chatter and made up their minds about things," Carolyn said. "Remember when you thought there were fairies in the garden because you didn't realize it was the birds stealing the fruits and vegetables? Children have no problem making up things."

"Sometimes they see things adults miss. Like the rhyme; you wouldn't be protesting so much if you didn't agree somewhat," Velma said, unwilling to let the matter go this time. Before, the rhyme had been a whim, but she had learned too much since then. If there was anything that could help, she would not overlook it. "We saw all sorts of things here in the inn."

Carolyn swung her chair around to face Velma. She held up her hands so her left palm faced upward and the other faced down. "If you insist so strongly, then let's do this the proper way."

With a grin, Velma mirrored her sister. Slowly, they began alternately clapping and striking the other's palm, pausing only as Carolyn corrected Velma's placement. Once they'd established the rhythm, Carolyn began reciting, her voice soft, then growing louder as she grew comfortable with the cadence. It went mostly how Velma remembered, until it didn't:

> Up, down, and in the ground.
> Up went Junior getting his fill fill fill
> Down came Sally in a spill spill spill
> In the ground went Mr. Jeremiah who made it so
> Will he come back we don't know know know
> One and two and two and one
> They came and got gone, gone, gone

"I don't remember those parts," Velma said as they finished. She leaned back on the chair, turning over the words and the differences she'd collected over the weeks.

"You never got it right," Carolyn said. "You always mixed it up with the other games or made up your own rhymes. I spent half the time correcting you."

"Granny said it was a call-and-response chant."

"She might have just said that so you would talk to me. It's one of her gentle nudges."

"I've been getting plenty of those," Velma remarked dryly.

They were quiet for a moment, the distant chatter of birds filling the air as they avoided the other's eye.

"What did we argue about anyway?" Carolyn asked.

"You wanted me to stay and run the inn with you. You said I could do Magnolia Muses work just as easily here as I did in Chicago," Velma said. "It spiraled from there."

"Yes, I remember. You said you didn't want to be stuck here with me," Carolyn said rather bluntly.

Velma winced. There were worse things Velma could have said to her sister, but none of them would have cut as deeply.

"I said some rude things too," Carolyn continued. "About you running from problems, being irresponsible and childish, and not someone I could trust."

"You were right to think that."

"Maybe, and you were right to not drop everything to work at the inn. As much as I would love to have you here, you're very good at the job you're doing now. The world is better for it."

"I didn't mean what I said back then," Velma admitted.

"I know—you're just stubborn."

Carolyn was smiling when Velma looked her way. The moment she saw that smile, whatever fears had kept Velma away all these months just vanished. This was her sister, after all. They'd knocked out each other's teeth, blasted holes in the walls, and wrestled with each other in the mud in the garden. It would take a lot more than a silly argument to destroy all of that.

"If I'm stubborn, I learned it from you," Velma teased. "Who holds a grudge for months on end?"

"Well, you were avoiding me since you missed the festival last year."

"That wasn't on purpose," Velma said. "I had a case around that time. Arista called me to Minnesota to help get a man and his family out of town."

"You never said that. I would have understood."

"Or would you think it an excuse?" Velma asked.

"Maybe," Carolyn admitted. "That's better than you saying nothing at all."

"I know," Velma added merrily. "Won't happen next time!"

"Next time!" Carolyn cast her eyes skyward. "Stars save us all! It's one adventure after the other with you!"

"I do plan to be here for the festival this year," Velma said very earnestly. "I'll move the stars themselves to make sure I'm here."

"What about your friend?" Carolyn asked, deceptively serene. "Shall I expect him to be back with you for the festival as well? I saw he bought a lantern."

"Who knows," Velma replied, aiming for a careless tone. "He's just here because he's helping with my case."

Carolyn chortled. "You're lucky that's there so much to prepare for this party, because that's a real stinker of a lie. Regardless of the finer details, you're going to have to introduce him to Mom and Dad. Will you see them tonight?"

"I will. I have something to show them. Quincy got his hands on the twins' elemental pistols—and he's altered them to use wands."

Velma showed her sister the altered pistols, and Carolyn's reaction was everything Velma had expected it to be.

"Just when I thought he couldn't sink lower." Carolyn reached to touch them but pulled back, her eyes dark and uneasy. "These were never meant to use wands. He might get some to work, but they won't last long. What if he stole wands from his sister? Wylda specializes in wands that work with celestial magic."

"These clearly won't work," Velma said.

"Maybe not these two," Carolyn pointed out. "Where are the others?"

"That's the question I'm afraid to get answered. You still have yours, right?"

"I do, but I'm going to go check just to ease my mind." As Carolyn left, the front door opened and Dillon stepped out. As they passed each other, they exchanged a few words, and Carolyn even laughed before she departed. Dillon, in contrast, appeared vastly worried, even more worried than during their previous travels.

Velma slowly rose from the wicker chair. "Ignore my sister—she's all bark."

Dillon gave an uneasy smile. "If I don't pretend to at least shudder, she may do worse. She'll get bored, I'm sure."

"Possibly," Velma lied, as Carolyn did not grow bored of her little games that easily. "If you have a moment, I wanted to ask you more about Members of Rational Clarity. I went through the notes you left and I have a few questions—"

"I'll get to them," Dillon interrupted. "I wanted a tour of the inn, to get a feel of where everything is."

"A tour? It's hardly that big of a place . . . ," Velma began, but something in Dillon's anxious expression changed her mind, influenced perhaps by Carolyn's subtle teasing. It would also be their first chance to be alone without relatives around, and maybe even the only chance for a time. "I suppose it wouldn't hurt if you knew where everything is before the excitement begins. Follow me."

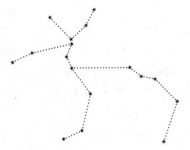

CHAPTER 28

The inn's layout was straightforward enough that there was no real need for a tour, but Velma took Dillon through each of the rooms anyway. In the hall sat the front desk, right next to the coat closet. The usual display of room keys had been moved, and only the most decorative elements remained on the desk. The grand sweeping stairs divided the floor into halves. On the left side was the lounge, dining room, and the two parlors: the more formal Hickory and the casual Dogwood. A hallway snaked around, leading to the kitchen, the inn's office, the door to the sunporch, and the Cardinal bedroom. There was an elevator tucked behind the stairs, next to the bathroom and a small linen closet. On the right side of the stairs were the drawing room, the library, and the conservatory.

"This is actually my favorite room," Velma said as she flung open the door to the conservatory. The glass-walled room gave an unobstructed view of the water, despite the great number of plants that hung from the ceiling. "At night I used to turn off all the lights and sit on the chair here. Somehow the stars were more impressive than if I sat on the roof. That's pretty much it. Upstairs are all the bedrooms. They are named after birds—Carolyn and I painted the signs you see on the doors. The topmost floor is the attic, and that's where my family lives."

Velma turned back to Dillon. He stood there in the center of the room gazing at the violets and tea roses that populated most of the pots. As she'd walked him around the inn, Dillon had asked questions as always, but there was no scrape of his pen nor flash of his camera. It was easy to pretend she had invited him here for typical circumstances, although it was hard to imagine any typical circumstances would ever occur with them.

"I'm glad you're here, Dillon," Velma said.

Brown eyes turned in her direction. "You did invite me."

Velma worried the toe of her boot against the floorboards. "I almost didn't. You were injured very badly because of me. I didn't want to risk that happening again."

"I think I have a good grasp of the danger. And I do many foolish things without asking," he said rather deliberately.

"You were awake." With a flush of embarrassment, Velma dimly recalled her words as he lay asleep. "But didn't the doctor in Kansas— didn't she dose you with sleeping powder?"

"Whatever was in the potion you gave me neutralized most of the impact. I was awake and heard you . . . not that you said anything too interesting. Although I was reassured I wasn't going to be left behind while I was on the mend."

"That would have been the case a few weeks earlier," Velma admitted. "I've grown fond of you since then."

"So she says reluctantly," Dillon teased.

"No, not reluctantly," Velma corrected. "Grudgingly, perhaps, because of our quarrel that played out in the newspaper. Annoyingly because you were like a mushroom cropping up in my cases and jeopardizing my work. But not reluctantly. Not even a little bit. I rather like you, and I think we can have a good time together no matter the circumstances we find ourselves in."

At the end of these words was an uncommon silence. A silence that left her with a trace of unease. Velma was not always good with her words. Not good at expressing feelings and emotions within the limit of human speech. It was why she ran away after Peter's funeral and her fight with Carolyn. Why she tried to defuse tension with a joke. Or even avoided conversations that would only draw minor trouble. Words didn't always make things clear. Sometimes they only complicated things even as you sought clarity.

But sometimes words put into form what action alone couldn't convey.

Dillon was pensive as his eyes met hers, but there was a smile on his face, tender and accepting of her words and more.

"Nothing to say?" Velma couldn't help but ask.

"I've been rendered speechless!" Dillon declared. "For what else is there to say?"

Before he could ramble further, Velma kissed him. This simple act succeeded in stopping the flow of words, although it was only a temporary measure. When they broke apart they remained entangled with the other, whatever boundaries they had placed between them now thoroughly vaulted over. It was too soon to call such tender feelings love, but it was certainly the blossoming of something special.

"To think all of this," Dillon gestured vaguely about the room, his eyes twinkling with good humor, "had to occur just for you to admit you actually like me."

"Well, it's easy to make a confession when you're somewhat confident affection would be returned," Velma replied.

"How did you know?" he asked.

"Besides the fact that you took a magic bullet for me and you kept making excuses to continue traveling with me? You kept the favor I gave you and used it when you had other cards to play."

"It was the perfect time to use it," Dillon said. "Velma, you know you never had to offer it in the first place. There is very little you could ask of me that I wouldn't agree to in the end."

"I know that now," Velma admitted. "I did ask you to fly my plane before I jumped out of it. That you didn't walk away afterward should have been a sign."

"Here I thought I showed my hand with the photographs!"

Recalling how often a camera flash went off around her, Velma affected a wearied sigh. "Dare I ask how many are there?"

"Less than you think and quite a few by chance," Dillon said. He pretended to scowl as Velma laughed at him. "It's not my fault something interesting always occurs with you in the frame."

"That's the excuse you'll be using?"

"That's my story and I'm sticking with it." As he moved to kiss her, something crashed distractingly nearby.

Dillon jumped, looking around for the source, but Velma knew exactly where to look.

Striding forward, she noticed with little surprise that the panel for the hidden door was sticking out just a tad. With a sigh, she wrenched it open and found Olivia sprawled at her feet.

"You need to stop listening at doors," Velma said to her cousin.

Olivia squirmed where she lay, avoiding Velma's eyes. "I was looking for secret passageways. Edythe said there're several in the house. I didn't mean to—I got stuck. The door wouldn't open upstairs, and I'm sorry—"

"Well, aren't you a regular Athena Vance?" Dillon cut in, saving the girl from further embarrassment. "I don't think any passageway here will go to a silver mine."

Olivia sat up, beaming. "You've read the books too!"

"I have a niece around your age. I read a few just to see what the fuss was about and was rather impressed. Secret passages, you say? Now, that sounds fun."

"It's not as exciting as you think," Velma protested. "They're just old servant corridors. They don't lead anywhere interesting."

"That's because it's old hat to you," Dillon said. "The tour isn't over yet."

Maybe it was his infectious smile, or the giddiness inside her, but Velma agreed with little protest. "I suppose we can continue the tour," Velma said. "There are eight passageways in use. This goes upstairs to the grandfather clock in the hallway. To open the door, you press the panel hidden behind the clock parts. To enter from this side, you have to do this." Velma shut the wall panel and then went over to the shelves, where several potted plants sat. She rearranged them into a five-pointed star, and once the last was put into place, the door popped open. "Order matters."

"Is this the trickiest one?" Olivia asked.

"Because it's in plain sight. They aren't all so complicated. I'll show you."

Crossing the hall into the dining room, they found the table set for tomorrow with fresh flowers in the vases and long tapered candles resting in the candelabra. Dillon and Olivia, however, were not admiring the decorations but looking intently around the room.

"It's behind the landscape painting!" Dillon declared.

"Olivia was supposed to figure it out," Velma teased as her cousin's face fell. "But you're right." Velma crossed over to the wall to the painting of the sea. She lifted the frame to reveal the hidden door-knob. "This one leads to the sunporch."

"Can we try one more?" Olivia asked. "I want to guess this time."

"Certainly," Velma said, hiding a smile at Dillon's exaggerated exasperation.

Velma took them into the kitchen. Other than the preparations for tomorrow's dinner laid out, the room was empty for the moment.

"There are three in here," Velma said, watching as Olivia's eyes flitted about. "You just need to find one."

Velma and Dillon stood in silence as they both watched Olivia carefully pace about the kitchen . . . until she spotted a small cabinet.

"Here," she said, and at Velma's encouraging nod, Olivia opened the cupboard doors to expose the lift hidden inside.

"This lift goes right up to the innkeeper quarters," Velma said. "We use it to bring up heavy trays or laundry from the downstairs guest room. Although of course Carolyn and I used to travel up in it. You just pull the ropes here."

As Olivia studied the lift intently, Dillon pointed to the area that led to the speakeasy. "Is this another passageway?"

Velma nodded. "It leads to our little speakeasy. Through it, a path leads back to town. It's a very long path, but people make the trip because my mother brews the best tonics around."

"Aunt Att is a bootlegger too?" Olivia said. "I didn't know that!"

"That's not important right now," Velma said hastily.

Velma brought them back into the hall, intending to show them the elevator tucked into the back, but Dillon stopped in the middle of the entrance hall. He made a small frame with his hands and slowly turned in a half circle.

"Can I install a camera in the front hall? I have my smaller camera with me. If I hide it at the right angle, we'll get photographs of the guests arriving and moving between the rooms."

"That's not a bad idea. Where do you think it should go?"

"The chandelier," Olivia said, pointing upward. "It's a bird's-eye view."

"That'll be very difficult to remove while the party is ongoing. You should stick it in a candle," Velma said, going to the front desk. "Perfect line of sight."

Setting up the camera didn't take too long. The tricky part was hiding the trigger under the rug in a way that didn't make it obvious it was there or put it in danger of getting broken as people walked across it.

As they worked, Velma looked up to see Edythe standing at the top of the stairs. Her face was cast in shadow, and it was hard to make out her expression as she watched.

The evening was a quiet one. Velma paid a quick visit to her parents at their home. Rodney and Beatrice were delighted to meet Dillon and warmly welcomed him. But they were not so distracted by his presence to restrain from asking dozens of questions about preparations, weighing Velma down with potions, grumbling about what Quincy did to the elemental pistols, and asking again if Velma truly didn't want them there for the evening.

"You'll be much more helpful if you stay in town," Velma assured her parents. "I bought lanterns from Miss Essie, and I'll place them in the attic window. One light, all is well. Two lights, it's dangerous, so stay away. And three, I need your help."

"I don't need any lights to tell me to help!" Rodney insisted.

"The girls know what they're doing." Beatrice placed a hand on Rodney's arm. "Plus, we must make sure these unscrupulous guests don't get up to mischief here in town. Can I see the photographs again, Dillon?"

Dinner at the inn was hurried, despite attempts at light conversation. Carolyn and Velma hashed out all the areas in the inn that needed to be closed and sealed to contain potential shenanigans. Olivia listened eagerly, but Dillon and Edythe both got up from the table early. Dillon made phone calls from the office, and through the open door Velma could hear his conversation with one of his newspaper contacts.

Edythe had vanished, and not even Carolyn knew where she'd gone.

To keep from dwelling on this, Velma spent the time after dinner sealing passageways and limiting access to portions of the house. She also went down into the hidden workshop. There was something she had overlooked, Velma knew, but she couldn't figure out what it was. Although, like Carolyn had said, there was no sign of the machine either in the items left behind on the tables or even in the blueprints left by the old man.

Dillon was still on the phone when Velma reappeared, but he hung up hastily to join her as she went to set spells outside the inn.

They walked the perimeter of the tidal island together while Velma flicked spells on the inn's grounds and quietly talked over the facts of the case one last time.

"Will these spells out here be enough?" Dillon asked.

"They'll squash any attempt to fly a broom to or away from the inn, and there are a series of quiet alarms that will ensure no one can leave or arrive without me knowing."

"What if something gets past your spells?"

"That's where I'm hoping you'll see something I won't. It's why you're here, after all."

"What a shame. I thought it was just my charming personality."

As Velma finished the circuit, she spotted pale golden smoke emitting from the center of the hidden maze in the garden.

"Why don't you go and try to charm my sister? I have one more thing out here."

"Don't stay out here long." Dillon pressed a kiss to her cheek.

As Dillon went back into the inn, Velma walked through the maze to where Edythe's writing cottage stood.

Light spilled out from the window, but the source of smoke was a small cauldron bubbling on the cottage's porch. Edythe sat, stirring the contents with a wooden spoon. She did not look up at Velma's approach, but the tensing of her shoulders said that Velma's arrival did not go unnoticed.

"I thought you might be working, but this is not what I expected," Velma said.

Edythe's reply was swift. "I'm making candles. You know I don't brew anymore."

"So I'm told."

Edythe looked up as smoke flowed around her like a shroud. "You don't believe me?"

"I don't like being lied to," Velma said. "It makes everything confusing, and I don't know what or who to trust. I need to know I can trust you."

Edythe's smile was wan. "Am I that suspicious?"

"You are, I'm afraid. That's not a bad thing and could be useful."

Edythe twirled her wooden spoon. "How useful?"

"Exceedingly. Laverna Addison knows you. If Delia got tangled up with any of this crew, they might know your name and face. I want you to play up that connection, even if it means acting as a red herring. Talk to them and gain their trust. Make them think you are on their side."

"I'm not an actor. When your family puts on those plays, I'm horrible."

"The key to playing a part is mixing the truth with a lie," Velma said. "Just find the right truth and use that as a core."

"And you trust me to do that?"

"You're family, I trust you," Velma replied, even though there was no other answer she could give.

"What if I told you that I know Kenneth Poole?"

Velma suppressed her surprise and forced her words to remain steady. "Then I'd ask why you didn't mention it before."

"I wasn't certain before. Not until you sent the photographs to Carolyn so she'd know if any one of them showed up early to the inn. I saw his photograph. He's using a different name now, but I know him as Malcolm Gladstone."

"*He's* Gladstone?" Velma asked. "Are you sure?"

Edythe nodded. "I swear under all that the moon's light touches, he's Gladstone."

"He's been hiding in plain sight this whole time. I've been looking for him. Though, in an odd turn of fate, it looks like I managed to invite him to the dinner party after all!"

"Gladstone's a slippery fellow," Edythe warned. "He's good at re-creating recipes and modifying previous work, but he couldn't make anything from scratch. I don't think that's changed. That's why I recognize his work after all these years. Same methods, same process."

"You're saying he's not very good at this? What about machine making?"

"I can't speak to now," Edythe said. "When I knew him, it was well known that his expertise was in waxes and glosses."

"Waxes and glosses," Velma murmured, thinking how Kenneth said he worked as a factory manager and how Velma thought he meant producing record players. But if he worked with waxes and glosses . . .

Velma snapped her fingers as thoughts collided in her mind. "I think I know what led to Wise Records shutting down! They got caught producing enchanted records!"

CHAPTER 29

T he last thing Velma did to prepare for the dinner was leave the
inn entirely. Both she and Dillon, actually. He went all the way
to the mainland to take the ferry in, while Velma meandered around
town, pretending to be a new arrival. She dressed the part, pairing
a blouse with billowing trousers for ease of movement. The vest she
wore on top allowed her to tuck the hatpin, the pocket watch, and
the sheet music in the pockets. The blouse's short sleeves didn't hide
her bracelets, but if the night went well, the visibility of her magic
wasn't going to be a worry.

Velma spent the better part of the day asking some old classmates
about their record collections, although none had the albums she
was looking for. When the hour approached to start making her way
back to the inn, Velma's plans changed abruptly when she spotted a
lone figure headed right for the path toward Beacon Inn.

Velma didn't have to come close to see it was Kenneth Poole. Or
at least, the man who had introduced himself by that name. How
lucky it was that she came across him first! Knowing he was Gladstone, she looked upon him with fresh eyes. He had told her several
things about Giles Pacer, but what was true and what had he told her
just to simply lead her astray? Had he been looking for more of Edwin
Addison's notes because he sought to re-create the mysterious, dangerous machine that Jeremiah Sitwell had made? How did someone
who made potions make the move to machines? Unless the machine
had an alchemical component.

All these questions and more fluttered around her head as she approached him.

"I see we meet again," Velma called. "Did you find what you were looking for?"

"You!" Kenneth sputtered. He clutched the briefcase he held even tighter at the sight of her. "What are you doing here?"

"I was invited to Beacon Inn," Velma said, pulling out the invitation she'd fashioned for herself. "And you?"

"The same. Although I did not think I arrived at the right place." Kenneth glanced across the water. "No one told me the inn came with its own moat."

"It's not a moat. I heard it's a tidal island," Velma said, taking on a rather lighthearted tone. "The path before us right now is only open when it's low tide. Isn't it so whimsical?"

"Sounds inconvenient to me," Kenneth said.

"Shall we cross? It's still a bit early, but I'd rather get inside," Velma said.

Kenneth nodded. "I agree, although I am in no rush to spur this evening on."

For someone who'd once trapped her in a circle of magic, he didn't do anything as rash this time around. He radiated nervousness, and Velma kept her eyes on the briefcase, sorely tempted to snatch it from him. As they walked, she discreetly flicked a small enchantment onto the case that would let her know when the seal was broken.

Arriving at the inn's front door, Kenneth rang the doorbell. Once and then twice. The door opened slowly, and Edythe stood there to greet them.

The understanding she had reached with her sister had almost been ruined when Velma suggested that Edythe act as innkeeper for the evening. It wasn't that Carolyn couldn't do the same. Velma wanted to eliminate the chance for sharp-eyed guests to notice the resemblance between Velma and Carolyn.

That was one reason. The other was what Velma hoped to see play out before her right now.

Upon seeing Edythe, Kenneth shuffled backward and gripped the briefcase even tighter, proving without a doubt that Edythe had been right. This was the same man she had known, who now dabbled in those enchanted coins that had caused so much trouble, and who Velma suspected had played a bigger role at Wise Records than originally claimed.

Edythe paused for a moment too long, long enough that Velma jumped in to start things off.

"We're here for the party," Velma said, showing off the invitation.

"You're early, but not by much. Shall we take your things?" Edythe called. Dutifully, Olivia made an appearance in a neat argyle skirt and blouse she tried not to tug at. Velma handed Olivia her empty satchel, but Kenneth held on to his briefcase.

"I'll keep this with me," he said.

"As you wish," Edythe replied. "This way, please. You can wait for the other guests in here." Edythe opened the door to the Dogwood parlor, ushering them inside. A tray of glasses and ice water had been placed on a low table. "Please ring the bell if you need further assistance."

Velma went to the side table to pour herself a drink. Kenneth found a chair as far away as possible and sat down, placing the briefcase between him and the wall.

"I'm starting to wish I did not arrive so early," Velma said.

Kenneth tugged at his collar. "I planned to be early."

"Hate being late?"

"I had to see what was in store."

"You came a pretty long way for that."

"I have some business in the area."

Velma eyed the briefcase but said nothing, not wanting to press too hard, too soon. They had just settled into an uneasy silence when the door opened and Portia Milburn entered.

The music shop owner and covert wandmaker who Velma had met at the auction was much as she remembered. And if Velma wasn't mistaken, the other woman was wearing the same gray dress she had worn the day they'd met. Portia's plain and ill-fitting attire made her look rather out of place, and even the faint touch of cosmetics proved that this might have been the best outfit she could manage.

The only difference was the wariness that entered and took root in her features.

"I thought I'd be the first," Portia said. "I suppose if you're here, Kenneth, it can't be all that bad."

"I'm glad you feel that way. Have you met Miss Velma Frye?"

Portia turned in Velma's direction, then she gasped as recognition filled her eyes. "You were at the auction!"

"I do keep getting invited to the strangest of places," Velma said gaily.

"Delia invited you?" Portia asked.

"She had. I just can't believe it," Kenneth said. "The last I heard, Delia wanted nothing to do with us. To see she's arranged all this, it doesn't make sense."

"She wants something," Portia mused.

"What would that be?" Velma asked.

"I don't know. I considered her one of my best friends and I didn't often know her mind," Portia replied ruefully. "That was a lifetime ago."

"Big movie star doesn't have time for the little people anymore," Kenneth said, "although she wouldn't have gotten as far without us. She was working for Holden Johnstone when she came into the studio with you. Would have stayed working for him if she wasn't noticed by—"

"That's all in the past," Portia interrupted. "And has nothing to do with why we are here right now."

"Maybe Delia is feeling nostalgic," Velma threw out, stirring this cauldron of brewing trouble she'd spotted behind the pair's words. "Old friends, new acquaintances, mutual partners."

"Mutual partners?" Portia asked.

"I knew Holden Johnstone as well," Velma said, very eager to pursue this newly revealed connection. "There hasn't been a better man to have a building dropped on him, in my opinion."

Kenneth snorted. "I thought that was a rumor! Although I agree. He had a stranglehold on distribution, and once he was gone, you could choose who got the goods."

"I thought you were based on the East Coast?" Portia asked Velma. "How do you know about a fellow like Johnstone?"

"You meet all sorts of people by chance as you travel around the world, I find. I suppose it's the same for you?" Velma said.

"Well, as interesting as the man was, we know he won't be here tonight," Portia said briskly. "I wonder who else was invited?"

"So do I," Kenneth said. "I'd like to know who I'm stuck with."

"Stuck?" Portia echoed.

"This inn has a fun quirk: when the tide is high, you can't cross back to the main island," Kenneth explained. "I can't imagine many people enjoy that here."

"The tide closes the path!" Portia cried. "That won't do at all. I've rented a room in town."

Intrigued by these very deliberately made plans, Velma asked, "This is an inn, why wouldn't you stay here?"

"I never planned to remain overnight. Strange invitations to even stranger places never bode well!"

An uneasy silence followed Portia's words, but it was broken almost at once by the door opening for the latest arrival.

Laverna Addison was bedecked in a tailored suit of a plum so dark it was nearly black, paired with garnet stones that shone at her ears and neck. She held a matching clutch purse in lace-gloved hands. Her arrival charged the air of the room as both Portia and Kenneth tensed up at her entrance.

"I should have known you would be here," Laverna said by way of greeting. "Mysterious notes. Strangers brought to a place on the far edge of the world. This is all your doing, Kenneth."

"Not at all," Kenneth replied. "I wouldn't invite you here on purpose, let alone by accident."

"Then you, Portia?"

"I don't go out of my way to have a terrible evening," Portia grumbled.

If Laverna was bothered by this show of unity, she brushed it off and turned her attention to Velma.

"What is the great Velma Frye doing here? I think the arrival of such a pilot would have spurred some news." Laverna flashed a brittle smile. One that acknowledged Velma's lie about when they'd first met and that Laverna had learned the truth in the weeks since. That Laverna chose not to reveal Velma's lies was an interesting choice, and Velma made a mental note to dig further for the explanation.

"I'm here for the same reason as you," Velma said. "I was invited."

"That's not why you're here," Laverna snarked.

"I suppose her reason is the same as the rest of us," Kenneth said. "Chasing after stories of stardust."

"We all got letters," Portia said. "Shall we compare them?"

Laverna shook her head. She settled in an armchair that was the most impressive yet most uncomfortable in the parlor. "What does it matter what they say? The only purpose was to get us here, and in that case they have done their job."

"If you are here," Kenneth said, "I have a good guess about the others who might join us. What are the odds of Strickland showing up?"

"Don't spoil the mood," Portia said. "I was hoping the blackguard got himself speared with the wrong end of a wand."

"Oh, I wish the same." Kenneth's foot nervously jumped next to his briefcase. "He'll be here, though. Maybe the others too."

"And a few surprises like Miss Frye here," Laverna said. "How do you know Delia?"

"I know her as well as you do," Velma replied.

Such light words betrayed the trio in three vastly different ways. Portia frowned, Kenneth blinked worriedly, and Laverna's gaze flickered with concern. Velma was still considering what to make of such reactions when Dillon strolled into the room.

"Who are you?" Laverna demanded. Her voice was sharp and deeply flustered. For good reason. While they had met and spoken with Velma, none could say the same of Dillon. He was an unknown to each of them, for all that he knew so much about their past and present endeavors.

"I was invited too." Dillon held up an invitation. "Although I wonder if my questions got me such a summons in the first place."

"Questions about what?" Laverna pressed.

"I'm a reporter," he said, "writing about the history of Wise Records, with an interest in its early talents such as Delia Moore, Marie Drew, and Posy Newman."

Dillon's words rang true enough that Laverna didn't press for more answers, although Portia continued to throw Dillon a suspicious look as he sat on the window seat.

"Why would you want to write about that?" Kenneth forced a boisterous laugh that shook uneasily. "No one would be interested in a book about a failed company."

"There's always an interest," Dillon said, "especially with such remarkable characters gathered here. I know that you, sir, were a manager at Wise's factory. Miss Addison here is the sole daughter and heir to Edwin Addison, who cofounded the company." Dillon slowly turned to face Portia. "And Posy Newman made blues records at Wise."

Portia's hand went to her necklace as she attempted a small laugh. "If you've done your research properly you'll know it was only one record. I barely had anything to do with the company."

"Which makes it even more interesting that you are here," Dillon replied. "Although we are missing a few others. Care to take a bet about who will pass through those doors next?"

"No," Kenneth remarked. "I don't do that anymore."

Portia grunted. "I suppose some things change for the best."

"I'll take that bet," Velma said. This was no game Dillon was playing at. He was warning her of something in the only way he could. "Who will also show up?"

"Given what I've seen so far, Brayton Strickland will make an appearance, and I wouldn't be surprised if he brought along Quincy Hodges."

Dillon paused here after uttering the name, and it was a good thing he was showboating, because surprise rippled through Velma with such extraordinary strength that she couldn't hide it. This was the worst possible news. The list of things Quincy could ruin, even on accident, was far too long. Then again, this was news she should have seen coming. Quincy had started this by stealing the items in the first place, so why shouldn't he be here tonight?

As Velma tried to compose herself, she found she wasn't the only one taken by surprise.

"Hodges!" Laverna exclaimed as Portia whispered the name as well. Kenneth had jumped to his feet in clear outrage. "Did you say Quincy Hodges? Are you sure?"

"It's only a guess," Dillon said, "but I'm often right. Just as I suspect you know him quite well from a job you did together."

"You're barking up trees you need to leave alone," Laverna said to Dillon. "If you want to publish any articles in the future, you need to forget it all."

Velma stretched languidly in her chair. "In my experience, when people say to leave things alone, that means the person in question knows something worth telling."

Velma's words had Portia turning to Laverna, who immediately accused the older woman: "You said you knew nothing. That Quincy knew more than you ever did. Did you lie?"

"Wouldn't be the first time," Kenneth said. "Pacer told me—"

"Giles Pacer is dead, so what he says doesn't matter!" Laverna cried.

"I don't know, Laverna," Velma said. "The dead have plenty to say. I was at the auction at his manor, and overheard quite a few interesting details."

Surprisingly, Laverna went quiet—and so did Kenneth and Portia. They knew Velma had been at the auction, having spoken to her. So why the guilt-stricken looks on their faces when Velma's words were meant for Laverna alone?

CHAPTER 30

Before Velma could prod the conversation in a favorable direction, the door swung open to reveal Marie Drew.

Resembling a faded siren of silent films who couldn't handle the move to talkies, Marie hardly looked like the respectable housewife Velma and Dillon had met in Dallas. Her copper-colored dress was ten years out of fashion, and her jewelry, mainly an ornate hairpin and gaudy earrings, only deepened that impression.

Marie took a half step back out of the room, staring at the gathered group before her, then shoved a hand into her pocket to withdraw a wand.

"You!" Marie stormed into the room, waving the wand in Laverna's face. "What are you all doing here?"

Laverna raised a hand and gently moved the tip of the wand away from her face, as if flicking away a tree branch that had swung into her view. "I should ask the same of you. I don't know who you're fooling with that wand. No one here is going to fight with you even though you sold my father's pocket watch to pay your bills."

"I lost it!" Marie said.

"Likely story given the debts you accrued," Kenneth replied.

"Yes, you've been 'losing' all sorts of things." Portia shook her head. "Like the glasses."

"They were taken!" Marie gulped as she finally took notice of Velma and Dillon. "Them! They took the glasses from me. Why are they here?" She backed away again, her wand useless in her hand. "I knew I shouldn't have come! I can't stay here. I'm not staying here with any of you! Nothing is worth it!" Whirling with righteous fury, Marie stormed out, slamming the door behind her for good measure.

"Oh dear, she left, how terrible," Laverna drawled.

Kenneth just shook his head. "She'll be back, though."

The grumbling was persistent in the room over this. Grumbling that Velma let continue. Not because it was interesting or revealing, but because she spotted movement in the window outside.

She tapped two fingers against her armrest. Seeing the gesture, Dillon sat forward, asking the group, "How badly in debt is she?"

These words were catnip to this group, and they quickly began to complain and speak of Marie's past endeavors and sins.

With their attention focused on Dillon, Velma barely needed to cast a spell to make her escape. She quietly stood up and slipped unnoticed out of the room and down the hallway.

At the front door, Marie Drew had met interference in the plan to escape in the form of Edythe. Velma's friend stood tall and unbothered by the wand Marie pointed at her, calmly arguing down the older woman. Even if she had done the implausible and made it into town, Marie could not leave. Velma had called in favors all over the island, including asking that the ferry would not depart with any stranger aboard. Nobody was leaving Bramble Crescent, so Marie and all the rest could do their worst.

Sidestepping this scene, Velma slipped out the side door by the conservatory and walked onto the porch. Tapping one of her earrings, she stirred the magic in one of the statues set out in the garden, newly cast by Dillon's sister.

"Are you sure this is the right place?" Brayton asked, his voice coming as clear as if Velma were standing right next to him, but she was only hearing him through the amplification spell.

"It is," Quincy said. "The door is out here, but they keep it locked tight. I couldn't get in there before."

"That won't be a problem. If the machine is here, I'll do anything to get to it."

"I can't promise it is," Quincy said, his voice quavering. "It's the only place left. . . . I've been everywhere else. Do you need the machine? Gladstone was able to replicate—"

"He replicated a copy that blew up. I want the real machine in my possession."

"What if it's broken?"

"Then I'll worry about that. You just make sure it's here. If not, I might pay your family a visit."

Their voices moved away from the statue, but Velma was already on her way around the inn, turning off the amplification spell as she speedily headed into the backyard.

Even if Velma hadn't overheard that conversation, she would have been suspicious of Brayton from the way he intently peered up at the inn.

Standing in Brayton's shadow, Quincy anxiously dabbed a hand-kerchief on his perspiring forehead. Upon hearing that Dillon had spotted Quincy on the island, Velma had been prepared to hex her cousin into the next year . . . but now, not so much. He had lied to her, betrayed the family trust twice over, and his actions had led to several deaths—but it seemed he might have been an unwilling puppet in all of this.

Velma cleared her throat rather loudly, and the pair spun around with great haste.

"I thought I saw someone outside. What do you think of the garden? The innkeeper spoke a great deal about the flowers."

Quincy blinked at Velma in exaggerated surprise. "Miss Velma Frye! What a surprise to see you!"

"I can say the same," Velma replied, hoping that Quincy would temper his words. He was never a good actor, prone to overexaggerating in the family plays.

"We are here for dinner," Brayton drawled. "Hodges mentioned visiting the inn before and thought I would be interested in taking a further look at the grounds. Although I'd be happy to tour this place with you instead. I'm delighted to see you again, and even more to finally get your name. I thought often of you and our interesting conversation."

"Perhaps we can tour the grounds later. I just stepped out for a moment of fresh air," Velma said demurely. She didn't step away, but she didn't move closer, either. She remembered her interaction with Strickland at the baseball game all too well. "I can't stay out here too long or the others will wonder where I went," Velma continued.

"Others?" Quincy asked.

"I don't know all their names quite well. They're very interesting," Velma said, pretending to think hard. "One sells musical instruments, one worked in a factory, one's a journalist, and there's a woman whose father owned a recording company."

Brayton scowled. "I think I have a fair idea who they are. Stars guide and protect me!"

Brayton strode off without a word more.

Once the other man was gone, Quincy said quickly to Velma, "Velma, I can—"

"You can apologize and explain later," Velma said. "For now, you must keep him distracted."

"Why did you invite them here?" Quincy said. "It's the worst thing you could have done! These people are after something dangerous, and they think it's somewhere in the inn!"

"Why are you blaming me? You gave them a taste. First with

the items you stole from the inn. Then you modified the elemental pistols. Where are the other ones?"

"Not with me," he said quickly. "How did you know about the pistols? I lost them."

"No, you didn't. Olivia has them."

"She followed me?" Quincy exclaimed.

"She's worried about you," Velma said. "And for good reason. You're in trouble."

Quincy's shoulders slumped. "I've been in trouble for months, but I couldn't say anything, even when you showed up at my house. He's been having me watched. I could only hope you figured it out like you always do. I tried to get out of the deal earlier, and that's why I moved my family. Strickland found me anyway. He has his goons watching them in case I don't follow through. Otherwise . . . " He let his words trail off, unable to say the rest.

"I'll help," Velma said simply. "But you must help me. Keep Brayton distracted. Keep the others distracted too. I have a plan in the works."

Quincy went on ahead before Brayton could take notice of his long absence. Although no one's absences would be especially noticed. Returning to the inn, Velma found that everyone had begun to wander around instead of remaining in the parlor. Voices were coming from different rooms, some louder than others. Before Velma could go investigate, she spotted Edythe shutting the door to the drawing room, her head turned to speak to whoever was in the room with her.

Velma went around the hall to the main closet. Pushing the heavy coats aside, she found the hidden doorknob. She twisted it open and stepped into the narrow passageway. Running along the height of the house from downstairs to the attic, the passageway used to open to the second floor, but that access had been blocked when electricity was added. The stairs, however, still ran against the draw-ing room.

Settling on a step, Velma took off one of her earrings and manip-ulated the amplification spell once more. She placed it against the wall and pressed her ear nearby. At once the muffled sounds became as clear as if she were sitting in the room with them.

"You know about it too," Kenneth said.

"Delia told me," Edythe replied.

"Everything? About the recordings?"

"She told me enough," Edythe assured him. "Delia and I are old friends. I owe it to her."

"You owe it to us. What we're doing needs all the help we can find."

"Yes, Delia told me that as well, but I have heard nothing from her about next steps."

"Other than this party," Kenneth said. "Which you know more about than I do—how did you manage to worm your way in here?"

"Delia helped me get into the innkeeper's good graces. They are so desperate for help, I could have said anything and gotten a job here."

"Have you looked for the machine?"

"Not as much as I could. I was kept busy, but it's hard. The inn was built over the original house."

"It has to be here—it has to be!" Kenneth insisted.

"How do you know?" Edythe said. "The innkeeper might have already found it."

"We'd all know if they did. Which is why we must follow the plan. No deviations."

"There won't be," Edythe said. "Give me the briefcase and I'll take care of these potions. You leave first. I'll be right behind you."

Velma listened for just a bit longer to the silence before she moved away from the wall.

The briefcase held potions. That wasn't far from Velma's speculations, although the revelation paled in comparison to the rest of the conversation. Velma hadn't expected Edythe to play the role of confidant so well either. If she hadn't asked Edythe to do this . . .

Velma fiddled with her earring, trying not to let her doubts rule here. Velma had doubts about everything this evening, except for things in her direct control, but she couldn't let them distract her.

Instead of exiting through the closet and risk being caught, Velma climbed the stairs all the way to the attic. Emerging from the panel in there, she went to the window and popped it open. Velma easily walked along the roof until she got to the big oak tree, then climbed down. With her feet once more on solid ground, she checked her appearance in her compact mirror and walked back to the inn.

Laverna stood on the far end of the porch looking up at the dangling bird feeder. She had lit a cigarette, and smoke encircled her head like a crown. Her gaze was in the opposite direction Velma had arrived from. She might have not seen Velma come down from the roof, but still, she wasn't surprised to see Velma out on the grounds.

"Miss Frye," Laverna replied. "I suppose this is all your doing?"

"What did I do?" Velma asked. "Delia was the one who sent the invitations."

"Delia isn't here, just like at the salon. Then, just as now, you went out of your way to speak with me, *Viola Heyward*. Don't think I didn't notice you watching me, or asking those silly artists all about me. You're lying still—Velma Frye isn't the name your parents gave you. I know because Beacon Inn has long been a name I've known." Laverna blew a puff of smoke into the air. "My father thought once to buy it some years ago, but was dissuaded by the fact that the couple who owned it had two young daughters. The eldest daughter, Carolyn Rose, works here now, and you are clearly the other one, Violet. After my father died, I couldn't afford this place. Ironically, I wanted it more since it's the last connection to my family because nothing remains of the town I grew up in."

"Ardenton, you mean," Velma said.

Laverna expelled a breath, pain streaking her face before retreating behind the mask of an unlucky heiress. "I haven't heard that name in a long time."

"What happened there?"

Laverna tossed Velma a disdainful look. "If you know the town's name, then you have a fair idea. Our life in Ardenton ended the night my father attempted to re-create his grandfather's greatest folly. It didn't go well, but my father learned his lesson and turned his talents elsewhere to greater success, short-lived as Wise Records ended up being."

"What about Ardenton?"

"What about it?" Laverna asked with a flash of vexation.

"Nothing grows there anymore. Nothing can live there anymore. He created a *record company* afterward—"

"My father was not one to dwell in the past. We suffered too. Mother had the magic sickness and it was painful watching her fade away. Starting Wise Records was my idea to get my father inventing again. Anyone can start a business, but keeping it going is the hard part. There's competition, there's sabotage, and there's merchandise no one buys. Wise might have lasted longer, but Father got one of his ideas on how to make the phonograph better."

"Make it better how?"

"If I knew, I'd be making a fortune selling them now," Laverna said.

"And not changing the world with Members of Rational Clarity instead?" Velma asked.

Laverna smirked. "You think I'm part of that group? Is that how I got invited?"

"They are all members, then?"

"Oh yes. All believers of the just cause, as I'm told. When Hodges found those items he gave them the tools to act on their plans. Once they saw how powerful the items could be, they reached out to me, thinking I'd know more. I knew about a few, luckily, and I was able to strike a deal, because you can't argue with fanatics."

"What about the arcane exposition? What are their plans for the machine?"

"If you want details about this group, you're not going to get them from me. I'm not part of it—I just told them I was so they would help me. They were already looking for the machine anyway, as they had seen my father's old papers."

"Why go through with the ruse?"

"I don't want them to get their hands on the machine. What happened in Ardenton was the work of an imperfect copy. If they get the real thing, imagine what could happen to Chicago."

As Velma sat with this piece of information, Laverna pressed on, sensing her advantage. "I know it's here. My grandmother said they left only with the clothes on their backs. She always said the machine destroyed itself, but they never checked. That's why I came here to look, especially when Delia told me the others were determined to find it."

"I know—you left behind your creepy dolls," Velma remarked archly.

"They never found much," Laverna said without shame. "The magic is strong here."

"Then maybe you should leave it alone."

"Not even the strongest of spells can stand against those willing to bludgeon it." Laverna returned, her eyes ablaze with earnestness.

"I want to destroy it, not use it. You want to destroy it even more than I do. If we work together, we can accomplish this."

Velma shook her head. "There is no machine here. We've never found anything. Trust me, we have been all over the inn."

"This place has secrets. I found patches and places where spell-work was strong and resistant. Help me help you. Because the only thing standing between the others tearing this place apart and locking you and the rest of your family in a cupboard somewhere is my word."

Velma doubted Laverna had such power, but nor could she dismiss the potential sway Laverna had over the others, even in the smallest of ways.

"What do I need to do?" Velma asked.

"I need time to search away from the group. If my harlequins are still around—"

"They're not," Velma cut in.

Laverna licked her lips nervously. "Well, I suppose I'll need more time to look. Can you give me that time?"

"I can make arrangements," Velma said, promising that and nothing more.

The front door swung open.

"I finally found you!" Olivia called as she stood in the doorway, but as she saw Laverna, Olivia hastily blurted out, "Dinner is ready. Everyone is waiting for you."

"Then we'll join them." Velma glanced at Laverna, wondering if she'd made a terrible gamble. "Can't keep them waiting."

CHAPTER 31

Everyone had corralled into the dining room, but no one had taken a seat yet at the table. Kenneth was gazing out the window toward the water while Brayton and Portia admired the splendor of the room. As they should. The dining room was the most impressive room in the inn, with a large window to grant a stellar view of town. An ornate rug covered the floor, and the large dining set still gleamed despite being many decades old.

What little conversation they made was stiff compared to the earlier, more explosive conversations in the parlor.

They were all playing a role, Velma saw, as she caught Dillon's eye. Her, him, everyone in the room. All engaged in this delicate dance as they waited until the proper moment to rip off their masks.

What was that signal? When they realized Delia wasn't coming? When Laverna gave the right word? Or was it when dinner concluded, so they could have full bellies as they went ripping apart the inn looking for a machine that might not even be there?

"Is this all of us?" Marie asked. "Where is our hostess? Has Delia not arrived yet?"

Edythe coolly replied, "We are following the instructions we were sent. They mention only when to begin the meal and said nothing about waiting for a particular person."

"You don't know any more than that?" Marie asked. "Where is the innkeeper? I wish to speak with him."

"You will have no luck there," Edythe said. "Enjoy the food." The guests reluctantly made their way toward the side table, which was covered with large platters and serving dishes. There was no overt display of magic over the food, but Brayton angled his cuff links over plates before making his selections. Portia chose only the blandest and least spicy items, and Kenneth didn't pick up anything Velma had not picked up first.

They seemed to have overlooked that the utensils could have been coated with poison, but Velma wasn't about to point that out. Carolyn had not included a truth-telling element in the food or drinks, as anything she had at her disposal would have been too noticeable. While Carolyn could have used subtler potions, Velma still didn't want to risk it. Cassandra plant worked in understated situations, but in circumstances like this, where everyone was equally suspicious of the other, it would do more harm than good.

"Let me help you," Brayton said as he pulled out a chair for Portia.

Portia walked past the proffered chair. "There's assigned seating."

"What does it matter? I want to talk to you."

"But I don't want to talk to *you*." Portia jerked away and sat down as far away from Brayton as possible.

Although Portia had noticed the place cards on the table, most had overlooked them, taking seats where they wished. Now Quincy picked up a card.

"Delia Moore," he said with a pronounced pause, long enough that Velma was afraid he was going to spoil things. "Is she here?"

Laverna trailed her fingers along the table. "It seems that despite having invited us, Delia couldn't make it."

"Not that it was possible with the tide being as it is," Kenneth added.

"Or without someone studied in the art of necromancy," Dillon said offhandedly as he reached for his glass of water.

"What are you talking about?" Brayton's demand quelled the conversation around the table.

Dillon studied his drink. "I suppose you must not have heard. I only came across the news myself as I did my research into Wise Records. Delia Moore is dead. Victim of a nasty mugging a few weeks back."

He delivered the news far better than Velma would have: his conversational tone meant it took several moments for the full meaning to become clear to everyone. When it did, the reactions were immediate. Kenneth dropped his fork, his shock vivid on his face. Portia sat back, a hand to her chest, her lips parted in a sound-less whisper. Brayton placed his hands firmly onto the table, while Laverna's lips were drawn into a thin line as she glanced right over to Velma, suppressed anger in her eyes.

"Dead!" Marie swayed in her chair, and might have toppled over if she had not gripped the table. "In a mugging, of all things!"

"I thought it was quite odd when I got the invitation to this," Dillon remarked rather mildly.

"If Delia is dead," Portia asked, "who invited us?"

"Maybe her ghost sent the invitations," Dillon said. "Stranger things have happened."

"You seem to know a great deal," Brayton said to Dillon.

Dillon met this suspicion with a grin. "Are you saying I arranged all of this? I'm flattered, but this is far too complicated for the likes of me."

"Someone did," Portia said. "Someone wanted to make sure we were here, that we were given those letters."

"Mine suggested dire trouble if I didn't come," Marie announced. "Something about my misdeeds coming to light."

"You were blackmailed?" Kenneth asked.

Brayton gave a vile little chuckle. "I doubt it. Blackmail means you're ashamed of what you've done in the past!"

"I suppose threats didn't work on you?" Portia asked primly. "That you only accepted the invitation because you were curious?"

"Of course I'm curious—and I'm not the only one!" Brayton sneered as he looked around the table. "Look at all of you pretending as if we aren't here about the machine! It's the only reason we've gathered here."

"Yet you came this way without a plan," Laverna said. "You don't even know where to begin. What you'll do if you find it. Or if someone places their hands on it before you do."

"I thought we agreed to keep quiet . . . ," Portia began.

"There is no reason to keep quiet," Laverna said. "We all know why we're here. We thought Delia invited us. That she realized it's better if we work together. But that's not the case now."

"What makes you so sure she would have?" Brayton asked testily. "What do you know?"

"Exactly what I told you," Laverna said.

"Is that so?" Brayton retorted. "For months you—"

"What's that music?" Marie exclaimed suddenly, lifting a hand to her ear.

The door to the dining room had been left open, and once it got quiet, it was easy to hear what it was. Music. Soft, with a familiar swing to it, a woman's voice filtered into the room. Velma's vague curiosity and welcome for the diversion vanished the moment she listened and understood the words.

The glass in her hand dropped to the table and shattered.

She knew this song. She knew the lyrics but had never heard them set to music before. As the haunting voice filled the room, the familiar words took on a new meaning:

At the house on the hill
Bad luck and trouble done spilled
One and two and two and one
The family of wicked fates
Leave them alone or it will be late late late
One and two and two and one
Leave now or be gone gone gone

CHAPTER 32

A s the record continued to play, Velma dashed out of the room, her thumping heart drowning out all other sounds.

She headed first to the drawing room, where the record player was set up. Nothing was in there except for a stack of her father's board games. The conservatory door was shut, so Velma went to the library, which was the closest, but the sound was muted there.

Velma spun around, running into Brayton as they collided in the doorway.

"Here, it's coming from here!" Kenneth called.

Velma returned to the hall and found that everyone else had also engaged in a desperate search for the music.

From behind the front desk, Brayton had pulled out the record player. He stopped it and yanked the record off.

"That's Delia's voice." Portia gripped the staircase railing as she swayed on her feet. "That is Delia singing. How is one of her records here?"

"I'd like to know that too," Velma said. The record player was the one kept in the Cardinal bedroom. Bulky and old, it was rarely moved from that room.

"I put the record on." Carolyn came forward, carefully steering her wheelchair into the hall. "The record came with the instructions, and I was told to turn it on during dinner."

"Instructions from whom?" Laverna asked.

"The hostess, Delia Moore," Carolyn said smoothly.

Why Carolyn thought it a good idea to lie about the record, Velma didn't know. Even if it did smooth the concerns of the moment, it brought too much attention back to her. Carolyn was supposed to blend into the backdrop, to better notice trouble from the guests.

Velma should have known Carolyn wouldn't be content to fade into the background.

"How did you get instructions from Delia in the first place?" Brayton demanded.

"Not in person. We received a letter detailing everything that needed to be done, down to the dinner menu."

"You've been fed a lie," Kenneth said. "Delia Moore is dead—she never sent anything. I don't know who you were in contact with."

Carolyn shrugged. "Doesn't matter to me. I'm just the cook."

Kenneth fumed at this words, but before he could cobble together a rebuke, Dillon interjected: "Well, dinner is done." He was the farthest away, standing by the conservatory door. "I suppose the party portion comes next, and we get to see who exactly brought us here. It might not have been Delia Moore, but someone wrote all those letters. We may soon find out why they wanted us here."

"I need a smoke before that happens. Where can I do that?" Brayton said, pulling out a cigar case.

"You can do that in the lounge," Edythe obliged.

"I wish to lie down," Laverna declared. "I need a room."

"Then you will have one," Edythe said. "I'll get the key, but the bedroom is just around the corner this way."

This was not part of the plan, but Velma had no choice but to let them go.

She'd made a deal of sorts with Laverna, after all, to allow her to poke around the inn. Protesting now would only draw suspicion. As if there wasn't enough already.

As Velma watched them depart, someone bumped into her. With his gaze straight ahead, Quincy pressed a note into her hand. He didn't look at her at all as he joined Kenneth, Marie, and Dillon's conversation about the record.

Not wanting to join them and more curious than she wanted to admit about the note, Velma slipped out onto the sunporch to read it. The porch was screened in, with a few ornamental plants and plenty of chairs to lounge on. She sat upon one and unfurled the note.

As usual with Quincy, it was blunt and straight to the point: *They are looking for a pen.*

The first pen that came to mind was the fountain pen they had found in Ardenton. None of the earlier squabbling had mentioned it or the town, but she supposed it was too much to expect that everything be revealed so easily through conversation.

Velma's study of the pen had never found anything unusual, but perhaps she'd missed something after all. She retrieved it from her vest pocket and turned it over in her hands with a keener eye. What could this pen do that made it so important? Could it unlock something, or was it part of a set?

Velma stared into the speckled green paint, but she could divine no answers.

With a sigh, she shoved it back into her pocket and set out to make her rounds. The sunporch opened right into the heart of the garden, and the setting sun bathed the lawn in a golden shimmer. While going out to the garden hadn't been expressly forbidden, the looming dark clouds in the distance might discourage people from romping around the grounds.

It would rain. Velma sniffed at those clouds. Well, a small storm would keep people from wandering too far, especially with the path to town closing in little less than an hour. Even now the water was hungrily lapping against the pathway as it slowly consumed the stone.

Completing her circuit, Velma headed back to check on the boat. The inn's rowboat was still tied up by the makeshift dock, and the spells that kept it further secure were untouched. Leaning in to study it more closely, Velma felt a prickle of eyes on her. She turned around, but there was nothing there. Just some birds flying overhead and the gentle buzz of passing insects.

The sight should have relieved her, but it only increased her throbbing concerns.

Velma tugged at the rope securing the boat and increased the spells she left upon it. Satisfied, she went to the broom shed at the back of the inn. She unlocked the door and grabbed the tool bag. While she'd expected it to be there, it wasn't the only item in the shed. Most of the yard tools had been moved around, and several broomsticks, including Velma's ancient one, had been shoved haphazardly in a bucket. She noticed the axe was missing, but given how Carolyn had been on a rampage against the clown dolls, she wouldn't be surprised if her sister was keeping it nearby. Velma went around the back to disconnect the microwave relay that allowed the inn's phone to reach town, the mainland, and beyond.

Once the relay had been successfully disconnected, Velma returned the tools and headed back into the inn. She entered not through the sunporch, but through the side door next to the conservatory. No one was in the room, and Velma took a moment to breathe deeply as she sat among the plants. She had just begun to ease some of the tension in her shoulders when the plants rustled and the secret doorway opened.

Velma grabbed a spider plant that had seen better days and was about to swing it around when Dillon stepped out.

Upon seeing her, he paused in the doorway. "Am I in trouble?"

"You're not supposed to go up there!" Velma slammed the plant back onto the table as he shut the door once more. "I don't want anyone upstairs—that's why there's a spell on the staircase, to keep everyone on this level."

"I needed to get my vial of developing fluid from my luggage. I would have asked for your permission, but you had vanished."

Velma ignored the gentle mocking as she asked instead, "Did anyone else notice?"

"Of course, but I think they were glad to be rid of us for a moment. We're the foreign element in their little group."

"Have you heard anything? Like why they dislike Marie?"

"That's easy." Dillon settled into one of the wicker chairs. "Nobody likes anyone. This group got arrested for indecent magic use shortly after Wise Records' demise. They blame Marie, mostly because she had stolen the Sitwell items and got caught when she sold them to settle debts. But the dislike runs in all directions, especially as the true value of the items were revealed. Your cousin unleashing more of the Sitwell items has them all crossing paths again, and they're wary of Marie. Of course, this is what I gathered between the lines and with the research I did on them. They aren't saying too much in front of me, and I have to be careful with my questions."

"Keep doing that as much as you can," Velma said. "I was suspicious enough that Laverna already figured out what I know—and possibly what I don't know. She's asked for my help in searching for the machine. She claims she wants to destroy it." Velma paused, waiting for Dillon to speak up. "This is the part where you argue with me about trusting her."

"I would, except you don't," Dillon said. "If you must pick an alliance with any of these folk, better her than Strickland. You noticed he's not doing that weird flirtation with you again."

"That's what concerns you now?" Velma asked, amused at his ham-fisted twist of subject.

Dillon nodded, no less serious. "He was doing it in Chattanooga, but he's not doing it now."

"He wasn't seriously flirting to begin with," Velma said, continuing to be amused by Dillon's observation. "It's about power."

"That's not—" Dillon just shook his head, giving up the argument. "Before we rejoin the others, can you lend me a hand? I'd like to get my other camera from its hiding spot so I can develop the photos and I need a distraction."

"I'm good at that."

Returning to the front hall, Velma found to her relief that it was empty of any lingering guests. Standing guard some distance away, Velma motioned for Dillon to get to work. As Dillon got behind the desk, one of the doors opened.

Velma sprung forward, ready to circumvent trouble, but it was only Olivia with a carefully balanced tray of drinks. As Olivia walked to the drawing room and struggled to get the door open while still holding the tray, Velma noticed all the doors downstairs were shut—when none were supposed to be.

"The camera, someone broke it," Dillon whispered.

They did more than that. The camera and the candle it had been hidden in were melted to such a degree that wax and metal had melded together, leaving an unsightly mess on the desk.

At this chilling sight, Velma gestured to her cousin. "Olivia, come here!"

The alarm in her voice must have rung clearly, for Olivia dashed over at once and placed the tray on the desk. "What's wrong, Velma?"

"My sister, was she in the kitchen with you just now?"

Olivia nodded. "Carolyn told me to give drinks to everyone, to keep them preoccupied until you came back. She's not happy you stepped out."

"Good," Velma said absently, and turned her attention to the doors around them.

The library door was unlocked and opened easily, but no one was in there. The Hickory parlor was the same. As was the Dogwood parlor. When Velma tried the dining room, the doorknob did not move.

Locked!

Without a moment's hesitation, Velma drew the arrow star sigil and shot it at the doorknob. Her spell bounced along the lock, and there was a soft click as the door opened.

The reek of fresh blood and her own expectations prepared Velma for what she would see, but not completely.

Lying underneath the window in the rays of the dying sun was Laverna Addison.

Her face held tinges of surprise as one hand reached for the butcher's knife rammed into her belly. The other was outstretched in a desperate final attempt to grab her killer.

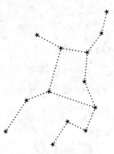

CHAPTER 33

The first murder case Velma had taken on had been by accident. It was quite like how she and Olivia had stumbled upon Delia Moore's body so many weeks ago. Velma had been on an errand when she'd come across a body in the middle of the street. She didn't remember all the gory details now, but she remembered one thing: how even with her first glance, the certainty Velma had of murder against all other options.

Velma crouched down next to Laverna's body to take the full measure of the sight before her. The gash across Laverna's stomach had not been the killing wound. It certainly would have killed given its location, but the lack of blood pointed to it being placed after the fact. The real killing blow was the wound to the back of Laverna's head: a blunt force with a few splinters left behind. She had been killed in this room, but she'd been moved so to make it appear that the knife had ended her life. A convincing tableau and one that pointed to both the killer's lack of planning and amateur craft.

"When did dinner end?" Velma asked.

"Not long ago enough for this to have happened!" Dillon stood some distance away, the bravado in his voice fully forced.

"The time," Velma repeated, more sharply.

Her words got through to him at last. Dillon glanced at his watch and haltingly gave the time. "That's just over a half hour, maybe a little less," he concluded.

"You were with Carolyn?" Velma asked Olivia.

Olivia nodded. "I didn't see anything or hear anyone."

"Happened too quickly," Velma said as she lifted Laverna's out-stretched hand.

"This window," Dillon said, striding toward it. "Is it usually left open in the summer months?"

"No, not during dinner," Velma said. She frowned, seeing where he stood. "Is it broken?"

The latch was undone, but that honestly wasn't enough for her to worry. A lot of the windows were left open during the day, only to be shut once the sun went down. This window opened out to the bushes, which was far from an appealing escape route.

"You're thinking someone came in through here?" Velma asked.

"Or left."

"I suppose it's possible," Velma said absently.

This was her fault.

She let herself get distracted and gave someone the opportunity to act. She had known this was a risk from the start, but she had not quite planned for murder, as if hoping no one would be so brazen as to make such an attempt.

"You stay here," Velma said to Dillon and Olivia. "I'm going to get my sister. We'll keep this quiet for now."

"For how long?" Dillon asked.

"Until there's no need."

Velma left the dining room, shutting the door carefully behind her before swiftly heading to the kitchen. Instead of knocking, she let herself in.

When Carolyn turned away from the sink, whatever she'd had to say fell away the moment she saw Velma's face.

"Where did it happen?" Carolyn asked.

"In the dining room," Velma said. "Laverna was struck on the back of the head and then stabbed with a knife."

"Who else knows?"

"Dillon and Olivia were with me," Velma said, "but no one else. Is there a knife missing? The butcher's knife found with her looks like it's from our set."

"All the knives are accounted for." Carolyn pushed her wheelchair to the nearest cabinet and waved her locket over the door to unlock it. Every knife they owned was stashed inside, including ones rarely used. "I did not want my good knives found in somebody's body," Carolyn continued.

"It was from ours, though," Velma said even as she wavered at seeing the butcher knife's twin in the cabinet.

"That knife is hardly one of a kind. Ask Paloma Tull. She got the same set for her inn, after her little spies spotted ours."

"I did speak to Paloma," Velma said, dredging up a passing remark from her encounter with Paloma. "When I was on the island last, she complained about thefts and pranks. What if the murderer stayed at her inn earlier, thinking it was ours by mistake?"

"Why take a knife . . . ," Carolyn began, before a high-pitched scream drowned out the rest of her words.

Velma ran out in time to see Marie stumbling into the hall, crashing right into Kenneth. The others crowded back into the hall, coming from every direction: Edythe and Portia from the lounge, Brayton from the drawing room, and Dillon and Olivia, not from the dining room but from the sunporch.

"She's dead!" Marie cried, shaking Kenneth. "Laverna's dead. Somebody killed her!" She staggered, nearly dragging Kenneth to the floor with her as she pointed. "In there!"

Quincy was the first person to enter the dining room, and everyone else followed, craning to get a look. Most backed away after getting a glimpse, but Edythe knelt next to the body.

"No pulse," Edythe declared after a few moments of examination. "Nothing else can be done."

"For her, yes." Portia was tugging at her necklace, her voice like violin strings pulled taut. "What about us? I don't want to be next!"

"Who said anything about being next?" Brayton said. He jabbed a finger at Laverna. "She's the root of all of this—she got what she deserved!"

"What she deserved?" Velma asked sharply.

"Yes, what she deserved," Brayton repeated. He turned on her, snarling. "Which you might have a better idea of than any of us! Where were you? You were missing while she was being killed!"

"I went to see if I could find the boat," Velma lied. "I wanted to make sure it was here."

"If it's still there, then good, I'm getting out of here," Brayton said.

"A woman is dead—you can't leave," Quincy spat. "None of us can."

As the bickering started, Velma spared a glance toward the framed portrait on the wall, hoping that with a dead body on the floor, no one would notice the askew frame. Dillon and Olivia had gone through there to not get caught near Laverna's body—she hoped. There was also the chance that whoever killed Laverna had gone through there as well. A very small chance, but one she had to consider all the same.

Portia's voice trembled even as she drew herself up to her full height. "What do you suggest, call the police?"

"Bramble Crescent does not have a police station," Carolyn interjected. "The people in charge of such things—"

"What sort of backward place is this island!" Brayton roared.

A burst of anger filled Carolyn's eyes. "Don't argue about the facts! We can report what happened, and someone from town will handle matters. It will take time and no one can leave until then."

"What about who did this?" Dillon drawled as he gestured in Laverna's direction. "She didn't fall on the knife. That's more than a bit of bad luck."

"Bad luck!" Brayton spun on his heel and charged out of the room before anyone could stop him. He barged into the drawing room, where the record player now was, and wrenched the record off the machine.

"No, don't do it!" Marie cried.

Heaving, Brayton held aloft the record, his intent clear from the defiance in his features. "I don't see why not."

"You're being reckless," Portia said. "You don't know what it will do!"

"It's a record—it's not enchanted when it's not being played," Brayton barked.

"You don't know that," Kenneth said quietly. "You never understood how they worked."

"If you break it, I hope the bad luck falls upon you!" Marie hugged her arms around herself, her eyes rimmed red. "You know better than to mess with things you don't understand."

"Aha!" Brayton jabbed a finger at her. "Hear that, mark it all! For if misfortune comes to me, she played a hand in it!"

"How dare you, Strickland—"

The rest of Marie's tirade was lost as Brayton slammed the record to the ground. As shards of the record went flying, Marie shrieked, while everyone looked fearfully about for latent magic.

Brayton stood firm over the shards, gasping as he glared at them.

"You've broken it." Edythe stepped forward, her ill ease rolling off her like the swift arrival of a sea storm. "Are you happy? Not that it changes a thing. You cannot leave!"

He rounded on her. "How are you going to make sure of that?"

"The tide is high," Velma said, pitching her voice to rise above all the others. "The doors are locked and warded, and the boat is bespelled to let no one remove it. None of you are leaving. And even if you could, I can't let you go now that Laverna is dead as well." Velma flashed a card at them, just long enough for them to spy the official-looking writing on it. "I'm a private investigator with the Kestrel Detective Agency, and I've been investigating Delia Moore's death. Along the way I've learned several things, including the plans Members of Rational Clarity have for the arcane exposition—some of which Laverna told me a great deal about. I want you all in the lounge right now, where you will remain until I call for you, for I have many questions and I will get my answers before the night is over."

"You can't . . . ," Brayton began.

"You'll find that I do indeed have that right and most importantly, the means," Velma replied without directing him any more attention than he deserved. "It's also for your safety that I suggest this. If none of you touched a hair on Laverna, and it's the fault of a stranger lurking around the inn, you staying in the same room is for the best. Arguing otherwise is just a waste."

Brayton again moved to protest, but Portia placed a hand on his arm. "Just listen to her, Bray. We can't go anywhere. There's no point in fighting."

At her words, Brayton relented and was led into the lounge. Portia and Brayton were followed by Kenneth, Marie, and Quincy. Edythe went in with them, and, with a nod to Velma, quickly closed the door. Perhaps because Edythe was in there, Carolyn and Dillon remained in the hallway, where Olivia lurked behind them.

"I said everyone," Velma remarked even though she knew it was a lost cause.

"There's no need to go through the farce of interrogating us," Carolyn said. "They are suspicious of Dillon, and I clearly know more than what I claimed."

"They won't talk easily in front of us," Dillon chimed in. "And do you want Olivia to be trapped in a room with a murderer?"

Carolyn nodded in agreement. "Exactly. There's no else here except for us."

"What compelling arguments you have," Velma said dryly as she faced this united front.

"Also, I'm not going to miss out on your interviews with this lot, *detective*," Dillon said.

Velma suppressed a smile. "I wouldn't imagine otherwise, but let me do the talking. Carolyn, can you and Olivia search the Cardinal bedroom and then around the inn for anything out of place? Don't worry about upstairs, unless you notice any tampering with the spells on the staircase. I'll be talking with everyone in the library. If you find anything, ring the bell."

Carolyn nodded. "Be careful. If Edythe wasn't in there, I'd say lock them up until morning."

"If only things were that simple," Velma said.

They split up then, leaving Velma and Dillon to hastily rearrange the library.

"I know you wanted to talk to them, but I wouldn't have high hopes for anything more than tidbits," Dillon said.

"I can work with tidbits," Velma assured him. "We'll talk to them one at a time. I'll need you to escort them from the lounge. I'd like to speak with Kenneth first. Then it's Edythe, Marie, Portia, Quincy, and finally Brayton. Try to keep that order if you can."

"And not let them run off."

"They wouldn't get far even if they could."

Velma lit the candles in the library, turning them slightly so that the sigils carved into them weren't as prominent. She had just settled at the table when Dillon returned with Kenneth.

Kenneth's eyes darted around the library, taking in the bookshelves, and he had to be directed to take a seat by Dillon. He sat stiffly in the chair, his left leg bouncing slightly from his foot rapidly tapping against the floor. Kenneth scarcely waited until Dillon had shut the door before he spoke up. "I knew there was a reason I ran into you at Giles's office! You're a private investigator. And to think I was ready to dismiss what Marie told me. Who hired you?"

"Let's just say Delia's death was enough to catch my interest," Velma said. "My original intent was to learn about her death, but that's changed now. What happened after dinner?"

Kenneth drummed his fingers against the armrest of his chair before he began speaking, a bit slower now. "I took a closer look at the record. I was in the drawing room the whole time until Marie started screaming. He can tell you that—he saw me go into the room," Kenneth added with a jerk of his thumb to Dillon.

Dillon scarcely looked up from his notes. "The detective is interested in what you have to say, not me."

"Just say that you saw me, she'll believe you—"

"You looked at the record and then what?" Velma interrupted.

"I played it again to listen to the entire song."

"Just listened? You didn't check to see what glazes were left on the record?"

Kenneth swallowed. "What are you talking about?"

Velma leaned forward against the table. "I think you know exactly what I mean, Malcolm Gladstone."

Kenneth's hands clenched involuntarily, but his unease didn't change. When he refused to speak, Velma went on. "You enchanted records for Wise and then moved on to a lucrative career selling bootleg potions. You brought some with you tonight. A simple examination of Laverna will reveal if any caused her death."

"She was stabbed!" Kenneth exclaimed. "How can you accuse me of poisoning her?"

"It's possible she was poisoned beforehand. The last thing Laverna told the group was that she wanted to rest." Seeing resistance form in his features, Velma took a different tack. "Either way, you're probably happy Laverna has been removed from the board. I've been to the workshop you abandoned in Sacramento. I know what you're working on."

"You don't know as much as you think," Kenneth replied. "I didn't kill Laverna. She's far from the top of my list. Besides, if she was right about the machine being here, the pressure is off me to make a new one."

"Why did you agree to make it in the first place?" Velma asked. "You nearly blew yourself up."

"Pride," Kenneth replied reluctantly. "I hated Edwin for the genius he was and how he limited his own vision. I wanted to outdo him. I never could make my own version of that glaze, but I thought with the machine I could."

"You failed."

"In some ways I'm happy I did. The spike when it went wrong . . ." He shuddered. "I don't have materials to try again anytime soon, and I'm glad for it."

He said little more of interest, and Velma ended the interview. Dillon escorted Kenneth out and returned with Edythe.

"How are things proceeding?" Velma asked her friend.

"I should be asking you," Edythe returned with some bemusement, "*private investigator*."

"I had to say something, and it was the first thing that came to mind. I didn't want to tell the truth."

"I think they know your relation to this house, or guess mostly. Laverna certainly knew. She mentioned it when I brought her to the Cardinal room."

"How did she appear?" Velma asked.

"Nervous. Although she attempted to hide it. She didn't have much to say to me in general, now that I think of it. She was rude. I showed her to the room and she immediately went in, all but slamming the door in my face."

"What did you do afterward?" Dillon asked.

"I checked in on Carolyn, and then Portia called me over about a broken ashtray," Edythe replied. "I cleaned it up and then stepped out to the sunporch and spotted Velma prowling the grounds. I came back inside to use the bathroom and was in there when the screaming started."

"That's next to the Cardinal bedroom. Did you notice anything?"

Edythe shook her head. "The door was shut when I got out."

"What about the potions that Kenneth brought?" Velma asked.

"I don't know anything about them," Edythe said. She stood up from the table before Velma could press her on the subject. "I should get back. They weren't trying to align their stories earlier, but we shouldn't allow them the chance."

"I suppose you're right," Velma conceded. Although puzzled by Edythe lying about the potions, she let her friend leave.

Marie was brought in next. She had calmed down slightly since earlier, but she trembled still as she sat across from Velma, her hands pressed against the table. She was out of sorts, missing an earring, and one of her hairpins was askew. "Do you think one of us murdered her? Am I in danger?" Marie asked.

"Why would you think that?" Velma asked mildly, ignoring as Dillon rapidly began to write in his notebook. "Do the others dislike you that much?"

"They liked Laverna more than me, so yes, I am a bit worried," Marie said. "When you were at my home, why didn't you say you were looking into Delia's death?"

"Why would I think to do that?" Velma let her question hang in the air, and Marie shrunk under the implications. "I had no reason to think you knew each other. All I know is that you bought something from Quincy Hodges."

"Nearly the worst thing I have ever done," Marie muttered.

"What's the worst?"

"Accepting the invitation for this dinner party, of course."

Velma sat back, watching the conflicting emotions spread across Marie's face, and then said, "Tell me what happened after dinner."

"I went to one of the parlors to get away from the others. After a while I realized one of my earrings was missing." Marie pointed to her empty earlobe. "I went back to the dining room, and then I saw her, and the blood—and—" Marie's words shook, and the rest of her did, and whatever sense Velma might get out of her was lost right then. Dillon got up to hand Marie a handkerchief and slid a torn piece of paper to Velma.

"I'll see her back to the others," Dillon said, guiding Marie out of the room.

Velma skimmed Dillon's note: *Ask about the time between*.

His words were unusually cryptic, and Velma barely had a chance to consider all their meaning when the door was flung open.

Velma hastily shoved the paper away as Quincy barged in. Dillon gave Velma an apologetic look as her elder cousin all but pounced on Velma.

"What do you think you're doing!" Quincy demanded.

"My job," Velma said, unmoved. "And you're making it harder."

"I doubt it. A woman is dead—in your home! I would have thought you'd be able to prevent that at the very least. Did you not get my note?"

"Are you saying she died because of a pen?"

"It's related to the machine they are looking for," Quincy said. "Instead of questioning them you should try to get your hands on it."

"Was that why you were prowling around after dinner?" Dillon asked. "Were you trying to help, or did you want to sell it to the highest bidder?"

Quincy ignored him, focusing on Velma. "You can't keep them locked in all night. Or at the very least I can't stay locked in with them. Let me look for the machine. I have found hidden places in the inn before."

Irritation shot through Velma. "You doing that is why we are in this particular situation in the first place."

Quincy's jaw tightened. "I am trying to make up for that. Don't be so shortsighted."

"Be patient. You'll have your time soon enough."

"Velma, he's lied to you before," Dillon said.

"But against the others," Velma said as she met her cousin's gaze, "I trust him. The only way I'll let you search is if everyone else is locked up in the room. What were you doing after dinner?"

"I was in here." Quincy waved a hand around. "I always did like this room. Most avoid it as it has too many books, leaving little else of interest." His eyes darted back to Velma. "You need to focus on what's important."

"By important you mean what's important to you," Velma said. "I told you. I won't let anything happen to your family. Strickland can't contact anyone. The phone line is cut, and there's enough magical interference to subvert any other attempt. Don't you trust me to keep my word?"

"As much as anything," Quincy said. "Don't drag things out. This isn't one of your air shows."

Just as abruptly as he'd arrived, Quincy escorted himself out of the room.

"He's going to be a problem," Dillon said as he hurried to follow.

"He already was," Velma replied, mostly to herself. Lost in thought, she let her gaze wander about the room and it fell upon the candles. One had melted to half its size since Velma had lit it.

Somebody had worked magic! A small charm or a pesky jinx, it didn't matter. Someone had attempted to cast a spell around her.

The entrance of Portia and Dillon curtailed her wondering, and Velma hastily gave Portia her attention. Unlike the others so far, Portia was reticent and as still as a seafaring ship on a day without wind.

"I was in the lounge," Portia said as soon she sat down. "I asked the housekeeper to get an ashtray after Brayton broke one. He didn't want to wait and left the room. Do you need to know how many cigarettes I smoked or what I used to light it? I heard from the others you want to know what we've been up to."

"It's helpful to know where everyone was, to better understand what happened," Velma said as she ignored the goading words.

"You would have known if you had remained inside the inn. I saw you on the grounds. All this magic that's keeping us trapped is yours, isn't it?"

"Some is even the inn itself," Velma said, avoiding a direct response. "That's the thing with old houses: the compounding of magic over the years can do extraordinary things."

"It's the people who make a home extraordinary," Portia said. "May I go? I have nothing interesting to tell you."

"I believe you do," Velma countered. "That one record you made with Wise Records—tell me more about it. Was it similar to the one Delia made?"

"Are you asking if it was enchanted? No, it wasn't. Why do you think I made only one?"

"I was curious if Brayton and his band accompanied Delia's singing as well."

At the mention of Brayton's name, the air tensed around Portia and her hand involuntarily went to her necklace. As she rubbed it, Velma noticed for the first time it was a treble clef. "It was only because of me that his band ended up at Wise Records. I needed a band to play with me, and I even gave his players the instruments from my family's music shop."

"Yet for all your efforts, he remained there afterward, until the end, while you went a different way."

"I'm better at making instruments," Portia said.

"You've done quite well—most of you have—but Brayton did far better than all of you combined, even when looking just at his legitimate businesses."

"Brayton was always very good at turning situations around," Portia said stiffly. "It's admirable sometimes."

"I'm surprised he showed up here tonight."

"He thought Delia invited him. Why wouldn't he show up?" Bitterness added texture to her words, then a dash of surprise—she had not meant to admit that.

As Velma realized this, Portia jumped to her feet. "Is that all the questions you have for me? How do you plan to find out who killed Laverna? Talking to us won't yield answers."

"In your opinion," Velma said.

Dillon escorted Portia out and soon returned with Brayton.

Brayton sauntered into the room and made the first blow with his defiant words: "I didn't kill Laverna, and you have no right to accuse me of such!"

Unbothered, Velma replied, "You didn't seem too cut up about her death."

"I'm a man of many vices, Miss Frye," Brayton said. "I don't claim to have a pure heart."

"I know—your friend hinted as much."

Brayton waved a hand about. "I suppose Hodges filled your head with the details of our agreement."

"Those are awfully pretty words for *blackmail* and *extortion*."

"It's what a man should expect. Hodges made promises he couldn't keep."

"Why are you interested in all of this?" Dillon asked from his corner. He clenched his pen but, instead of writing, he focused on Brayton and Brayton alone. "The others I can understand, but you? What are you after?"

"None of your business."

"Answer the question," Velma said, "or you'll find accusations are the least of your worries."

Brayton's mouth turned upward, and there was nothing charming about his patronizing tone. "Well, detective, you were there at the baseball game. You saw what's in store. We will change the world and get what we as a people justly deserve."

Despite the murder taking place, this was the surprise of the evening: Brayton, the crime lord, nightclub owner, potion smuggler, and King of Sin, was a true believer!

As his eyes fixed on her, Velma could see the fervent belief swelling in them. He might be lying about several things, but not this. There was an energy radiating from him, and a clear desire for her to see things his way.

"Very few people have heard about your little club," Velma declared. "What makes you think you can impact anything?"

"Don't make jokes." Brayton turned his hands over, and the sea serpent star sigil lashed about in his palm. His spell coiled around him, stretching toward Velma. "Word of advice: when you stick your nose out, it's more likely to get chopped off."

"If you're threatening me," Velma said, watching the sea serpent drift around her, "you're going to be disappointed."

"This is a warning of the potential consequences for you and your family. After all, accidents can happen if you aren't careful."

The sea serpent shot out toward Dillon, grabbing him by the throat.

Velma wasn't sure if the rumbling thunder was real or just in her ears. It didn't quite matter. The table had flown out of the way as Velma as strode forward, the candles burning so hotly a pool of wax spilled onto the shelves.

With a lift of her hand, the Pegasus constellation flew through the binding magic, severing its hold on Dillon.

"Let me clarify something for you," Velma said as the winged horse fell into place at her side as she stood before Brayton. "There are no threats—or, as you call them, *warnings*—that could make me do your bidding. You try something and you'll find yourself wishing you hadn't even thought of it."

Brayton laughed at her, and only stopped laughing when Velma's magic clamped down onto his shoulder and threw him across the room. He hit the wall hard, but not hard enough to do more than rattle him.

"You may have noble ideals," Velma said, "but everything you've done has undercut them. You want to make an impact and change the world? Find a different way. You won't do it by hurting those you claim to help. Forget about the machine—I will never allow it to be used to harm, no matter who the target is."

"Then you'll never get the chance!" Brayton spat.

As if to prove the universe had a keen ear, a tumultuous clap of thunder filled the air. Lightning must have struck somewhere, for it felt as if the entire island shook and rattled about, and a few books on the shelves behind her fell to the floor.

Not far away glass shattered, striking such a sharp note Velma nearly covered her ears, and the room—and perhaps even the world—plunged into darkness, followed by an even more ominous bang.

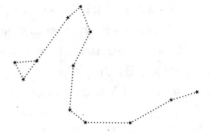

CHAPTER 34

Velma found the library door by touch alone and flung it open. Moonlight streamed down from the window and fell upon what was left of the chandelier that had watched over three generations of Newberrys.

Velma started to cast a light spell. Even before she could begin, she felt a chill where there was usually warmth. Pressure began building along the back of her neck as well, a familiar sort of pressure.

No, it can't be. Nothing is wrong, she told herself.

Except she tried again to cast a spell . . . and again nothing happened. No matter what star sigil she drew or what spell she sought to cast.

Nothing happened.

"Velma?" Olivia's trembling cry cut through the air, and her little cousin stood at the foot of the stairs, illuminated by the storm lantern she held aloft.

Upon seeing the lantern, Velma finally pieced together what was going on.

This was a Quelling, a suppression of magical energy. This sort of spellwork had been around since the first spells were crafted, but had been weaponized over the centuries. Usually a restraining device or another spell did the trick, but advancements during the Great War allowed for certain refinements so such suppressive magic could be deployed at a moment's whim. The effects were immediate, but varied on how long they lasted.

Olivia called out to her again, and this time Velma answered.

"I'm here—stay where you are. I'm coming to you."

Following that steady light, Velma got a closer view of the damage done to the chandelier and hall.

In the middle of the hall sat Carolyn, frustrated tears welling up in her eyes.

Edythe reached over and squeezed Carolyn's shoulder. "It's all right," Edythe whispered. "No one was hurt."

"That chandelier is original to the house!" Carolyn wailed, but her despair wasn't from the damage. The chandelier could be fixed, the floor repaired. What could not change was that after all these years and all the storms the inn had weathered, this evening was what had brought it to ruin.

"Can you do magic?" Velma called into the darkness. "Any of you?"

"Oh, thank goodness it's not just me." Dillon's voice floated nearby, but he was too much in shadow for Velma to determine if he was just using humor to cover his ill ease.

His words seemed to get Carolyn to rally. "It's a Quelling. It'll fade in time."

"Until then we're in the dark." Velma peered into the shadows, wishing for better light so she could count heads. Whoever had done this was taking advantage, but she couldn't run after people in the dark—that was how you ran into knives. "The Quelling kicked off the lights."

"We need to get the power back," Carolyn said.

"I'll take care of it," Velma replied.

Edythe spoke up. "Olivia should go with you, since she has the light."

This was sensible, even though Velma wondered how the lantern had ended up in Olivia's hands so quickly in the first place. The lantern had been in the office—to get it so quickly in the dark meant someone had already been there. Had that been Edythe?

"Lead the way," Velma said to Olivia as she shoved back her conflicting thoughts.

They went out the front door and walked down the short ramp to head into the backyard.

A passing thought niggled at Velma as they walked past the bushes until she realized something with a start.

The ground wasn't damp, despite the storm she'd heard.

Velma stopped and turned back toward the inn, a slow trickle of horror working its way through her.

"That wasn't a storm," Velma whispered, looking at the dry ground around her. When she'd heard that boom, she'd mistaken it for thunder. Then she remembered her earrings and the amplification spells she had connected to them.

The statue that had been made to furtively listen in on anyone who came into the garden was in pieces on the ground. Like the hidden camera in the candle, it too had been discovered.

Edythe didn't know about this one, Velma thought, and berated herself for the unkind thought.

"Someone's been in the garden!" Olivia cried from a few feet away. The light spilling from the lantern revealed footprints that turned a vivid pink under the filtered light. "Why do they look like this?"

"It's by design," Velma explained. "The lantern uses different colors to reveal footprints, magical residue, blood, and eucalyptus."

"That's very specific," Olivia observed.

"The plant shows up quite often in cleaning potions. Let's see where these footsteps go."

The hedges were a mess, trampled over like elephants had run amuck. Thankfully, the mess went not toward the hidden garden and Edythe's cottage, but away.

"Did you and Carolyn find anything while searching the house?" Velma asked.

"Not much," Olivia dutifully replied. "No one came in through the windows or forced their way into any of the other rooms. Carolyn spent a while looking at the elevator. A table had been moved. She said she could tell because her wheelchair bumped into it as she turned the corner."

"The elevator?" Velma pondered. During more usual times at the inn, the elevator door was easily overlooked, as Grandmother Newberry wanted it to blend into the wall. Tonight they had camouflaged it further by sending the lift to the second floor so they would hear it being used. If the table had been moved, had someone attempted to climb up the shaft?

"Velma, isn't there supposed to be a boat over here?" Olivia asked, drawing Velma out of her thoughts.

"Yes, it's tied up near the dock."

"I don't think that's true anymore." Instead of elaborating further, the girl pointed toward the water.

Silhouetted by lights in town, a bobbing rowboat was well on its way to getting stuck in Nettle Cove.

"Someone took it," Olivia suggested.

"I should have known if they did, but it's too far away to have been let loose now," Velma said.

"Unless someone is still out here!"

Like the literary detective Olivia so admired, the girl ran off with the lantern held high to ward off danger.

Hurrying after the moving speck of light, Velma caught up with Olivia near the gazebo, where the girl waved the lantern over the nearby ground.

"Look at all this," Olivia said before Velma could even begin to protest. "These aren't footprints."

They weren't. The slick smears of orange, blue, and silver magic residue along the ground were far too spaced out to be footprints.

"Give me the lantern," Velma said, and Olivia couldn't hand it over fast enough.

Carefully, Velma followed the splotches illuminated by the lantern. At first she was afraid she and Olivia would end up in the magical herbs section. Instead the splotches were near the shed, where a shoe stuck out. Velma took a deep breath and held the lantern out farther.

Light illuminated the graying hair and Kenneth's glazed-over eyes.

Lying as if he had been flung to the ground from the skies, Kenneth's body was arched in an impossible backbend as silver streaks of magical residue radiated from the hole in his chest.

Velma could only stare as the streaks of silver glistened under the light. These streaks had just changed everything about how this night was going to end.

"What does silver mean?" Olivia asked, her voice squeaking only a little.

"Silver means sorcery," Velma said. "The streaks show where it impacted."

"And where the magic killed him," Olivia said. "That's where his heart is."

"Not quite. It's too high." Velma frowned. "It's a very bad wound, but it's not what killed him. Even if the magic cauterized the wound, there should be more blood."

"Was he pushed out of the window to hide that fact?" Olivia asked.

Velma turned around and looked back at the inn. With no lights, it was hard to tell if any of the windows upstairs were broken.

"Not sure yet," Velma answered, "but we can find out after we get the power back on."

Velma opened the breaker box and started flipping switches and turning knobs that would swap the inn's power to the solar generator.

"When we get back inside," Velma remarked, "I'm going to lock you in the office."

"No!" Olivia cried, all but pleading with Velma. "It won't be safe. It's better if I stay with you!"

"You might see something you aren't supposed to see." Then Velma took a different tack as she spotted the bubbling protests on Olivia's lips. "Something worse than you already have, I mean."

"You're supposed to be teaching me," Olivia said. "I'm the only one of the children interested in learning about the family business. If you can't show me what to do now, how will I manage otherwise?"

Olivia really had eavesdropped on every conversation Velma had at Juniper Street. Still, she couldn't help but smirk at the girl's persistence. "You can stay with me. If someone charges at me with a knife, you get out of the way and let me handle it?"

Olivia nodded.

The generator came on, and Velma flipped a switch. Lights flickered, brightening the inn's windows one by one. All the lights downstairs flicked on as Velma expected, then the lights turned on upstairs.

The only light there should have been from the paper lantern up in the attic, but lamps had been turned on in guest rooms on the second floor. All in rooms no one should be in.

"We're headed upstairs to add lanterns?" Olivia asked, correctly interpreting the troubling sight before them.

"Looks like it," Velma said. "But only one lantern."

They returned through the front door to find the hall empty. After the rush of excitement, the quietness that had settled around the inn now set Velma's teeth on edge. She should have heard someone, even from the back of the inn. Where had everyone gone?

A few doors were open along the hall and the first door that caught her eye was to the dining room.

Curious as to why this door was open, Velma went to shut it, only to notice a chair out of place. The dining room table had been moved as well, and the painting that hid the passageway sat on the floor propped up against the wall, but that wasn't the most troubling sight.

Laverna's body, which had been left in the room, was missing.

"She was still alive!" Olivia cried.

"No, somebody moved her," Velma said, even as her thoughts jumped to a similar conclusion. Velma *had* confirmed the death, but her study had been quick and rushed. She had trusted her gut and the fact that Edythe had also confirmed the death. Laverna couldn't be alive, unless Edythe had lied. . . .

A bang from the back of the house pulled Velma out of her thoughts.

"That's the sunporch." Velma dragged a chair in front of the passageway to firmly seal it shut. "Let's go check."

"We're going to go look?" Olivia gulped.

"You said you wanted to learn—this is part of it," Velma said.

Lights were on in the sunporch. While a few chairs had been moved about, nothing stood out to Velma other than a jagged cut in one of the screened-in windows. Velma tapped the frayed edges. What could have caused this?

"Look out!" Olivia cried.

Velma stepped back, just in time for an axe to swing past her head.

The missing axe, Velma dimly realized, as she turned to face her assailant.

Expecting it to be in the hands of Brayton, Velma prepared to fend off the attack, only to find her script upended. Velma would have been better prepared to fight an axe floating in the air or in the hands of a random stranger who had miraculously gotten onto the island. A brawl with a tag team of Marie and Portia she could handle with a few adjustments. Tangling with Quincy, or even Edythe, was slightly feasible after a moment's pause. Even a curiously undead Laverna she could handle. Velma was prepared for all these hypothetical situations.

Except not for one that included Dillon.

But it was Dillon who held the axe.

Dillon who had come within inches of chopping off her nose.

Dillon who had very deliberately taken aim at her and was already swinging the axe back to try again at chopping her to bits.

Whatever Velma was going to do, she promptly forgot.

"Hide," Velma managed to say to Olivia.

If Olivia obeyed her or not, it was the farthest thing from Velma's mind as the axe came her way again.

Impossible, she thought. There was no way Dillon was involved in any of this. He had been with her the whole time during her travels. He had helped her find information. . . . What if he had been feeding her false information? She had no way to check. She had only his word. He could have lied to her. He could have lied so many times, and she would have had no way to know. What if he wasn't writing an article about Members of Rational Clarity and he was part of the group instead? He had been using her. He was after the machine. Everything he'd said to her. Everything he'd confessed and declared. It was all a lie.

She'd gotten it wrong.

Velma slipped on the rug and tumbled against the wall. As whispers of poor judgment filled her ears, Velma noticed that Dillon's glasses were different. The frames were round and the lenses were opaque—no, not opaque. They were tinted green.

The glasses Marie Drew had!

Green was for the nightmare glasses.

Dillon was seeing whatever images the glasses were producing. He wasn't fighting her . . . but what the glasses were conjuring up!

As these thoughts connected, Velma's senses flooded back, and instead of retreating when the axe came her way, Velma raised her arm and blocked it. The axe caught against her bracelet, sparking as metal clashed against metal, and Velma shoved Dillon back.

"Dillon," Velma said, slowly stepping around the ruin of the sunporch. "It's me. I'm right here. What you're seeing isn't real." Velma kicked over a chair, pushing it in his way. "Listen to me. What you're seeing right now isn't happening at this moment."

Dillon paused for a moment but then advanced, the axe coming closer and closer.

Velma could block or avoid his swings, but she couldn't get close enough to strike back or, more important, knock the glasses off his face. Dillon was fast, faster than she'd anticipated. He wasn't necessarily stronger than she was, but the axe's magically enhanced sharp edge and his agile footwork gave him an advantage. He was also reliving one of the worst nights of his life, and if she could puncture that living nightmare, she could get through without hurting him.

What did Dillon tell her about Roslyn Keys? He didn't say much, just the facts. Surely there was something she could use?

"Your family is safe," Velma said. "Your parents, your siblings, you got them away."

Dillon froze, the axe still held up above his head. "What about Hitchcock?"

"Hitchcock is fine too," Velma said without a clue who that was. "He got on the truck with them."

"You're lying," Dillon said. "He never made it."

Velma stumbled back, tripping over the ruins of the chair. She fell hard onto the ground, and Dillon bounded over, the axe raised overhead. He wouldn't miss at this range, and she couldn't move in time.

"Hey, Uncle Dill!" Olivia cried.

Dillon froze mid-swing, locking in place. "Marilyn? What are you doing here? You weren't born when it happened."

His confusion held him still long enough for Velma to hook her foot around his leg and knock him over.

Dillon toppled backward, dropping the axe. Velma rolled up to her feet and caught the axe before it fell on him.

Velma firmly placed the butt of the axe against his windpipe. Dillon attempted to grab her once again, but by then the glasses had slipped. He stopped as he saw her around the fringes of the lenses.

Velma removed the axe and then reached down to yank the tinted glasses off his face.

"It is you," Dillon said, blinking up at Velma. "I thought I heard your voice, but it felt like a distant memory." He continued to blink more as Velma sat down next to him. "Are you mad at me?"

"A little, but at least you didn't cut me in half." Velma waved the tinted glasses at him. "Why did you put these on?"

"Would you believe me if I said it was by mistake?" His eyes were slightly unfocused as he sat up, his hands clenching and unclenching as he spoke. "I bumped into something in the dark and knocked off my glasses. I put on this pair thinking it was mine, and when the lights flickered on, I was there on that last night in Roslyn Keys. I'm sorry—"

Velma looped her fingers through his. "It's fine," she assured him as she squeezed his hand. She waited until his breath steadied. "Did you pick up the glasses or did someone give them to you?"

"I got them from . . . Carolyn!" Dillon surged up to his feet, spinning around the sunporch, looking not at the door back to the house but to a wall. It took only a moment for Velma to realize where he meant to look.

One of the chaises barricaded the opening into the passage that ran into the dining room. Velma shoved it aside, and Carolyn opened the door.

"Finally," she huffed, navigating her wheelchair around, slightly out of sorts. "Dillon, I have your glasses. That's what I came to give you before you shoved me in there. You're lucky I heard everything, because otherwise you'd be in a world of trouble."

"Was that you I heard earlier making all that noise?" Velma asked.

"That's not important," Olivia said. "Laverna Addison is missing! It's like she got up and walked away!"

"How is that possible?" Dillon stammered, nearly stabbing himself in the eye with his glasses. "She's still dead?"

"As far as I know she still is," Velma replied. "We just looked in the dining room. Her body is gone, but I think someone moved her."

"I haven't been back in the room, so it wasn't me." Carolyn frowned. "Dillon and I were out here when the lights came back on."

Dillon turned toward the wall. "The passageway was already open. I mistook it for a door. That's what triggered the memory, I think."

"What's with these glasses?" Carolyn gestured toward the green-tinted ones Velma held.

"They're nightmare glasses. I collected a pair just like them."

"They're not *like* them—they're the same pair." Dillon shook his head. "Look at their tags."

On the temple of the glasses was a small tag with a case number on it from the Muses office.

"This was stolen from the archives." Velma gasped. "If these glasses were taken, anything I gathered there might have been too."

"Your friend is in charge of the archives," Carolyn remarked.

"Lois would never . . . ," Velma began even as she considered it. Lois knew the routes. Lois knew all the major facts of the case. Lois had access to everything Velma had brought. Lois didn't tell her every bit of news. Lois had said the communications went down. . . .

"Lois is a terrible liar," Dillon said, snapping Velma out of her thoughts. "She's not the only one who works there. It's a big organization. There is an explanation for this—let's go with what we know. Somebody brought them here. My vote is on Kenneth."

"Kenneth is dead," Olivia announced, her voice strained but steady. "Velma and I found his body in the garden."

"He had a briefcase with him. I think it's time to see what's in there," Velma said.

"That might not be helpful," Carolyn reminded her. "It could be anywhere in the inn, and with the Quelling you can't find it easily with a spell. Or anything else for that matter."

"Which is why we're doing a thorough search of the house," Brayton announced from the doorway.

He had in his hand one of the altered elemental pistols. Pieces of wand wood were inside the cannister, and unlike the broken ones, this pistol appeared to work. He certainly had the confidence it would as he pointed it directly at them.

"Why would we do that?" Carolyn asked.

"Because it would be easier if you did." Edythe stepped forward, an elemental pistol pointed directly at them.

"Edythe," Carolyn cried. "Why are you . . . ?"

"I'm only doing what I came here to do," Edythe replied steadily. "If you help them, this will go easier for everyone."

"I don't think so," Velma said as she took a step forward.

Edythe's finger jumped to the pistol's trigger. "I made a deal with Strickland. No more bloodshed and nobody gets hurt as long as you cooperate."

"Surely you can't trust Strickland to keep to his word," Dillon scoffed. "The things I could tell you about this man . . ."

"Save story time for later," Brayton said.

"I think it's rather relevant," Dillon persisted. "I find it hard to believe why someone of your caliber would get involved with Members of Rational Clarity. Edythe, you should know that this man has killed many who have gotten in his way. He doesn't honor his promises and will gladly ring the bell in your graveyard."

"If I'm not around to hear it, would it matter?" Edythe replied.

Dillon shrugged. "Perhaps not." Then he kicked the lantern lying on the floor. It sailed in the air right at Brayton, striking him on the shoulder.

"Run!" Velma urged Olivia. The girl dashed out the back door and into the night.

Velma would have followed, but a clang of metal in the background caught her attention.

Dillon sat on the ground, his hands behind his head as Edythe aimed the pistol at him.

"Not so fast!" Brayton had his pistol pressed against Carolyn's forehead, his other hand gripping the back of Carolyn's wheelchair. "You leave and she's the next victim!"

There was no need to threaten Velma. The fact that he had gotten that close at all was reason enough to cooperate. The roses carved in her chair were charmed to turn into thorns if someone attempted to push her wheelchair, but those charms were dormant. Carolyn herself was just as prickly as those charms—she once stabbed a mugger with a brooch, broke a man's kneecaps with an umbrella, and, most memorably, pushed Paloma Tull into a pond.

Velma's sister never went down without taking her attacker with her. Carolyn fought everyone and everything, because to her, life wasn't worth living if you weren't willing to put your all into it.

Now Carolyn just sagged in Brayton's grip, not even resisting as he shook her.

Velma held up her hands, unable to look away from her sister. "Let her go. I'll cooperate. What do you need me to do?"

CHAPTER 35

L et's try this one last time," Brayton said. "We're going to search the house, and you'll be helping. It'll be for the best if none of you do anything foolish." He looked directly at Velma. "I'm warning you."

Velma could only glower at Brayton. She wasn't sure how this abomination of a pistol would work, but the Quelling continued to be well in effect. She still couldn't do any magic. And without her spells, there was too much—and too many people dear to her—for her to risk an attempt otherwise.

Carolyn had been released and led the way down the hallway. Brayton was right behind, the pistol trained on her.

Velma and Dillon followed, with Edythe taking up the rear.

"Why are you helping them?" Velma asked, unable to believe Edythe had betrayed her. That Edythe could deceive her at such lengths. Velma had asked her friend to gain the confidence of Brayton and the others, but she had not asked for such a complete betrayal. Nothing like this, and nothing that would hurt Carolyn so deeply.

"I already told you," Edythe said. "I made a deal. This is the only way tonight will end."

Velma turned to confront her. "That's not true."

"Don't," Edythe whispered. "Things are already in play."

"Portia!" Brayton called up the stairs. "We've got them. Have you found anything in the rooms?"

"Not a single thing," Portia said as she descended the stairs. Marie and Quincy weren't far behind her. "We checked all the rooms— nothing is there. Looks like what Kenneth told us was wrong."

"As to be expected," Marie said. She looked askance at Quincy. "Although I doubt *his* words."

"He said his cousin would come through the back if she saw the lights on," Brayton said. "And she did."

"A game of alliances," Velma whispered to herself, recalling her father's lecture on game mechanics. "You were all working together, right from the start."

"Which made the invitation you sent all the more convenient," Brayton said.

"Where is Olivia?" Quincy demanded just then. "You promised she would be unharmed!"

"I'm not a monster," Brayton said. "The brat has run off. As long as she stays out of the way, she'll be fine. It's not like she can go anywhere."

Under the threat of violence for refusing, one by one they all trickled into the library.

"It's in here." Edythe looked at Velma, her chilly expression familiar from their days smuggling tonics. "She knows where."

Brayton trained his pistol on Dillon. "Show us, and no funny business."

"Trust me, I wouldn't dare," Velma said.

Not yet, at least.

Velma went to the bookshelf and pulled down the book on celestial mechanics. The hidden door swung open.

Brayton urged Velma forward with the pistol. "You go first. In case there's some sort of trap lying in wait."

Velma stepped inside a small, lackluster storage space. It was dusty, tight, and full of cobwebs. No magic stirred at her entry, and certainly no useful curses to fling back at Brayton and his crew.

"See, nothing is here," Velma said, her irritation out in full force. "This was blocked up ages ago."

Even as she spoke, Velma knew something was wrong.

At first the dimly lit space was as it always had been. A small space that stored a few things, too plain for any adventure. Standing here now, Velma saw something she had never seen before.

Scratches along the stone on the wall, deep enough to be gouges.

The Quelling had done more damage than Velma had realized. Not only had it stripped their magics on the house, it had ripped away the magic originally laid by Jeremiah Sitwell himself.

Brayton stepped up to the wall and pushed. The wall split apart at his touch and, like a curtain rising before the opening of a play, revealed an entrance for a room that should not have existed.

Velma swallowed hard at the sight, fearing what could be tucked away in that room.

Worse was the sneer on Brayton's face, filled with insatiable greed as he turned to them.

"Looks like there's something here after all!"

If there was a reason this hidden space had been tucked away, it was clear the moment Velma got a good look at the room. The concrete floor had a large circle in the middle of it. Nearly filling the room, it was barely a foot deep, but cracks around its rim ran along the ground and fed into the ragged streaks along the walls, like a river and its tributaries.

Something had sat in the recess of the floor. It might have been heavy. Or the impact of its magic had been great enough to leave something behind.

It didn't matter.

From just looking around, Velma knew in her very bones this was where Jeremiah Sitwell had worked on the experiment gone wrong. That had gone so wrong that his family fled the island and changed their name. And then his grandson had found his notes and not only repeated history, but did it worse.

It all started here, with a machine of untold power.

"Is this where—" Dillon began, only for Velma to gently shush him.

Like a tiger, Brayton prowled around the ring, sniffing for any hint of what he was seeking. Marie and Portia were poking around at the tables pushed to the side as they sought anything of value. Edythe lingered on the fringes, her eyes sweeping about.

"Is this where you found the objects you recovered before?" Brayton demanded of Quincy.

"I did say it was a workshop. I stumbled across it by chance." The slight shake in Quincy's voice did little to ease Brayton's suspicions.

"I don't think anything is here, Brayton," Portia called, inadvertently saving Quincy from his lies being exposed. "Or if it was, it's long gone."

Brayton turned on Edythe then. "You know something!"

"I know nothing!" Edythe said. "I've told you everything."

"She's lying. She's been lying to you all night," Quincy insisted. "She told Kenneth she's been looking but found nothing. She told Laverna she found old blueprints. She's a sly fox that will betray everyone for the mere sip of a tonic."

Edythe turned, and maybe it was the light in the space and the odd shadows it brought, but the rancor that filled her features was enough to render her nearly unrecognizable.

"You're the liar, not me," Edythe declared before she fired her elemental pistol toward the nearest wall.

Hers was a true elemental pistol instead of one of the abominations. Velma knew that the moment it fired and a cloud emitted from its end.

This was one of Carolyn's pistols, and while there were others of a more offensive nature, this was perfect for the situation at hand.

A thick fog shrouded the entire scene, covering everyone and everything from sight. Somewhere around her, Velma heard scrambling to counter the spell, including a few incantations by Marie, who still had that cheap wand of hers. The pistol's magic was stronger than sorcery and certainly stronger than Marie's feeble attempts.

That didn't stop her and the others from trying.

Green light whizzed past and struck the wall hard enough that the world shifted around her. Velma lost her balance but didn't fall.

Dillon's voice came out from the surrounding fog as he held on to her. "I got you. You good?"

"So far," Velma said. "How—" She'd begun to ask how he'd found her, but saw that the etched star sigils in her bracelets glowed brightly in the gloom. Her magic was back. A very good thing normally, not so much now since it revealed where she was. "Oh dear."

"Exactly," Dillon said. "I think the exit is—"

The earth grumbled under them, and then the solid ground they had been standing on vanished.

It was a short drop, passing so quickly that Velma had only just realized she was falling when she landed on cold-packed dirt face-first.

Grimacing at her stinging palms, Velma sat up and ran her hands along her limbs and joints, checking for injury. "Are you okay?" she asked Dillon.

"I've been better," he groaned somewhere to her right. "Let me lie here for a moment before you run about seeking revenge."

Ignoring him, Velma drew the crow star sigil. The star-speckled bird emerged joyfully into the air, mirroring her own delight.

The light of her spellwork illuminated the dirt and stone around them. Yet another hidden space underneath the inn, although this was not a room. Shadows extended beyond the light of her magic, suggesting not just more space but a path ahead.

"Up, down, and in the ground," Velma repeated to herself.

Was this how the Sitwell family had escaped without being seen?

There weren't any footprints to prove such a theory. There was only Dillon lying on his back, studying the ceiling above their heads.

"Looks like we're locked in," Dillon remarked.

"Not for long!" Velma slapped her hands together and thrust her magic above their heads. It rebounded, her spell ricocheting hard enough to the floor that they both barely jumped back in time to avoid getting hit.

"So we can't go out that way," Dillon said as smoke rose from the scorched mark on the floor between them. "Time to find a new exit."

"If we can," Velma said. "We could be trapped."

"I wouldn't fret about that." Dillon rubbed his palms together, and a star-speckled fox emerged. The little creature encircled him before darting forward into the darkness.

"If we reach a dead end, we'll just blast our way through." Pretending to whisper, he added, "This is the part where you choose to agree with me or argue?"

"Why would I do that when I know you're right?" she replied.

Side by side, they ventured deeper into the tunnel, able to see only what was immediately around them.

"So, about Edythe," Dillon remarked. "You never told me much about her. Was that on purpose, or did you assume my sister tells me everything about her friends?"

"I didn't want to prejudice you against her. On paper she's very suspicious. She was an old friend of Delia's, the person who put me in contact with Yoshi about the coins, and was a brewer out in Sacramento. The *Golden Lily* fire was because of one of her tonics, and the potions she makes haven't always had good reputations. She's put it all behind her to write poetry."

"And she's a very convincing actress," Dillon pointed out.

"She was known to some of tonight's players. She knew Kenneth as Malcolm Gladstone—she's the one who told me that news, actually. I may have misled you about my source. Edythe also met Laverna at the salon held earlier and interacted with her a fair bit."

"The two people who happened to be murdered tonight," Dillon pointed out.

"Edythe didn't have a hand in it."

"Are you sure? That was very dramatic what happened upstairs. Betrayal, collusion, backstabbing, and more."

"She helped us get away," Velma said. "I asked her to play this role, to keep an eye on the suspects. You and I couldn't do it. I couldn't risk Olivia. Carolyn wouldn't be convincing. It had to be Edythe."

"She played the part a bit too well," Dillon said. "If I hadn't recognized her quoting *Peril in a Fortnight*, I would have been deeply suspicious."

"What are you talking about?"

"A book by Melvin Winterberry," Dillon said, "the mystery novelist. His first book described a manor very much like this inn, except the rooms are swapped around and it's set in Detroit. It's owned by a pair of sisters: one of them is a balloonist, and they run a speakeasy in the basement. I'm pretty sure Edythe wrote the books, but for obvious reasons I haven't asked her yet."

"These are popular books?"

"The doctor who patched us up had copies." Dillon shrugged. "They're everywhere. I just haven't had a chance to read them until lately. When Edythe confronted us, she repeated lines from her own book. I guess it made it easier for her to play the part."

"Edythe has nothing to do with this!" Velma said with relief.

"I know," Dillon remarked mischievously. "She's your friend after all. The dearest of friends will do anything to help."

Velma was scowling at his purposefully provoking words, only to be distracted as a thought occurred to her. The suspects upstairs weren't just working together—there had once been friendships among the group. Friendships . . . and more.

As the thought blossomed, Velma spotted the star-speckled fox Dillon had sent ahead. It pawed at a wall with a carving of a sun during a solar eclipse.

With a gasp, Velma jammed her hand into her vest pocket.

"Dillon, take a look at this!"

"What am I looking for?"

"This carving on the wall is the same as this." Velma held up the hatpin. "Look at the design—it's the same."

"That's a very decorative hatpin," Dillon said. He frowned as he added, "Although I don't think it's an ordinary one."

"What do you mean?"

Dillon just pointed to her bracelet, which was glowing once again. The faint glow was not one easily seen in bright light, which was probably why she'd missed it before. Now it was unmistakable, and it grew brighter as Velma touched the embellishment on the hatpin.

Velma twisted it and the hatpin split apart to form, rather surprisingly, a tuning fork.

"I was expecting a key," Dillon said. "How disappointing."

"Don't be disappointed yet." Velma tapped it against her bracelet, and the pure, mellow tone of a bell filled the air. "Because I think you might be right."

As the sound echoed, the carving they stood before sprouted intricate star sigils. Misty tendrils appeared first, taking the form of the familiar vertices and lines of each of the twelve zodiac star sigils. The animals, Aries, Taurus, Pisces, Cancer, Scorpio, and Leo, floated side by side with the human figures of Virgo, Gemini, and Aquarius and the objects and beings that fell into categories of their own. The spells flared around Velma and Dillon, crowding the space.

Velma struck the tuning fork again.

The sigils brightened and flowed into the wall before them, and then the stone vanished, leaving behind an archway.

Night air blew into Velma's face, but it was only when she heard waves splashing against rocks that she turned to Dillon, grinning. "I guess you were right after all—there is another way out!"

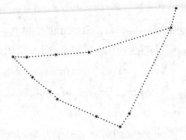

CHAPTER 36

Only a slender ledge was before them, and it was barely wide enough to keep a person from plummeting over the edge into the water below, let alone walk across.

"I don't know about you," Dillon said, "but I'm not up for a swim."

"We can't. The rock protrudes too much this way and the current is wicked." Velma poked her head out of the opening. Looking toward the sky, she sought to find the familiar contours of the inn from an angle she had never seen before. Then she spotted their way out.

Grinning, Velma asked, "How do you feel about flying?"

She removed her bracelets and tapped them together. As she pulled them apart, they remained connected by a glowing silver chain.

Holding on to one bracelet, she spun it around like a grappling hook and then flung it upward. The bracelet soared like a comet in the night sky, pulling the glowing chain behind it. As luck would have it, the bracelet found purchase on the first toss. She tugged on it, then pressed her other bracelet to lock the chain in place so she could adjust her grip.

She held out her hand to Dillon, who was properly awed at the sight of her.

He grabbed ahold of the glowing chain and, taking advantage of the situation, wrapped his other arm around her waist to bring them nose to nose. "Never a dull moment with you, is there?"

"Would you have it any other way?"

"Of course not."

Dillon kissed her as the chain retracted and they flew upward. With the added weight, it would take a little bit longer, but that was hardly trouble at all.

Velma had managed to hook her bracelet on the oak tree, grabbing on to one of the branches that stretched over the water like a helping hand. Once they were high enough, Velma and Dillon dangled for a moment before dropping gently onto the grass.

Velma patted the tree in silent thanks as she removed the bracelet from the branch and undid her spells.

"My poor jacket," Dillon said as he pulled it off, frowning at the rip.

"I'll get you a new one after all this," Velma said.

"I'm going to hold you to that. It's going to be the most expensive jacket you've ever bought."

"I look forward to it."

The inn was still as a graveyard as they entered through the front door. Pieces of the ruined chandelier were scattered in an even more chaotic pattern than she'd recalled. While lights continued to flicker from the candles in the hallway, there were no voices or sounds of movement. Not even from the library.

It seemed they had just missed a tussle, though. A bookshelf had been knocked over, and there was enough lingering magic that Velma could follow the shimmers left behind. The trail ran right to the kitchen. Instead of stopping, it continued through the kicked-in door.

Chaos had kept company in this room as well. The kitchen table was upturned, herb plants had been knocked to the ground, and shards of glass lay sprinkled in a far corner. The tiles on the floor bore several footprints made in Carolyn's finest jams, and an unsightly gash marred a cabinet door. While the back door and even the kitchen window remained untampered with, the door to the cellar was ajar.

"Stars and shards," Velma whispered.

"What's wrong now?" Dillon asked.

"Someone's in the cellar. That's where the hidden workshop with all the Sitwell artifacts was first found."

"In the cellar?" Dillon echoed. "How many ways are there to get under this house?"

"Not that many," Velma said as she opened the door wider.

The lift had been retracted, and at the very bottom Velma spotted light.

Without even considering other options, Velma jumped down the shaft. Her magic softened her landing and she didn't even pause as she darted down the corridor. Ready to face unknown fiends, Velma swung out to a stop when she saw it was only her sister.

"Were you about to hit me?" Carolyn asked with true irritation.

Never had Velma been relieved to hear such prickly words. She embraced her sister, hugging Carolyn until she pushed Velma—although not that forcefully—away.

"What happened?" Velma asked. "Dillon and I fell through some sort of trapdoor. We had to find another way out."

"Glad you found it, because I was about to go looking for you," Carolyn said. "After you vanished, things were about to turn sour when one of the women found something on the desk, and they got all excited, declaring they knew where the machine was. They ran out, leaving me behind."

"And Edythe?" Velma asked tentatively.

"Edythe locked me in the room!" Carolyn bristled. "She said it was for my own good, and to keep me out of danger. That's what she's been doing all evening. We're going to have words after all of this is over! How dare she pull such a trick on me. Did you put her up to this?"

"I may have suggested that she be friendly to the suspects." Seeing Carolyn's glare, Velma hastily asked, "How did you end up over here if you were locked in on the other side?"

Carolyn gestured to the hidden workshop. "The room under the library connects to this room. Or maybe it was part of it the whole time. One moment I was banging around trying to get out, and then there was this small corridor. A skeleton was tucked in there. A woman, I guess, based on her dress." Carolyn paused. "A very old dress."

Velma gaped. "You mean Clarice Sitwell?"

"It seems that the rhyme was wrong, she didn't drown after all. The fracture in her skull holds some clue, but whether Jeremiah killed her or not we'll just have to find out later."

Velma nodded. "I haven't seen them yet, but I know Brayton and the others are around elsewhere causing more mischief."

"Edythe is with them and we need to rescue her. After we find Olivia."

"If she's hiding somewhere, wouldn't it be best to let her stay there until it's all over?" Velma asked.

Carolyn shook her head as she went to the lift, jamming the button. "Based on her running amuck all evening, Olivia won't hide for long. She wants to help, after all."

Dillon was waiting for them up in the kitchen, flipping through his notebook.

"There's a gap in their stories," Dillon said, "about what happened after dinner. I noticed something too in how—"

"We can go over your notes later, but we need to find Olivia first," Velma said.

Dillon shut his notebook with a shrug. "I wouldn't worry about her. She knows to find a good hiding spot."

"There're so many places to— Oh!" Velma lurched across the kitchen, her heart thudding in her chest as she threw open the cabinet door with a flourish.

The platform was gone and only dangling ropes remained.

"She's upstairs!" Velma declared. "She remembered about the lift!"

"Go and get her," Carolyn said, "I'll hold down the fort here."

"If the others come back . . . ," Velma began.

In answer, Carolyn drew a swirling mass of magic into her hands, her eyes sparking with the light of her spellcraft. "I'll manage."

Velma took the stairs two at a time, Dillon right behind her, not slowing down until she was on the third floor and had opened the door that led into the family apartment. Just as she suspected and hoped, the chute that Olivia had used to escape was open.

Olivia was not in either of the rooms, and instead light spilled along the hall from the attic. Velma hurried past the wardrobe and the untidy stack of boxes that held her father's old baseball equipment to find Olivia near the window holding one of the paper lanterns they had bought yesterday.

"There you are!" Velma said. "We wondered where you went!"

"I didn't know where else to go," Olivia said, not moving from the spot. "I hid in the passageways. I heard people talking. They said the hatpin was important after all, and shouldn't have been left behind."

"Hatpin." Velma paused. "Not a fountain pen?"

"Yes," Olivia said, "that's what I heard. Do you know something about it?"

As Velma began to answer, she noticed that while Olivia was speaking, her hands were also moving. "Look behind you!" she signed.

Velma spun around as the wardrobe door flung open and Quincy emerged, holding a modified elemental pistol pointed at them.

"If you have it, hand it over," Quincy demanded. "It's the key. It's the key to everything."

"Yes, those words are very convincing," Dillon drawled. "I can just see her helping you after you betrayed everyone!"

Quincy aimed the pistol right at Dillon's heart. "I will give her one good reason," Quincy said. "You haven't seen a demonstration of this yet. You may call them an abomination, Violet, but they pack a punch. I don't want to traumatize my sister's daughter, even more than you already have, cousin of mine. So make it easy and help me."

"I think you—" Dillon began.

The pistol clicked and Dillon went silent.

"Quincy, what are you trying to do?" Velma asked.

"I'm trying to put things to rights," Quincy said. "You've been messing it up from the start. You lied to me."

"Me?" Velma said. "You lied to my face! You're the one who stole things."

"I had to." Quincy's eyes were fixed on Velma. "I had to help Stickland and others. My family was threatened!"

"Do I not count?" Velma demanded.

"There are always acceptable losses."

Quincy's hand was unsteady on that elemental pistol. He might shoot. He might not. This wasn't like anything Velma had seen from him before. Quincy wasn't rash. He was deliberate in his actions as well as his words. All evening he had been unpredictable and on edge . . . and utterly out of control.

He hadn't been himself all evening. . . .

"Give me the hatpin. I know you have it." Quincy's arm twitched, and Velma noticed for the first time his other hand was clenched into a fist.

"I don't have it," Velma said, letting her attention waver for a moment from her older cousin. "I can't help you, even if I wanted to."

"She threw it away. It's in the ocean," Dillon said. "Or is it the sea that's outside the window?"

"What?" Quincy called incredulously, and turned around just as Dillon swung an old baseball bat at him.

Because he was aiming to injure only, the bat collided with Quincy's arm, knocking the pistol out of his hand. It flew up and went off accidentally.

Magic sparked inside the cannister and imploded its magic toward the ceiling.

"I got it," Dillon called, swallowing up the loose magic with some quick spellwork.

"And I have you," Quincy said, drawing out a penknife instead.

"Not in this attic, you don't!" Velma flung Canis Minor at the stacked crates and they toppled over, stopping Quincy in his tracks. Velma sent the various items around at him in a hailstorm of animated fury until she finally lunged at her cousin, tackling him against the wardrobe.

He shoved her back with a wild swipe that she easily ducked. Velma blocked the first of his punches, then danced out of the way of the second to get Quincy to move around the room. Then she struck back, aggressively moving forward with a series of punches and strikes that got him dodging until he was in the right position for the elbow she rammed into his ribs.

He howled, dropping to the floor, but still his limbs stubbornly thrashed. Quincy's hand unfurled, but he didn't drop a coin. No quarters, no pennies, not even a dime fell away from him.

Nor would she find a coin tucked on his person, Velma realized, seeing the lucidity within his eyes.

Despite everything Velma had hoped he'd been coerced, but he had played her like a fiddle.

Without even looking at him, Velma drew the arrow star sigil and lobbed a sleep spell to make sure he wouldn't bother her for a while.

"Is Uncle Quincy okay?"

Olivia's eyes shimmered with tears as her fears and concerns bubbled up to the surface. These tears were not for herself, but for Velma, who had no more tears to shed over a cousin who had once been dear to her.

"He's sleeping," Velma said. "What did he say to you?"

"He told me he was helping you tonight. I knew that wasn't true. I spotted him going through the briefcase Edythe had hidden away. He got into the office—"

"Because he was family," Velma interrupted. "I forgot to change the spells when he showed up!"

"He set off the Quelling," Olivia continued, stumbling over the term. "Uncle Quincy said you told him to do it, but I didn't believe him. I guess everyone was right about him? That he's a bad person."

"He's not a bad person," Velma said for Olivia's benefit, and for a much younger Velma, who had once admired her eldest cousin. "He just made bad choices . . . ," Velma began, only to stop as a realization struck her.

"I know who the murderer is," she said suddenly. "I know why this is happening. This is about Ardenton. It's always been about Ardenton. Dillon, can I see the pictures you took of the town again?"

CHAPTER 37

Seated in the gazebo, Velma played her piano. Her fingers danced along the keys as the handclap song filled the air. The song had seen many variations, and Velma created a new one as she played it with her own flair set upon it, rendering this old tune anew in the face of clarifying knowledge.

As she played, wisps of blue silver stretched and grew until they were dressed in fashions confined to painted portraits. Then the portraits came to life. A couple walked into a home with a young family. A young man introduced a young lady carrying a small trunk. An older, distinguished man presented the same woman with a pair of scissors. The woman, in despair, writing in a book. A family fleeing through a secret passageway. More and more images sprouted, depicting disjointed memories, each one a tale of the doomed Sitwells dancing, laughing, and crying as Velma played on.

As she continued, Dillon stood in the gazebo with her, holding a wind pistol. Carolyn and Olivia were tucked away in the outer ring of the maze, hidden by the hedges and armed with potions. While Olivia fumed about being placed out of the way, Carolyn didn't fuss; she knew she was placed there to prevent further disaster.

The scheme was aimed to lure Brayton and the others to them, but Velma didn't know how well it would work. They were still nearby, but if they were deep in the bowels of the inn, the music might not reach them.

Those worries vanished at once when a door banged open and excited, raised voices soon followed.

"Looks like our gamble paid off," Dillon whispered. "They're coming."

"Wouldn't you investigate such a curious thing?" Velma said.

"After a night like this, maybe not."

But Brayton, Marie, and Portia were driven by something bigger than mere curiosity. Velma leaned into her playing, infusing the notes with the promises the trio sought. Drawn by these notes, and captured by the illusions swirling around, the group was brought to exactly where Velma wanted them to be.

"Here it is!" Brayton's eyes were dazzled by Velma's enchantments. "The machine is here. It was right here the entire time! All our plans, they're coming together."

"None that will ever bear fruit," Edythe said. Her hands were tied together, and she was more than a bit mussed, but her words were steady. "Look again. Or rather, listen again."

Velma lifted her hands from the piano. Once the music stopped, the illusions faded, revealing the gazebo.

Marie gasped, stepping back. "It's a trick!"

"The whole evening has been one of tricks," Velma said as she stepped out of the gazebo. "I brought you here with invitations filled with falsehoods, and employed further tricks at my disposal. My chief objective had always been to figure out who murdered Delia Moore. Because everything comes back to her one way or another. Her search for the items, her music, her connections to people. Two of the people she contacted before her death are now dead, and the third has been harassed by you all evening. Her voice alone was chosen for a line of records that were enchanted, and one of her records is a song that started as a children's handclap game. It's a local favorite of this island's children, about Jeremiah Sitwell and the ruin he brought. A song that holds little meaning to most people except those who know the names. Laverna knew them as distant relatives . . . and so did you, Portia, from growing up in your family's music shop in Ardenton."

Marie let out another cry of surprise, but Velma was no longer paying either Marie or Brayton any attention. Velma's focus was on Portia, who was even more inscrutable than before.

"Delia sung the song that Laverna and Marie had written," Velma continued. "She must have been excited since it was her first recording, and so she sang it for you when you asked to hear it. When you listened, you recognized names you hadn't heard since Ardenton."

"Delia claimed it was a coincidence," Portia said.

"Which you believed until you spoke with Laverna and found out the truth."

Portia's mouth twisted up into a mocking smile. "Laverna lied about a lot of things, but she didn't lie about that. She claimed her family for who they were without regret. All those years ago I thought she respected the force that magic was. Only to find out she was exactly like her father. Ardenton wasn't an accident. It was not the work of some mad scientist whose creation overwhelmed him. Edwin Addison brokered a deal—he'd gain a small fortune and access to rare supplies if he betrayed an entire town. Ardenton held off three waves of injustice only to fall due to the greed of one man. Laverna was the same. Her intended plans for the machine were just like her father's, only the names on the bill of sale were different. If I'd only known back then that she was cut from the same cloth as her father, I would have arranged for them both to be at the factory that day!"

Brayton turned toward Portia, his shock rattling through him. "You did that—the accident at the factory—"

"Edwin deserved it," Portia said. "He ruined the lives of hundreds of people and then opened a record company! His works and ideas could have been put to good use. Instead of using the records to expand minds and bring enlightenment, he only wanted to make money. I told Pacer about this. He didn't act in a timely fashion, so I took matters into my own hands. Giles was a good man. I'm sorry he had to die."

"Did you kill him?" Velma asked.

"No, that was Kenneth. Pacer held on to all of Kenneth's notes, and he wanted them back. If Pacer hadn't been so organized, we might not have found Edwin Addison's old notes or realized what was contained in them. Kenneth became obsessed with re-creating the machine—although Quincy muddled the waters with the fake blueprints he gave us. Kenneth was a very good partner in all of this . . . until he became a liability."

"She killed Laverna," Marie whispered, "and Kenneth—"

"No, no." Portia tapped her treble clef necklace. "I killed Laverna. *You* killed Kenneth."

Marie reared back, outraged. "I never—"

Marie's words fell to pieces as Portia brushed her thumb along her necklace. Marie stiffened, and the hairpin in her hair gleamed as the stone in the center turned copper-penny brown.

Far too relaxed, Portia added, "Marie killed Kenneth. She just doesn't remember, as these coins have a way of jumbling up memories. Kenneth had many flaws, but he was decent at making these glazes."

"You used it on her?" Brayton declared. He leveled the elemental pistol at Portia now, his arm shaking. With all his bravado gone, he was just a man who'd had his whole world turned upside down. "You were controlling her with that coin. We promised we'd never used them against each other. You joked about it when you gave me money—"

"I never promised you anything," Portia replied as a bitter and long-stewing anger crept into her words. "Not after you said no to getting rid of Delia. That, as an actress, she was too important to the organization. She was going to expose our plans not just for the exposition, but everything we had been building upon for the past two years, and you didn't believe me. Delia was always too important—first at Wise Records, and even now. You always picked her over me. Don't look so upset. You don't remember driving that stake into her back anyway!"

Brayton staggered away from Portia. "This wasn't the plan."

"Nothing ever goes to plan. It's like you always say: if you see an opportunity, take it. I took it. Don't worry—the coins you had have long since worn off. Anything you've done tonight was under your own volition."

"That's not what I'm worried about." Brayton lowered the pistol. "You didn't have to do this. We could have achieved our goals. Instead you only compromised everything. No one had to die."

"I guess we have to agree to disagree."

Without fanfare, Marie withdrew a pistol and shot Brayton.

It was the first time Velma had seen it fired with intent, and it worked more quickly than she would have thought. Magic sparked to life in the cannister, and a blast too solid to be just light struck Brayton in the chest.

Seven spikes slammed into his torso. He was flung backward, but the spikes had skewered him so completely that he didn't go far. His limbs twitched, and he let out one last gurgle as blood dripped from his mouth. There was no chance of healing him. Brayton was already dead before the spikes retracted and he fell to the ground.

The pistol in Marie's hand darted to Edythe, but a potion bottle sailed in and icicles rained down with winter's fury.

Edythe rammed her shoulder into Marie and the pistol flew out of her grip and fell harmlessly into the bushes. As Edythe tackled the older woman to the ground, Portia whipped out the final modified pistol and took aim.

The burst of flames was extinguished by a gust of wind as Dillon shot off the wind pistol just in time.

"This has a bit of kick to it," he said, and adjusted his aim to better center on Portia. "So don't do that again."

As he held Portia in position, Carolyn emerged from the hedges, helping Edythe to her feet. She held on to her beloved for as many moments as she dared to steal, muttering threats that were undermined by tender words.

Velma grabbed Marie. Depositing the older woman near the hedges, Velma plucked out the hairpin, bent it, and then sent Marie into an enchanted slumber.

"The boat's gone." Velma turned to face Portia with a star-speckled wolf at her side. "What you're planning next, you should forget it. Your family made beautiful instruments. Are you sure they would have wanted this?"

"My family is dead!" Portia snarled. "Edwin Addison killed them! First with the machine and then disease!"

"Then why plan to unleash the machine at the world's fair? To bring that same level of destruction there?"

"Because this time it will be used properly," Portia said. "The machine will be used in the way it should have been intended all along. To devastate a community founded on hate and betrayal and show to all the world the might and majesty of magic that cannot be ignored!"

"That's not how you show the majesty of magic," Velma said. "Violence just creates a cycle that never ends."

"Yet you watch on and do nothing as the reports arrive about extrajudicial murder. You stand still as families have their farmland stolen. You utter not a word when your fancy plane and money can't promise you safety if you stay in certain towns after sunset. You work for the Magnolia Muses but have you done anything to make a real impact?"

Velma's conversation with her boss echoed in her ears along with her growing frustrations. There was so much injustice to deal with in this world, but protocols and the wishes of people who cared more about internal politics stopped change from happening. She did what she could, but what had Velma accomplished in the past six years that would create long-lasting improvements?

Portia's eyes glittered as she pressed her advantage. "How many towns, how many cities have burned? If we show our power, then we can change everything to how it should be."

"You're just using that as an excuse for violence," Dillon cut in. "If you truly cared, you wouldn't have had several people killed, including your boyfriend. Delia was right to try to stop you."

"You'll fail just like she did!" Portia snarled. She flung out her arm, tossing sparks of raw celestial magic into the ground. It shook underneath them, and a boulder sprung up and flew in their direction.

Velma got her arms up in time, and the enchantments on her bracelets glowed and expanded into a shield that shattered the boulder. Tiny stones rained around the yard, but instead of falling, the stones hovered in the air with a malicious ruby red tint.

With a cackle, Portia flicked her fingers and the rocks became a swarm that descended upon Velma and Dillon.

Dillon ducked back into the gazebo for cover, while the less lucky Velma had to deflect the flying stones with her bracelets. She bounced most off the metal as she spun around in a dizzying dance, moving as swiftly as her eyes caught sight of the flying stones. When the last one sailed past her, she came to a stop in front of Portia.

The other woman panted as she pressed an elemental pistol against Velma's neck. The pistol was overburdened by the uncontained magic from the wand wood, and its tip was unbearably hot against Velma's skin.

"You told me that this was a trick to bring us all together," Portia hissed. "Then you proceeded to tell us there was no machine, that no one's found anything, and that no one ever would. You're wrong—it does exist. You had it in your possession."

"You're mistaken. I don't have a machine."

Portia chuckled. "You don't now. Your cousin was useless for the most part beyond keeping you distracted, but he told me enough. I just need the key."

"I'm not going to hand it over, even if you ask nicely."

"Then I'll just have to take it from your cold, dead hands!"

"Leave her alone!" Olivia popped out of thin air just then, dropping her invisibility spell. She swung the baseball bat right for Portia's arm.

It was a great swing, and delayed the casting of the surely fatal magic.

But the bat didn't connect.

Portia moved back just in time, and the bat skimmed the air.

Olivia stumbled, dropping the baseball bat, and Portia grabbed ahold of her.

"Wait a moment," Portia said as Velma darted forward. Portia hunched over, holding Olivia close to her, causing the girl to squirm painfully. The pistol in her hand was pointed at Velma, but with only a slight twitch of her wrist Portia could turn it upon Olivia. "I wouldn't do anything risky."

"Taking risks is what I do."

Portia smiled. "Oh, I know. But even you have your limits."

She fired the pistol, but aimed it not at Velma or Olivia, but right at Dillon, who had just clambered out of the ruined gazebo.

Velma lunged across the garden, throwing up her hands so her bracelets could take the brunt of the spell. The blast of magic tore through them, ripping away the magic and rendering them nothing more than pieces of plain jewelry.

Then a shimmering shield of starlight snapped into place.

Carolyn was at Velma's side, her arms outstretched as she held back the roiling mass of raw magic. "She's getting away! Go after her!" Carolyn yelled. "She ran for the broom shed!"

"Portia won't get anywhere," Velma said. "I cast spells everywhere to stop her."

"You did," Carolyn reminded her, "but the Quelling, it knocked *everything* out. Those spells aren't there anymore."

Velma didn't need telling twice.

Yanking off her ruined bracelets, Velma ran, stopping only to grab the baseball bat.

Any hope she had of thwarting Portia before the woman got too far was gone as a broomstick lifted into the air.

As she ran, Velma drew the rabbit star sigil and flung it forward before she even finished, using the spell to propel herself into the air. She landed on the roof of the inn and charged to the very top, enchantments cast on her shoes like Hermes's sandals.

Once she ran out of roof, Velma threw herself into the skies.

For a moment, while she was aloft, Velma thought she could stretch and grab the broomstick's bristles.

Velma's fingers reached only air, and Portia crossed over the water. The spells around Velma wavered and then collapsed.

Instead of falling to the ground, she landed face-first on a floating platform made from clumps of earth stitched together with starlight.

Dillon was underneath, his outstretched hand suspending the magic. As Velma pulled herself up with the bat, she remembered his boasts about his baseball talents.

"Can you toss up the wind pistol?" Velma called.

"I can, but Olivia is on the broom with—"

"I'll catch her," Velma promised. "Just get it there when I stop moving!"

Velma slapped her hand along the platform, her magic melding with Dillon's as she propelled the platform higher into the air. She stood up and swung the bat over her shoulder as she focused on getting the platform to the right height.

As soon as she got there, the wind pistol flew up, reaching the exact height she needed.

Velma swung and lobbed it right at Olivia.

Olivia grabbed the wind pistol. She didn't hesitate as she flipped it around and aimed it at Portia. A small whirlwind stirred up between them, blowing them apart. Olivia fell, while Portia still retained a desperate grip on the broomstick as she dangled from one hand. Portia swung up and then jerkily flew off into the night, vanishing from sight.

Velma tossed the baseball bat away and lunged forward, barely aware that the platform of earth turned into water as she closed the distance between her and Olivia.

Stubbornly fighting the very stones beneath the water, Velma ran. The ancient enchantments would not tolerate any magic working around it, even from the sky itself, but she would overcome them. She had to. Velma exerted her will, forcing her spellwork to hold together as she ran and ran, so swiftly she wasn't even aware of the exertion. Olivia couldn't swim. Olivia was too panicked to cast any spells. Olivia's mother would never forgive Velma if something happened. Olivia trusted that Velma would catch her.

Velma's magic gave way past the midway point and she lunged, grabbing ahold of Olivia.

"I got you," she said as they fell. "Don't look down."

"Too late," Olivia whispered, shutting her eyes as she buried her face into Velma's chest.

Velma just chuckled as she took the wind pistol from Olivia and fired. The puff of air that expelled from it was barely anything, but it was enough to give Velma a moment. A moment for her to hang in the air, giving her time to think and plan.

Clutching Olivia, Velma twisted them around in midair to create a lattice of starlight. Hexagonal shapes formed a bubble shield that locked into place just as they hit the water.

The impact knocked Velma backward, but she grimly kept the magic stitched together through sheer will, even as she fell to her knees and the magic in the water threatened to flatten her into dust.

"You can open your eyes now," Velma managed to say. "I need your help, Olivia. I can't walk this bubble back to shore."

"A bubble?" Olivia's eyes snapped open as she stared at Velma's spellwork in stunned delight.

"You got good ideas, kiddo. Show me how it works. If not, I'm going to have to teach you how to swim very quickly."

Olivia stood up, squared her shoulders, and placed her hands on the shields. Her magic flowed into the bubble around them, further stabilizing the spells. "It goes like this."

CHAPTER 38

V elma didn't recall much of the walk back to the inn. She just knew that when the bubble hit the rocks, it cracked and her spellwork fell apart. Stretched past her limits, she could only watch as it slipped out of her hands, while she desperately tried to weave it back together.

Before any panic could set in, arms grabbed around her waist. Velma's head broke the water's surface, and Carolyn adjusted her grip around Velma as she swam them to shore.

"At least you had the courtesy of going about things in the most ostentatious way." Carolyn bristled as they crawled along the sandy barrier that separated the inn from the sea. "Your little light show helped us track you in the water. If you'd been paying attention, we could have grabbed you from the boat."

Velma flopped onto the ground, breathing deeply. The sounds of the inn's boat docking and the voices of the others felt far away even though Velma could see them doused under the light of the lantern Dillon carried.

"Thank you, Caro," Velma said, and coughed.

Carolyn's bristling stopped as she quickly gripped Velma in a one-armed hug. "What else was I going to do, Violet?"

"The boat was gone." Velma sat up, coughing a bit more. "Olivia and I saw it floating away."

"It was not floating—you saw us earlier," Beatrice said.

"*You* took the boat!" Velma cried, only a little stunned and hardly surprised at the sight of her parents standing before her.

"You know your mother's only good at making people, not large floating objects, vanish from sight," Rodney added. "We were here part of the evening, until the dinner. We turned the record on, set up a few spells and potions around the inn, and left. You almost caught us, when we went to get the boat. We were going to stay in town for most of the evening, but then the lights went out."

"We moved the bodies while you were distracted," Beatrice said. "They're both currently in the morgue. We'd just gotten back from dropping off the second body when your light show started."

"Why didn't you tell me you were doing that?" Velma demanded. "There was so much confusion."

"Where do you think you got your flair for theatrics?" Beatrice replied as she and Rodney exchanged smug smiles.

"I didn't know about them taking the bodies, but I knew about everything else and thought it was a good idea." Carolyn shrugged. "As you said, it added to the confusion you wanted, and Mom and Dad were never going to stay far away while this was going on."

They'd clearly only said otherwise just to avoid wasting time with an argument, Velma guessed. She was deeply annoyed, greatly touched, and overall very glad to know that her parents had been behind the few lingering mysteries. "Where did the record even come from?" Velma asked instead.

"Turns out there was someone on the island who not only had a record made by Wise Records, but the one we needed," Rodney said as if chewing glass. "Paloma Tull."

Velma shuddered at the name of the rival innkeeper. "Does it mean we have to be nice to her now?"

"For her help, she said we need to stop slandering the Candlewyck."

"Just tell her it wasn't useful," Carolyn offered. "Then we won't owe her anything."

Beatrice remarked dryly. "And you're fine with stoking the flames of this feud between the inns for another sixty years?"

"Yes!" Rodney declared, and Velma and Carolyn also chimed in.

Beatrice sighed, though she shot them all a fond smile. "Why do I even ask?"

"So I'm to believe you put Olivia's bubble idea into practice, but my ice idea wasn't seen as valuable?" Dillon asked as he came around with the lantern. He winked at Velma, although he didn't get closer given the proximity of her parents. Still, tucked behind his usual cheer was a reassurance as comforting as any embrace.

"Next time I do a stunt like that, I will try your option."

"Please don't," Edythe called as sat she down next to Carolyn and nestled her head on Carolyn's shoulder. "It was the most terrifying sight all evening."

"For you, perhaps," Carolyn said quietly. She frowned, looking around at the gathered group. "Why are we making jokes? Portia got away. I saw her crashing through the protections set around the island. Aren't we going to go after her?"

"No need," Velma said. "I know where she's headed: to the International Exposition of Arcane Arts and Sciences. She's going to enact her foolish plan."

"They never found the machine," Dillon said. "So how do you know for certain?"

"Portia wanted a key, and she knew I had the hatpin. She wouldn't insist if the machine wasn't found."

"Trust me, they didn't find it while I was with them," Edythe said. "I sent them all over the inn, using Beatrice's potions to confuse a few things. That space under the library was the closest to any evidence. The machine might have been in there, but it was removed a long time ago."

"Under the library!" Rodney thundered. "There's never been anything there!"

As arguments and explanations went around, Velma quietly turned over the facts.

The machine existed—the recess in that room proved it. Like all those objects that Quincy had taken, it had been hidden in the inn and then removed. Small things, big things. Some ended up with the Muses.

Except that the tinted glasses had been taken by some conspirator working with Portia. Who knew what else had been stolen? Which was a particularly sore spot, since Velma had gone through a great effort to get some of the larger ones—

A piece slotted into place, and she understood Portia's smug belief that the plans for the arcane expo would occur without a hitch.

"Was she the one who found something in the laboratory?" Velma asked her sister suddenly. "You said one of the women found something in the desks. Was it Portia?"

"Yes," Carolyn said, at first hesitant but then certain. "Portia found blueprints. I got a quick look at them."

"What were they?"

Carolyn frowned. "You know, it looked like something our grandmother would have had."

"A sewing machine?" Edythe asked.

"No, something related to astronomy, but the name escapes me."

"An orrery?" Olivia suggested.

"What's wrong now?" Carolyn asked as Velma staggered to her feet.

Dillon moved over to help her, and she leaned on him as she headed toward the house. "I need to make a call. I never asked *when* they recovered the orrery!"

It didn't take long to get Henrietta on the phone despite the late hour. In fact, her grandmother had picked up as if knowing Velma would call that night.

"You've always told me that assumptions can lead to trouble," Velma said. "I made a mistake I should have realized sooner. When you told me you'd recovered the orrery, you made it sound as if it had happened recently on purpose. But you'd found it years and years ago, didn't you?"

The amused chuckle that filtered through the phone's receiver was all the answer Velma needed.

"You can be forgiven," Henrietta said. "You were a baby when it happened, after all."

"It was that night the intruders came to the inn. That's when you found the orrery."

"We weren't there that night but arrived as soon as we heard. We took the time to explore the inn, and that's how we found the workshop and the remains of that young man, the husband of the infamous Clarice. The room was hidden very well, and we took pains for it to remain so. Something about the orrery caught my eye from the start, and we decided to take it with us. Beatrice and Rodney were so focused on you and your sister, they didn't even notice."

Benjamin's voice came through the phone next. "The enchantments on it were rather dormant. We left it alone, and eventually it ended up in the cellar. It didn't work like an orrery was supposed to. Something told me not to get rid of it, though. It might have stayed lost if Zadie and Gregory hadn't gotten busy cleaning the cellar earlier this year."

"Did you know the orrery was the machine that destroyed the old manor?" Velma asked.

"We didn't," Henrietta said after a pause. "Stars above, Velma. We love our mysteries, but we can't solve *everything*. You figured it out, didn't you?"

"Although not soon enough. There's Quincy to deal with."

"Oh yes, we must deal with him," Henrietta said sternly. "Focus on what you need to do next, my dear, and we'll take care of the remainder."

"Is Gregory around? I need to talk to him."

"I'll have him call you," her grandmother said, and then hung up before Velma could say a word more.

Bemused, Velma dialed the number for Lois's home.

"Is the party over?" Lois asked, skipping right past niceties.

"Not quite," Velma said. "Besides you, who else is in charge of the archives?"

"I oversee them all with the help from Wanda, Bojun, and Jim—plus my assistants. Or should I say one assistant. Morris quit so abruptly, it can't be my fault, no matter what Phyllis says."

Velma tuned out her friend's ranting as she recalled her last interactions with Lois's former assistant. "Morris didn't abruptly quit," Velma interrupted. "He was planted to steal information and items. The item that came in from Philadelphia—I need you to see if it's there. It's a matter of life and death."

"I knew you were going to say that," Lois moaned. "What do I do if it's not there?"

"Wait for me. I'll be there soon to handle it."

Velma waited by the phone for Lois's confirmation. She sat slumped in the chair as everyone moved about, cleaning up the remains of the night's activities. Velma tried to sweep up the glass from the chandelier, but her sister shooed her back to her seat.

"You need your rest. You have a long flight tomorrow."

"I could stay an extra day," Velma said.

"No, you have things to do," Carolyn replied. "Also, you'll be back soon."

"Soon as I can," Velma said just as the phone rang.

Snatching up the phone, Velma asked, "Lois, what's the verdict?"

"That once again you needed help despite me telling you how busy we are," Gregory said.

"Oh, it's you," Velma said. "Gregory, could you come and help us at the inn? I know it's a big ask, but I'd appreciate it so much. I'll make it up to you, I promise—I'll cover your work at the funeral home so you and Zadie can go and paint somewhere."

"Well, that's a generous offer, but I'm afraid I can't take it. We're in Chicago, and you need to get back by tomorrow because we found out when Members of Rational Clarity will strike."

CHAPTER 39

<small>Chicago, Illinois</small>

I thought you said this was my case?" was the first thing out of Velma's mouth when she met her cousin at the airfield in Chicago.

No matter how the last few days had been, Velma could not have anticipated this series of events, one in which Gregory and his wife arrived in Chicago just hours after she left and did the legwork around town to determine the movements of Members of Rational Clarity for her. Gregory had explained nothing, obstinately getting back at her for doing the same to him numerous times before. He was having too much fun, evident by how he waved at her from her own car when her plane came into view.

"You also asked for my help," Gregory reminded her. "Besides, do you think Olivia and her friend went off to New York City without me knowing? We've been keeping tabs on her, and you told me enough about your work that I could figure out the rest. Also, Rational Clarity showed up in our strange four-people-murdered-four-different-ways case, if you can believe it."

"I suppose I'll have to," Velma said. "Thank you for helping."

"I'm just giving you an assist. You've already done most of the work. Is it just you and Olivia?"

"And me," Dillon said as he got out of the plane with Olivia. "I'm—"

"You're the fellow with the camera at Velma's flight shows," Gregory interrupted with a grin. "My wife and I see you at them all the time. Granted that happened only three times, but it's not unremarkable. I suppose you're a fan. Though your articles, Dillon, paint a very different story. I'm very curious about that. We can talk about that later in greater detail, though. I have a feeling you're going to be around for a while."

Dillon turned to Velma with a slightly pained expression. "Is meeting everyone in your family going to be like this?"

"Yes, especially with the relatives that like me a great deal," Velma said. She fixed Gregory with a stern glance when she caught a smirk tugging at his mouth. "You can tease him later, but save it for after we stop the bombing at the world's fair."

Waiting at Velma's house were Zadie, Lois, and Cornelius. Lois had brought with her confirmation of the theft of the orrery and other items from the archives. As Velma finished explaining every-thing she couldn't by phone, Dillon's siblings, Madelyn and Fitzhugh, arrived with intel about the arcane expo's grounds.

"The exposition is spread among five buildings all connected by an open courtyard," Madelyn explained. "Three buildings are dedicated to the areas of magical expression, craft, and knowledge. The fourth highlights U.S. manufactory and makers, and the last is for international participants. This machine—orrery—could be anywhere, as they were loading a few items into each of the build-ings."

"Hidden in plain sight," Lois said as she peered at the map. "I've tracked the shipments to and from the place, but found nothing re-cent to describe the size you told me, Velma."

"How did you manage to find that out?" Fitzhugh asked.

"She's a librarian," Cornelius answered easily. "They know every-thing."

"The orrery would have been newly brought in," Gregory added before they could get sidetracked. "They are still adding a few things to the displays—the expo wasn't quite ready to open when it did, but they wanted to stick to the opening day because they have a senator here. Which is why the group is going forward with their plans."

"Are there any demonstrations scheduled?" Dillon asked. "It sounds like they wanted a show."

Zadie held out a piece of paper. "There are a few, but none seem to be connected to the orrery. We'll have to search every building."

"I wanted to see the expo, but not like this," Fitzhugh remarked.

"We'll need to split up into groups. Pairs, even," Madelyn said. "And we shouldn't focus on the international building."

"We should consider everything," Dillon protested.

"No, your sister is right," Gregory said. "This group has goals that inform its plans. If they do anything, it'll be done to make a point. So let's start with this: What do they aim to accomplish?"

"Show the world the 'majesty of magic,' specifically in areas of race relations to make a statement that cannot be ignored," Velma said.

"Then we need to focus on just one building." Lois tapped the map. "Manufactory."

With such a big group, they were able to spread out. Lois and Olivia would remain in the courtyard outside as a central point of contact. Cornelius, Fitzhugh, and Madelyn would search the other buildings just in case, while Velma, Dillon, Gregory, and Zadie would be in the manufactory building. Velma's cousins would circulate through the room, focusing on the loading area as they looked for the orrery, while Velma and Dillon looked for Portia.

"There's a surprisingly large number of people here," Dillon remarked as they moved through the space together. With such thick crowds, they nearly had to walk arm in arm to avoid being separated in some parts of the room. "This might make things difficult."

"Don't be pessimistic," Velma said. "You're the one with the eye to see things that others can't even without magic."

"It's not perfect, though."

"No one's asking for that."

They continued to walk, passing the booths and pushing through the crowd. It was easy to see why this space was a target. In a room where innovation and new products that would shape the future were on display, it would be quite a statement if something occurred here.

Velma was tempted to let it occur. There were inventions that could improve lives found along these tables, but there were many more inventions that would only turn into weapons in the wrong hands.

If she let Portia act, who was to say the outcome would be so tidy? And the orrery was a device she knew nothing about, beyond the devastating results it had left behind in its wake. Devastation she did *not* want to see again.

Two times was enough. There would not be a third.

They turned down the next aisle, and at the end Gregory wildly gestured to get their attention. He and Zadie were both pointing to a distant corner, not caring about the odd looks they were both receiving.

"I think we're getting close," Velma said.

"Not just us, either," Dillon added. "To your right."

Velma looked and spotted a familiar figure moving parallel across the room.

Portia was able to move faster, as the aisle she was in had fewer people, but given how she was shoving and elbowing others out of the way, she was already attracting attention.

Dillon placed a firmer hold on Velma's arm. "Don't run," he whispered. "You'll get stopped."

"But she'll get there before I do."

"She might, but you jumping over the tables will only help her."

"How do you suppose I get there in time?" Velma asked.

"You make things move for you," he suggested as he held out the lemniscate. "Like you always do."

Velma grinned as she took the once-enchanted favor from him. "Then try to keep up, because once I get going, there's no stopping me."

Velma turned over the metal, and the moment it was under her fingers, the remaining magic thrummed to life. With one swipe of her thumb, she had the nearest tables shifting around to make a small path. A turn of the infinity symbol in a different direction had adults and children moving out of the way. Thus she and Dillon proceeded until they finally reached the aisle where a man pushed a metal cart holding the orrery.

Because he wore the same uniform as the other people working in the room, Velma hesitated. Then he turned slightly and she recognized Morris Broadleaf.

As Velma made this connection, Portia rounded the corner, locked eyes with Morris, and tapped a fist to her shoulder.

Morris responded by crudely spinning the outer planets of the orrery.

Velma didn't think it would work, but she heard a click and then a whirl as a spark danced between the planets.

This was different from Velma's previous, idle tap of the orrery. Back then she had only bumped the planets slightly. This haphazard jerk had the orrery spinning at such speed it was hard to make out the whirling planets. The air became charged with magic, growing thick and suffocating. Velma's ring suddenly heated up, and before she could even become greatly concerned, her feet suddenly lifted from the ground.

Velma wasn't the only thing or person floating several inches in the air. Dillon was hovering as well, along with Morris and Portia. Objects and nearby tables rose, and loose items farther away had begun to rattle.

The only thing that remained firmly on the ground was the orrery.

With each turn of the orrery, Velma thought this strange weight-lessness would extend farther out into the crowd, but a shimmer of starlight fell to halt its path.

Not far away, Zadie dragged her paintbrush along a set of tables, the enchanted paint forming a boundary to hold back the assault from the orrery. A small bang cracked the air apart as Gregory fired his elemental pistol. Seedpod capsules burst above the crowd's heads as flowers sprouted into an unexplainable rain of daisies, capturing both the awe and surprise of those nearby.

With this distraction in play, Velma half swam, half rolled over toward Morris, shoving him away.

She grabbed ahold of the cart as Portia propelled herself forward.

"No, you can't stop it!" Portia cried. "It's impossible!"

"Nothing is until you try." Velma pushed the orrery out of reach.

Portia's face twisted into desperate rage as she summoned her spellwork, but Dillon hurtled into view and snapped his camera, aiming the flash right at Portia's face.

Not expecting it, Portia squawked and jerked backward into a stack of boxes.

Almost lazily, Velma lobbed a tiny arrow made of stars at the woman to bind her, and then turned her attention back to the orrery.

It was still spinning, and the effects were growing with each passing second. The notes from Clarice Sitwell flashed in Velma's mind, as well as the destruction she had seen and imagined. Shoving such thoughts aside, Velma removed her ring.

She gave it a rueful squeeze and then let go.

The ring floated above the orrery, suspended by the crackling magic. Velma focused on the sigil she carved, manipulating the spells to transform it into something new.

This was the true majesty of celestial magic. The ability to change as needed by whim or desperation, all at the caster's desire. Magic was the second great mystery, and use of it had forged, destroyed, and remade the world in an endless cycle. Velma's greatest spell would just be a tiny stitch in the fabric of all that magic, but it was hers and overflowing with all her best intentions.

At the exertion of her will, the ring became a magnet, siphoning the energy radiating from the orrery. At first it didn't seem like it made much of an impact, but then the sigil on the stone began to glow bright and the orrery wound down like a fan abruptly turned off.

Velma's feet hit the ground with a small thump, and echoes of similar thumps occurred as the other floating objects returned to the earth. The ring clattered atop the orrery, cold to the touch, neatly split in two from its heavy burden.

"No!" Portia howled as she banged on her invisible cage. "You can stop me, but there are others, more members in the group. There will be other places, other venues—"

"Cut off one, more will spring up, and so on and so forth. Heard it all before, and it won't happen," Dillon jeered. "The game's over and the scores are being reported."

Portia snapped back at him with a stream of curses that were more foul than magical. Dillon flicked his hand, and the magic shield around Portia became opaque, making it so they couldn't hear or see her anymore.

As this was going on. Velma took out the tuning fork. This was the key that had brought the orrery to life so many years ago. It had destroyed a home and its copy had ruined a town. Velma's fingers twitched over the tuning fork, and she wondered what would happen if she could strike one of the planets right then. Would it work differently from what Portia and her accomplice had attempted to do?

Her grandparents told her it didn't work like an actual orrery, so did that mean, if Velma tapped it right now, she would reveal the true power of the orrery? Edwin had built his to destroy a town, but what had been Jeremiah Sitwell's original intention? It couldn't have been for destruction. No, he wanted to display something so wonderous, so beautiful, so powerful, so . . .

Dillon's hand fell over hers. "I wouldn't strike that if I were you," he said quietly. "It doesn't have a good track record, after all."

He held out his other hand.

The tuning fork flashed, and the sight broke Velma from the thrall the orrery had cast on her. She hastily loosened her grip, dropping the fork into his palm.

"You'll be okay holding it this close to the machine?" Velma asked.

Dillon winked at her. "I have my lucky charm with me. I think I'll be fine." As he carefully wrapped it up, Dillon nodded toward the cart. "What about the orrery? Does it get locked in a warehouse somewhere or does it get destroyed?"

"The orrery is dangerous," Velma said, stepping away from it. "It must be destroyed. I know there are other objects we haven't found yet, but taking care of the orrery is the most important thing. As for everything else, I'll figure it out."

Dillon tsk-tsked, not quite hiding his amusement as he shook a finger at her. "You don't have a plan, do you?"

"I make plans," Velma protested. "I just don't mind when they change on me. After all, sometimes it's best to travel with the wind as it blows, for it can lead to places you would have never discovered on your own."

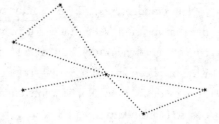

CHAPTER 40

Velma's final report was heavily edited.

Not because the details of what had happened needed to be hidden—although Velma did make sure Quincy's involvement was as a nameless antiques dealer who she was unable to locate. Most of Quincy's crimes were against the family and personal to her; there was no need to get the Muses involved when her family knew how to deal with Quincy.

The report that Velma submitted spent more time detailing the information about Members of Rational Clarity—the only information of value they did get from Marie. The woman was very eager to assist them, as she had become disillusioned with how the organization was acting, despite agreeing with the main goals on principle. Marie told them all about the organization's goals, missions, plans, and past incidents, and her information reopened an old case file—one which Velma would have loved to have known about weeks ago, but the reason she hadn't was because of Morris Broadleaf.

Delia's report about the enchanted necklace had alerted Portia to potential interference by the Muses. So, she tasked Morris to disrupt the Muses' operations, and due to bureaucratic entanglements Morris had been quite successful. Not only had he leaked information, he'd meddled with Velma's case. He'd kept important information out of her hands, doctored both Lois's and Jasper's reports, revealed who she was to Portia, and leaked Velma's trip to Ardenton. He was also the reason Velma had lost communications in Colorado.

Portia was currently in a holding cell somewhere. Officially, Velma was not part of the effort to uncover the woman's connections and information. Unofficially, Lois kept Velma updated every step of the way.

As for the orrery, Velma confirmed its destruction in her report but made no mention of the true powers of the device. After all, not every detail needed explaining.

Velma's report earned her a long holiday. Not just for the work done well, but because the aftermath had sent ripples throughout the Magnolia Muses, with many voices calling for change to make such an infiltration less likely. Wanting to be part of the conversation, Velma put off taking that holiday until ten days following the events at the arcane exposition, when Dillon's article about Members of Rational Clarity hit the newsstands.

In a few words, he undid the myth the organization had created around itself, revealing not just what Portia's faction had attempted, but all the misdeeds the group had done across the country, revealing scams, subterfuge, and other incidents of grave concern, including Brayton Strickland's connection. To the general populace, who had previously seen the group as one giving a voice to those without much hope, such revelations caused an uproar.

Although no death threats came with this article, once again Dillon had to leave town in a hurry. They rode out the frenzy at Bramble Crescent—just in time for the lantern festival, as it turned out. Dillon would never admit he'd timed the article's release on purpose, and Velma suspected this would not be the first or last such occurrence.

As summer turned to fall, Velma's work in the field lessened, leaving her with time to help Carolyn with the repairs and renovations at Beacon Inn, play the new game her father was working on, and test the new concoctions her mother came up with for her plane. Edythe confessed to writing detective novels as Melvin Winterberry to help with the inn's expenses, and Carolyn was so relieved at hearing this was Edythe's big secret that she kept her teasing to a minimum. The book of poetry was still in progress, and Velma suggested that Edythe should make the poems mystery themed, a suggestion that first earned scorn, then laughter, and then thoughtful consideration. Velma had a long visit to Philadelphia, where she flew her grandparents to whatever destination they picked out on the map and went stargazing. She also introduced them to Dillon, who they took a liking to right away, especially as he was eager to listen to all their old stories. Olivia remained at the house on Juniper Street, being mentored in magic and mystery, with Velma as one of her main tutors whenever she was in town. Edythe held another artists' salon with Gregory and Zadie as major guests during Velma's visit, and when they returned there was talk about possible changes in the funeral home's future.

Upon returning to Chicago Velma met Dillon's older brother, Beaumont, when he and his daughter Marilyn arrived to see the arcane expo—and to retrieve the mailbag that Dillon had forgotten to send back. Lois finally told her brother that she worked for the Magnolia Muses, but Cornelius and Velma noted she neglected a few key details. When confronted about this, Lois only shrugged and replied: "A girl has to have some secrets."

Velma got a promotion of sorts, with mediation added to her field agent duties. With the authority to help folks the way she'd always wanted, she could prevent deadly incidents and also sow some much-needed chaos. This was the first of many changes on the horizon, as Velma's boss had moved into a director role in order to ensure that the Muses took a more proactive role. One of their first projects was to dismantle the Bureau of Magical Detection, pointing to the

THE IMPROVISERS   439

lopsided enforcement and abuse of power in light of the coming end of prohibition.

Despite all the news and excitement, for Velma the most note-worthy arrived before her air show, when Dillon published a public apology for all his previous comments on aviation.

"'To fly has always been a practice of trust, and a willingness to strive to places few have ventured previously. To do so by plane is no different, but it's a symbol of the change that is arriving at our doors. It would be trite to declare that this winged metal bird will change the world in unforeseen ways, but it has changed this re-porter's world. I can admit I was wrong. . . .'" Velma looked up from the article. "You could have stopped there, but you went on for five more paragraphs."

"Two are promotions for today's event, and another singing praises of your pilot friends," Dillon said as he reclined on the other end of the cockpit of Velma's plane, pretending to polish his camera instead of watching her read his article. "Should I have cut them?"

"No, it's just that you didn't have to write all of that—besides the promotion of my event, of course. I know you have been enlightened by the wonders of aviation."

"If I'm going to be spotted at your air shows, I should make it clear that my opinion has changed, and that it's not your admittedly lovely charms playing a role."

"I don't think one article will be enough."

"Then an interview. The subject I have in mind, though, is no-toriously hard to get a hold of, very secretive, and prone to bending truths. All to be expected, as she never even learned to drive because she grew up on an island."

"This sounds like it's going to be a very difficult interview. Luck-ily, I can help you. Although," Velma added as she leaned over to kiss him, "it comes with a price."

"That's a very nice price," Dillon replied. "Although I'm open to negotiating terms."

"We can do that after the show," Velma chuckled. "Are you sure you want to be aboard while I'm doing my feature? The view would be better from the ground. Plus, everyone's here. Our friends, our family. People we're friendly with. People who either dislike one or both of us. Probably even an enemy or two."

"I'll see the rest of the show from the ground," Dillon assured her. "For this part, though, I wanted to get pictures while up in the air. Just give me a little warning before pulling a stunt. Which reminds me—what's the theme of the air show again?"

"Oh, that's quite simple." Velma peered up at the skies, filled with the planes of her fellow pilots and friends. Skies that were open and waiting for her to join in. Skies that held no limits for her and her ambitions. Skies that held even more wonders now with someone alongside her who was just as eager as she was to discover their secrets.

Velma took a deep breath, anticipating all the other flights ahead of her, no matter where they took her in the world. "It's all about how we soar."

ACKNOWLEDGMENTS

If you have a passing interest in aviation, you'd probably heard about Bessie Coleman. Famously the first Black and Native American woman to gain a pilot's license, she's wildly heralded as an inspiration to both her contemporaries as well as future pilots headed for the skies and stars. I first learned about her by chance during a school assignment and was instantly captivated by someone so driven to achieve her goals that she overcame every obstacle in her way.

Velma's story is largely inspired by Bessie Coleman's, as well as those of Janet Bragg, James Banning, Willa Brown, Cornelius Coffey, and other pilots of the era. While it was tempting to do a World War II story to bring in the Tuskegee Airmen, placing this book in the early 1930s allowed me to explore the adolescent years of aviation with some overlap with the upcoming end of prohibition and the uncertainty of the era. The world of *The Improvisers* is one close to ours, but the presence of magic allows me to play with history in many ways, using it as a canvas to explore a story I couldn't quite tell any other way.

For help with the hard work of getting this book together, I have to thank the usual suspects. My family most of all for the support, thoughtful words, and even confusion about how this whole author thing works.

Thanks as always for my agent, Jennie Goloboy, whose sensible advice and words of encouragement got me through many drafts of this book.

Thanks to my editor, David Pomerico, who in a few short words had my mind spinning with ideas taking me in all sorts of directions, including the right one. Also much appreciation to the rest of the HarperCollins and Voyager team who played a part in this book. There's so much that goes into making a book once I hand it over, and I'm grateful for the work done along the way.

Thanks to Jamie Levine. This book literally wouldn't exist without you. Thank you for all you've done—I appreciate everything.

Thanks to the National Museum of African American History in Washington, D.C., for once again being a source of inspiration. When I stumbled across the Oak Bluffs exhibition at the museum, I had never heard about the town before, although I knew of Martha's Vineyard (which, by the way, is not named for any famous Martha you may be thinking of!). It is in the history of this town frequented by many famous Black folk that I found the inspiration for Bramble Crescent and to bring to life an island where magic runs rampant and where a number of extraordinary things simply become ordinary.

Other sources of inspiration include *Atlas Obscura*, who always had an article for the somewhat obscure topic I was looking for and was a launchpad for deeper research, as well as the *AirSpace* podcast, whose episodes on Black aviators ("Chicago Flyer" and "Leaving for Paris") showed up in my feed around the time I was putting together the pitches for my next book and reminded me of an old draft I had lurking in my files.

Last, but not least, thanks to all you readers out there in the world. Let us soar together.

ABOUT THE AUTHOR

Nicole Glover works as a UX researcher in Virginia. She believes that libraries are magical places and that problems seem smaller with a cup of tea in hand. Her life outside of books includes bicycles, video games, and baking the perfect banana bread. *The Conductors* was her debut novel. She can be found at nicole-glover.com.

DIVE INTO THE
MURDER AND MAGIC SERIES!

THE UNDERTAKERS

Nothing bothers Hetty and Benjy Rhodes more than a case where the answers, motives, and the murder itself feel a bit too neat. Raimond Duval, a victim of one of the many fires that have erupted recently in Philadelphia, is officially declared dead after the accident, but Hetty and Benjy's investigation points to a powerful fire company known to let homes in the Black community burn to the ground. Before long, another death breathes new life into the Duval investigation: Raimond's son is also found dead.

THE CONDUCTORS

"A seamless blending of magic, mystery, and history. . . . Glover's worldbuilding, characters, and attention to historical detail create a delightfully genre-bending debut!" —Tananarive Due, American Book Award winner, author of *Ghost Summer: Stories*